Praise for *The Framed Women of Ardemore House*

"The book is more than just a mystery: It's an autistic woman's journey of self-discovery."

—*THE WASHINGTON POST*

"A delight."

—*THE WALL STREET JOURNAL*

"A thoughtful mystery that does justice to generations of women who see life differently."

—*THE CHRISTIAN SCIENCE MONITOR*

"Brandy Schillace's cozy murder mystery is supplemented with equally fun characters."

—*HUFFPOST*

"Twisty, engaging, and thoroughly unexpected . . . a must-read for any mystery lover. Featuring a unique cast of characters and a village full of dirty little secrets, this book delivers a fresh take on the English cozy."

—DEANNA RAYBOURN, *New York Times* bestselling author of *KILLERS OF A CERTAIN AGE*

"Intricately plotted and thematically rich, with characters I grew to really care about. I'll be recommending it to every mystery reader I know."

—ALEX GRECIAN, *New York Times* bestselling author of *THE YARD*

"A New York editor on the spectrum clashing with a dogged British detective. Makes a mystery like an English garden: wild, masterly crafted and full of secrets, beauty and marvels."

—MARIO GIORDANO, author of The Auntie Poldi Adventure series

"A classic murder mystery, an amateur sleuth like no other; Josephine Jones will change the way you look at the world."

—**STEPHEN GALLAGHER, author of *THE BEDLAM DETECTIVE* and writer for BBC'S *DOCTOR WHO***

"A marvelous contemporary murder mystery seasoned with a dash of romance . . . *The Framed Women of Ardemore House* has both a protagonist whose imperfections are part of her charm and locals with a host of secrets among them, so it is sure to delight fans of British crime fiction."

—***SHELF AWARENESS***

"The intricate plot and memorable local characters here are a delight."

—***BOOKLIST***

"Schillace, who's autistic herself, draws a marvelously believable heroine in Jo, and sets her up with an expertly constructed mystery. Readers will be hungry for a sequel."

—***PUBLISHERS WEEKLY***

"Quite the romp. . . . There's as much action as feeling in *The Framed Women of Ardemore House*. It's enough to satisfy every reader, especially mystery lovers."

—***BOOKREPORTER***

The DEAD COME to STAY

Also by Brandy Schillace

The Framed Women of Ardemore House

Mr. Humble and Dr. Butcher

Death's Summer Coat

Clockwork Futures

The DEAD COME *to* STAY

BRANDY SCHILLACE

HANOVER
SQUARE
PRESS

HANOVER SQUARE PRESS™

Recycling programs for this product may not exist in your area.

ISBN-13: 978-1-335-12187-5

The Dead Come to Stay

Hanover Square Press
22 Adelaide St. West, 41st Floor
Toronto, Ontario M5H 4E3, Canada
HanoverSqPress.com

HarperCollins Publishers
Macken House, 39/40 Mayor Street Upper,
Dublin 1, D01 C9W8, Ireland
www.HarperCollins.com

Printed in U.S.A.

The DEAD COME to STAY

CHAPTER 1

The man on the doorstep of Jo's cottage dripped rainwater; it trickled from wet-plastered hair to overcoat gun flap and onto the overnight bag clutched under one arm. Jo had remembered to say hello, but that didn't stop him staring at her, all wide-eyed and open-mouthed. He reminded her of a disheveled pigeon after colliding with a windowpane.

"Mr. Ronan Foley?" Jo asked, stepping back to give him entry room.

"I—Yes." He shuffled onto the flagstone cottage entry. "I—I thought keys would be in a lockbox?"

"Um?" Jo had practiced every opening line, but not this one. She blinked twice. "I have the keys for you. It's for an attic en suite . . . in my . . . house."

"You *live* here?" The way he looked around himself wasn't entirely complimentary; Jo chose the high road.

"Don't worry! You'll have total privacy," she insisted. That was the point of going through all that trouble of installing a full bath on the second level (including hoisting a freestanding tub through the attic casements, quite a feat when you're five foot four and one hundred fifteen pounds soaking wet).

"Of course, of course," muttered Mr. Foley. "You . . . meet all your guests in person?"

Jo decided not to tell him he was her first guest. Or that she'd locked her knees to keep from bouncing up and down with nervous energy. She also fought to urge to ask if he was Irish. Instead, she dangled the keys.

"The door at the top of the stairs locks with the minikey," she said. "The brass ones are for the front door and dead bolt."

"Thank you, Ms. . . . ?"

"Jones. Jo Jones." She smiled, probably a little too much. He had a broad face and smile lines, but he wasn't smiling now. "Always ask if you can get them something," Tula had said when she informed her about her decision to rent the cottage. "It's welcoming." Wise words from the Red Lion innkeeper and the one person Jo considered a truly close friend. She might have suggest *what* to offer.

"I could get you . . . something? I can cook. Well. I can warm things up. Actually, I can drive into town and get food. Or maybe you're thirsty?"

"Tea," the man said, and of course he would say tea. They were in Yorkshire.

"Yes! Yes, that I can do. And cookies. You don't call them cookies—but little shortbreads with the jam in the middle?"

Maybe it was the fact that Jo had forgotten to call them tea biscuits, or maybe it had to do with the fact she wasn't taking breaths between sentences, but the startled pigeon suddenly began to . . . laugh. It worked a change in him, shaking all the stiffness out.

"Tea *biscuits*. You're American—you are, aren't you?"

"Erm" was the best she could do, but now, *now* he smiled.

"Delighted," he said, shaking her hand. "May I?" He pointed up the stairwell, but Jo looked at his wet mackintosh. Obviously, he needed to clean up. And she should, as they say, *put the kettle on* instead of jawing at him like an idiot. He hadn't actually waited for an answer, though, just gave the keys a jingle and disappeared up the stairs.

This wasn't how she'd pictured her first experience as a host—and she'd run every possible scenario right down to the mise-en-scène. She'd try again when he came downstairs. Better make it a *big* plate of biscuits.

★★★

Jo hadn't *wanted* to rent out her little cottage, but the attic was empty, and her bank account soon would be as well if she didn't find some work. A year ago when she'd first moved to England, Jo had envisioned herself freelance editing, but that still hadn't taken off yet. Plus, she had been spending all of her time in the Abington Archive searching for any scant information about her ancestors with the long-suffering elder museum curator, Roberta Wilkinson. Needless to say, it wasn't exactly a moneymaking endeavor. It was obsession.

But she couldn't help it: Jo had moved to the Ardemore property last year in a surprise inheritance following the death of her mother, who conveniently never mentioned that her will would leave Jo with a giant crumbling manor home (unlivable), the small cottage attached (slightly more livable) or the gardens upon which they were built, which turned out to be quite famous. The cottage made for a simple, straightforward home that suited Jo nicely, but she'd learned in a hurry that the manor across the hill housed only secrets.

The mysteries of her ancestors William and Gwen, for example, who had lived in the estate house a century prior. They were lord and lady so to speak; their portraits had hung regally in the estate house as a constant reminder of their strange marriage and even stranger living arrangement with Gwen's sister,

Evelyn. Some handwritten letters revealed that Evelyn and William were having an affair. How much sister Gwen knew about it all was unclear.

Jo had been the one to bring all this to light last year when she discovered, buried beneath the crumbling estate, the remains of Evelyn herself—and the telltale signs of pregnancy etched in her bones. Curiously, no remains of a child were found with her, only a hope chest filled with baby clothes buried in the garden and the letters between her and William.

The questions surrounding the strange love triangle at Ardemore estate a century ago and what exactly happened to Evelyn's child haunted Jo, but the constant dead ends threatened to drive her mad. Even Roberta, who worked in a museum after all, was ready to let it go.

"Face facts," said the crusty old woman; the Ardemores had always been a "bad lot" who didn't care about community, and Evelyn and her baby "obviously" died in childbirth. Time to focus on the better part of the Ardmore property: Jekyll Gardens, about to open to the public in an event that would be historic for the town of Abington.

The kettle whistled and Jo jumped; she usually tried to stop it before the unholy screech. She poured hot water in the pot and steeped; if her sojourn in the north of England had taught anything, it was to *never* leave the tea bag in.

Her guest was awkward. But so was she. This could work.

She reached into the cupboard for the package of Jammie Dodgers. Jo bought them because, as a New Yorker, "Dodgers" would always mean Brooklyn, even though they had been in LA since 1957. Of course, there was the Artful Dodger, too, from Charles Dickens's *Oliver Twist.* A silly name for cookies, maybe, but the mix of American baseball and Victorian pickpocket appealed to her sense of incongruity.

She emptied the whole box onto the tea tray, and by the time she reached the living room, the man was standing in front of her. Clean and tidy and now in proper lighting, he offered her the chance for a better look.

Face: full, square at the jaw. Hair: dark and wet, combed back behind the ears. Mud-flecked black trousers had been changed to another pair, also black. Rather baggy. The blue button-down shirt was damp at the collar.

"How long were you standing in the rain?" Jo asked. "You were very wet."

"Sorry? "Oh. Yes. It's—I didn't have an umbrella." He touched the curl at his temple with a wandering fingertip.

Had she been rude? She held out the plate of biscuits to offer him one. He gave her the smile again. Salesman smile, she thought, but his eyes settled on the Dodgers with evident pleasure.

"You're out of the way, living up here."

"Sort of. We're close to the trails, though, and you can't get any nearer the Jekyll Gardens." Jo flapped a hand toward the window. "You'll practically be on the doorstep for tomorrow's opening ceremony."

That had been the entire point of finishing preparations for renting the cottage by May: the Jekyll Gardens Opening Celebration. Jo may have lost her ancestral home to a fire, but finding out that it was built on a garden designed by the renowned Gertrude Jekyll . . . Well, it was one for the books. The falling-down house at the edge of town had suddenly become a site of national historical significance. The whole National Trust seemed to have checked into the Red Lion inn.

"You're lucky," Jo added, hugging her knees in the rocking chair. "I barely got the weblink up before you booked in—otherwise there'd be stiff competition for a room, I'd bet."

He hadn't answered either comment, or her attempt at a joke, just chewed a sticky biscuit and drank tea. Jo felt a prickle run down her spine; was she not supposed to make chitchat? Wasn't that part of hosting duties? He'd looked at the clock twice, but after swallowing, he refocused on her.

"I'm afraid I didn't know about it. Just traveling through on business."

"Oh! But you're here at just the right time! The National Trust is opening the garden tomorrow—it's where the manor house used to be. Big party!"

"Sorry, a manor? I didn't see anything nearby . . ."

Jo jumped up and joined him by the window, pointing to the dark distance. "Well, you can't really see it from here. But just beyond the trees is Ardemore House. What was once Ardemore House, at least."

"So, it's a ruin?" her guest asked, and gulped his tea.

"Well, it is *now.* It was deserted for almost a century. The property was *supposed* to be in the care of my uncle Aiden in the nineties, but he never really tended to it. Didn't even live here, in fact." Jo looked up to see her guest gaping at her and stopped short.

"So you are a newcomer to Yorkshire, then?" he asked. Jo almost laughed. He wasn't exactly hanging on every word, was he?

"A yearling, I guess," she admitted. "I came here to start over after my divorce and the death of my mom last year. I didn't realize inheriting the estate would be so . . . complicated."

She felt herself at risk of rambling again, so she pulled out her phone and flipped to her photo library. "Here's the Ardemore House *before.* Here it is after the fire last year, still smoking. I was inside it when it burned down."

"You—What?"

Jo's finger kept swiping through the pictures. "That's the garden workmen over summer, and here is the original Gertrude Jekyll plan, and *this*—" Jo stopped at last on the National Trust page "—this is the announcement of its opening tomorrow! I'm sort of, em—part of the—committee."

Mr. Ronan Foley looked down dutifully at a bright summer green event ad: open time at 10:00 a.m., official ceremony at noon, under pavilion, rain or shine. He didn't say anything. Again. And Jo felt her heart hammering. Uncertain about chitchat, she'd instead launched into full-blown special interest lecture. *Nice, Jo.*

Or was it her reference to the fire? She'd got used to everyone knowing about all of that; it had caused quite a commotion in Abington. There'd even been interviews for the paper.

"Very interesting." His eyes roved about the room in a full circuit. Then he smiled, genuinely and wide. A surprised smile. "Well, it would be my pleasure to come."

Crap, Jo thought. She'd got a hapless rain-soaked businessman who booked the cottage *only* because he couldn't get into a hotel . . . and now she'd accidentally invited him to the gardens.

"You know, you really don't have to—" she began.

"No, I do. It's a wonderful idea. So many locals will be there, new people to meet. You can expect me . . ." His eyes strayed to the enormous painting over the fireplace even as he spoke. "My goodness. Beautiful painting."

Evelyn's portrait. It would be hard to miss. The near-life-size painting took up most of the chimney. The gilt frame glinted, offering the perfect contrast to the moody scene within: a woman with strange, distant eyes, a face simultaneously demure and retiring, fierce and resistant. She sat against a backdrop of flowers—yet the sky was a haze of storm.

"Yes. Evelyn Davies," Jo said. "An ancenstor."

Do not recite your family history. Do not mention that she was buried under the house.

Ronan took a closer look, tugging up his ill-fitting second trousers. From the side she could see his jaw was more pronounced, and he ran a thumb down its stubble, briefly lost in thought. Jo had often seen James MacAdams do that.

Which reminded her to text him with a reminder of the

details of the ceremony opening. Again. For good measure. Storybook detectives solved murders with wits, extraordinary attention to detail and the reflective power of eidetic memory. MacAdams relied on wits alone.

"Something about the eyes," Foley remarked, still staring at the portrait. "They don't quite square with the angle that her body is facing."

"Yes! I thought the same when I first saw it. The painting was damaged badly. Likely by acid. But I found out my uncle Aiden had it repaired when he lived here, and that's why the eyes look a bit 'off' from the rest."

"The artist's style is quite distinct," Foley was saying.

"It's an Augustus John painting," Jo said proudly. "You have a good eye. Are you into the arts at all?"

"No. Not in the least. I actually work in real estate development for an architecture firm. Boring stuff. You can call me Ronan, by the way."

"Ronan. Is that an Irish name?"

"I'm Irish originally. Live up in Newcastle now."

"I thought you might be," Jo admitted.

"We all look alike?" he laughed, a sort of bubbling chuckle in his throat.

"I don't know about that," Jo assured him. "But you do *sound* like my friend Tula Byrne. She owns the Red Lion."

"Tula?" He raised his eyebrows, mulling it over. "Irish indeed. How interesting. All the people in Abington seem quite . . . cozy."

Jo wasn't sure what to say to this. She watched him drink the rest of his tea while standing, then he pocketed some of biscuits.

"I'll be along tomorrow. Easy to spot—I'm on my last clean shirt and it's blazing red silk."

"Oh?" Jo wondered if this was his attempt at humor, and whether she should laugh.

He checked his watch with darting eyes. “It’s very late. I’m sure you’ll need to get up early.”

It *was* late, about eleven. And she did have to get up early, because she promised Tula she would. And given how stressed she’d been about meeting Mr. Late-coming Foley, Jo now needed another shower.

“Right. Good night, Mr.—” she replied, but he’d already disappeared up the narrow stair.

CHAPTER 2

Jo liked to think of herself as a morning person, awake in the space between dark and daylight, when the world was dew soaked and silent and new. But thinking didn't make it so. Her alarm had gone off twice already. It was six thirty-five and she'd promised to help load catering. At seven. *Dammit.* She'd been looking forward to the opening of the Jekyll Gardens for months, but she would have given her left arm to wriggle out of it now. That was the way of public engagements. Like mornings, they were better in theory than practice.

Perfunctory clean-up, hair in a short knot of ponytail. She was about to face a bunch of strangers, so the outfit of safety included her black jeans and a gray T-shirt. Jo tugged her Doc Martens on in the kitchen. So far, the skies looked clear but it was going to be squishy. She filled the electric kettle and set an assortment of teas on the counter with more biscuits. It looked a bit sad—like airline fare. She was going to have to up her game in future, but then again, her lodger hadn't even thought she'd be there. Technically she already exceeded expectations.

Jo peeked up the stairs: door still shut, no noises. Probably dead asleep. She crept quietly out the door. Jo was *almost* not late.

★ ★ ★

"Will wonders never cease!" Tula said, tossing Jo an apron as she walked into the Red Lion. "It's as early as I've seen you since the jet lag wore off. Be a dear, take the sausage tray out of the oven, would you? Ben's servicing the coffee rig."

Espresso machine, Jo translated. It was Ben's pride and joy, and Jo very much encouraged its use. But so far, it seemed best suited for creative malfunction.

Jo followed orders and retrieved an enormous tray overladen with varieties of rolls and pasties. Tula had already prepped breakfast for a dozen lodgers and half filled the travel cart with meat pies. Normally a welcome sight—but a bit much pork grease on an empty stomach.

"How many people are you expecting to turn up?" Jo asked, handing it over with pot-holders.

"The whole town had better, or I'll go after 'em with a switch and broom," Tula said, pushing a stray curl behind her ear. "Best thing to happen in Abington since I don't know when—we'll be booked all through the summer!"

That was the general sentiment: the discovery that the Gertrude Jekyll Gardens held historic significance meant a boost to tourism. Jo had achieved semicelebrity status among the town, particularly the small business owners.

"Anyway," Tula insisted, pulling the warming cover over her delicacies. "It's our first fete in ages. Sutton—from the poulterers, you know him—is bringing the generator; the cider house should be there, crafters. I ain't about to run out of eatables."

Judging from the number of tents ordered, it was going to be an honest to god circus up there. It caused a worrying clench in Jo's guts. "Fete, fallow, fiduciary," she whispered on repeat. All she had to do was cut a ribbon; Roberta Wilkinson promised to do the talking. And Gwilym, who was vying for the role of neurodivergent Watson to Jo's Sherlock, would be there, too. He'd booked his room about six months ago.

Tula signaled to Ben, steered Jo and the meat cart, and they were off on the first delivery trip.

There would be four of those, in the end, partly because Tula's Scout had the guns to get uphill well laden, and Sutton's delivery cart did not. Jo walked the green in her wellies; crushed gravel steamed in spring sunshine and temperatures promised to rise. White party tents glistened where Ardemore's circular drive had been, a combination market, fair and celebration.

Even the local vintner had a table, sporting cowslip wine. Which wasn't wine at all, but a fermented concoction of yellow petals and sugar (and sometimes brandy). Jo made a slight face; recalling that *cowslip* actually referred to the manure the flowers grew within. It took the romance right out of it. She settled on the tea tent instead, ordered black with milk and perched on a folding plastic chair. In the shadow of the tent flap, she could watch the general goings-on without being the center of attention.

"If I may say, you look conspiratorial."

Jo looked up to see Emery Lane, an acquaintance who worked at the Abington solicitor's office, in a white-and-blue suit, sporting a pink bow tie and boater hat. But he didn't look like an assistant to the town solicitor. He looked like—

"*Luncheon of the Boating Party*," she finished out loud.

Emery smiled under his pencil mustache. "Renoir?" he asked. "Very good."

"Sorry. But it's perfect—you could be painted in front of the garden terrace!"

"I was afraid you were going to say you discovered yet another unknown painting in Abington," he said, taking the seat next to her. "Speaking of which. How is your Augustus John original?"

"Evelyn is presiding over my living room magisterially," Jo said, blowing on her tea. "Is Rupert coming?"

"He is." Emery half hid behind his teacup. "But I am guessing that isn't who you're waiting for?"

"I'm not waiting for anyone."

"Not even James MacAdams, over there?" Emery asked, looking over her head.

"He's here?" Jo swiveled in place, but did *not* see a rumpled-looking detective. Instead, she saw only a vest-clad, hill-walking Welshman with a ginger man-bun.

Behind her, Emery chuckled.

"My mistake," he said innocently. "Hello, Gwilym!"

"Emery!" Gwilym gave the man an enthusiastic handshake that almost turned into a hug, but when he turned to Jo, the smile went lopsided. "Erm, I have some news—and I don't think you'll like it."

Jo gave Gwilym a look. No conversation should *ever* start like that. Especially not today. Jo braced herself, but Gwilym's attention had already been diverted. He took Emery's seat and cast his eyes at the tea tent's baked goods.

"Scones and clotted cream!" he announced.

"Bad news, you said," Jo reminded him. She could already guess. MacAdams wasn't going to be there; he'd told Tula, who told Gwilym, who took it upon himself to—

"It's Roberta," he said.

Jo heart pancaked against her sternum.

"Oh my God. Is she all right?" she asked, half rising in her seat. Roberta might be stalwart and stern, but she was *also* elderly and—

"What? Yes! Oh, yes—*she's* all right. It's just that she found a body on her way here and had to call the police to handle it, so she might be running late to the garden ceremony."

Jo sat down again, hard. So far, this had been a deeply unfair chain of emotional stimulants. She blinked, opened her mouth, then shut it again. Gwilym kept talking.

"Since she's been delayed, she thought you could give the

opening remarks. I mean, you were the one who found the garden plans—"

"A body. Like, a *dead* body?" Jo interrupted.

"Yes?"

"Whose?"

"She didn't know—or didn't say. The mobile service isn't great out there."

"Out where?"

"Oh. She was walking the trail from town. You can give the talk, right?"

Jo swallowed tea. Spur-of-the-moment presentation on Gertrude Jekyll. *Could* she? Obviously; she'd done most of the research for the brochure and could quote a few of the sources verbatim. But *Roberta found a body and would be delayed* needed to be processed at some point, alongside *the police had been informed.*

And of course, in Abington, *police* meant James MacAdams.

"Great," she said, and meant nothing of the sort.

CHAPTER 3

Detective Chief Inspector MacAdams stood at the edge of a weedy ditch. Below, marbled patches of black dirt, gray mud and bent grass turned to soup from the previous night's deluge. The town medical examiner, Eric Struthers, stooped to take a closer look at the body.

A man, dark haired, lay face down in the wet earth. No coat. No bag. A bit of a tumbled-over look, as if he'd rolled into position. Not especially remarkable, except for the gash in his skull, visible even from where MacAdams was standing.

Eric blinked up at him. "I'm going to need a hand getting out of here, James," he said.

MacAdams braced one foot against the gravel and the other on the firmer bank before giving Struthers a good tug. His boots pulled free with a bone-sucking sound.

"Cold and stiff," he said, scraping mud.

"Meaning?"

"Warm and stiff, three to eight hours. Cold and stiff, eight to thirty-six. I can tell you more after I get him to the lab." He peeled off his glove and looked to the sky above him. "Weather plays a role. Warm now but was cold and wet last night. But since rigor mortis hasn't worn off yet, it's safe to say he hasn't been here more than twenty-four hours. Maybe even as early as last night."

"Any chance it was a hit-and-run?" MacAdams asked dubiously. Struthers gave him a plastic smile.

"Wishful thinking, I'm afraid. I'll know more after we get him under the lights, but in the absence of broken bones, torn clothing or tire marks? I'd say murder."

Of course. MacAdams turned his attention to the bright horizon; the sun had come up against a cloudless sky, all hint of storm forgotten. The Jekyll Gardens opening was no doubt off to a glorious start.

"Ah-hem, Detective." Roberta Wilkinson stared at him through her yellow-lamplight glasses and struck the ground with her walking stick for emphasis. "I *do* have somewhere to be, you know."

"I've taken a statement," said Detective Sergeant Sheila Green, MacAdams's partner, waving a notepad over the shorter woman's gray-white head.

"I'll get Uniform to drop you at the, ah . . ."

"Jekyll Gardens," Roberta barked, sniffing the air with a stately my-kin-were-born-to-the-land frown. "Forget it. Came this far. I'll just walk. Though I take it *you'll* be late."

There was a nearly 100 percent chance that he wouldn't make it at all, despite being dressed for it. He didn't say so, and Roberta hadn't waited for a reply anyway before she started down the road.

"She takes right to roam very seriously," Green said, slapping her notebook against her left palm. "Started this morning from the Mill, nine o'clock sharp. Took the trail up over the stiles, but apparently part of it was flooded, so she came up this way to the road."

MacAdams nodded. There were two lanes: one that led directly to Jo's cottage and the gardens, and one that ran along the walking path.

"She walked right past him. Then called us."

It had been spotty, a crackling voice cutting in and out, though MacAdams was more surprised by the fact Roberta Wilkinson owned a mobile than that she'd managed to get a signal. He'd been halfway through breakfast.

Green closed the notebook. "Nothing else of use, frankly. Didn't see anyone, no sign of cars or other walkers, etc. If Roberta hadn't been along, there's no telling when we might have found him."

"It would be a quieter Saturday if she hadn't," MacAdams said dryly.

"Sir? I think he might still have ID on him," a uniformed police officer shouted from the ditch. Three of them were attempting the task of getting the body onto a gurney. The lad picked something up from the ground below.

"Yeah? And an earring. I think?"

"A what?" Green asked—but Struthers nearly leaped back into the ditch.

"Leave it!" he barked. "Leave it, *please*. It's evidence and you aren't even wearing gloves." He snatched the leather wallet from the officer and bagged it. Then he leaned into the mud once more. "Earring or pendant. Gold."

"Maybe torn off in a struggle?" MacAdams asked.

"Don't think so. Delicate little thing." He pulled it free with tweezers and dropped it into another plastic envelope. "I'll process everything and call you. You'll be in your office?"

MacAdams sighed. *So it would seem.*

★ ★ ★

Abington CID hadn't changed very much in a year, though it was in want of a chief. The old boss, Cora Clapham, had abruptly left the precinct in light of the familial corruption that came to light in their last case. She was now in Southampton, last MacAdams heard. The job opening had been advertised rather *aggressively* in MacAdams's direction, but he wasn't fool enough to take it. Then again, he'd ended up as de facto interim chief without the attendant promotion . . . so perhaps he was a fool, at that.

"Gridley's making coffee," said Detective Constable Tommy Andrews when they made it back to the station. Kate Gridley was better at coffee than most. Almost a promotional capability, something to remember when it was time to consider a second sergeant.

"Good, could use some." MacAdams tossed his coat over a chair.

"You, eh, had other plans, I thought?"

"It's a village fete," MacAdams said, as if this explained the freshly ironed light gray slacks and rather more festive than usual tie. "Bit like May Day."

Green only shrugged, sat backward on a swivel chair. "Today isn't May Day—and *you* didn't answer my question, boss."

"Yes," MacAdams said, demurring to his attire. "I had other plans. And now, I have a murder investigation. Shall we?"

Kate Gridley had reappeared from the kitchenette; by far the most tech savvy of the bunch, she already had several search engines running and ready, and still managed to start coffee. MacAdams seized his chance for a moment of silence—and a coffee mug. Then he opened his messaging app. The last one had been from Jo, reminding him of the opening time. MacAdams scrolled to the chat window, thought better of it and returned the phone to his pocket. He had at least three reasons for this. One: a (completely unlikely) hope that he could make it to Jo—rather, the gardens—before festivities were over. Two: the dead body in Struthers's forensic lab, and three—

"Boss!" Green leaned through the doorway. "ID from Struthers. Driver's license and credit cards."

"I guess that means it wasn't a robbery," MacAdams sighed. He pulled the glass pot before it was finished, leaving drips to hiss on the hot plate as he poured a slug of black. "All right, let's meet our victim."

Gridley responded by taking a rubber band from her wrist and pulling back shoulder-length hair—her way of settling in for the long haul.

"Murder is murdery," Andrews said, sitting down beside her. "What are his details?"

MacAdams reached into the bag for the trifold wallet. Inside was a folded twenty-pound note, three credit cards and a driver's license. Predictably, he didn't recognize the name. His eyes jumped down to the license number and location: 06 03 1962 Belfast.

"Ireland," MacAdams said. "Issued in 2019."

"So not a current address?" Green asked.

"We'll find out. We can run these credit cards, too. See what he's been up to in the last twenty-four hours."

He cleaned off the whiteboard and wrote out the deceased's name and age at the top. Then, he left them to it and returned to his office to hunt up a current photograph.

The man proved surprisingly easy to find. Despite the address listed on the dated license, his name popped up repeatedly alongside a firm in Newcastle: Hammersmith, just like the London train line. The company website listed three contacts, an executive named Stanley Burnhope and two agents—one of whom matched the license photo. The man's hair was not yet grizzled, with an incongruity that suggested hair dye. Strong jaw, gaunt face, wide-set eyes, slightly hooded, hawkish nose. Not unattractive, but not striking. The sort you could lose in a crowd.

"Heya, boss." Green leaned against his door frame, muscular arms crossed, signature eyebrow-raise. "It's almost noon. You could *definitely* still get to the garden opening."

"Sheila," MacAdams said, taking the still-warm printout by the corner. "You put off your honeymoon with Rachel for a money-laundering case."

"And Covid. Remember?"

"All the same."

"Not all the same," she insisted, turning her severe chin toward Andrews and Gridley. "Bet you two would like a lunch brought back, right? You know Tula does meat pies."

"And sausage rolls," Andrews suggested.

"And cakes," Gridley agreed, waving from behind her computer.

"Right. And I want curried chips. Extra curry." Green gave him a toothy smile of appreciation. "You would be doing us *all* a favor."

MacAdams did not, as a rule, outwardly express much emotion. Genetic predisposition, probably, as his father's face showed about as much feeling as a cricket bat. He did, however, have the uncomfortable sense that his team mistook the local fete for a date he was not having. And the room seemed a trifle warm, if he were honest.

"We have a lot of legwork to do," he said firmly. "The first few hours after a crime can make or break an investigation, so no—I'm not running up a take-away order to Jekyll Gardens."

"Actually," Gridley interrupted, holding up one finger. "I think you had *better* go, boss. I just found the last transaction on his credit card, and you aren't going to like this one bit."

MacAdams leaned over her shoulder to view the wide-screen monitor. The charge, made late on Friday, hadn't even cleared yet. It remained gray, pending, from a Ronan Foley to the account of one Josephine Jones, *Netherleigh Cottage.*

CHAPTER 4

This was not how MacAdams had imagined his day. He'd put the mackintosh back on, despite the warmth, and stood in back of a surprisingly attentive crowd. Up on stage, Jo Jones held forth about botany, architecture and Gertrude Jekyll as though it was her principal stock in trade. The utter ease with which she interwove the histories she'd only just learned herself was admittedly impressive, all while bouncing enthusiastically on short legs, ponytail bobbing wildly. He could see the ever-eager Gwilym, too. He seemed to be holding up placards with images too distant to make out, and mainly staying out of her way.

On second thought, this *was* how he intended to spend the fete—just not with the intent of questioning her about *another* dead body, or demanding yet *another* search of her premises. Why could she not just steer clear of murder?

"To quote Jekyll herself," Jo said, her voice rising in crescendo. "'The love of gardening is a seed that once sown never dies. There is no spot of ground, however arid, bare or ugly, that cannot be tamed into such a state as may give an impression of beauty and delight.' Thank you."

★ ★ ★

When the applause subsided, Roberta Wilkinson—who had made it, after all—handed Jo a pair of oversize scissors. The yellow ribbon fell away and Jekyll Gardens opened at last to the public. There were party crackers and cheers, and MacAdams began the inglorious work of threading through the crowd.

"Well, well! You came after all," said a spring-fresh Emery Lane. He towed along a more conservatively attired Rupert Selkirk, his partner both in life and at the law firm.

"Official business, unfortunately," MacAdams said.

Rupert's bushy brows gave the slightest rise.

"Nothing serious, I hope." He said it genially enough, though a certain coolness had developed between them since the murder of Sid Randles last year. It was an investigation that required a bit of "special research" into Rupert's personal affairs to guarantee his cooperation.

"I'm just trying to reach Ms. Jones." The couple gave way and let MacAdams get on with it. He was certainly trying. An excited throng mobbed the little stage and Jo was in the thick of it—wide-eyed, semifrozen.

"So your ancestor was a thief and a forger? Is that how he got rich?"

"Are *you* rich?"

"This is where that house burned down, isn't it?"

"Were you really *inside* when he—"

"Ladies and Gentlemen!" MacAdams barked in his best clear-the-way baritone. He spotted Gwilym, took him by the shoulders and placed him bodily in front of Jo Jones. "This gentleman here will answer all of your questions."

"I will?" Gwilym asked—but MacAdams already had a hand on Jo's shoulder and was steering her into the clear.

"Is there somewhere we can talk?" he asked, scanning the increasingly noisy party grounds. Jo still had a fish-eyed look, but she followed him in acquiescence. Once inside a tea tent nearby, she perched herself on a corner folding chair, and MacAdams flagged the hostess: Teresa, if he remembered right. Kate Gridley's niece.

"Milky tea with a lot of sugar," he said, pointing to Jo. "Then I need you to close shop for a bit, Teresa."

"James! It's my first event—you know we just opened. I need this!" she protested.

This was a fact. MacAdams sighed and fished out his credit card. Probably a good thing he never had kids with his ex-wife; there were plenty of others happy to spend his money.

"Run this for thirty quid and then go for a walk."

Teresa crossed her arms and did the new-adult version of pouting.

"Fine! Run it for fifty. It's police business."

"I'm gonna ask Auntie," she said, but very happily ran his card on her mobile register. He watched her bounce away then partly closed the tent flap for a bit of privacy. Jo—well, Jo drank tea.

"That's a lot of sugar," she said.

"Helps the nerves—" MacAdams began, but she finished for him.

"L-Theanine, amino acid in black tea. It induces a sense of relaxed calm and lowers cortisol levels. The sugar just releases serotonin into the bloodstream," she said, swallowing. "But you don't need quite this much."

"Thank you for that."

"Your welco—Actually, thank *you*. My hero and everything."

"Don't speak too soon," MacAdams muttered, pulling out his notebook. Jo put the cup back on its saucer.

"Oh. The dead body," she said. MacAdams scratched his chin with the end of his pencil. *Roberta*. No doubt the whole town would know all about it by day's end.

"Yes, a body was found. And I have some additional bad news," he said.

Jo nodded before delivering the matter-of-fact pronouncement: "It's my lodger, isn't it?"

★ ★ ★

Jo didn't remember what she'd said on stage. Or, rather, she remembered the material, just not her performance of it. She'd never had a fear of public speaking—if anything, she excelled at it in school. Just not for the reasons people thought. Up there, she wasn't making small talk or even conversing with another person. It was just Jo, her special interest and the irresistible desire to share it. While in the middle of it, a sort of synethesia took over; she could see the arc of her story lit up by animated pictures, each fact bursting with color and light. When it was over, she felt a bit punch-drunk and was, as a result, completely unprepared for a people onslaught after stepping off the stage.

When Jo had seen MacAdams making his way through the crowd, her immediate response had been one of wild relief. Second, and upon its heels, though—a feeling of presentiment. There was a body, Gwilym had said. A man's body, in a red shirt, Roberta had added. Now that the post-speech haze had lifted, everything else she'd been thinking between events came pouring out.

"This morning! I just thought it was so early, he must still *be* there. But I should have checked!"

MacAdams had not moved since she started spilling details, and still seemed in suspended animation. When she stuttered to a halt, however, he put both hands in the air.

"You had no reason to think anything was wrong—"

"But I did. Because of the car," Jo interrupted.

"What car?"

"There wasn't one."

MacAdams opened his mouth, shut it again, then fetched

himself a cup of sugar tea and slugged it like a shot. When he returned he picked up the pencil and notebook.

"Can we start over, please? You started in the middle of a conversation we weren't having yet." He paused with forced bemusement. "Again. *Yet* again."

Jo knew he was trying to put her at ease and failing a *lot*. Jo took a breath and red-penciled the narrative in her head.

"He booked late in the afternoon, but didn't turn up until just after ten. In the storm. He was soaked."

"Did he seem agitated?" MacAdams asked.

Jo shut her eyes. She could see him so plainly, framed against her doorway and backed by sheets of rain. She'd thought of surprised pigeons and body snatchers. Those did not seem like good examples.

"*Great Expectations*—you've read it, right? Mr. Pocket keeps trying to lift himself up by his own hair. That's how he looked."

"Could we try a suitable adjective?" MacAdams asked. Jo's nose twitched.

"Surprised? Harried? He thought it was a self-catering cottage. And he didn't come to Abington for the gardens at all—just on business, he said. But when I told him about it, he said he'd be there, wearing a fancy red shirt."

"And when was the last you saw of him?"

"Last night. Had a blue shirt and a rumpled, wet raincoat. Greenish—khaki, I guess? He changed out of muddy pants, ate a lot of biscuits and went up to bed before eleven." She paused, thinking about the steamed dial of her bathroom clock. "I know, because I was in the shower by eleven ten."

MacAdams's pencil had been busily scratching, but now he looked up.

"How does that relate to the car—that wasn't?" he asked. Jo blanked for a moment; it seemed so obvious now, almost beyond saying. Yet she'd missed it, too.

"When I left this morning, there wasn't any sign that he had a car. I mean, I didn't see one last night, either, but he got here somehow, didn't he? I should have realized something was . . . well, wrong."

MacAdams sat straighter, smoothing his own coat lapels after her description of Foley.

"You know we'll need to search the cottage," he said.

"You aren't going to ban me from my home this time, are you? He didn't get murdered there!"

MacAdams winced. "It's not officially a murder until forensics—"

"Roberta said someone bashed his head in," Jo interrupted. The wince hadn't faded; it instead acquired a grimace.

"Yes, she is very forthright, is Roberta," MacAdams said. "I will want a full statement from you, everything you remember. And I'll need your keys for now."

Jo put her hand inside her pocket, but didn't withdraw them. "Nah-ah. I'm coming with you."

Of course she was. Saying no would change nothing, and to be honest, he wasn't inclined to refuse her, anyway. He dialed the station for a forensic search team to follow, and asked her to lead on.

★ ★ ★

Jo fumbled slightly with the lock and dead bolt. MacAdams had wanted to go in first, but it was her house—and if anything was wrong, she'd know straight off.

"Here we are," she said, stepping through. Nothing moved, not her books, not the furniture . . . not the tea and biscuits on the island that separated the tiny kitchen from the living room.

"This was your first guest?" MacAdams was asking behind her, but Jo had just reached the unopened Jammie Dodgers, and her answer stuck in her throat. Somehow, the little cookies unlocked emotions that the death announcement itself had not. She'd learned that lesson first when her mother died; the strawberries Jo bought for her spoiled in the fridge. Death was hard to grasp, uneaten meals painfully tangible.

"Sorry. Yes—he, um, he really liked these." She waved the package.

"And his room?" MacAdams asked.

Technically, he'd seen the place before as a work in progress. He *may* have participated in some of the work himself, especially the bathtub business. She'd meant to show it off in a more official way once complete, really impress him with it, but hadn't got around to it. Now she hovered at the door, wondering if something awful might be on the other side. MacAdams was still behind her, on the stairs (and so also partly in the living room). *Click-clack-click*. The door swung open to reveal—nothing much.

They stepped into the breezy, yellow-green room, glinting in sunlight. It looked almost *exactly* as it had before Ronan Foley ever arrived: new half bath in one corner, full-size bed, bureau, minitable, chintz armchair . . . and fresh wallpaper in green floral. It made Jo think of *The Wind in the Willows* and sundry fur creatures huddled under quilts with steaming mugs of tea.

"Did you remake the bed?" MacAdams asked.

"Not me. And *he* didn't, either—I know how I make a bed." Jo pointed to the careful seams and tidily tucked corners. "He never slept in it."

MacAdams didn't reply; his attention had been drawn to the man's duffel. It lay unzipped at one end of the mattress.

"You saw him close his door at eleven?"

"Yes. Then I showered. Was in bed by midnight."

"And everything—this door, the cottage door—was locked up this morning?" MacAdams asked.

"I didn't check this one. The front door was unlocked," she said. MacAdams did almost a full circle turn, like a clumsy pirouette.

"Why didn't you say so?" he asked, and Jo felt her face get warm. She grew up in Chicago and New York, learning to install all the best locks and dead bolts. But a year in the quiet countryside had made her forgetful—so much so, that leaving the doors unlocked of an evening had become a semiregular thing.

"Because I'm the one who didn't lock it."

CHAPTER 5

A victim had been murdered a crow's mile from Jo's cottage. A year earlier, and a man had been murdered *in* Jo's cottage. Would nothing trigger even an ounce of self-preservation in this woman?

"How, Jo? *How* can you forget to lock up?" he demanded.

"I swear, I meant to! Especially with a guest staying," she said, as though this weren't even more baffling.

"All right. So he left sometime in the night." His eyes fell upon the bedstand where two keys glinted in morning sun. "And you're lucky he didn't take those with him, or the murderer might have them right now." He resisted saying *again*.

"I just don't understand," Jo said, looking around. "He seemed in such a hurry to get to bed, then doesn't sleep here?"

MacAdams turned his attention to the overnight bag, pulling a latex glove from one pocket.

"Don't touch anything," he cautioned. "You said he was on business. Did he say what kind?"

"No. Do you always keep forensic gloves in your pocket?" Jo asked, peering into the bag from the other side of the bed.

He didn't unless he started the day off with a corpse in a ditch.

The nagging irritation was spreading like an itch. MacAdams pushed back the duffel flap with more violence than necessary and fished out a knit vest, an unworn long-sleeved tee, the blue button-down and one very soiled and still damp pair of trousers. They'd been shoved in on top of the cleaner clothes, which didn't make much sense. He looked closer at the fabric—all of it spattered in mud.

"That's what he had been wearing," Jo said. "Plus a rather short raincoat. It only went to his hips."

The man must've walked to the cottage last night, like Roberta had done. It might explain why Jo hadn't noticed a vehicle. But who walks across the fields in a downpour?

"Where's the raincoat?" MacAdams asked, peering into the empty bag and then casting his eyes around the room. Jo closed her eyes and flapped her hands at the wrist.

"Double breasted, dark buttons. A sort of Sherlock cape thing at the back—gun flap." She opened them again. "Not here, is it?"

It was not. And the body wasn't wearing it, either. MacAdams called Green. It was a clue, if an absent one. He rang off to find Jo in the closet-small toilet.

"I don't believe it," she said, voice muffled. "He stole my soap and washcloth—" she looked at the clawfoot tub "—*and* the towel?"

MacAdams made a quick survey of the toilet and bath, even crouching to look under the bed. No towels. The duffel had an assortment of toiletries tossed in the bottom. A very strange business trip indeed.

"This doesn't make any *sense*," Jo complained. "He left in the middle of the night without his bag, but takes my *towels*?" She had walked to the nearby chair and prepared to sit in it; MacAdams caught her by both elbows.

"Evidence," he cautioned. Jo grasped back and hung suspended from his forearms with a *sorry!* expression. He leaned backward, pulling her upright next to him, if a foot shorter.

"Detective?" A uniformed officer stood in the doorway. "Was unlocked, sir."

MacAdams let go of Jo a little abruptly.

"Thank you, Officer," he said, crossing the room. "Get the team in here and get the contents of that bag to Struthers."

"Yes, sir."

"No one in or out till we're through, Jo. I mean that. No strangers, no guests, no random businessmen."

"He wasn't 'some stranger,'" Jo interrupted. "He was a *guest* at my *rental cottage*."

"Yes, and I need to see his booking." Possibly, he'd switched rather suddenly into hard-boiled. *Consequence of the job*, he told himself, unconvincingly. And Jo was catching the edge of his ill humor. But she sent him the booking details as requested, and handed over her keys before they returned to what should have been a celebratory event.

★ ★ ★

Forensics (minus the head of the department, Struthers, who was busy with their victim) bagged Foley's belongings and made the usual sweep. Nothing else of note. MacAdams met Green at the station with Jo's keys in his pocket, and in a very unpleasant mood.

"What's the news?" he demanded.

Green waved her phone at him.

"Gimme a minute. Getting Uniform over to his apartment," she said. MacAdams waited until she closed the call, though not very patiently.

"Okay, so, Foley's flat. Turns out to be an extended-stay place. The kind that comes already furnished."

"How long was he there?" MacAdams asked.

"Last six months. Sold a flat in Whickham, apparently. Struthers isn't finished with his analysis on the duffel yet, by the way."

"Well, we have the death window, regardless. Jo saw him close his door at eleven."

"And Roberta found him at eight thirty." Green nodded. "What about the cottage?"

"They're looking at his clothes right now. Trousers were muddy, suggests a walk." MacAdams looked to the whiteboard.

Someone had written "Hammersmith" in bright blue, and both "Ronan Foley" and the "CEO" were stuck by magnet underneath.

"Where is this place?" he asked.

"Gallowgate in Newcastle," Green explained. "A Knight Frank kind of setup for commercial real estate, but smaller scale."

"And his executive, Stanley Burnhope?" MacAdams asked, tapping the photo of a dark-haired, smiling city boy type.

"We tried his office," Gridley said, emerging from her ramen and egg. "Closed on weekends, and I figured you might want to make a house call anyway. Opens Monday at 9:00 a.m."

MacAdams tapped rhythmically on the back of a plastic chair. It meant they would lose all Sunday for that angle; weekend murders were very inconvenient.

"On the bright side, we got cleared for the work email. It matches the one on the booking form you forwarded," Andrews said, handing him a printout. "It's basic—rfoley@hammersmith. No personal stuff, apparently. Must have another email for that."

The subject headings mostly concerned a series of overseas properties—and an unfinished job in York. MacAdams made a mental note.

"Look at this latest one, though," Andrews said. "It's from Foley to Burnhope; it says 'partner meeting.' Except the website doesn't list Foley as a partner. And check this out—the email header says, 'Meet Friday at 4:00 p.m. to discuss business.'"

MacAdams wrote a timeline on the board.

"Meeting at four, he reserves the cottage by five according

to the registration, arrived at ten—dies after eleven, found by eight thirty Saturday morning."

"Right. But he really *shouldn't* have been," Green said. She'd returned to her desk with a pile of curried chips in Styrofoam. In fact, everyone had managed to get lunch except MacAdams, despite his proximity to sausage rolls. "The murderer picked a damn good spot. That access road isn't traveled all that much."

"Hard to get to as well," Gridley added. "I mean, what with the rain."

"Hard to get to," MacAdams repeated. "Like the cottage itself. Did he walk up there? If he drove, in what? Where is the car now? And why are the towels missing?"

"The towels?" Green asked.

MacAdams filled them in on the missing items, which included the coat, as well.

Gridley cracked her knuckles. "A thought. It was storming, right? Maybe he started to drive to the cottage, got stuck and walked the rest of the way."

MacAdams rubbed his chin and paced under the fluorescents. Surely he'd have mentioned it to Jo when he arrived to the cottage?

"Keep going with the theory. His car is stuck and . . . ?" he encouraged.

"Hang on, I'm getting a map." There was a nearby stack of brochures for the garden's opening that had the town map printed in friendly cartoon colors on the back. She grabbed one and used it as a guide to draw a rudimentary copy in dry erase marker.

"Okay, here's the road and here's the lane. I've been up there walking, and it's steep. Gravel gets waterlogged and muddy, let's say his car gets halfway. Maybe he even tried to push the car out."

"It would explain the spattered pants," MacAdams agreed.

"Right. So, then the rain stops and he thinks about going back for it."

"In the middle of the night?" Andrews asked. "Surely you would wait for morning."

"Unless you were lured back out," MacAdams said. "But it doesn't make sense. If someone calls him out, or even if he chooses to go back on his own, why wearing your only dry pants? And why take soap and towel?" There were holes a-plenty, but the team wasn't quite ready to give it up.

"You said he left the cottage keys, right? Maybe he wasn't going back for the car," Green suggested. "Maybe he was leaving. Bugging out. You said yourself there wasn't much in the overnight bag, and most of the essentials he took with him."

MacAdams frowned. That much about the empty duffel was true, and it bothered him a bit. What had he really been traveling here for?

"We have his wallet, but no phone. We know his work email, but nothing personal about him. He's a blank. We've had the local constabulary search his flat, and nothing of import so far."

"There's the earring," Green said. "Struthers still has it, but maybe that will lead somewhere."

MacAdams nodded. It was the outlier, and incongruous as the red silk shirt. There would be more, little bits and pieces for a fuller picture.

"We'll go to his flat ourselves. That's where we'll go tomorrow, then." He thumbed at his jaw. "About the missing car—if ever it was stuck on the lane, it isn't there now."

"We could check CCTV, maybe?" Andrews asked.

Gridley was two steps ahead and merely turned her computer screen to face them.

"Once you get past the Mill, there isn't much going. I have pulled files for a petrol station and the Mill's security camera. Anyone headed that way late at night in a thunderstorm might be of interest."

"Give that to Andrews," MacAdams suggested. Youngest of the team, Tommy had a good eye for details, but wasn't as experienced on the tech side of things. "Gridley, you chase up Ronan's details and whatever you can get on his company, Hammersmith. Green, we'll go hunting up the flat, and let's look into his boss Burnhope, too."

"Got it. I take it we don't have much hope, then, for helpful evidence from the cottage?"

MacAdams felt his earlier annoyance suddenly returning. "No. And yes. *Why* stay at Jo's cottage, of all places? Why *there*?"

"The Red Lion was booked," Andrews reminded him.

MacAdams shot him a glance. "There's a whole hotel on the south side called Abington Arms. Were they booked, too? I know the opening was well attended, but most everyone was still a local." MacAdams rolled his shirtsleeves up. "Ronan's movements don't make sense. Middle-of-the-night business trip is strange enough. But why pick the worst possible place to stay?"

Green had just made a slight noise in the back of her throat. It did not bode well, but it was Gridley who spoke.

"I don't know, boss. I've seen Jo's cottage. Charming—Teresa wants to host a tea event there. And it's on the doorstep of the gardens. It's a nice last-minute option."

"For day trippers, maybe. Up a muddy lane, well outside of town. Alone." He checked himself. "It's out of the way, is my point."

"You're reaching," Green cautioned. Behind her, Andrews put the phone receiver against his chest before speaking.

"The Abington Arms wasn't booked up," he said. "Rooms available, and a few low-end ones are cheaper than Jo priced the cottage, according to Airbnb." MacAdams gave Green a validated look.

"All right," she agreed. "But it could *still* have come down to incidentals—like ease and last-minute timing. We know he had a business meeting. We don't know that it went *well*."

"As in, he's been fired or such, and is now in a hurry to . . . do what?" MacAdams took a breath. His stomach was growling. He found himself looking around half-consciously for stray biscuits, half wishing he'd taken Jo's leftover Jammie Dodgers. "Something's been coming, and I think he knew it. Sells a house, lives in a furnished rental, takes flight in a hurry with a badly packed bag—ends up dead."

He had more to add, but his phone was ringing. A quick look told him all he needed to know. Struthers was ready for them.

CHAPTER 6

Struthers's forensic lab occupied space below the Abington clinic, walking distance from the station, technically connected if you took the right hallways. MacAdams thought he could probably navigate by smell: antiseptic and the not-quite-something-else he'd learned to associate with morgues in general.

"Come in, come in—just scrubbing up," Struthers said. He looked fresher than he had that morning, though his fair hair now stuck up at odd angles.

"Record time, Eric," MacAdams said.

"Well, it's just the autopsy so far. I have more work to do on the clothing you sent, but come see our chap up close and personal."

Struthers led him to the metal slab and a now-nude cadaver, covered to the waist in a blue sheet.

"We're lucky the blow came from behind," he was saying. "Otherwise, it would have caved in the nose and eye-sockets."

"Thanks for that." MacAdams grimaced. "I imagine he didn't see it coming?"

"No defensive wounds to speak of, no. And as predicted, no broken bones or bruising that might have been consistent with car strike. The impact had to be made by something heavy, possibly with a flat edge to one side." Struthers turned on the backlit screen to show off the X-rays.

"That could be anything," MacAdams said as he looked at the gray-white screen.

"Not *anything.*" Struthers mimicked a downward striking motion. "The blow was downward arcing."

"Meaning it came from above?"

"I think so, based on the point of entry. The object would have been solid, with at least one edge, but not uniform in shape."

"So not a hammer?" Green asked.

"A hammer leaves a proper indent, and fractures in a standard way, usually leaving a nice clean hole. I am still trying to ascertain the shape, but whatever it was, I'd say a hell of a blow." Eric pointed to two trays farther along. "Still going through his belongings—not much to report. Expensive shirt, that. Silk. Trousers don't really go with the ensemble. Bit humdrum."

"What about the piece of jewelry?"

"Ah. That's more interesting, but also seems a tad out of place. No prints or anything useful, but I sent one of the lads to the jeweler in town for a look."

"Earring, wasn't it?" Green asked.

"Seems to be. Not for him, though. Ears weren't pierced."

MacAdams made a mental note. "Belonged to the killer, then? Yanked out in the scuffle?"

"Only if the dead man managed to put the back on it again after. No, I'd say it was in a shirt pocket or something. The other might be at the bottom of the mud pit. That's it for the outer possessions." He gestured to the table farthest. "Now, the viscera. Might help with the time of death. His liver and lungs tell a story, at least."

MacAdams cleared his throat. "Drinker and smoke, then?"

Struthers wagged a finger at him. "*Used* to be. I'd say this chap was cleaning up his life. Plenty of regeneration. Longtime smoker, but not recently—maybe even a teetotaler."

"Is his hair natural?" Green took a closer look at the body.

"Dyed, but he still had plenty of it at least. Good muscle structure, heart in decent shape. Sixty-two by the driver's license but looks younger inside and out. Shame to do all that work for nothing."

"A cautionary tale," Green suggested. "What are those marks from?"

MacAdams leaned forward over the sternum. Grayish skin, the usual amount of chest hair. There were, however, oddly shaped patches of white.

"A skin condition?" MacAdams asked.

"Like vitiligo, maybe?" Green added. Struthers followed her gaze, and put on another pair of gloves. He slid one finger over the discoloration.

"Not sure yet. They happened after death—and I can't rule out the boys' manhandling him out of the ditch." He smiled at her. "You have sharp eyes. I didn't think you'd even notice them."

Green really did have sharp eyes—and used them a lot on MacAdams. She saved her beyond-case query for the elevator.

"Okay, boss. What happened? You skipped lunch, your neck tendons look like iron cables and you've been talking without moving your jaw."

"A murder happened, Green."

"Yes, that keeps us in our jobs. I mean what happened when you saw Jo?"

MacAdams had given them all a detailed description of what happened . . . so he knew very well her question wasn't about protocol. And she knew him well enough to spot a lie.

"You would think after everything that happened last year, she wouldn't open her house to murder victims."

Green gave him a slow blink. "I'm pretty sure that wasn't in either of their plans."

"It's not safe. You've seen how small she is."

"Oh my God. James." Green put her back to the wall beside him as if she needed a breather. "What's safe? We've got break-ins, theft, vandalism. Hell, stalkers. And what about Tula? She rents ten rooms at a time to perfect strangers. Anything could happen. It usually doesn't."

"Yes. But Tula has *Ben*," MacAdams protested. And with that, he'd stepped in something he couldn't back out of. Green stood straight and bucked her razor chin in his direction.

"Oh. *I* see."

"Not what I meant," he protested. Green shook her head.

"It *is* what you meant. She's a woman. That's it, isn't it? After everything, you still think that woman can't take care of herself?"

Of course women could take care of themselves. They also took care of everything and everyone else. And he'd had that, once.

There were times when MacAdams wondered if he should have just stayed married to Annie, taken a lateral move to desk work and moved to York like she wanted. They might have had a family. She could have been the one with ideas, and MacAdams could have become the sort of man who complains about *kids these days* but otherwise avoids having strong opinions.

Instead, he was a single DCI with a DS who knew where to kick him and somewhat complicated feelings for a woman who kept embroiling herself in local murders. Green's nostrils had flared and her pupils dilated; he had truly offended her, and now he was the one in need of a breather.

"Okay," he said slowly.

"Okay? How about *I'm sorry for being a patriarchal son of a bitch*?" Green asked. This was tipping into insubordination territory, but MacAdams assumed he deserved it.

"I'm sorry. I *am*," he admitted. "She just—troubles me."

Green looked far from appeased, but she'd stopped looking daggers at him.

"That's why you like her, in'it?"

★ ★ ★

Gwilym had bought Jo's whiskey, or tried to, except Tula made everything she ordered "on the house." If she didn't watch very carefully, she'd end up too far gone to drive home.

"Was brilliant, I'm saying, you wowed everyone," he was saying. Again.

"Aye, even Roberta was impressed, and that's no mean feat!" Tula gave Jo's shoulder a good shake. She'd removed her apron and declared herself off the clock. Patrons were welcome to the (few) remaining sausage rolls, and Ben could pour the drinks if necessary. It wasn't very busy for a Saturday night, the beer tent having been well-patronized during the fete. Most people had left the day's events happy, well-fed and a bit sunburned. Gwilym certainly was.

"I honestly think the day's event outperformed the . . . local gossip," Ben said.

"Local *murder*," Jo corrected. "At my cottage." Jo raised her glass, just not her spirits. Dead bodies had a way of dampening things. Including the cottage's future prospects as a restful retreat.

"Now, wasn't actually killed there this time, remember?" Tula soothed.

"Plus, *I'd* stay in a murder cottage," Gwilym offered.

"Course you would," Tula smirked. She turned and disappeared through the kitchen door for a moment before returning with a tartan flask and shot glasses. "Celebrating, aren't we? A toast to Jekyll Gardens, tourist season and Jo Jones."

"I'm having a guess this is moonshine?" Gwilym asked, twirling the Guy Fawkes mustache he sported these days. Tula gave him a solemn look.

"Gwilym Morgan of Wales," she said sternly, "I would never countenance illegal trade in this fine establishment.

"Nor thwart the liquor tax," Ben added with a wink.

Nor have a still in the woodshed behind the Red Lion, Jo thought.

"Forgive mine ignorance," Gwilym said with a bow.

Tula unscrewed the cap and poured out colorless liquid.

"To Jo," she said, raising hers. "For a rousing speech. To Jekyll, for many tourists to come . . . And to James MacAdams for that spectacular tie."

Jo tilted her head at the last bit—but Ben was now pointing toward the door. Jo followed his gaze to see MacAdams; he was *here*, probably to deliver her keys. She decided to take the shot before turning around.

"Jesus!" she sputtered, coughing. It didn't just burn; it was fire incarnate. It also made her nose run, so she sought for a napkin. By then, MacAdams had crossed the room and taken a seat at the bar beside her.

"Tula's medicine?" he asked, forcing what looked like an attempt to smile.

"You missed your turn. We're all empty." Gwilym seemed about to offer his own shot to MacAdams, but caught a deadly look in Tula's slate-gray eyes. Down went the liquor, and to his credit, he handled it much better than Jo.

"Good lad," Tula told him. "And what can we get *you*, Detective?"

"A single," he said, then turned to Jo, presenting keys. "You've eaten?"

Still standing, Gwilym's stare was impossible to ignore. Tula set upon him before he had a chance to open his mouth and ushered him to the kitchen, but that did not make it remotely less awkward. Just less crowded.

"Right." MacAdams hazarded a glance in her direction. "You're not still cross with me about the cottage, though? We're good, aren't we?"

Were they? Probably. It was always rather hard to tell, but he probably wasn't inviting her to reason that out. The proper response to these things tended to be "Yes?"

"Good."

Jo waited for a follow-up. MacAdams drank whiskey.

"Are . . . you okay?" she asked, finally. MacAdams ran one hand through his hair, which, given the humidity, made it stand on end. Now it was his turn to say the expected *yes*, but he didn't.

"So, Airbnb? I thought you were planning on a freelance career. In editing."

Jo slow-blinked. Yes, that had been the plan. Except her old clients had indemnity clauses that her ex had worked into noncompete contracts, and authors from other houses didn't want to pay for external editing when they could get it in-house for free. She'd advertised: "Editor for hire: hyperlexic, speed reading, photographic memory, mental Rolodex of facts to hand." And so far? The only takers had been romance novelists. And . . . and . . .

"I can't edit romance," Jo admitted. MacAdams pursed his lips.

"Beg your pardon?"

"That's the market." Jo rubbed her forehead vigorously. "I'm a developmental editor, a fact-finder. I can find out who died of what in 1687. I can tell you a LOT about poison plants, Egyptian embalming and how to make your own plywood. But—and this is a direct client quote—I *don't know what romance requires*. And . . . and . . ." Jo felt a blush coming, so said the last bit very fast. "And reading steamy sex scenes make me want to jump out a window."

MacAdams finished his whiskey.

"You've done that," he said. "The jumping out of windows."

"Just the once," Jo said.

"Well, I'd like that not to be repeated. Any of it."

"So, no being chased by a murderer through a burning building. I think I can manage that."

"Good. I'm glad we got sorted," he said, and as if by the magic of eavesdropping, Tula reappeared.

"James, I do believe you had some questions for me about your investigation?"

"Do I," he said, repossessing himself. Then he took out the notepad and clocked out of polite civility. "Last week—did anyone call here looking for a room by the name of Foley? Ronan Foley?"

"Afraid not," Tula said, shaking her head. "Common enough name in Ireland, though. Through a fistful of barley and you'd hit at least one."

"Fair. I'll have Green bring by a photograph, anyway. Just in case. And Jo? I'll be looking forward to the full details of that statement."

He tipped the hat he wasn't wearing and turned around for the door. Jo jingled the keys in her pocket. Was he worried about her? Did she want him to be? She caught a sideways look from Tula. Jo didn't understand what was being communicated, though, and in a moment he was through the door and gone. Tula shook her head.

"The detective has a new *tie*," she said. Jo knew that; she'd stared at it at the tea tent. It was the pictographic sort, yellow stone arch, burst of green above, tall stands of hollyhock below. It reminded her of something.

"What about it?"

"Love, the man hasn't worn a new tie in five years. I suspect he wore it on purpose for opening day of the gardens." And because she knew Jo a little too well to leave it to chance— "For *you*."

Jo pinked right to her ears.

"Oh." She'd lost the opportunity of complimenting him, which made her feel both embarrassed and like she'd dodged a bullet at the same time. Even so, the whole weird day seemed strangely salvaged knowing he'd meant to come after all.

And it *was* a nice tie.

CHAPTER 7

Jo liked the northeast corner of the cottage best. Morning light came in through the panes, painting fat yellow squares on the wood floor, and if you sat at an angle (which she was presently doing), you could see out the window to your left and still have a view of the fireplace to the right. It offered good thinking room, and so she'd conscripted Gwilym into finding a tiny antique writing desk that would fit.

That summer, if she wasn't in Roberta's archive, she was in her own—surrounding by stacks of books now high enough to serve as end tables in a pinch. One of them supported a slate coaster and her by-now-cold coffee. She was elbows deep into the last of her uncle's archive boxes, and had forgotten it.

Uncle Aiden: he had always been a shadow figure in Jo's life. Her late mother rarely ever spoke of him, and never positively. Some sort of major fallout had occurred, though Jo never could work out what about. Despite all that, she had begun to think of him as a kind of ally. After all, he was the one who restored Evelyn's painting. And he was the one who preserved her photograph. Roberta had collected the things Aiden donated to the museum for Jo: a mishmash of books about Abington, maps of the Pennines, a history of Newcastle and a copy of *Burke's Peerage*, possibly for tracking the Ardemore baronetcy. Despite her love of books, however, none of those had absorbed her attention half so much as the loose sheets of paper that lined the bottom. *"Rubbish,"* said Roberta.

And she wasn't all wrong. Old flyers, a crumpled cash receipt from Abington's Sainsbury's, several used envelopes. But each had been pressed into service as notepaper, Aiden's handwriting scribbled in pencil.

They didn't offer stunning revelations. Two of them appeared to be grocery lists; others offered up random notes in a stream of consciousness that endeared him to Jo: "if you are going to call it a cab service, you should at least know the way to the station, or don't try your luck on the roundabout." Pleasant. Distracted. Conscious of details, though not always to the right ones. Jo stretched her back and looked at Evelyn's painting.

"Where are *you* in all of this?" she asked, standing. It was getting to be nine-ish, and coffee was no kind of breakfast. She tidied the stack of motley notepaper and hunted for a book to put it in—no sense in tossing them back in the bottom.

But there was already a note in the bottom. Jo rubbed her nose; had she missed one? A bit of paper poked up through the cardboard folds. The flap had been glued down; whatever it was had to be thin and stiff enough to slide inside. She carried her mug to the kitchen and returned with a knife. Roberta would have to forgive her. Sharp end to the back and a good prying popped the seam—and out dropped two halves of a photograph: the wedding portrait of William and Gwen, with a missing square where Aiden had snipped out Evelyn.

Uncle Aiden had used the cutout and given it to the artist in charge of repairing Evelyn's painting. He hadn't discarded the cut up remains, and they had ended up with his other "rubbish," care of the Abington Museum. Well. They weren't going back there. Jo would have to keep them. For posterity.

She turned them over to look for the photographer's insignia. There wasn't one. Instead, fine pencil lines scrawled across the flat finish: "save the painting for repair," it read, running into the empty center. On the other side, it picked up once more: "for when Evelyn comes home."

A partial message, cryptic, it sent a thrill of electricity right to Jo's toes. It *meant* something. She just didn't know what.

★ ★ ★

Day two of the investigation began bright and early at the Abington Arms hotel. Sunday breakfast was underway, the downstairs dining room awash in linen tablecloths and smartly clad servers in blue uniforms.

"I've never actually been in here," Green admitted, admiring the high ceilings and their scalloped plaster. "Fancy." MacAdams couldn't disagree; mahogany balustrades, wide front stair, ornamental rugs—the Abington Arms was a far cry from the comfortable environs of the Red Lion. As was the price to stay.

"It caters to a certain sort."

"Gotta be out-of-towners. Have a cucumber water, will you?" she asked, bucking her chin at the glass bell jar.

"Country men, and the various types they court from high society." Particularly those with under-the-table dealings, though he didn't say this out loud. Mainly because he'd been cautioned to quit bringing up the past (and their last case). "Ah—there's our man."

A green-suited gentleman with a close-cropped mustache had just appeared at the reception desk. He was slightly balding these days and wearing spectacles that didn't fit his face, but largely looked the same as ever: fastidious, ingratiating—and ruffled. Evans.

"Oh! Detective MacAdams," he said with a rising tenor. "You—Did you come for breakfast?"

"Afraid not," MacAdams said, reaching for his police ID. Evans stopped him with a flutter of fingers.

"Not necessary—I of course know you," he said (but, MacAdams knew, really meant: *please do not flash that around in front of the guests*). "How can I help?"

"We have some questions," Green said. Evans had noticeably ignored her but was quickly rectifying it. "About a guest."

MacAdams enjoyed the way Green's voice carried even above the dinging noises—more so Evans's horror at the same. His eyes ferreted between them and the guests beyond.

"Could, eh, could we do this in the lounge?" he asked. MacAdams remained stubbornly where he was.

"Here is just fine. Talk to me about the booking process. Website? Telephone? Email?" he asked. Evans gave up trying to shoo them out of sight.

"We *do* have a website, as all businesses must these days. But we still do our booking by phone—and occasionally, email." He gave a presuming little smile. "Our guests prefer the *personal* touch."

Didn't they just, MacAdams thought. The good and the great, meaning the rich and the richer, of course expected such treatment. A place like Abington Arms handpicked its guests almost more than the guests picked the rooms. Of course, he reminded himself, he shouldn't make assumptions.

"And who takes these calls?"

"The phone is answered by the host on duty." Evans said, smoothing his sideburns. "Someone is always on duty; names and notes are recorded here." He jogged the computer mouse to wake up the screen and brought up a spreadsheet. "Emails go to a general inbox that all hosts can access."

"Good." MacAdams flipped open his notebook. "I need to see if you received an email or call from one Ronan Foley on Friday. Part of a murder investigation."

Evans suddenly looked like he might fall through the floor.

"You *can't* mean the gentleman found dead at the festival?"

"He wasn't found at the festival," MacAdams corrected. "And he wasn't a guest here, as far as we know."

"Oh thank *God*—"

"But," Green interrupted, wisely keeping up the tension, "he could have been. He apparently tried to get rooms around town; the Red Lion was full. We want to know if he called here, when and why." Her delivery was perfect, given that this was MacAdams's hunch they were following up. Evans pursed his lips and called up the records on his computer. He wasn't enjoying any part of this, but neither did he want them to say the word *murder* again.

"Three email requests on Friday, all accounted for, but none from that name," Evans said, inviting them to view the subjects over his shoulder.

"And phone records?" MacAdams asked. Evans toggled back to the spreadsheet and scrolled to Friday.

"Eleven outside calls," Evans said. "I *really* don't like sharing details, Detective, our guests have a right to privacy—"

MacAdams ignored this milk-and-water protest and took over the mouse. The first ten calls had been received before five in the afternoon. The eleventh at five thirty. Name: Ronan Foley.

"Got him," MacAdams said. "I don't see his number registered, though. Green—call up Andrews and have him request records for Abington Arms."

"Detective!" Evans protested. MacAdams turned around swiftly, taking him enough by surprise that the man took a step back.

"Who took the calls after five on Friday?" he asked. "You or someone else?"

"Ms. Templeton," Evans stuttered. "She took the late shift due to a call-off."

"Templeton," Green repeated with a head tilt.

"Yes. She's overseeing the Sunday brunch, just now—"

MacAdams didn't wait for more. He walked directly through to the dining room, where several dining couples in luxurious Sunday best raised curious heads. Evans had chased after, but MacAdams had already spotted a likely candidate. Tall, ropy-limbed and wearing another management-level green suit. She turned as they approached, and he watched her expression take three leaps: confusion, professionalism—recognition.

"If it isn't Sheila Green," she said, shaking her sleek ponytail over one shoulder.

Green returned a laconic smile. "Hello, Arianna. We have a few questions about a call you received here Friday night."

The woman cast a glance at Evans, but she remained unperturbed, and invited them to sit with her at an empty table.

"Tea? Or perhaps coffee?" she asked, as if they had been ushered into her own very grand living room.

"Two coffees. With cream," MacAdams said, and enjoyed watching a rankled Evans dart off to fetch it. With him gone, Arianna's smile iced over slightly.

"What can I do for you, Sheila?"

"DS Green," Green corrected, coolly composed. This was apparently her act and scene, so MacAdams gave her the lead. While he and Green knew most details of each others' pasts and histories, Arianna was a new name, and was curious to read their dynamic. "Friday night, you took a shift as host, is that right?"

"Yes. We were busy helping our guests—twenty arriving almost at once. You know we're a premier venue; weddings, events. Our clients expect the best." She said this with evident pleasure. MacAdams steered her back to the questions at hand.

"And five thirty, you took a call from a man named Ronan Foley."

"I don't remember his name, but sure. I'm assuming you have already checked the phone register."

"Nothing gets past you, does it?" Green asked her.

Arianna smiled toothily—and Evans returned with coffee. MacAdams took a grateful sip. An awful lot was being communicated here, but none of it about the murdered man. Green pushed her coffee away, course correcting.

"Ronan Foley called here on Friday night. Saturday morning, he was found dead on Upper Lane. We need to know *exactly* what he said to you."

Arianna's expression and posture remained unchanged as she absorbed the news, and its implications.

"God. How awful," she said, but without much feeling.

"*Do* you remember him?" MacAdams pressed.

She nodded. "I do. But he didn't want a room. He didn't even ask if we had any available."

MacAdams was poised with his pencil, ready to write down her statement, but this caught him out.

"He called a hotel, but didn't want a room," he repeated, making sure he'd heard that right.

"Honestly, it's probably why I remember it," Arianna said, lacing her fingers in front of her. "He asked if we already *had* a booking for him. But we didn't."

"I want you to think back very carefully, Ms. Templeton. What *exactly* did he say," MacAdams asked.

"I already said—"

"You summarized," Green interrupted. MacAdams didn't need Arianna to bristle, however; he put up a placating hand.

"Here, try this—" MacAdams wrote a series of letters down in his notepad: *T, F, T, F.* "*T* for Templeton, *F* for Foley. Can you fill in the basic conversation as closely as you can?"

She took the pad and pencil and a deep breath.

"I answered as I usually do." She scribbled a note. "'This is Abington Arms, how may I help you?' Next, he said his name was Foley—he gave his first name, too, but I didn't remember till you told me. 'Did I have any rooms under my name?' Mumbled something about his secretary possibly booking it for him, and he wanted to verify. I told him we didn't have anything booked for him, *but* we still had available suites. He didn't ask about pricing. He wanted to know if we were *busy*. I told him the whole town was booked. One of our guests checking in complained that everywhere 'affordable' was taken for the night. That's when—Oh." Arianna tapped the notepad, but didn't write anything down. "He wanted to know if there were self-catering places."

"Self-catering," MacAdams repeated. Places where you check in and out on your own, flats where no one greeted you, almost fully anonymous. "What did you tell him?"

"Sorry, you said he was found on Upper Lane?" Arianna narrowed her eyes. "That's by the new gardens, isn't it. And the—the American's cottage."

"What did you *tell* Mr. Foley?" Green repeated with an impatience MacAdams now shared.

"The place was in the paper; that's the only reason I knew about it. Part of the old Ardemore estate."

★ ★ ★

"He chose her cottage on purpose," MacAdams said, climbing back into the sedan, "because he didn't think anyone would be there."

"And the Hammersmith meeting seems connected," Green said. "He had a meeting Friday and booked about an hour later. But why ask if there were rooms booked *for* him at Abington Arms?"

MacAdams was already batting that question around his brain. "The easy answer is that he expected there to be. As in, someone else made reservations for him."

"*And* he does the opposite. I mean, he doesn't stay there, and he chooses an out-of-the-way cottage he expects to be empty," Green said, warming up to his idea. "You still think he was expecting trouble, don't you?"

"Or he doesn't want to be recognized," MacAdams said. They hadn't found any indication of train travel (Gridley checked), and so far no word on abandoned vehicles. Then again, if he were trying to be inconspicuous . . . "Let's check car hire; he got here somehow. And he was being quiet about it."

"Shame we have to wait till Monday to tackle Hammersmith."

It was, at that, but it gave them time to do some digging in Newcastle. He turned onto the main road and flipped on the wipers against a warm drizzle. The next stop would be Ronan Foley's apartment and—if they were lucky to find him at home—Burnhope's uptown residence as well. They had an hour to kill, however, so he determined to venture into guarded territory.

"About Arianna Templeton. History?"

Green gave him a side-long look.

"I could ask you the same thing about Evans."

It was a fair point. MacAdams leaned back against the headrest.

"Yes. I always wondered how old boss Clapham got his money after it came out that he was selling off his military equipment," he explained. "It was clearly through connections, because every pound and penny were squeaky clean. Well, Evans was a personal friend of our Clapham. He was also an accountant at a London firm."

"A city boy? Running a hotel?"

"Yes, about that. His firm was nailed for fraud. But not Evans."

"So he either has an exceptional moral compass, or somebody bailed him out in exchange for special accounting." Green nodded out the window. "Neat little theory."

"And still *only* a theory," MacAdams said. "But there were

goings-on. I suspected back then, I know now—and I doubt we've heard the end of it. Anyway, there's my little story. Are you going to tell me what's up with you and Ms. Templeton?"

"Nope," she said, then put the car in gear and pulled out of the hotel parking lot.

CHAPTER 8

Wellington boots made for excellent footwear to keep your feet dry. Why they didn't also come with actual tread to keep you from falling on your ass, Jo didn't know, but the fact remained. It was one she unfortunately learned the hard way.

Gwilym managed to pull her up without falling down himself, but only just. The previous day's sunshine may have dried out the puddles, but the trail remained slippery and muddy. It was lonely, too. The effect might be softened by late-spring greenery, but these were the environs of *Wuthering Heights* and every bit as isolated.

"How did Roberta walk this whole trail by herself?" Gwilym asked.

"Fourteen generations of Wilkinsons," Jo explained. Roberta had genetic fortitude. Jo, on the other hand, had a wet backside. She'd spent most of her life between Chicago and New York, scarce able to catch a bit of unbroken sky between high-rises, or more than a few stray stars above the pink haze of light pollution. Out here, the land rolled away like the gathered edge of a bed skirt dotted blue yellow with furze and heather. Clouds had moved in, but across a fat stretch of sky wide enough to bend at the edges. If Roberta could still hike it at eighty-three, she would, too. "Where was I?"

"Your uncle Aiden."

"Right. So, we already knew he was the one with Evelyn's photo. He also *kept* the original—and he wanted to bring Evelyn 'home,' whatever that means. But here's the weird part. Even though the Ardemore estate was technically under his management back in the eighties, he never lived there. Didn't even seem to want to take care of it. When did he suddenly get interested in our family history?"

"I guess about the time he went to such great lengths to get the painting repaired," Gwilym offered. "But since we're talking about him, if not the Ardemore estate, where *did* he live?"

"Had his own flat in York, which was sold after his death. But according to the neighbor, he was almost never there, either."

"Another home someplace?"

Home. Funny word; it had never been the sort Jo collected for cutting her teeth on, but neither was it as straightforward as it pretended. Had she ever felt at home in Chicago, with her mother and aunt? Had she felt at home in the Brooklyn flat with her ex?

"Where is home, though, anyway?" she asked. "Is Swansea home for you?"

"I suppose. I'm Welsh."

"Tula's Irish, but Ireland isn't her home."

"Fair point. Always meant to ask about that," Gwilym admitted, sidestepping a particularly opaque puddle.

"She probably wouldn't tell you much," Jo said. "But Abington is *her* home. Mine too, I guess, now. What about Evelyn?"

"As in, Painting Evelyn?"

"As in, Ancestor Evelyn, yes."

"Well, she's also from Wales, if I recall from our research, but I see your point. Note on the photo you found from your uncle says 'Evelyn comes home,' but who's home?"

These were the questions that kept Jo up nights, and that was no euphemism. Did it refer to Evelyn's home in Wales, before she moved in with Gwen and William?

"We searched for months and never found evidence of Evelyn living anywhere else," she reminded him.

"Or any mention of a baby mysteriously turning up in Abington," Gwilym agreed. "I mean, assuming the baby lived, you would think an orphan would get *some* kind of attention around here."

He kicked a dirt clod from the path. That had been his hobbyhorse: orphan hunting. Jo had focused on William and Gwen, but no child of any sort ever darkened their door—there weren't even nieces or nephews to hand. And not a mention of Evelyn herself, either, alive or dead.

"Maybe Aiden meant Evelyn's home here in Abington, you know? Ardemore House? Assuming you gained home status by being buried somewhere."

"Ugh. That is not a nice thought." Jo frowned. "Maybe Aiden meant his own home. Either York or . . . somewhere else. I'm not giving up."

"Of course you aren't! *We* aren't. But you have to admit, murders in ditches during town celebrations are very distracting."

Wasn't that the truth.

"There it is, I think," she said. Just beyond them was a rise in the landscape; the North Pennines surrounded Abington on three sides, and the Pennine Way could be picked up from Upper Lane. She'd learned all that from Tula and Ben, and been forced to walk it more than once with Roberta. Up ahead, police tape flapped in the wind, and Gwilym gave his hoodie strings an enthusiastic tug.

"Oh gosh. That's banging! C'mon!" He skipped down the trail till he reached its nadir. Jo leaned over with care. *Ditch* wasn't quite the right word—*culvert*? Steep sides and a mucky middle that police boot prints had turned into a slovenly pond.

"That can't have been easy," Jo said, trying to imagine getting a body out of it. Gwilym was imagining it, too, but with greater appreciation.

"Like excavating a bog body or something. On the other hand, plenty easy to put him *in*. There's a good incline—you'd just have to roll him out and let gravity do the work."

Unpleasant. But he had a point.

"Why here, though? Just the solitude?"

"Sure! No one would find him right away. Oh. Well. I mean, in theory." Gwilym turned in place. "It beats odds, doesn't it? Roberta walking right up on him."

Jo scanned the horizon. Maybe—or maybe not. It was close to a pull-off; people parked there sometimes. In fact, someone appeared to be parked there now. Up ahead on the road, something stood out against the brown and green. Two somethings, as it happened. A hiker, maybe, and something bigger . . .

"Look up there. Is that a car?" Gwilym squinted but couldn't differentiate at a distance.

"I see a yellow blur and a white blur?"

"Windbreaker and the backside of something—an SUV maybe." It was a lonely place, but not deserted after all. Of course, if you weren't familiar with the area, you might not *know* that.

"I see her now." Gwilym raised his arms and cheerfully hallooed.

"Please don't do that." Jo grimaced. She was not in new-people mode. This did not stop Gwilym, who was always in new-people mode.

He started jogging to catch up. Now Jo had to scamper after him. When they had covered about twenty yards, he gave another shouted greeting, and this time the hiker turned around. Jo caught a distant glimpse of her face, but she didn't stop. She didn't even slow down.

"Headed for the van, I guess?" Gwilym asked, slowing to a

walk. "That *is* a van, isn't it?" Jo's vision was better, but they were still half a football pitch away.

"Seems to be," she said. "It has letters on one side: *B-U-T-T-Y.*" The word lived nowhere in Jo's extensive mental catalog, however. "Butt-tee? Boot-ee?"

Gwilym erupted in laughter.

"Laird, have you never eaten a bacon butty?" he asked. "I love a bacon butty, me—and a chip butty. Gorgeous. Like a *cwtch* for your insides."

"Is this a Welsh thing?" Jo asked.

"It is a *sandwich*, Jo. A right guilty one. Butter and back bacon on thick white bread—didn't expect a butty van out here, but I'll take it! Let's get one, shall we? You'll love it."

Jo had experienced the British equivalent of bacon and wasn't sure *love* was the right word. Maybe they also did chips. Essentially a food truck, a window opened to one side, and a tiny counter jutted out with condiments of various kinds. Gwilym tapped on the window and the thick jowls of a mostly bald man appeared.

"What can I do for ye?" he asked.

The accent was thick; Jo tried to place it—*glottal stops*, she thought. The audible release of air after complete closure of the glottis. Cockney? No. Something else. Gwilym asked about her order, but her brain couldn't get past the *other* blur they had just seen.

"Where's the hiker?" she asked.

Gwilym took a quick look around. "Maybe she already ordered?"

"But she's not *here*," Jo insisted. She stood on her tiptoes to better see the proprietor. "Excuse me, did you see a woman in a yellow rain slicker?"

"Nar."

"Did you see *anyone*?" Gwilym asked.

"Nar, I seed. Ye gan order something or nowt?"

"Oh! Yes, um. Bacon butty, please," Gwilym said, hunting his clothes for cash.

"Aye. In a min't."

Gwilym dutifully awaited his sandwich. It seemed to be taking a very long time, so Jo climbed a little rise next the road and peered out over the moors. No one. Not anywhere. It shouldn't bother her. But like other unexplained errors in the general skein of things . . . it did. A lot.

* * *

An hour and four minutes on the 694—surprisingly breezy driving for a Sunday. MacAdams stopped first in Whickham to put eyes on Foley's *former* address, a brick terraced house with sizable garage and impressive garden.

"Nice village. Good parks," Green said. "Geet place, as the Geordies say."

"Means big, yes?"

"You could keep a lot of kit in there, is what I mean. Leaves all this behind for a by-month rental?"

"A *furnished* one, at that," MacAdams added, pulling away from the curb again.

"Right. So, where's his stuff?"

It was an excellent question. Newcastle Uniform did a preliminary sweep the day before; everything, right down to the ice trays, came with the flat.

"We've probably looking for storage, a unit. Something," he said. An officer met them at the door, and proffered paper booties for their shoes. It wasn't a crime scene. At least, MacAdams didn't think so. But then again . . . He tugged them over his oxfords.

The inside had the appeal of a cheap chain hotel. Furnishings were perfectly serviceable—everything a shade of familiar beige.

"Where do you want to start?" Green asked.

"Divide and conquer," MacAdams said, pointing her to the

kitchen and heading down the short, narrow hall to the only bedroom. Here, at least, the linens were personalized: pale green sateen and a comforter with blue stripes. It had clearly been slept in recently; they waited on forensics, but chances were good it had been Foley. MacAdams peered into the closet. Button-downs, pressed trousers, all reasonable quality. Jo had described him as disheveled on the night of, but his sartorial choices were smart business casual. Only one suit. It might have been a good match for his silk shirt, but hadn't been worn. The tags were still on it.

"Kitchen's barely worth notice. Not much a cook, apparently." She paused, looking down at him from the doorway. "Why are you on the floor?"

"Shoes," MacAdams explained, his head partway into closet corner. "What did Struthers say? The shirt needed a different ensemble. Found a suit. And—" He backed out of the closet, pulling a pair of white-and-buff brogues. "Hello there. *Very* expensive shoes."

"These are fancy?"

"Oh yes. Foster & Son. Bespoke." He ran a thumb down the hand detailing. "That's a two-thousand-pound shoe. Starting."

"No shit." She pushed aside a few hangers. "The other clothes are all off-the-rack, though. I mean, nice brands. But not tailored."

MacAdams put the shoes on the bureau to get a better look. "Basic apartment. But one very top-shelf pair of shoes—an unworn suit and a flashy red silk shirt to be murdered in."

"I'll bite. What's that tell us?"

"I don't know," MacAdams admitted. "Except something doesn't fit."

"What's this?" Green reached into the left shoe and tugged out the purple silk fabric with a gloved hand. It was a woman's scarf.

"That's surely not Foley's," MacAdams said.

"No judgment if it is, but there's perfume on it." Green held it under his nose: sweet, vanilla, floral.

MacAdams headed for the apartment's shower room and opened the medicine cabinet. A pair of nail clippers fell out, and can of shaving cream nearly did; he caught it with one hand. He didn't find perfume. But that didn't make it uninteresting.

"Green, have a look at this," he said, holding the cabinet door open.

"Messy," she said. Then she sniffed at the whipped white goop smearing the internal shelf. "Shaving cream?"

"Yes. I suspect it fell over in there." MacAdams showed her the canister, where additional foam had crusted from the dispensing head. "Tell me what's missing."

"Razor and toothbrush, which we found in the bag." Green frowned. "But—then why leave the toothpaste and cream?"

"And cologne," MacAdams added, picking up the bottle with gloved fingers. It had fallen on its side.

"Packed in a hurry?" Green tapped her chin with an index finger. "Or maybe in a panic? Starts tossing things into a bag?"

MacAdams nodded, *tossing* being the operative word. Almost as if he'd swept a hand along the shelf and kept whatever fell out.

"He packs one nice shirt but not the suit, brings less than half of his toiletries." He replaced the shaving cream. "This isn't just hurry. These are the actions of someone on the *run*. Bag this up along with the shoes, and let's see if we can get DNA from the scarf."

"Right. Together with the earring, I'm guessing a lady friend." Green collected evidence bags from the Newcastle officer and wrapped the Foster & Sons in plastic. She handed them to MacAdams with a smirk.

"You know, I didn't have you down as a shoe man," she said.

"I'm not," he said. But Annie was. She bought him a pair for their first anniversary. He'd still never worn them. "We're here, let's look up Burnhope."

In truth, MacAdams still planned—even preferred—to meet Burnhope at his offices for Hammersmith. Everything suggested the meeting there had galvanized Foley's runner to Abington (even if it didn't explain the gap between a five-forty booking and turning up at 10:00 p.m. for a commute that should've been under two hours). All the same, he wanted to get eyes on Burnhope's housing situation. Had he, like Foley, recently sold up? It was easy enough to find out with a drive across town.

★ ★ ★

Twenty minutes later, MacAdams determined the answer, apparently, was *no*.

They pulled up to a four-story detached manor-style house awash in gardens and situated on almost an acre in Jesmond. The last alone would have fetched over a million before a brick had been laid.

"My God, there's a pool," Green said, noting the enclosed solarium to the southwest. "Who the fuck has a pool in Newcastle?"

"In all of Northumberland," MacAdams agreed as he rang the bell.

A moment later, a young woman answered the door. She had deep olive skin, black hair parted in the center and an accent MacAdams couldn't place. "Can I help you?"

"I'm Detective Chief Inspector MacAdams, and I'm looking for Stanley Burnhope," MacAdams said.

"Not here," she said abruptly—but a velvety voice rang from somewhere farther inside.

"Mary, who is that?" The words were followed by a willowy woman dressed in white from head to house-slipper, coupled with platinum hair and near-translucent skin. It didn't seem possible that she owned the heady voice which now greeted them.

"Mary, who have we here?"

"It's police, ma'am," the woman said unsteadily. Mrs. Burnhope, or so MacAdams presumed, put a hand upon her shoulder.

"That's all right Maryam; please look to the children," she said, then turned her gaze upon them. "Can you tell me what this is about?"

"It would be better if we could come in, Mrs. Burnhope," MacAdams said, but she was already fading backward to allow it.

"Of course."

The entryway glistened in polished marble, but despite the manorly look from outside, the inner sanctum had been re-created in sleek modern elegance. Deep mahogany wood offset by a grand white marble fireplace that somehow spoke of old money without any semblance of old style. And there was a *lot* of glass, some of it architectural, some of it clearly artwork . . . and some which might be both of either. But they hadn't seen anything yet. Mrs. Burnhope led them through to a bright room with a grand piano and stands of music, overseen by what appeared to be a trio of molten-glass figures, at least four feet tall. Their sweeping arms caught the light, translucent, pearlescent.

"Wow," was Green's very natural reaction.

"My muses," she said. "I play here. It's my room, you might say. Art and music." She shut the door behind them.

"You'll understand, I hope, that I don't want to upset Mary. She'd been through quite enough."

MacAdams and Green exchanged glances. Both of them more or less blank.

"Quite enough of what, Mrs.—"

"Call me Ava. And I'm quite sure we have done all the necessary work to provide her with stability at last. So if this is a matter of paperwork, we can handle that through better channels than house calls."

Her behavior wasn't exactly unfriendly; it wasn't stony, either—but definitely unyielding. Commanding, too, in the demure but expectant way only those of the upper crust could be.

"We are not here regarding Mary at all," MacAdams said. "We are investigating a murder."

"A—murder?"

He now watched Ava perform a mental backstep, and then sink into a seated position on the sofa. He used the moment to his advantage; bad news was better sitting down.

"Did you know your husband's business partner?" MacAdams asked.

"Sophie Wagner? Something's happened at the club?" Ava's tone bore honest concern, but MacAdams had the peculiar sensation that he'd just stumbled into someone else's investigation.

"Sorry, his partner at Hammersmith."

Ava simply stared, eyes like the glass chandeliers. "He doesn't have a partner at Hammersmith. I thought this was about the charity, Fresh Start? It's for sponsoring refugees. Maryam, for example, she's been here a year, from Syria. But then what's this about? Who's been murdered?"

"Ronan Foley," MacAdams said.

Ava shook her head. "I don't know who you're talking about."

So far, the interview had been an exercise in non-sequitur. Green, above and to the left of Ava, had given up on stoicism; he could almost read the words *what the fuck?* on her cheekbones.

"Ronan Foley worked with—or for—your husband at Hammersmith. He handled properties in York and abroad. We know he met with Mr. Burnhope on Friday at four thirty; between roughly eleven thirty Friday night and 3:00 a.m. Saturday morning, he was murdered. We would like to speak to Mr. Burnhope; can you tell us where he is?"

It was a lot of information at once, but he'd delivered it in emotionless bullet points. Ava—who had preserved a mostly emotionless veneer so far—was animated at last, but the principal feeling seemed to be one of confusion.

"Murdered," she repeated, the velvet voice wrapping the word up at both ends. "I'm sorry. But I still don't know the man. Maybe if I saw a photograph? Stanley consults with a lot of people for his firm; I can't remember them all. We keep our careers mostly separate, anyway."

"And your career, Ms. Burnhope?" Green asked.

Ava half turned to look at her, the platinum wave falling forward over her shoulder.

"I am a vocalist and concert pianist," she said, gesturing to the piano. "We work together for the charity. That's where we were on Friday. I performed for the ball at Sable Green. The golf club. And it's where Stanley is at the moment."

"Meeting with—Sophie Wagner?" MacAdams asked, consulting his notes.

"Golfing," she corrected. Then she stood up. "I can show you out." The interview was clearly over. MacAdams didn't need to extend it—yet.

"Thank you," he said aloud as they re-passed the glass kitchen. "We'll be in touch if we have further inquiries."

Ava merely opened the front door and wished them a colorless "good afternoon."

Back outside, Green sucked air through her teeth.

"That was weird."

"It was," MacAdams agreed. "Foley's email specifically requested a meeting between himself and Stanley as partners."

"Not that. Or, not *only* that." Green was scrolling through her phone. "Ava Burnhope—is also Ava Thompson. Look." She held up the phone to reveal Ava attired in brilliant red at a piano under a spotlight. "I didn't put it together at first, but she was well-known in the city. Daughter of Newcastle's chief executive officer, Andrew Thompson—he's outlasted two Lord Mayors."

MacAdams took the phone and scrolled; two images down Stanley appeared at her side, both of them posing with another woman in front of a banner that read Fresh Start.

"I take it that's Sophie." He handed the phone back. "We'll go there next."

CHAPTER 9

It *still* wasn't bacon, in Jo's opinion. And it didn't compare with Tula's sausage rolls. But it was hard not to enjoy something warm and buttery, especially when you were walking on your own through damp, open country.

Jo parted with Gwilym at the branch between Upper and Lower Lane; he was headed back to the Red Lion—she just wanted to put her feet up at home. The first time she'd taken the right to roam train from cottage to town, it seemed endlessly long. Now she did it regularly, sometimes once a week in the warmer months. Lone walks gave her brain a chance to unspool—no conversation to keep up with, no one asking for explanations. Just her own thoughts. And a bacon butty, which would have benefited from fresher bread.

The disappearing hiker had been walking alone, too. Nothing strange about that, though mostly the hill hikers came in pairs or groups. The Pennines could be surprisingly tricky. One hill looked *a lot* like the next hill, cell service was spotty, fog rolling in unexpectedly. People did get lost. A woman and her dog got lost on the peak of Ingleborough in the late fall; freezing weather moved in, and a rescue team had to track them down. Then there was the runner who fell; they didn't find *him* until it was too late. Granted, Abington hugged a corner in the southeast, where the geography happened to be a lot more forgiving.

Still, watching a hiker disappear almost before your eyes . . .

Jo stopped walking and spit out a bit of unchewable back-bacon fat. That more or less ruined the experience. She rewrapped the sandwich in the least-greasy bit of paper and shoved it into a pocket. The wind had picked up a bit; it smelled fresh and green. A friendly sign stood prominently near the road proclaiming Jekyll Gardens. She wasn't far from home now. And there was that word again.

Home. Jo rolled it around in her mouth, repeated it and held the last *mmm* until her lips tickled. *Dwelling, domicile, residence, room* . . . even *house* just didn't have the same feeling. And that was it; home *felt* like something, didn't it? Her nose twitched and she rubbed it absently. Where did she feel *at* home?

She picked up her pace, hurrying up the lane until she could see the trees that backed Netherleigh Cottage and catch the first glimpse of the chimney. There, in the stomach, she felt the tug. When had that begun? It had been the scene of one murder and was the last place Ronan Foley ever stayed the night (*if* he stayed the night). But for Jo, it was definitely home. She was practically running now, fast as she could in rubber boots on slippery grass. Her hearth, her little reading nook, her books and books and books—

Buzz buzz.

And her cell phone signal. Back from the dead zone, she would have catching up to do. Gwilym telling her he'd got back, and what Tula made for Sunday dinner, probably. She unlocked the dead bolt and dropped the keys in the dish by the door. The bacon butty went into the garbage; the cell phone she scooped out of her jeans pocket while slipping out of her raincoat.

It wasn't Gwilym. An email had arrived. Jo opened the app,

one arm still ensleeved. Sender: "Arthur Alston." Subject: "Are you the niece of Aiden Jones?"

Jo stopped breathing for twenty-three seconds, the time it took for the message to load.

Dear Ms. Jones,

I read about you and the gardens in the Newcastle Times. I apologize for dropping you a line out of the blue, but I knew Aiden Jones very well. I would like to meet you. If ever you're in town, I'm at Loft 8, Hadrian Hall, Quayside, in Newcastle.

Yours sincerely,
Arthur

Jo put her coat back on. She also checked the train app.

Dear Arthur, she wrote. *I'll be there in one hour and forty-seven minutes.* Which gave her exactly three minutes to pack and eleven to drive to Abington Station. She charged the ticket fare on her way out the door.

CHAPTER 10

The newest building of the country club stretched long, low and glass-covered; MacAdams half expected to see planes landing on the tidy lawns. The new-modern sensibility followed them indoors, where a front desk stood to one side of a glass wall bubbled to look as though water cascaded down through it. The signage emblazoned upon pointed out the spa on the lower level, bar and restaurant to the rear in a portal of white marble and steel.

"Like Burnhope's house," Green mused. "I'm beginning to prefer Abington Arms."

They had asked after Sophie and received a negative; she was a busy woman. Producing his police ID and mentioning a murder investigation had placed them on better footing. The guest clerk told them to await Ms. Wagner in the bar, which was, on balance, the best reception that they'd received so far. It also gave them opportunity to look about.

"Morning, sir. Can I get you a drink?" A youthful, tweed-vested barman had appeared before them.

"Not quite lunch hour. A bit early, isn't it?"

"Depends on preference," he said, tugging a bar towel over one shoulder. "And beverage—we've a coffee machine."

"Thank you, no," MacAdams said. "Instead, I'd like for you to tell me about the gala on Friday."

He'd opened his identification once more, as did Green. The bartender examined their cards and seemed to warm to them both.

"Is something up? Everything went to plan, actually. We had everyone out before two, and that's a feat. No problems at all."

"So you were in attendance?"

"Sure. Did a lot of drink mixing—there's a separate bar for events. You've seen the ballroom?"

They hadn't, and he was keen to show them. MacAdams left Green to await Ms. Wagner and followed the young man down a corridor awash in daylight.

"Is this all part of an annex?" he asked.

"We were *in* the annex; this is actually the original club on this side. Needed a lot of doing up over the years."

He pushed through a set of double doors, and whatever the building had been before, its afterlife presented only the shell. Bare stone walls reached two—maybe three—stories tall but with no floors between. The square wooden beam braces remained, securing the structure together, but seemingly without a roof. The timbers had been replaced by a vaulted glass ceiling, as though they stood in an enormous greenhouse.

A bit gutted, maybe, but far from empty; tables stretched down the length of both sides and several young women were draping them in linen.

"Rented out for a golf club awards ceremony on Tuesday," the bartender-turned-tour-guide offered. "Then a wedding at the weekend. A stage goes up over there, and the rear doors are for the band. Tidy little setup, if I do say so."

"You are surprisingly knowledgeable about the workings."

"I should be! I manage the events."

"And you tend bar?" MacAdams asked.

"When I'm needed," he said, a smile breaking forth. "I'm Simon—Simon Wagner. I do a lot of the runabout for the family. Sophie Wagner is my mum. So, if something's up, I like to know what."

This perhaps made sense of the unusually helpful demeaner; he wanted to keep an eye on the prying police officers, no doubt. But someone else was keeping an eye on them, too. One of the women laying table service had been casting glances back at MacAdams.

"Anyone else here family?" he asked, subtly tilting his head in her direction.

"No, sir. You're looking at Anje. She came through the charity."

"Come again?"

"We sponsor refugees as a part of our employment program."

"I thought there was supposed to be some separation between those who sponsor and the actual labor of sponsored refugees," MacAdams said. "Otherwise it *might* look like you are bringing people over for your own benefit and profit."

"Tsk. Do you know how difficult it is to start over again in another country, Detective?"

This reply came not from Simon, but from a voice behind him.

Sophie Wagner walked breezily through the rows of tables in a jewel colored kaftan with Sheila Green in her wake. A comfortable-looking woman, probably midfifties, with a pair of sunglasses hanging rather precipitously from an ample bosom; he gathered she suffered no fools.

"Many don't speak English, or not well enough. And then you have racism, classism, visa bureaucracy and all the rest. Imagine trying to get gainful employment with all of that against you." It was delivered flawlessly, artfully almost. MacAdams had the distinct impression she had given this speech before.

"Anje here and her mother both work for us; they also take courses to learn the language. And we have Dmytro and Artem as well. All four from Ukraine. So you see, Detective, we are trying to do our part, using wealth for the greater good."

MacAdams heard all the words, but it was hard to miss what she *wasn't* saying, too. *We, the upper crust, the better half, reaching out to the lowly.*

"No conflict of interest being the head of a charity and the lead employer of those you bring through?" MacAdams asked.

Sophie gave an easy laugh. "We aren't the only employer—there are businesses all over Newcastle who support the work by bringing on wage earners. Is that what you're here about? Another upstanding citizen upset they got their tea from an immigrant?"

It occurred to MacAdams that Fresh Start must have faced its share of bad press. Perhaps this was an attempt at a more magnanimous veneer?

"Not today, Ms. Wagner. I want to ask you about Stanley Burnhope—to start. You had a gathering here on Friday; did he attend?"

The laugh returned, renewed. "Stanley and I *ran* the event. He gave the opening and closing speech, an honor granted by his unwavering support for everything we do."

"Can you take us through the day's events, please?" he asked. Sophie was companionable and far more willing to bend than Burnhope's wife, Ava, but he could see that she was growing tired of the game.

"There's a brochure I can fetch you," she said, leading them back through the corridor. "Open house at seven-thirty, silent auction, performance, dancing, etc. Why does it matter?"

"Because, Ms. Wagner, it provides an alibi."

Sophie stopped so abruptly, he nearly tread upon the kaftan. "An alibi? For *what*?"

"Murder," Green said, coming up abreast of them. "Of Mr. Burnhope's business . . . associate . . . Ronan Foley."

Was that a flicker of recognition that passed through her wide-eyed stare?

"Foley," she said slowly. "Murdered? Does Stanley know?"

"You knew him, then," Macadams followed up, but she shook her head.

"Knew of; he works at Hammersmith. A sort of deal closer or something. That's awful—but Stanley wouldn't have anything to do with . . . Is that what you're suggesting? That he needs an alibi for murder?"

"We're just trying to log everyone's movements," MacAdams said by rote. "And to discover who was last to see him."

Technically that wasn't true, MacAdams couldn't help but think. Apart from his murderer, the last to see him was Jo Jones.

★ ★ ★

"Christ, that place is all about the white man's burden." Green shook her head. "Imagine failing to see the problem of hiring the people you're sponsoring."

"Not very likely to report any bad dealings, are they?" MacAdams agreed.

"Or abuse, or extralong hours, or missing paychecks. But they must have good PR. Look at the headlines: 'Local Businessman Is a Leading Light for Change.' Oh God, they call him a *thought leader*."

"Meaning others turn to him for business guidance?" MacAdams asked from the driver's seat. It was technically Green's turn to drive, but he hated reading on a tablet screen.

"Meaning he paid somebody to write the article, probably." Green scrolled on. "Ava has done quite a bit in the way of charity, too; lots of events among the great and the good to drum up fiscals. Golden boy, blah blah. Sophie Wagner is more interesting."

MacAdams reached for the toasty he'd picked up at Tesco. "She's the charity's originator, I take it."

"Established in 2011. Been sponsoring refugees from Somalia, Sudan, Afghanistan. Lately from Ukraine. Get this, though; she wasn't lying about the job placement. It's not just her golf club. They're employing people all over the north, around ninety-five percent placement. That's better than you get among local graduates, these days."

"So the four people working for her—"

"Are a tiny fraction of the whole."

"And Burnhope's involvement?"

"That's a little harder to parse, but to be honest? I'm guessing he's just dollars. And according to Sophie, Foley never even made an appearance on that end of things."

MacAdams took the exit for Abington. They could investigate all of this further on Monday—*tomorrow*, MacAdams reminded himself. They still had frustratingly little to go on, and despite establishing an alibi via Sophie Wagner, they hadn't managed to actually meet Stanley Burnhope himself. Yes, he'd "golfed." No, he wasn't on the green when they arrived. Convenient, if coincidental; it also meant they lost the element of surprise. News of Foley's death would be in the papers by morning, and of course, he and Green had played their cards already.

What happened between that four-thirty meeting and Foley's trip to Abington? Why had he sold his house—and what did the oddly vacant flat tell them about the man's future plans? There was an awful lot riding on the scarf, shoes and Foley's inquiry at the Abington Arms. He hoped Andrews had more luck with CCTV.

"Not going to the station?" Green asked when he turned onto the High Street.

"Red Lion," MacAdams said, patting his shirt pocket. "Jo said Foley seemed to recognize Tula's name; I want her to see the photograph."

The pub room was busy, boisterous and loud. A dozen people were gathered around the television and rooting for Man City, the partridge pie special was making rounds to crowded tables in the front room and a full line stood at the bar.

"I could eat," Green told him as the smell of warm pastry and sizzling drippings drifted overhead.

"I'll bet. Tula—when you have a minute?" MacAdams said as he approached Tula, who had three pints in her hand and was pouring another.

"Next week on Tuesday, love," she replied and winked.

"We still have a full house," Ben added. He'd come in through the kitchen with two baskets of fries. "Your usual, Sergeant Green?"

"I wish—my wife can smell curry a mile away."

"You ate curry chips yesterday, didn't you?" MacAdams asked.

Green gave him a pointed look. "And Rachel will have a fit if I do again today. Not healthy, and all that—Oh, look who's here." She bucked her head toward the door, and MacAdams followed her gaze over a dozen heads.

A flash of red—and a mustache straight out of *The Three Musketeers*. Gwilym. He looked wind-blown and muddy. MacAdams gave him a nod, but Tula had finally returned.

"I know you're busy," he started.

"Well spotted," Tula said, sidling up to the bar where Green and MacAdams waited. "Talk quick."

"As promised, the photograph of Ronan Foley, to confirm whether you recognize his face from the last couple weeks—or not," he said, pulling it from his pocket. He'd barely handed it over when the Welshman tucked in at his elbow.

"The garden ladies had a *lot* of questions, you know," he said. "I feared they might eat me when I didn't know my Cambridgeshire from Canary Bird."

MacAdams didn't have a chance to ask what the hell he was

on about; the Man City crowd shouted, *"Goal!"* Someone in a corner booth nearly overturned their chips—and behind the bar, a glass shattered.

"Shite," Tula barked. She rushed toward the glass fragments and beer, the remains of a half-filled Imperial pint. "Ben, bring the dustbin, would you? And the mop."

"You all right?" Green asked.

Tula ducked behind the bar for a moment; when she came up again, she had the photograph. It had been dropped in the momentary chaos. Tula pushed a mop of curls out of her pink and sweat-steamed face.

"Aye, sorry 'bout that," She handed the photo back to MacAdams.

"You don't recognize him?" he asked.

Tula shook her head. "Never met your Foley," she said.

"It was a long shot," MacAdams agreed.

CHAPTER 11

Jo walked along the quay along the banks of the River Tyne. The river flowed beneath the Gateshead Monument Bridge; her side of the river boasted restaurants and nightlight hot spots. She'd known that Newcastle had once been an enormous commercial port for shipbuilding, glassmaking and—thanks to Lord Armstrong—munitions. She didn't know it boasted an art scene. A center for the arts massed along one side of the quay, and despite MacAdams designating Newcastle as the "cheap" city by comparison to York, the lofts rising over the Tyne suggested ready money. Hadrian Hall looked positively luxurious.

The main entry resembled a hotel lobby, so much so that Jo almost went out again to check the address. She wished she was wearing something a bit more flashy; her classic Doc Martens, black jeans and a scoop-neck tee felt a bit like inappropriate in the present environment. *Fargesia, ficus, freesia,* she thought to herself—the recent dive into botany having provided a good supply of new words to chew on. *Artemesia, asphodel—*

"Can I help?" the clerk asked. Jo made her best attempt at a breezy, carefree smile and made her approach.

"I'm Jo Jones. I'm here to see Arthur Alston in Loft 8? He's expecting me."

"One moment." She picked up the telephone receiver and dialed in a code. "Mr. Alston? A Ms. Jones to see you."

Jo's palms had begun to sweat. She felt like she was being buzzed in for an interview. Did everyone here get the same treatment? Or was Mr. Alston special? *Breathe*, she told herself. Which was terrible advice, as she promptly forgot how to do it properly.

The woman hung up the phone and pointed. "Choose the fourth floor. Loft eight will be to your right."

Jo repositioned her backpack and hurried past the porter. There were six floors total; she made a reasonable guess that meant two lofts per level. If so, the apartments inside were utterly huge. In New York calculation, a place like this—on the water, no less—would be well into the millions. It did nothing to assuage her galloping heart.

The elevator dinged whimsically and opened into a long hall with windows at either end. She approached the right door, but it opened before she could ring the bell, accompanied by a lot of excited barking.

The man in the doorway looked to be in his fifties, dark hair streaked with iron gray and swept back from the temples like a silver screen icon. Lean, graceful limbs draped in a silk kimono dressing gown over slacks, dress shirt, neck scarf. If he wasn't an avant-garde painter, he was missing his calling. In a moment, he swooped down to capture a Pomeranian attempting escape, then made a gesture of welcome.

"You must be Aiden's niece," he said, backing away to allow her inside. Jo swallowed the interior in a single gulp of extravagance and nodded as she entered the apartment. "It's good to meet you. I am Aiden's widower."

Jo found her way to a sofa she'd originally taken for an art piece and sat down gingerly. Outside the bank of windows, the sun was starting to sink.

"I'll make tea, shall I?" Arthur held up tiny Japanese cups. The Pomeranian was still circling Jo, and she'd just noticed a sad-looking Boston terrier snoozing on a shag rug. She ought to be putting a list of useful questions together in her head, but she was still trying to take in the art-laden walls, Persian carpet, squat little Moroccan footstools. The mantelpiece shone in glorious white marble, with a nested Russian doll curio and vase of orchids in the middle.

"Please, yes," she said. "I didn't know Aiden was married."

"Ah. I should explain," Arthur said, sitting across from her. "We were *not* married, in fact—though, for all practical purposes . . ." He poured tea. "We'd been together eighteen years. That's before gay marriage had been legalized, but there were other reasons for keeping things unofficial."

"What were they?" Jo asked. Then regretted it; probably this was impolite. Arthur sipped tea with engineering precision and a wry smile.

"So, jumping right in. Perhaps we should start a little further back," he said. "How much do you know about your uncle?"

"My mother never spoke of him."

"Never? I see. And what about your grandfather?"

Jo bit her lip. She didn't even know who her *own* father was, much less anyone further back on either side.

"Nothing," she said.

Arthur didn't look surprised; he nodded his head and stood up, sending the dressing gown into butterfly flutters. He strolled along the wide windows, stopping at a large square painting on the opposite wall. Mostly red, with streaks of gray and a small black dot in the center.

"This is an original painting by a local artist: Chen Benton-Li. It's called *Hiding.* Aiden bought it at an art auction. It's where we met."

"You're an artist," Jo said, but he laughed it off.

"No, alas. But I support the arts."

"You're a millionaire," Jo said, not intentionally. Arthur laughed again, and it sounded to Jo a bit more natural.

"Oh goodness, if we were I'd be living in Jesmond, wouldn't we, boys?" Jo half turned to take in the modern eclectic *Vogue* shoot behind her, and Arthur went on. "Despite appearance, surprisingly affordable at the time of purchase. I do have somewhat expensive tastes."

"This is a Persian Kerman Lavar from Esfahan," Jo said, mentally adding *A Guide to Eastern Rugs, 2014*. It took her two extra weeks to edit because she kept falling down subject interest rabbit holes.

"Very good! *Very*. And you've caught me out; I am a rather uninteresting investment banker." He winked. "Though a well-paid one."

"And that's not a reproduction on the mantel, is it?"

"Antique Russian iconography nesting dolls, tipped in gold. A present from your uncle, in fact." The darkness outside was descending, so he turned on the lights, which simultaneously lit up the red painting. Then he returned to his leather club chair. "I realized you are seeing me at home, where I have the obligatory gay man's dogs and kimono. But out in the world I do not cut an especially flamboyant figure. Which certainly appealed to Aiden. Your uncle, you see, was not out, Ms. Jones."

"Jo, please." She took a breath. "He didn't want people to know you were together?"

"He began life not wanting his father to know. Then I think it became a habit with him."

"But you lived together—here?" Jo said, trying to explain it to herself.

Arthur nodded. "Yes. You see, *straight* Aiden lived in York, at a flat he sublet most of the time. The real Aiden lived here, with me." He swept his hand toward the red painting. "In *Hiding*."

Jo stared at the square, this time focused on the small black dot behind a gray streak. A great deal had just clicked into place.

"My mother kept secrets, too. I was left a crumbling estate that I didn't even know existed, until she died and I inherited it."

"I know." Arthur picked up a newspaper and handed it to her. Jo stared at a headline—and her own face. It was the interview she'd done before the garden opening.

"Oh."

"American inherits mystery property, almost gets burned alive inside it, bequeathes a garden to the National Trust. You can understand why I wanted to meet you. Aiden would have wanted to, as well," Arthur said.

Jo put the paper down and wet her lips.

"You said there were—letters," she managed.

Arthur nodded, passed the gas fireplace and headed into the farther stretch of apartment. He returned with several envelopes and placed them into her hands. One of them had been addressed in Jo's own handwriting.

"Oh God," she panted. "This is mine? I sent it when I was twelve—"

"Yes. The other is his answer to you. It was returned unopened."

"Wh-what do they say?" she whispered.

Arthur gave her a quiet sort of smile. "I only know what I've been told. I didn't pry. Aiden was a very private man. Even with me."

Jo was listening. She was also opening envelopes—starting with the response to her own.

Dear Josephine,

I'm so happy you wrote to me about the school trip. I would be delighted to meet you when you arrive. Here is my telephone number; if you give me the details, I can even meet you at the airport in London. Send love to your mother; my very best,
Uncle Aiden

“He wanted to see me,” Jo said, almost to herself. Arthur was kind enough to say nothing. She picked up the second letter; it had been sent to her aunt in Chicago.

Dearest Aunt Susan,

I know we have not spoken in some time. Not long ago, young Josephine wrote me; I tried to respond. I may not have the correct address. Can you please direct me?

“That one had been opened—by someone,” Arthur said. “It came back in a new envelope, postage paid. But without a single word.”

Jo understood the message too well. Both her mother and aunt had been silent sentinels as Jo was growing up. *We don’t speak of the ugly thing, the hurtful thing.* As if that would make it safe. But it was worse that than; Jo knew her mother was a holder of grudges. She knew keeping the letters secret would hurt Aiden. Apparently it never occurred to her that it would hurt Jo, too.

“And this one?” she asked; a smooth, white envelope, unmarked.

“Unsent,” Arthur said. “He kept it with the others. I feel like it’s for you. Just you.” He handed her a letter opener to break the seal; Jo’s hands were shaking, but she took it anyway and managed to split the seam.

The paper inside was from a notebook, faint blue lines on a sheet torn from something else. The writing looked the same, but not the same. A note left for the self, and not for others.

Dear Josephine,

I recognize even as I write this that I’ll probably never send it. I suppose I needed to put the feelings into words, somehow.

> I could have wept when I received your letter. You have excellent penmanship, by the way. A wonderful, grown-up way of expressing yourself, too. I imagine that you look like your mother did, at your age, full of life and adventure. I had thought the past was behind us, that your letter was an olive branch. I wanted—

But those two words had been crossed out. On a new line, he'd begun again:

> I think about you, waiting to get my letter. It hurts me to know you never will. I wonder what possessed her to allow you to write at all—to set up your hopes only that I may disappoint them. Then I realize this was no doubt the intent all along—for I am "not to be trusted."
>
> I will keep your letter in fondness.
> With love, Uncle Aiden

Jo felt pain—sharp edged but hard to articulate. It was the tragedy of Miss Havisham in *Great Expectations*, the rotting wedding feast of joyous anticipation. It was the party that never happened, the gift never given. Jo spent her life trying to meet expectations of others, but always seemed to see the need too late or met it the wrong way. This time, she had been Aiden's joyous anticipation. She thought of his excitement at her letter, making little plans, hoping for a reunion that would never come—and it hurt her. *God*, did it hurt. For once in her life, she had been the gift, the promise. And she could never, ever fulfill it.

Jo's mother once accused her of having no feelings. The truth was much harder to live with. She had too many, had learned to turn them off to keep from drowning. She was certainly trying to now, folding away the feelings with the envelopes and training her mind on practical questions and tidy lists.

"He said he wasn't to be trusted. That my mother may have been trying to . . ." She struggled to get the words right, and ended up with the baldest honesty. "To disappoint me on purpose so I would never try to reach out again. It's awful. That's *awful.* Why would she *do* that?"

"I did not know your mother," he said after a long breath. He hesitated, lips pressed tight together, as if he feared something not very nice might come out. He was sparing her. But at the moment, she wasn't sure she wanted to be spared.

"What happened between them? I know my mother left England in her twenties, alone and pregnant with me. It was as if she was banished from their family. She never spoke of Aiden, and she didn't go to his funeral. You know more, though, don't you? I need to know." Jo's tone had wandered into desperate demanding and she wrestled it back. He just gave her a faint smile.

"Your grandfather was a vicious, hateful man. At some point, he discovered that Aiden was gay—I'm not sure when; after that, Aiden was as good as dead to him. Then there was your mother."

"Pregnant and unwed," Jo added.

Arthur nodded. "Aiden was very cagey about it. But I suspect she met a similar fate. Both of them cast off by their only living parent."

"Wouldn't that make them allies?" Jo asked.

"In a perfect world, I'm sure. Of course, in a perfect world they wouldn't be cast out at all." He set his cup down and scooped up the Pomeranian again. "Aiden lived a great deal in his own head, but he kept things locked up there."

"In his mental attic," Jo said, slipping into Sherlock parlance. Arthur gave a slight chuckle, possibly in response to an ear lick rather than the turn of phrase.

"I suppose. He could be private to the point of secrecy. Your letter came when we were first dating, and he was surprised into giving me the details I just gave you. There was a falling-out over trust. That's all I know. But I feel somehow the family patriarch must surely be to blame."

Jo rolled this around her head, looking for a good shelf to keep it on. She was upset. She understood the mental attic problem. She felt anger at her mother, confusion, and disappointment, but she couldn't deal with that now; instead, she clung to a sliver of maybe good news. Aiden kept secrets. He had a painting he called *Hiding*. Maybe he also believed in seeking.

"Did Aiden like puzzles?" she asked. "Problem solving, clues?"

"How do you mean?"

"I have a painting, too," Jo said slowly. "I discovered it last year in the Ardemore estate. It's by Augustus John, we think."

"Really?" Arthur sat a little straighter, and Jo felt an odd sort of pride that he knew what she was talking about.

"Yes, but it had been damaged. Badly. Aiden had it restored. I never found out the artist he hired to do it. Thing is, the woman in the painting is a mystery, a family member of mine—and Aiden's—that no one talks about. I can scarcely find any historical records. Did Aiden tell you about the Ardemores? About the love triangle between our ancestors—Gwen and William and Evelyn Davies? The baby?"

It was fortuitous that Arthur was not, at that moment, drinking tea. He would have choked.

"Baby? Whose baby, now?"

"Oh boy." Jo bit her lip. Was there a way to be concise here? *Just the facts, ma'am* . . . "So, Evelyn was the sister of our ancestor Gwen Ardemore. And she had a baby with Gwen's husband, William. And then Evelyn died, we think from childbirth. And got buried under the house."

Jo heard Arthur's sharp intake of breath.

"*That* wasn't in the paper."

"No," Jo agreed. She had left that bit out for the interview, partly at MacAdams's suggestion. It had been an ongoing investigation at the time. "I found a hope chest in the garden full of baby clothes and love letters between Evelyn and William Ardemore." Jo tried not to squirm. It sounded incredibly bald when you said it in shorthand. She rushed through the rest, forgetting to pause between sentences.

"We didn't find the baby—so maybe it lived or was buried somewhere else—I've been looking everywhere—and I think was Aiden looking, too, when he was alive, because I've heard that he spent time in Abington and was looking in archives and maybe even found something—because—because—" She gulped a breath. "Because he left a *note*."

Arthur said nothing for a long moment. Then he nodded and pressed his fingers together, prayer-hands style.

"You're looking for Evelyn's child, and you think Aiden might have been, too?"

Jo swallowed. She felt deeply embarrassed all of a sudden. She *was* and she *did*, but her only evidence was an archive box, the torn photo and half a sentence.

"I'm so sorry," she sputtered, but Arthur raised a hand.

"Tut, now. If anyone should apologize, it's me. I realize you've come to me for answers, and that so far I've been something of a bust. Let's just get some facts together. You said Aiden was in Abington. When, exactly?"

Jo didn't have an exactly. But she gave him the approximate date.

"Yes. Okay. He would have been diagnosed by then," he said. "Pancreatic cancer. Treatment for a year. We had hope at first, but in the end, there wasn't a lot they could do. He was away a lot, settling his affairs. I know his solicitor was in Abington, but he never asked me to go with him. And he never said anything about Evelyn or the painting. I might *still* be of some help, though, if you're looking for the artist Aiden hired. I have some some artist connections. And after all, not everyone could convincingly match the style of an Augustus John."

Jo had done everything to try to find out more about the painting, including taking it to an art restoration organization in York. But she only came up empty again and again, with no clearer understanding of who repaired it or why it was even ruined in the first place.

Arthur went on. "It's not as simple as copying someone's work; that's what all this business about artificial intelligence gets wrong. Yes, of course, you can copy the content itself; we see two-dimensional prints all the time, posters and greeting cards. But even a copy machine is only capturing the color and lines."

"Right," Jo agreed. "There would be brush strokes, and some paints and varnishes can be aged. The person I took the painting to used microscopes, types of X-ray."

"Layers, yes. A mere copy lacks depth. Optical and stereo microscopy . . . spectrometry to identify pigments . . . infrared. But there's more." Arthur handed her a teaspoon. "Take a look at this spoon."

Ornate, silver, it had a flower design worked into the handle. She gave it back to him, and he held it up between them.

"A jewelry artist designed and forged this for me. With the right equipment, you could copy the design and have it mass-produced. The end result might look a lot like the original. But it won't have a *soul.* The particular sheen and ripples of metal. All art works this way."

He set the spoon once more upon his saucer. "I'm not a collector of Augustus John paintings, but I know plenty about him. He was known for darker, moodier portrayals, revealing these piercing, even unkind, psychological insights in his portraits. He did Yeats, you know? Dylan Thomas."

"I've seen it online," Jo said, but Arthur shook his head.

"Then you have only seen a *copy* of it. The real thing, the real work—if it's *his* work—makes you feel the suffering. The point of all this," Arthur said, standing up and finally rousing the Boston terrier, "isn't the art lesson. It's that I know—and more importantly, Aiden knew—an artist who considered Augustus John the greatest master of the form."

"Oh my God, you're serious?" Jo gulped air, nearly swallowed spit wrong. She was going to have the worst emotion hangover in the morning.

"I know her personally. And if you'll consent to stay the night—I've an extra bedroom—I can introduce you tomorrow."

"I can get a hotel—I don't want to impose," she said, silently appending *and I might need to have a good cry somewhere private because what the fuck is this day?* Arthur, however, shook his head.

"Pepper," Arthur said, pointing to the Boston terrier panting beneath the coffee table, "loves guests. And the little prince here, Hans—he loves an early-morning walk. If you would be so kind, I would consider it full repayment for room and board."

Jo conceded the point; it would save the night's stay, too . . . and the flat was nicer than any penthouse.

"The artist, though—who?"

"Ah! Didn't I say? You've already seen her work," he said. "She painted *Hiding.* Chen Benton-Li."

CHAPTER 12

Monday morning with take-away coffee from Teresa's mobile tea-and-cakes van. It wasn't very good coffee. But at least she'd given it to MacAdams for free after his generous "go away" tip from Saturday.

"It's not a bad business model," Green said. "Gridley says it's better for her than university."

"Life in a food trolley?" MacAdams asked.

"To start, why not? We've apparently got a butty van somewhere around; Gwilym said he and Jo saw one near the trail."

MacAdams took their exit, chewing over this last remark.

"Isn't that near where Roberta found the body?" he asked, but Green's phone had just buzzed.

"Oi, that's Gridley." She picked up her mobile and listened intently. "Ah. Figures. The telephone number we lifted from the Abington Arms call history? No trace; must be a burner phone."

There were only so many reasons for a throw-away, untraceable number, and most of them were *not* aboveboard. It added a new element.

"Stanley Burnhope should have his regular mobile number; that might tell us something," MacAdams suggested.

"As to Burnhope, since we missed him yesterday, Rachel and I had a good poke around the internet last night."

"Everybody's best boy," MacAdams said. "What did you find?"

"Stanley Scott Burnhope, son of MacAlister Burnhope—diplomat. Mother was what you might call industry aristocrat."

"Grew up with wealth, then."

"They owned yachts," said Green, in whose opinion yacht owners didn't *go* to hell; they ran the administration. "Degrees from Eton College and Oxford, surprise, surprise. Started out in an old-school architecture firm, then started his own commercial development company. They win awards for places no one would want to live. That sort of thing."

MacAdams thought of the Gherkin—formerly the Swiss Re Building—of pickle-shaped fame.

"No blemishes on the record anywhere?" he asked.

"If there are, they have been thoroughly swept under money rugs," Green said, "though there was a discord at Eton, apparently. Hang on . . ." She scrolled through her notes. "Right, so he never gets actually sent up for this, but there had been allegations that he and four other pupils received leaked exam information. Only one of them punished. The scholarship kid."

"The not-as-rich one."

"So it seems. Anyway, everything against Burnhope was dropped. A quick look through his time at Oxford doesn't turn up much, but I am pretty sure money got him the initial job in the firm."

"And money to set up Burnhope's award-winning development company," MacAdams said. "That also has no blemishes."

"Or none we can find. Money makes problems go away."

"You are deeply skeptical, Sheila Green," MacAdams said, pulling into an immaculate but mostly empty car park. Of course, MacAdams largely agreed. Entirely made of glass that seemed to ripple around the curved exterior, Hammersmith and Company certainly dripped with money. The real impression was waiting for them, however, on the inside.

Something between rotunda and Parthenon, all offices faced inward to an open piazza. Within was a four-story waterfall, all of it lit by a glass ceiling some fifteen floors above. Green craned her neck for the full view of the latter.

"A bit on the nose, isn't it?" she asked, then looked again at her notes. "Company supposedly has twenty thousand employees all told."

"Interesting. A lot of offices up there are dark." MacAdams swept his eyes across the vast lobby. A café occupied the rear wall, on-grounds service. The inverse of Teresa's tea mobile, he couldn't help but think. In the center, left of the waterfall, was a proper reception desk—and a crisp-looking woman in lavender.

"Good morning, welcome to Hammersmith and Company. Can I direct you?" she asked. MacAdams read her bronze name pin.

"Ms. Simmons," he said, producing his police ID. "We would like to speak with Stanley Burnhope, please."

"Oh my, has something happened?" she asked. Her tone wasn't alarmed necessarily, but no hint of expectation, either. Burnhope no doubt knew of Foley's death now, but perhaps it hadn't made the rounds.

"If you could just point us in the right direction."

"I'll ring you up," Ms. Simmons agreed, and MacAdams took the opportunity to brief Green quietly.

"Dig." He nodded toward the knot of people forming in front of the café. "Find out who knew Foley and if anyone's heard . . . anything."

"Boss," Green said, using the title as an affirmative. Meanwhile, Ms. Simmons gestured to the far left.

"The lift is just past the fountain. Eleventh floor."

★★★

Like everything else at Hammersmith, the lift was a glassed-in affair, a music box on pulleys offering visitors a near 360-degree view of the rotunda and several floors of sudden death, should a cable snap. MacAdams wasn't afraid of heights, but he didn't care to *see* the mechanisms by which mankind evaded gravity, in the same way he didn't want to see the interior workings of a jumbo jet.

MacAdams expected to step off into a reception area with secretary gatekeeper, as below. Instead, the doors opened into a sunken floor plan with two steps down to short-backed, shiny sofas with an obelisk coffee table. The raised terrace around it boasted architectural drawings and shelves with best-in-the-business awards. MacAdams investigated the first; shaped like a pyramid, it offered commendation for architectural design.

"Good morning, Detective."

MacAdams turned to see a man in his fifties, dark hair a bit longer than his online photo and inclined to wave. Slim build in a tailored suit, wearing an expensive watch. Well turned out, but not ostentatious—with a face that married the reserve of Gridley with the affability of Struthers.

"A pleasure," MacAdams said briskly. He pointed to the framed drawings. "So Hammersmith is both architecture and real estate?"

"Yes, more control of the process. As you can see, it's paid off. Our design team is a hundred strong now, award winning. Have you seen our builds?"

"I've seen this one. And the country club. And your house."

"Ah." Burnhope's hooded eyes closed a moment, his smile regressing. "Yes. Ava told me—and I spoke to Sophie. About Foley."

"Your wife didn't seem to know him," MacAdams said. "Or even really much about your work at all."

"She knows we build stunning buildings," Burnhope said. "That's enough, don't you think?"

"Do you?"

"Certainly. I know Ava is a celebrated concert pianist. I don't have to know the difference between a B-flat and an F-sharp. I respect her work, she respects mine. Separate spheres."

"So I see." MacAdams did not see, but all the same. "Back to Foley, then. His last email to you called for a *partners'* meeting. On Friday, the day he was killed. Can you elaborate?"

Burnhope nodded, then backed toward the farther glass wall. "Would you step into my office? I have something to show you."

MacAdams obliged, taking a seat in the chair opposite Burnhope's credenza. "You aren't from Newcastle yourself, I take it."

"Is it so obvious?"

"You don't have the accent. Your wife does, but we know she's local." MacAdams watched his smile reappear.

"Daughter to city CEO Thompson, yes, Newcastle born and bred. I come from London."

"Not Ireland?" MacAdams asked, referring to his very slight brogue. Honest surprise dawned on Burnhope's face.

"I'm not, but well spotted, Detective. Are you a linguist?"

"Detective Chief Inspector. And I'm not, but I'm familiar with the Irish accent. Yours is faint, but I can hear it." In all honesty, he'd guessed—and only because Burnhope pronounced the word *cannot* the same way Tula Byrne did: *cannae.* Burnhope rested his hands upon his desk.

"You'll be surprised to know I only spent a year there, but it was a formative one. I was three. Do you have children?"

"I don't."

"Well, you would be shocked what a toddler picks up and can't let go. I learned to speak there, and retain a bit of those linguistic leanings." Burnhope turned on his laptop and appeared to be scrolling. "I did receive that email from Foley, as you said, and we met up. I don't know why he called it a partners' meeting, except that he had been angling for a promotion. Been asking for at least six months."

The half year seemed to be increasingly important.

"You weren't keen on the idea?" MacAdams asked.

Burnhope's eyes had returned to their usual demure hoods, and he frowned slightly.

"I'm afraid not, no. Don't mistake me—Foley had a certain set of very important skills. But he wasn't right for partnership."

MacAdams tapped his pencil against the notepad. He wanted to talk about the meeting on Friday, but this seemed important.

"What *does* it take, Mr. Burnhope? Why wasn't he the right sort?"

Burnhope looked out the window and away from MacAdams before he replied.

"I started this company in 1993," he said. "Now we're international. We employ thousands of people; we do a build from design to finish. It's better for Newcastle, better for everyone. We have a public face and a debt to the community."

"I believe you *are* the public face," MacAdams countered. "The golden boy of industry, or so says the *Chronicle*."

Burnhope laughed. "I wouldn't put it that way myself. I'm a businessman, and we all want fiscal success; I'm not denying it. I just *also* want something good to come of it. It sounds cliché, but I want the world to be a better place for my children. Sophie Wagner wants that—Ava wants that. It's our focus."

"You haven't really answered the question," MacAdams reminded him.

"What I'm saying is that it takes different personalities to run a company. Foley had single-minded focus. He was aggressive; he wasn't afraid to push. I used to call him the bulldog." Burnhope's expression grew serious. "Foley could shout down a contractor; he could bully the toughest supervisors, he wouldn't be crossed, denied or made a fool of. But you can't treat financers and governing bodies that way. I gave him his six months to turn it around with a property in York. It took him half that time to gravely irritate the Lord Mayor, in a way that gets the project shut down. I'd made up my mind before the meeting that he simply wasn't partner material."

And with that, they had circled back to Friday.

"Start from his arrival at four thirty," MacAdams said. "Don't leave anything out."

Burnhope sighed and laced his fingers. "There isn't much to tell. He arrived; we had a coffee. It started cordially enough, but when I told him it wasn't in our vision for him to make partner, he became angry."

"And did things escalate?"

"He shouted a bit, then said he didn't need Hammersmith."

"He quit, you mean?"

"I don't think he meant to, and it's no way to tender resignation, anyway. I told him to have a cool off at the weekend; we'd talk about it more later. He agreed, still heated, and left. That's all."

"What time did he go?" MacAdams asked.

"It wasn't even five."

"Anyone verify that?"

"Doubtful," Burnhope said. "I let everyone leave at 4:00 p.m.; a number of them were invited to the charity ball."

"For refugees," MacAdams said. "I understand your nanny is one."

"Maryam. Yes." Burnhope's brows darkened a moment. "You say that as though it's an accusation, Detective."

"Not to worry," MacAdams said dryly. "Ms. Wagner has already given me a detailed report on why it's aboveboard."

"I see." Burnhope stood up and adjusted his sport coat, a clear signal the meeting was coming to an end. "You're one of those who think charity begins at home, I suppose? No hiring of immigrants?"

MacAdams stood, though in other respects remained unmoved. "Did Ronan Foley ever take part in the charity?"

Burnhope's hackles smoothed again. He led the way to the lift.

"Detective, I don't want to speak ill of the dead. But Foley was not the sort to do charity work. He worked like a dynamo, was a good job lead. But I did not have a *personal* relationship with him."

"And you clearly kept him away from your family," MacAdams said.

"I suppose? Work-life separation. There wasn't a reason for him to meet Ava." He frowned again. "Has the obituary been printed? I haven't yet made an announcement to the staff. Our secretary should be told."

"I think my DS may have taken care of that," Macadams suggested when the lift announced itself. He held it with his foot and pulled out his notepad again. "One more thing. This is the number we have for Foley. Did he have any others?"

Burnhope scanned the yellow pad.

"Not that I know of, I'm afraid. It's the one I've got for him."

"And it's always been the same, has it?"

Burnhope's hooded eyes narrowed. "Since he started with us, yes. Why ask?"

MacAdams declined to give a reason. Instead, he entered into the glass coffin and descended to the ground floor. Green had migrated to the sitting area behind the fountain with Ms. Simmons, who appeared to be weeping openly. She looked up as they approached, dabbing at her mascara with a handful of tissues.

"Oh it's so awful," she hiccupped.

"It's a great shock," he agreed as Green got to her feet.

"Thank you for your time, Ms. Simmons," Green said, though her eyebrows suggested a great deal more. "If you think of anything else, you can call."

"Trisha," she said, taking Green's card. "Thank you."

★ ★ ★

Once outside, Green let out a long breath.

"That was a *lot* more emotional than I expected."

MacAdams ears pricked. "Go on."

"Well, most people I spoke to knew who he was; he definitely turned up here plenty, but I gather his was the away-game, on-site sort of thing. But shite, when I asked Trisha Simmons, she just completely fell apart."

"Enough to suggest they might have been more than colleagues?" he asked.

"You're thinking of the earring."

"Or the silk scarf."

"I got there, too; especially if *she* is the assistant who may or may not have made the Abington Arms reservation. We could get a DNA swab, but if so, she wasn't wearing the perfume today." Green got into the driver's side. "Simmons is something of a personal assistant to all of the upper-level folks, not just Burnhope. She'd also a single mum raising a daughter and having a struggle of it—especially since the pandemic. Foley apparently brought her flowers on Mother's Day, even picked up her kid from school on occasion. That sort of thing."

"Strange. According to Burnhope, Foley didn't think of anyone but himself."

"So not friends?"

"Honestly? He described Ronan Foley as a bully—a bull *dog.* And he didn't want the man around his wife and kids." MacAdams buckled himself in and Green started the engine.

"Descriptions don't exactly square, do they?" she asked.

MacAdams made a noncommittal noise in his throat.

"Could be work versus personal life," he said. "Then again, if he and Trisha weren't more intimately involved, then she ought to fall on the work side. We need more input, someone else who knew Foley well."

"Afraid most of what I picked up at the office was more or less neutral and distant. If he was a bully, it must have been leveled at outside contracts."

"About that," MacAdams said. "Burnhope said he received big complaints from a property in York."

"So what's our next move?" Green asked, picking up her mobile.

"*Your* next move is to get that burner trace. I . . . need to make a phone call."

MacAdams did *not* add that his call would be to Annie. Her new husband, Ashok, worked as a commercial architect; he might have a handle on professional gossip about the York build. It meant doing pleasantries with his ex-wife's partner in ways that MacAdams would much rather avoid; then again, it also meant making inquiries in the quietest way possible. "I also want a list of attendees to the charity ball."

"You think Burnhope has a motive?" she asked.

MacAdams didn't. Or, rather, he could see Foley having a motive to wish harm onto Burnhope more than the reverse. At the same time, despite the coincidental timing, Foley's demand for a promotion didn't explain why he might sell his possessions so quickly before his death. Was he in fiscal trouble? Nothing in his accounts suggested it, but if he was in trouble—if he owed money to dangerous people—if he were involved in some sort of—

"Hey boss? It's Jo Jones."

"What? Where?"

He looked up to find, indeed, a Jo Jones. Here in Newcastle. With coffee. And two small dogs.

CHAPTER 13

Hans did not understand *heel*. Or *stay* or *stop* or *whoa*. Pepper, on the other hand, refused the indignity of walking after a block and a half. Happily, their destination was in sight: the Right Café, with its welcoming outdoor seating among potted ferns. It's where she intended to meet Chen Benton-Li, and she'd been reading about her the whole way.

The artist had been born in Newcastle to Chinese immigrants of modest means. Her father passed while she was still a child, and she and her mum lived in the low-rent district. Chen had only intermittent education until her mother remarried; she first entered public school at the age of thirteen, and announced publicly that *she* was a *she*. Assigned male at birth, Chen lived the rest of her life as a woman. Jo did the mental math; now seventy-one, Chen transitioned in the '60s following pioneers like April Ashley (who modeled for *Vogue* before being outed). Coming out of the closet was hard enough in the present; she imagined Chen must be made of stern stuff.

And, according to Jo's research, her artwork was impeccable. Jo couldn't wait to meet her—even if the prospect also gave her new-people anxiety. The joys and woes of excito-terror.

"Can I come in with the dogs?" Jo asked at the front door. "I'm supposed to meet someone—we can sit outside."

"No problem. Those are Arthur's pups, aren't they?" the server asked. "He's here all the time."

"Yes. I'm just walking them. To brunch." That sounded especially odd, but then again, they weren't even the only dogs inside the place. Jo's eyes adjusted to pick out a herding dog of some variety near the back—and the flutter of a hand in her peripheral vision. The café was white: white walls, white tables, bamboo-colored chairs. But just beneath the stylized café name, a bright mandala bloomed in teal and aquamarine. A jacket, Jo realized, with structured shoulders and a vanishingly thin waist. Tucked into it and wearing a contrast of summer yellow was an elegant woman, gracefully poised. She held one hand aloft, supporting a nickel-sized sapphire stone, and rolled her wrist to beckon.

"Wow," Jo said before she could school herself not to.

"Pleased to meet you, too, child," said Chen. Jo already knew Chen was native to Newcastle, but that she talked like Ann Cleeves's Vera Stanhope was both incongruous and delightful. "Shall we dine alfresco? It's a rare thing."

Jo nodded affirmative, and Hans registered his approval by circling Chen excitedly.

"Arthur wouldn't leave his babies to just anyone, you know," she said. "You must be very special."

"Oh" was Jo's so-cultured response. *Think faster, please*, she instructed her brain. "It's really wonderful that you could see me," she added as the server led them to the sun-soaked beer garden.

"Of course. I adore Arthur. And besides," Chen said, lowering magenta sunglasses and looking at Jo over the rim, "I'm interested. You see, no one else *knows*."

"About . . . ?" Jo put Pepper down in the shadow of the table and tied off Hans's leash.

Chen waited until she was settled. "Evelyn's painting."

"You—saw it? You were you at the estate?"

Chen smiled. "Oh. Hadn't you guessed it was my work?"

Jo bit her lip. No, and yes. Dared to hope.

Chen went on. "Aiden invited me; he wanted my opinion about their origins. As I gather you already know, Evelyn's is an Augustus John. The other two paintings of his ancestors were *not*. Very strange mystery indeed. Evelyn's painting was decent work, mind. But not expertly done."

"So it's all true. Aiden knew it was an Augustus John! I thought he must have. Was it hard to replicate?" Jo began. She wanted to ask about the message on the torn photo, but the server was standing over her now. "Um, coffee?"

"Try the omelet, pet," Chen suggested, then to the waitress, "I'll have my usual," then back to Jo, "Aiden had a small photo on silver paper in a tiny gilt frame. Very helpful for the repair."

Chen went on, pausing now and then to make quiet little hums—appreciative vibrations. It was oddly soothing.

"Aiden invited me to the Ardemore estate. He was sick then, and I rather younger and fitter. I worked right there, in the library—was sorry to hear of its demise. Aiden sat in a wing-back chair, blanket on his knees, and watched me paint." She smiled gently. "I'm glad I had the time with him. He supported me when it mattered. I was only too happy to return favors."

The omelet had come, but Jo pushed the plate to one side.

"I want to know everything," she said.

"Tut. You want to eat your breakfast is what, pet. There's a girl. And then, you want to come to this." Chen burrowed into an oversize bag, half disappearing into its yawning mouth. She returned with a folded brochure. "It's an exhibition."

Jo looked at the title: *Fractured Genius: Augustus John and the Slade School of Art*. It started tomorrow, Tuesday, at the York Art Gallery. Jo lifted her eyes to Chen. "This is . . . interesting timing."

"Oh, there's always a show somewhere featuring the Slade

pupils. It's a celebrated bunch, and you'll see the work of Derwent Lees and William Orpen. Even Augustus's sister, Gwen."

Jo nearly choked. Why was everyone called William and Gwen? Across from her, Chen put down her toast and jam.

"Join me," she said.

"At the museum?"

"Quite. You want to know more about Aiden—you need to see the paintings. Consider it the price of admission." She winked. "Now, eat up. Those pups will want to be home again before it gets too warm."

★★★

Chen wasn't wrong about the temperatures; by the time Jo left the café, she'd started to sweat in earnest. On the street, she saw summer shorts and preposterously white legs to prove how rare a day it was. And Pepper was having none of it. Looking up the museum while carrying an inverted eight-pound dog was not improving the heat index. She retraced her steps at a clip even Hans could appreciate, cutting across the park to one of the main streets . . . just in time to be honked at.

Loudly, Jo dropped her phone, managed *not* to drop the dog, and quite possibly her heart had exploded. The phone remained thankfully intact. *Car horns should be banned.* Any horn, frankly. Manic, random noisemakers.

Looking up, she did *not* see a cranky driver riding away as she'd expected. What she saw, instead, was a white butty van.

Not the same one, obviously. The one with a single window, dinged metal counter, out-of-date condiments—the one that delivered a sizable bacon sandwich but on stale bread Gwilym complained about the whole way back. The one with a bejowled driver with a thick Geordie accent.

Except, somehow, it *was.* Jo approached the window, dogs in tow.

"Hi, excuse me?" Jo asked. The man had been looking at his phone.

"Closed," he said.

"Oh. I'm not ordering. I just had a question." Jo was, in fact, trying to formulate a question just then, but it was hard to know how to begin. *Were you parked up at a murder scene yesterday?* didn't seem like a good opener; *Have you seen the vanishing hiker?* didn't strike her as much better.

"Closed, I said." He reached for the sliding glass door—and Jo did something drastic and more than a trifle embarrassing. She blocked it with the bone-shaped dispenser for tiny dog-poo bags she'd been carrying around. That made him shove all the harder, but he'd been thwarted by femoral knob.

"Please, I really just—"

"Look, ye nebby hinny, go off. We ain't selling today." With that, he wrenched loose the blockade, shut the window and put up the official closed sign. Jo stared at it, wondering what had got into her lately. The van wasn't her problem. The hiker wasn't, either. She had enough mystery women to track down without adding new ones to her repertoire.

And anyway, she needed to prepare for an art opening. She opened a text window and searched for Gwilym. It was time to divide and conquer.

I need everything you can dig up on Augustus John.

The ellipsis of creation appeared immediately.

You're the boss, he wrote.

★ ★ ★

When MacAdams and Green returned to Abington CID, Gridley and Andrews met them at the door.

"About our burner phone," Andrews said, waving a sheaf of

paper. "Guess what? Most of the calls go to *another* burner, or several—"

"Which you are also tracing," MacAdams interrupted.

"Yes, sir. But we did get a bit of good news. The reports show a series of calls to a landline, every few weeks over the last six months. The Abington Arms."

That got MacAdams's attention, and Green's, too, he noted.

"Wait just a minute," she said. "Arianna said he'd never called before, that she didn't recognize the name."

MacAdams responded by putting Arianna and Evans back on the incident board in the Active category.

"We'll get them in for questioning. What about Sophie Wagner's charity?"

Gridley hopped up from the table she'd been sitting on. "That checks out; cleared with Home Office and registered for community sponsorship. Not as big an organization as something like Citizens UK, but they seem to have helped resettle a few dozen families."

"Is that a lot?" Andrews asked.

Gridley picked up a marker. "You bet. It's thousands of pounds per person. If—super conservatively—we say 5K per, that's over 130,000 sterling." She wrote that on the board. "But that's not even the biggest part of it. There's finding the right housing, getting it approved, sorting the paperwork, job center training, language classes. That's why it's usually a communal effort."

"And not usually attached to a country club," MacAdams said.

"Fair," Gridley agreed. "But even though Sophie started the Fresh Start charity, she has a board of directors. It's not under the business she operates; they just happen to be licensed for job placement. FYI, though. Burnhope is on the board. So is Ava."

Burnhope had said as much to MacAdams. Tight little family, they had there. Each standing in as supportive alibi for the rest.

"It might be worth looking into the club, anyway. It's called Lime Tree Greens. Wagner's son works there, too."

"Are they suspects?" Gridley asked.

"Not yet. But add them to the list of people surrounding Foley. Where are we on next of kin for Foley?"

Andrews waved a hand. He was nosing over his tablet and chewing his bottom lip. "Nothing. I mean, *nobody*. No mother, no father, no siblings. Actually, no Ronan Foley earlier than 1998."

MacAdams picked a stale doughnut, then put it down again. "Explain."

"Well, his ID card tells us he was born in Belfast in 1962. I put in a call to Ireland's General Registry Office, but they don't have a birth record for a Ronan Foley in Belfast."

"Have you checked the driver registration?" Gridley asked before stealing the doughnut MacAdams had his eye on. She took a chalky bite before continuing. "To get a driving ID, you have to have a public services card and verified government ID. And if you don't have those, the list is long—he'd need his personal public services number, at least. Someone's got to have his details."

"Tommy, chase it. Also, one of you poke around more in Burnhope's past. Let's see if we have any more like the Eton near-miss."

MacAdams had been trying to capture the important pieces on the incident board. Sophie, Ava, Stanley and Fresh Start. Foley as a dark horse, friendly to single mum Trisha, had a mystery lady leaving things in his flat, but was otherwise a bully who couldn't get on with authority. Burnhope had said "work-life balance"—an odd thing to remark about a now-deceased employee—and it stuck in MacAdams's mind. Was the murder in question business or pleasure related?

"Phone, boss," Gridley said, "Struthers. He wants you to come down—says he's got something you need to see."

Please be useful evidence, MacAdams thought.

"Green? Prepare the interview rooms and get Arianna and Evans in here."

"On it," she said, and MacAdams slipped out the door. It was better to go it alone, anyway. He needed to call Annie.

"It's me," he said when she'd given the flower shop's sing-song greeting.

"Oh! James—is everything all right?"

"It is. I need a favor."

"Goodness, certainly. But you *never* ring me; gives me a heart attack. I always think someone must have died."

"Listen, I need some insight into architecture and commercial real estate for a case. I thought maybe Ashok—"

"Oh my God, James! You're calling *and* you want to speak with Ashok?"

"Sorry—"

"Are you kidding? It's wonderful. Hold on . . ." In the distance he heard her shout "Ashok! It's James." MacAdams pressed his phone to his forehead as if that would recall the situation. "Okay, I'm back. He's just coming down."

"Annie, please, I'm about to walk into the morgue," he said.

"Ah. So someone *has* died. But you want to speak to him?"

"I do. I would like to, when—"

"Wonderful. We'll have you to dinner. How's Thursday?" Her voice was fainter as she asked, "Ashok, Thursday—that works for you, doesn't it?" MacAdams had reached the elevator and, if he were very lucky, the end of wireless service.

"Tuesday," he said, as the doors closed. Thursday might almost be too long to wait. The call dropped, the doors opened and, for once, MacAdams was almost happy to see the hallway leading to Struthers's lab.

"Hello, James! Sorry to bother you at luncheon," he said, waving a home-packed sandwich on the side table. MacAdams wondered, not for the first time, what sort of childhood trauma made for a good coroner.

"Is this about the murder weapon?" he asked.

"Partly, yes. And something else. Right this way—I've been

experimenting." Arranged on a steel tray was a curious menagerie: a hammer, a long lead pipe . . . and what appeared to be a fancy ashtray. "I've been trying to find a match for our wounds using an assortment of random objects, comparing their weight and force to what we saw in the damage to Foley's head."

"Not the hammer," MacAdams hazarded.

"Very good! Serviceable, yes, especially from a long-armed assailant. I thought it might make sense of the downward-glancing blow. Alas, as you note, the wound is much too broad." Struthers picked up the lead pipe. "This was no better; whatever struck him wasn't a uniform shape like this. Not the way to crack a coconut."

"A what?" MacAdams asked.

"Coconuts! Cantaloupe are better for shape and weight, but I needed something closer to five on the Mohs' scale of hardness."

MacAdams had a fleeting curiosity whether Jo would know what the Mohs' scale was. Probably she would, he decided.

"I needed something heavy enough to do the deed in a single blow, but still do more damage at one corner," Struthers said. "I used to golf, you know. Had a whack with a heavy iron. It does damage, but still not the right kind."

"So *not* a golf club?" MacAdams asked, halfway to calling in a search of Lime Tree Greens. Struthers wagged a finger.

"Cracks the shell, but the wound is all wrong. Weird as it may seem, this came closest." He handed the glass ashtray to MacAdams.

"It's heavy enough," he agreed. "But—"

"But ashtrays don't make good murder weapons, eh? I agree." Struthers sighed.

MacAdams looked at the object in his hand. Ungainly. Yes, he could probably wield it, but it would be better as a missile.

"Do you think someone threw it at him?"

"I do not. You lose a lot of force that way. But—" He took it back and swung it downward, for effect. "Say your opponent is already down. On his knees, maybe. Or you are on higher ground. That would do it."

"You're saying this is my murder weapon?"

"I am *not*," Struthers said, taking it back. "But heavy glass would do the trick, and might explain the complete lack of residue, fiber or filings in the wound. People have been killed with all sorts of strange objects. I once presided over a man done in by a tennis trophy."

MacAdams wasn't sure coconut smashing counted as forensics, but it proved one thing at least—

"No one *plans* to kill someone with a thing like this, do they? Planners use practical, surefire weapons."

"Unpremeditated, you mean?" Struthers asked.

MacAdams nodded. "If the murderer used something like this, they chose whatever was to hand." He looked at the chunk of glass, thinking of the modern glass sculptures populating Ava's music room. Defensive, wasn't she? Ready to deny all knowledge of her husband's business—and his partner. He'd found it hard to believe then. Now that suspicion took a slightly darker hue.

"You said you had something else to show me?" he asked.

"Two somethings. We'll start with the curious and graduate to the strange. Come have a look." He led MacAdams to the table with his sandwich, a small cardboard box—and a microscope. "First, your golden earring. I'm shocked it wasn't pummeled to bits by our boots. Lucky anyone noticed it."

He lifted the tiny object from the box and placed it on a piece of black foam. MacAdams judged it to be about the size of a pound coin, maybe smaller. Sort of a half-moon shape, it had been adorned with filigree work.

"Very pure, maybe twenty-four or twenty-six karat. That's called box construction, according to our jeweler friend. More specifically, 'open-work S-curve crescent with an arabesque design.'" Struthers turned it sideways, to show the "box"; the earring was hollow, like a basket.

"Does that help us identify it?" MacAdams asked.

"That's the curious bit. The design, I'm told, was popular in Egypt and North Africa, Spain, India and Turkey . . . in the eleventh century."

MacAdams's attention to the objet d'art had wandered, but this news recalled it. He stared again at the exotic-looking disk.

"You're telling me that's a thousand years old?" he asked.

"Well, the *design* is. There's no hallmark stamp, and you can't carbon-date *gold*. It might have been made last week to mimic the design. In any case, it's a pricey piece, handmade and not mass-produced. If you know an antiques dealer, they might be able to say with more certainty."

In fact, MacAdams did know one. He made a mental note to see if jewelry was one of Gwilym's many specialties.

"I don't suppose this jeweler friend had any guesses as to who might have made it?" MacAdams asked.

Struthers shook his head. "None he knew of—he reiterated how rare it was, then actually suggested we seek out a museum professional."

MacAdams sighed. *Curious*, yes, but not especially helpful. "All right, show me the *strange*."

"Ah. You know those white patches noted by DS Green? Not vitiligo. I've performed a few tests, and it's true, the skin has been damaged. But it's not an abrasion, disease or fungus."

Struthers indicated the microscope, and MacAdams peered through the lens at tissue on a slide. At high magnification, he saw mainly ridges. When he came up for air, Struthers was smiling giddily.

"The tissue has been severely dehydrated *after* death," Struthers said. "And punctured by crystals. Does that help?"

MacAdams looked back to the sample. "It doesn't."

"Freezer burn," Struthers said, and MacAdams blinked hard. It had just called up the brown-white of beef left too long in the back of the icebox.

"You're telling me the body was frozen?"

"No, the damage would have been everywhere. I'd say it was packed in ice—and not dry ice, either. *That* freezes too hard and fast for crystal formation. Shame, actually, since dry ice is harder to get hold of and easier to track."

MacAdams pushed his hands out in front of him, as if that would make it easier to catch the stray thought that kept buzzing around inside him.

"This doesn't make sense. Someone killed him after midnight, then packed him in ice, then dumped him in a ditch before 3:00 a.m.? Why bother? It wouldn't be long enough to disguise the time of death, would it?"

"Not really," Struthers agreed. "Rigor mortis sets in a few hours after death and lasts at least twenty-four."

MacAdams made a four-cornered circuit of the lab. It clarified nothing. The midnight-to-three window remained.

"Is there anything else to determine exact time of death?"

"Stomach contents."

"Fine." MacAdams tapped his fingers against the steel table. "See what you can do to narrow this down."

"Will do," Struthers said, peeling his gloves off and making advances on his sandwich.

MacAdams left the long hall feeling far less buoyant than he had on arrival. Shoving a bunch of ice bags on a corpse (in a rainstorm), maybe dealing a blow with glass sculpture; it made no real sense.

CHAPTER 14

Evans had been placed in the interview room—the only proper one, really. Arianna awaited them in the sometimes-storage cupboard.

"You're going to take Evans," MacAdams explained.

"Because?" Green asked testily.

"You and Arianna have history, and—" he held up his hand to forestall remonstrance "—*and* Evans and I have history. It doesn't matter what kind or why, but it's better if neither is on their guard." He peered through the window at Evans; he hadn't risen from his chair, but managed to be in constant motion anyway. MacAdams had seen long distance runners burn fewer calories. "*Less* on their guard."

Green wasn't exactly mollified, but she uncrossed her arms and smoothed the lapels of her blazer.

"So I should be nice," she said.

MacAdams handed her two cups of tea to carry in with her. "Be your usual charming self," he said. Then he returned to the kettle for two more. Perhaps milk and sugar would placate Ms. Templeton, who had been far less nervous but also more recalcitrant about coming to the station.

She sat very straight in her chair, ponytail pulled back tight at the temples. It had looked professional in situ; without her uniform—and with her present expression—it just looked severe.

"I'm sorry to keep you waiting," he said, passing her a cup of tea. "Here you go. You were kind enough to offer me some when we came to the Abington Arms."

Arianna had seemed about to decline, but he'd scored a point by recalling her own charity.

"Thank you, yes."

"I know this wasn't your plan for a day off," he said (they'd found her at home, in the midst of doing laundry). "But it will be very helpful for our inquiries."

She took a sip of tea and looked about the small, spare room. "I've never been inside a police station."

"It doesn't really improve on further acquaintance," MacAdams admitted. "I just need to clarify some details."

"Sheila thinks I lied. I didn't. I told you then—I'm telling you now—I never heard of Ronan Foley until he rang on Friday. You can tell her *that*."

MacAdams patted himself on the back for not allowing Green to run this particular interview.

"We don't think you lied—not intentionally." MacAdams laid the hotel registration book on the table in front of her. "You said Foley asked if there were reservations in his name."

"Yes. And there weren't any."

"Not under his name. But I want you to look at the numbers." He'd circled Foley's. And then he'd circled a dozen more. Arianna stared in blank confusion.

"How—What? But that's Mr. and Mrs. Connolly! A married couple from Manchester; they come every few weekends."

MacAdams had managed to get that far after seizing the register. Now he needed the rest of the story.

"Was Mr. Connolly an Irish gentleman?"

"Well, yes. But—"

MacAdams slid across the photograph of Ronan Foley printed from the Hammersmith website, with his name visible underneath. Arianna caught her breath and covered her mouth with one hand.

"Oh my God. That's—that's the man you found dead?"

"Is it a match?" MacAdams asked. She nodded slowly, her face blanching behind her makeup.

"What's happened to his wife?" she whispered.

Wife? MacAdams felt his pulse spike. Ronan Foley didn't have a wife, not a legally listed one anyway. Was "Mrs. Connolly" the owner of the earring or scarf? He kept his tone neutral.

"It would help the investigation to know more about her," he said.

Arianna drank the rest of her tea in a single go. Her demeanor had changed, or changed again. From hostess to disgruntled potential witness to something more human. And fragile.

"Slight," she said. "A tiny thing. Really young, but I never really spoke to her."

"How so?"

"Nathan—Ronan. Whatever his name is. Was." She took a breath. "He always arranged everything, and he was *so* attentive. Like she was a china doll. He bought flowers and champagne, chocolate, roses. Always some little present or surprise ahead of their coming." It had, MacAdams realized, really made an impression on her.

"I take it such behavior is rare at Abington Arms?" he asked.

"We cater to high society, remember? MPs and judges and their wives. They—Of course, they're always very well turned out. But presents and flowers? That's not for married people." Arianna had looked away when she said this, so the last was delivered to the left-hand wall.

MacAdams extrapolated. "Mr. Connolly treated his wife the way most of your guests treat a mistress?" he asked.

Arianna's eyes flitted back. "I didn't say that. Look, the first time they came was their honeymoon. Newlyweds. He called her his 'little Alina.'" She pursed her lips. "Dammit. If Connolly wasn't his real name, though, was he lying about the rest, too? I mean, were they married at all? Or just cheating under false names?"

MacAdams had written all of this down, but he had a very different idea taking shape. As there was no Ronan Foley in the records . . . perhaps *that* was the false name, and this the real one? He'd have Gridley run a search on Alina and Nathan Connolly.

"If there's anything else—anything—let us know," MacAdams said. "I'll see you out."

Arianna stood up but didn't move toward the door.

"Don't go telling Green I was dizzy on romance. I just thought they were a nice couple, is all."

"Understood," MacAdams said, still trying to usher her out of the room.

Arianna pointed at him with a well-manicured finger. "She's not my ex, by the way, in case you're thinking it. Sheila Green is *not* my type."

★ ★ ★

MacAdams poured himself an honest cup of coffee, in a mug and everything, and retreated to his office. He had time to process Arianna's last remark as he waited on Green's report. Arianna was probably not Sheila's type, either; that would be Rachel, fierce feminist fireplug nutritionist who favored scrubs and fleece and for whom *fuck* was a universal adjective, noun and conjunction. He wondered why Arianna thought it important to tell him; he decided it wasn't worth sharing with Green.

He also had time to process the fact that Jo Jones had somehow been less than a block away from Hammersmith, the erstwhile employer of their murder victim . . . who had also been her temporary lodger . . . and whom she had seen alive during his final hours. Instincts and long practice told him that this, of course, made *Jo* a person of interest in the case. But he would no more suspect her than he would Annie. And also he should stop putting the two of them in the same category.

"Boss?" Green asked; she was leaning in through the open door. "Ready for an interesting story?"

"Do tell," MacAdams said, beckoning her into the admittedly ramshackle state of his office. She scanned the chairs, all of which now served as shelves, and chose the one with the fewest things to clear away.

"Well, first off, Evan's full name is Errol Evan Jacob Evans, and that really *ought* to be a fake name, but isn't. Second, he identified Foley's photo. Said that Foley was a well-paying regular customer from Manchester, *with* a wife, and expecting a kid."

MacAdams sat straighter. "Come again? Arianna never said anything about that—"

"Arianna knows as much about pregnancy as a sentient vacuum cleaner," Green said.

It was by far the weirdest insult MacAdams had ever heard, but somehow managed to convey both an empty center and being full of it, while preserving the basic premise that she sucked. Impressive, to be honest.

"Details, Green."

"Evans noticed that Mrs. Connolly-not-Foley wasn't looking well the last time they stayed—which was two weeks ago, in the Empire Suite. He asked Foley about it privately, and he said they were expecting but it was early days."

"Damn."

"Right? Except—and here is where things get interesting—Evans said he *knew* Connolly was a false name. And he suspected they weren't married." Green sat back triumphantly; she knew this was a nibble MacAdams couldn't resist. He'd already produced his notepad.

"Wait, okay, let's start with the name. How could he *know* Connolly was false?"

"Google it," Green encouraged. "I just did. Nathanial Connolly is the lead guitarist for the Belfast band Snow Patrol."

"Fuck." No wonder it sounded familiar. "Okay, what were Evans's expert deductions about their marital status?"

"Well, for a start, why a false name? But Evans also thought the age difference was suspicious. Matter of opinion, obviously. He assumed Foley was a married man courting a younger woman on the side with money and presents."

"Astute, except we have no record of Foley being married. Arianna told me that he doted on his maybe-wife, assumed they were newlyweds. Seemed to find him charming."

"Evans didn't. He described him as . . ." Green thumbed her own notes. "A well-monied and uncultured plebian."

"Oh of course," MacAdams groaned. Evans had always been a status chaser, the toady of their old boss Admiral Clapham, but also an obsequious slave to title and nobility. "But he obviously paid court to Foley's pocketbook. He knows the man is a liar, suspects him of philandering, doesn't do any background checks beyond making sure the written ones don't bounce. Does that cover it?"

"Just about."

"That, Detective Sergeant, is why Evans was Clapham's man."

"Boss. Clapham is over and gone."

"The case is, yes. But that doesn't mean the Abington Arms has changed its ways. Fill up the hotel with guests who look the part, ask no questions, look away when necessary . . ." MacAdams trailed off. Green was right, though. They had enough going with the current, active murder. They didn't even have a motive yet. He peered through the glass to where Gridley sat; she noticed and waved with enthusiasm. Hopefully it meant she'd found something they could use.

"Guess what?" she asked when they returned to the common room. "Struthers says he can lift DNA from the scarf; there was a hair on it. It's not a match for Foley, appears to be darker. Do we want to get a swab from the colleague he took care of, Trisha Simmons?"

"I'd rather get a swab from Burnhope," MacAdams said.

Green blinked at him. "You think Stanley Burnhope is the mystery woman? I mean. No judgment. But it's not his color."

"*Ava* Burnhope," he corrected, though he would like to have Stanley's, too—why not? The answer being, of course, Stanley and Ava would have to submit willingly to a rather intimate ask despite having watertight alibies and friends in parliament.

"You're serious?" Green asked. "You suspect Ava?"

MacAdams examined the incident board (with now-cold coffee). "Foley has a lady friend, but doesn't tell anyone about it. They sneak around. He wouldn't have to sneak with the secretary, would he?"

"Ah shite." Green scrunched up her nose. "That's a bit of a drop, isn't it? For a woman like Ava? Slumming it, almost."

"Not impossible, though, is it?" MacAdams asked.

Green chewed her lip. "Okay, I'll walk with you on this a minute. She could have affairs with anyone, why choose Foley—*unless* it's to get under Stanley's skin. You said he didn't like the man. But that would still make *Stanley* the prime suspect, wouldn't it?"

"Only if he knew about it," MacAdams said.

"Knowing is the point of revenge affairs, boss."

MacAdams wouldn't usually suspect Green of bias, but her responses had a decided lean to them.

"You really don't want Ava to be involved," he said.

Green gave him a half smile. "Oh, I think she's probably *involved*. Born with a silver spoon, married to money with all the benefits. I just can't see her stooping. You've met her; that's not a woman who bends." Green rubbed her chin. "You haven't mentioned the *other* woman in all of this: Sophie Wagner."

"Fair. And we might have less hassle convincing *her* for a DNA sample." He stepped to the board and arranged Sophie's photo next to Ava and the secretary, Trisha. To the other side was Stanley Burnhope and a bracket for the mystery woman.

What about prints at the apartment?" he asked.

"Most usable fingerprints were Foley's," Green explained. "They did lift two marks from the doorknob that aren't his, but also aren't in the database. Oh, and Foley's aren't in the database, either, by the way—no previous." She bit her lip. "There's a problem searching his alias for Abington Arms, too."

"Yes, guitarist," MacAdams said. Behind him, Andrews—so far quiet—had a fit of giggles. Gridley cleared her throat but didn't quite drown it out.

"I know we have to treat everyone as a suspect, but we *do* have some details for Foley's lover that might help," she said, "Evans claims she had dark hair, was probably between eighteen and twenty-three and didn't speak to staff. That doesn't sound like Ava, Sophie or Trisha. Unless—hang on. Do we know how old Trisha's daughter is?"

"You don't mean—" Andrews grimaced in disgust, but Gridley was busy hunting up Trisha's Facebook page.

"Hey, it's possible. One reason for sneaking is that the woman is married, yeah. Another is that she isn't a grown woman."

"Evans said she was *very* young," Green said darkly.

"That would certainly change things," MacAdams agreed. "It would explain sneaking around. And someone, at least, would have a motive for doing him in."

"A father, a brother," Andrews suggested.

"A *mother*," Green added.

"A sister—hell, an aunt," Gridley added. "My niece Teresa *is* of age, but I'd be after any old guy trying to seduce her."

"All right, all right," MacAdams interrupted. "Let's follow up on Trisha's daughter and see if we can get a swab of—somebody. And add possible predation to the board; if Foley went after an underage girl, it's probably not the first time. But don't put too much stock in Evans's description; the other three women are still in the running. Now, let's get back to why he used his real name when he called the Abington Arms."

"His real name? Ooo, I see. That is odd," Gridley said, returning to her desk. "If you stay there all the time as Connolly, why inquire if there are rooms for Foley?"

"Exactly," MacAdams said, pointing at her. "You're going to stay in Abington on Friday night. You call the local hotel where you usually stay and ask if there is a booking under a different name than you typically use. Why?"

Andrews scrubbed a hand through sandy hair and looked hard at the floor.

"Foley must think there *is* one under his real name for some reason."

"Good," MacAdams encouraged. "Keep going."

"He thinks there's a booking under Foley but one he didn't make—because he uses an alias. So, he checks to be sure. Given the state of his apartment, we already suspected he was on the run from someone. Maybe he thought they'd got the jump on him, had blown his cover—or were already a step ahead. Of course, there isn't a booking, so it eases his mind. But not enough. So he stays somewhere he's never been instead."

Green clapped her hands. "I can get into this," she said. "Foley must suspect he's been followed. And he's right, too, since that someone *also* murders him."

"So why not give it up? Go back to Newcastle?" Gridley asks.

"He might have, if he'd found a booking under his own name," Green offered. "Instead,he books a quiet out-of-the-way spot just to be safe. Damn. That's it, isn't it?"

It made sense. That didn't make it true. MacAdams paced in front of the board, trying to put it together.

"All right. He's hiding out at the cottage. He must still plan to meet his woman . . . ?"

"Doesn't get a chance," Gridley said. "He arrives and *bam*, there's Jo Jones. It's not safe and secret anymore. He has to leave."

"In a rainstorm, in the middle of the night," Green added. "And he ends up not far away in a ditch between eleven and three."

"Timeline problem," MacAdams said. He'd forgotten to tell them Struthers's little secret. "The body was iced. It doesn't make a massive difference, but Struthers suggests he must have been killed *very* soon after Jo last saw him. As in just after eleven or so."

"With . . . ?" Green asked. "Do we know what the murder weapon is?"

MacAdams did not relish explaining the coconut problem. "Something heavy," he said, "in a downward blow."

CHAPTER 15

Jo made it back home by five thirty in the afternoon. She needed fresh clothes for the trip to York, which meant she needed to do laundry, and halfway through *that* it occurred to her that dinner would need to happen. She spend a good ten minutes staring at dairy whip and cheese slices before deciding a trip into town might be necessary. She could probably count on Gwilym to bring her some takeaway, but that seemed an unfair side quest since she'd already sent him after research. He may very well be back in Wales, since that was Augustus John's place of origin . . . one couldn't find *everything* in Roberta's archive. So, onward to Sainsbury's.

It wasn't busy on a Monday evening—almost empty, in fact. Jo had a passing worry that they may not be open but the door was unlocked and the lights still on. *Just the basics*, she told herself. Milk, eggs, bread, veg. Except the prospect of cooking something no longer appealed. She wandered to the cheater section of pre-prepared meals and was just choosing between crispy potatoes and chicken pasta when a familiar voice asked about razors.

The man wasn't, it turned out, speaking to Jo. MacAdams

stood at the end of the aisle, shopping basket over one arm and a minibottle of mouthwash in his free hand.

"Aisle four," said shelf stock. Except it wasn't. Jo waited for the clerk to wander away, then set about course correction.

"End of aisle six, actually," she said. MacAdams looked up with what, for him, counted as a startle response. "Used to be in four, but they rearranged things in March."

"Oh. That's—I don't even know why I'm surprised you know."

"I hate it when they rearrange things," Jo admitted. She shopped only one store for a reason: the comfort of knowing frozen peas were where you last left them. "I had to rememorize the place in April. It's annoying, because I have to overwrite the original orientation—and some things didn't change—so it's sorting out which memory map is the right one." She pointed at her head, as though this better explained it. "Sorry. You didn't ask."

"Well, I would have." MacAdams dropped the mouthwash into the basket. "And I do need the razors. And dinner."

"Same," Jo said. "I was just in Newcastle." For some reason, this caused a sort of face cramp in MacAdams's wooden features.

"Yes. I know. I saw you there. You had . . . dogs."

Now it was Jo's turn to be surprised. "Why were *you* in Newcastle?" she asked. "The dogs are Arthur's."

"Arthur . . . ?"

"My uncle's widow—It's a long story."

"Do you like shepherd's pie?" MacAdams asked. Jo was good for a non sequitur but this was unexpected even for her.

"Yes?"

"We can get two, then. And you can tell it."

MacAdams kindly paid for both pies—and Jo returned the favor by reminding him to buy the razors he'd come for. They'd arrived at a tacit agreement that baking them at his house made more sense than trekking back to Netherleigh, so Jo trekked her own groceries into his kitchen and camped them in MacAdams's mostly empty refrigerator. A SMEG model. There was a nice, weird word—just slightly perverse. Jo pocketed it for later use.

"It'll be a minute," MacAdams said, firing up the oven. Jo perched on a bar stool at the kitchen island. She'd sat there before, just over a year ago. The view had changed.

"New curtains," she said.

"Yes, they are." They were yellow and MacAdams gave them an appraising glance before sitting down on the opposite stool. "Arthur and his dogs, you say."

"Right. He and my uncle were—I don't know what you call it here. Common-law married? Unofficial, but long term."

"I thought your uncle Aiden lived in York?"

"He did! Sort of. Mainly his *address* lived in York. He mostly stayed in Newcastle. I didn't know anything about it until yesterday; he emailed me. There were letters, um, left to me." Jo had not actually had time to process the various feels regarding all that and didn't want to get too near the subject. "Anyway, I stayed in the guest room and then walked the dogs to meet Chen Benton-Li; she's the one who repaired Evelyn's painting."

"That's a lot of new information."

"You have no idea," Jo groaned slightly. "Where did you happen to see me?"

"Near Hammersmith and Company. It's the firm Ronan Foley worked for; I believe Green tried to get your attention," MacAdams said—and Jo made the connection.

"Never, ever, ever, honk at me," she said.

"I didn't, but I'll pass it on." MacAdams pursed his lips a moment. "There's no other reason you were in Newcastle?"

"No? Why?" But she'd just managed to catch his sideways drift. "You thought I was getting involved in the murder investigation, didn't you?"

"I thought you were getting *more* involved," he said, which—fair—Foley did die not far from her doorstep.

"At least I'm not a suspect. I'm not, right?" she asked. MacAdams let out a protracted breath.

"No. And I'll drink to that. Whiskey?"

Jo kicked her heels and watched him dig ice out of a SMEG. He handed her a glass and poured a single.

"Caol Ila," he said. "Distillery near Port Askaig on the isle of Islay. Copper stills, but only half filled to maximize contact."

"Moving on from Talisker?"

"Expanding horizons," MacAdams corrected, clinking the rim of her glass. Jo took a sip; it was less peaty than she expected, like salt and caramel and smoke.

"Oh fancy, I like it. Here's to not being on the incident board." She waited till after MacAdams finished his first taste before adding, "I might be investigating something in a not-murder-case kind of way, however."

"Does this have to do with a butty van?" he asked. "Gwilym told Sheila."

"Did he tell you about the vanishing hiker?" Jo asked. MacAdams had the whiskey glass halfway to his lips. Now he stopped, and Jo went on in a hurry. "It's probably nothing. But we saw her walk to the van, and then when we arrived, no one was there. Gwilym thinks they just kept on, slipped out of sight while we weren't looking. Except I saw a van *again*, a similar one, this time in Newcastle."

"Hold on," MacAdams said, pointing his index finger (while still holding the whiskey glass). "How can you be sure it was the same kind?"

"Because I knocked on the window. He got angry as soon as he saw me and called me a—a nebby hinny?"

"Nosy woman, more or less," MacAdams said.

"Am I being silly? It's here near where Roberta found the body, then a woman vanishes, then I see it again in Newcastle and—"

"A *woman*. The hiker was a woman?" A subtle change had just come over him. It looked like interest.

"Oh—it's important," Jo said.

"Maybe, maybe not."

"Your face says it is."

"I am assured that my face says very little," MacAdams insisted, and Jo laughed.

"Not true. Well, it is true. But the little details matter. That's my whole life—I mean, yes, people accuse me of not reading a room. But actually, I'm the only one who really *does*. Looking for the secret handshake you all take for granted so much. *Your* eyebrow just twitched up and your hand went so still the whiskey stopped swishing."

The timer went off, announcing that their food was ready. MacAdams picked up pot holders.

"You missed your calling in life," he said, pulling the pies out. "Foley had a girlfriend we're trying to track down. She is a person of interest. But you were talking about the artist your uncle hired—"

"Chen. She's an expert on Augustus John," Jo said, hopping off the stool to hunt in her bag. MacAdams seemed to be hunting too—for knives and forks. "There's an exhibition. See? I need to go to York tomorrow."

★ ★ ★

MacAdams dropped the silverware. A knife managed to skitter under the refrigerator, but it could stay there. He retrieved a second set and plated dinner.

Jo was going to York tomorrow. Of course she was. For someone who wasn't a suspect, she ended up in the most curiously suspicious places.

"An exhibition," he repeated.

Jo handed him the brochure. "On the Slade art school. There are paintings on loan from all over. Have you been?"

"To York?"

"To the gallery there." Jo cut into the pie, releasing a cloud of steam. She probably meant the York Art Gallery, and yes, he had.

"A long time ago." After the wedding, in fact. He took a bite that was much, *much* too hot and attempted to float hot mashed potato in his mouth while hurrying to fill a water glass. "I'll be in York tomorrow myself," he said, when he managed to swallow it down.

"Can you drive?" Jo asked. Apparently his not-so-expressive face was registering its confusion, because she blushed and clarified. "Sorry! It's just . . . I only drove there the one time. I got stuck on that outer circle—couldn't work out how to exit—and stalled out on the bridge. I'd rather chew glass."

"Um," MacAdams said. Jo was spooning gravy and mash into her mouth with gusto, unaware of the dilemma she'd just put him in. This was police business, after all. He was going there to speak to his ex and her partner about Hammersmith, and he'd planned to stay the night somewhere.

"I won't be back till Wednesday," he said.

"That's okay, I probably am, too. Just have to find a hotel." She stopped eating. "Oh—would you rather I didn't? With you, I mean. I could take the train."

Yes, take the train and let him feel like the complete jackass he undoubtedly was. It was his turn to do some reading; Jo didn't look mad—or even hurt. She looked expectant, bright, unsinkable as usual, looking up through mussed bangs and suspending a forkful of shepherd's pie in want of an answer. It would be fine. They might stay at the same hotel, which was also fine. Everything was perfectly fine. *For fuck's sake, James, pull your finger out.*

"What time can you be ready?" he asked.

CHAPTER 16

"So you're going to York with Jo Jones, in order to talk shop with your ex-wife's better half," said Green. They were in line at Teresa's tea wagon; it was eight thirty in the morning.

"Your discretion is admirable," MacAdams said.

"Just clarifying, boss. Same hotel?"

It was, and a budget sort of place, too, because short-notice bookings weren't exactly easy to make in York during wedding season. MacAdams didn't say this out loud, just watched the quirk of Green's lips. They were lined in lipstick, dark brown with plum in the mix. Business makeup. Green was headed up to Newcastle to get a DNA swab of Trisha and to see her old police chief to inquire about Hammersmith.

"Don't you look professional," Teresa said when Green made it to the counter at last. She ordered ham-and-egg croissants with coffees, handing take-away cups to MacAdams.

"Just a picnic," Green said with a wink. He supposed that was true; they were about to pay a visit to Abington trail off Lower Road.

"Gridley is running through the CCT footage again," Green

said. "So far no singular hikers; mostly groups have turned up on the Petrol camera. And no missing persons reported, either."

MacAdams knew that a connection between Foley's lady and a vanishing hiker was, in fact, unlikely. The largely tree-less Pennines had a way of fooling the eye. They hid away folds and dips in shadow and heath. A walker might descend quickly out of sight or disappear in the oft-creeping mist. Jo probably just lost visual for a completely usual reason. Then again, Backbone of Britain, the Pennines' stony spine, offered a bleak sort of beauty, sublime, and was not uncommonly dangerous to outsiders or unskilled walkers. Maybe there was something to it, even if not tied to Foley's murder. And speaking of—

"Any new records for our victim?" he asked.

Green swallowed a mouthful of croissant before answering. "Still struggling to uncover his movements before 1998—though it seems that's when he arrived. Andrews hunted passenger charts and found his name on a Belfast-Newcastle. Gridley's checking cognates of his name, in case he altered it once out of Ireland."

The worry, of course, was that he may have changed it altogether, despite his driving records attesting to documents on the up and up.

"Might be time to publish an obituary in Newcastle papers, "McAdam said. "See if we can turn up next of kin using his photo."

"What are we going to do with the man himself? "Green asked. "He can't just stay in the morgue forever, can he?"

MacAdams was surprised by just how long people could stay in Struthers's morgue. Evelyn Davies was, technically, still there. Struthers had begun to refer to her as his colleague.

The Lower Road had dried firm once more, narrow but serviceable. The spot where Foley had been found wasn't far.

"Will wonders never cease," he said, driving past the van to where the road widened for better parking. Jo called this spot a trailhead, but it wasn't. The path Roberta frequented was instead part of extensive right-to-roam trails that skirted farmland and crossed the moor. It did intersect with the Way as it crisscrossed lonely hills, but it wasn't much used. Hikers tended to take Upper Road, instead, with its shorter distance to better vistas.

So what was a food truck doing *here*?

MacAdams closed the car door gently and hitched up his trousers.

"We do not look like hikers, boss," she said. They looked exactly like two police officers, in fact.

"I wasn't expecting to find it," he admitted. There wasn't anything special about the van; in fact, almost the reverse. Very basic, white, with words on one side in plain black letters. The window was open, however, so someone was presumably there to sell sandwiches. He and Green approached together.

"Hello?" MacAdams said when he reached the window. He expected the character Jo had described: heavy brow and jowls, bit of a bruiser. Instead, a youth scarcely older than seventeen popped into view.

"Morning!" he said, dusting hands against his trousers. "Got no butties ready yet. Have you a coffee, yeah?"

MacAdams chose to stick to questions.

"Is this *your* van?" he asked.

"God no. Gap year, me." He turned a freckled face to Green. "Coffee? Tea?"

"Nothing, thanks, "she said, casting an are-we-getting-the-badges-out? look to MacAdams. He was weighing that himself and decided against it.

"Bag of crisps, plain," MacAdams said. "Who does own it—the van?"

"Dunno. I got hired by the Geordie."

"Sorry?"

"That's what people call him, I guess." The kid handed him change. "I just started, to be honest. Couple days ago."

"Thank you for the crisps," MacAdams said, leaving him a pound in tip.

Green waited till they were out of earshot to make hay. "You didn't even ask about the supposedly missing woman hiker. Or why he was parked up here."

MacAdams handed her the crisps.

"He'll tell us he doesn't know. He's not the driver Jo met. Possibly not the same van, and that's a lesson in itself. That's a lot of activity on a quiet stretch of road a long way from customer density."

Green hmmm'd. "It does seem a bit off when you put it like that. You really think something's up?"

"Hard to say," MacAdams said, tearing out the notebook page he'd copied down the license number onto. "Send this to Gridley when we have signal again." MacAdams checked his watch. "I'll drop you at the station so you can pick up a CID car."

He'd promised to pick up Jo by ten.

* * *

Getting to York by car was a *lot* faster than taking the train, Jo decided. At least, when she wasn't driving. Most everything had been booked solid, but she'd found a place called the York Astoria; the name sounded promising. The present-day Waldorf-Astoria on Park avenue, New York, was the very height of luxury and glamour. Hotel spas, signature restaurant, grand ballroom. Of course, these days no one rented rooms in the landmark building. You could buy a thousand square feet of apartment for a cool four million, however.

"You know, the original Waldorf-Astoria was an unofficial palace before it was torn down and relocated," Jo said, as they followed the satnav into a narrow street. "Built on Fifth Avenue in 1893 by Waldorf Astor. But then his cousin built a taller hotel next door. They eventually stopped fighting about that and connected the two with a marble corridor called Peacock Alley."

"Why did they call it that? "MacAdams asked, making the final left-hand turn.

"I don't know actually."

"I almost find it disconcerting when you don't know something," MacAdams said. "Which reminds me, do you know what the Mohs' hardness scale is?"

"For identifying minerals? Hardness as resistance to scratching?"

"Or cracking open." MacAdams ran his thumb along his jawline thoughtfully. "Human skull is about a five."

"I didn't know that, either," Jo admitted. It happened a lot more than people supposed. Like right now, as Jo took in the view before them. The York Astoria was *not* living up to its name.

"Oh."

They pulled into a badly mended car park in front of a yellow-brick-and-stucco facade. It did not look like the Waldorf. It looked like a Day's Inn in Gary, Indiana.

The interior did little to alter this impression. There also wasn't a clerk on duty—which meant running down a member of the cleaning staff. They eventually located the stairs and found themselves on the third floor. The carpeting zigzagged in awful red-and-salmon stripes like something out of *The Shining.*

"That . . . gives me a headache," she said.

"We can hope it doesn't continue inside." MacAdams dangled door keys. "I think we're neighbors."

Jo opened the door and looked in. A very compact room with striped wall panels instead of paper or paint. But at least the carpeting was a dull solid blue.

"It's not bad," Jo said.

"Serviceable," MacAdams agreed; he dropped his bag inside

his door and shut it again. "I've got to go meet Ashok now. Enjoy the exhibit."

He tipped his hat (which he wore despite the favorable weather) and headed back down the hall. Jo would herself be walking—they were near the train station and it wasn't that far. She gave a little chirrup of excitement. Chen promised to tell her about Uncle Aiden! But there was something wonderful and terrifying about fruition; she needed to be properly attired. Jo pulled out a tightly rolled black dress; sleeveless, high neck, a sheath. Next to her funeral dress, it was probably her favorite, and just slightly fancier. There was something deeply uncomfortable about being dressed wrong for an occasion; she hated standing out when she wanted to blend in. To really complete the look, a pair of heels would have been nice—but Doc Martens were technically always in style, weren't they?

The York Art Gallery looked out upon Exhibition Square, both opened to the public in 1879. Jo had come by way of the lane and—improbably—a footpath called Dame Judy Dench Walk. It meant her phone navigation just instructed her to "turn left on Dame Judy." The walk did her nerves some good, and before long she spotted her target. Planters with flowers ranged along the arches of its front doors, and already she could see a small knot of people outside. One of them waved a glass-handled umbrella at her.

Chen still wore the mandala jacket, though beneath was a striking orange pantsuit. She tapped the umbrella cane against the pavement.

"Support for the hips and the weather," she said. "Are you ready to meet Augustus?" Jo was ready to meet Aiden, but this seemed the entrée.

"Very," she agreed, following her through the doors and into a grand exhibition hall.

"It's a special opening," Chen explained. "Will be more crowded tomorrow, during regular hours."

It was *already* crowded in Jo's opinion. A diffuse background hum of private conversation surrounded them. Chen bypassed the sketches near the front, however. She crossed the room with purpose, and despite being the most striking person in the room, didn't raise much of a glance. Between that and her expert navigation, Jo gathered, she was at the York museum rather a lot.

"Here we be," Chen said, stopping in front of a large portrait. Seated as subject was a corpulent man in black, his abdomen filling the bottom of the frame, one arm resting on a near-invisible chair. His face, long, flat, topped with a wave crest of white hair and ending in a double chin, appeared vaguely surprised. "What do you know of Lord Leverhulme?"

Jo ran through her mental Rolodex. *Leverhulme.* There was a story she'd read . . .

"He hated the painting of himself, didn't he?" Jo asked.

Chen clapped her delicate hands.

"Very good and very sanitized," she said. "Have a close look at the canvas, not the man."

Jo did so. A faint line appeared above the man's head, and beneath, and on either side.

"You are standing before the headless painting," Chen explained. "Leverhulme didn't dislike it, he despised it. Was ashamed of it, even. Told Augustus John it didn't favor him at all. John told him to pick up a paintbrush and fix it himself. He picked up scissors instead." Chen's eyes sparkled, and she flourished the sapphire-bearing hand toward the now-hard-to-mistake rectangle. "Cut his own head right out of the canvas, but by some mistake, the housekeeper packaged it up and returned it to Augustus John. *He* called it the grossest insult and took the story to the papers."

She stepped to the side of the portrait to reveal more of the museum curator's comments along with a reproduction newsprint: *Beheaded Portrait*, it read.

"Imagine, pet. Artists went on strike. People protested in

the streets. They even burned Leverhulme in effigy. How very *dare* he?"

Jo looked again at the painting. The man in the picture did not look pleasant. Self-important, perhaps, self-indulgent, but also curiously vacant.

"He looks—repulsive."

"Oh yes," Chen agreed. "Augustus John painted the inside on the outside, you see? A psychological portrait. *That* is what made him singular; that's why he's a master. He never painted to please the sitter. Now come, child. The gem of the collection is a portrait of Dylan Thomas, fellow Welshman."

That, at least, was a name Jo knew well.

"'Do not go gentle into that good night,'" she quoted—words the poet wrote as a plea for a dying father.

"That's the one," Chen agreed, turning her cheekbones up toward the canvas. "What do you make of young Dylan?"

Jo found herself mentally tracing brush strokes. This later painting lacked the careful rendering he'd done for Evelyn's. It was as though his style grew disheveled, the subjects revealing themselves in bolder but less precise strokes. Yet looking at the portrait, Jo felt she *knew* Dylan Thomas. It was so different from the heavier, swallow-cheeked man whose brow shadowed large eyes in famous black-and-white photos. Instead, here was a youth, almost feminine, bright red curls hugging a high forehead, full lips like a rosebud, slightly parted. And the eyes: strange faraway eyes, wide with something like naive expectation married to the acceptance of fate. Behind him, black-and-blue clouds were streaked in angry white. Here was storm, uncertainty and yet acceptance and a willingness to walk on. *Do not go gentle.*

"Like Joan of Arc offering humanity to nothingness," Jo said.

"Ah, pet! That is the perfect interpretation," Chen said, her eyes moist and approving.

Jo felt a blush surging up the back of her neck.

"Can—can I ask about *your* painting? The one Aiden bought," she said—not very slyly returning to her still-unanswered questions. "Why is it called *Hiding*?"

Chen's eyes creased at the edges. "Can you visualize it?"

"Oh yes."

"Good. Tell it to me. Just like you did with this portrait."

Jo felt slight panic. "I'm not—definitely not an art critic."

"Try," Chen encouraged, her voice humming approbation. "Just speak it." There was something strangely disarming about the way Chen asked, and it galvanized Jo's natural need to answer. So she closed her eyes and brought the painting into view.

"The black dot reminds me of a lost shoe," she said. "Like Miss Havisham's lost shoe. We only ever see her wearing the one; the other is left behind. That can't be the *point*. But it's the first thing I think about."

"Very well. And what do you make of the red background?" Chen asked.

Jo chuffed at her bare arms. "It's bright but it's not warm. And it's *loud*. I don't know why it's so loud, but I look at the gray streaks to give my eyes a break." Jo found herself thinking of the hotel carpeting. "I think it's angry."

"Ah," said Chen, "a small, forgotten thing, clinging to a thin veil in the midst of a red, red rage? I think you understand the painting very well."

Jo opened her eyes.

"But what's hidden in it?" she asked. "I can't tell that."

The old bell was ringing; there were connections, but she just couldn't see them yet. *Colophon, Calliope, Centennial . . . Smeg . . .* Chen reached out a gentle hand and laid it upon Jo's, which had accidentally turned into a thumb-hiding fist.

"The artist," she said, her voice a quiet rasp. "*I* was hiding. Being out, being yourself in the bad old world, it's hard and it's grim. When I had my first art gallery opening, I couldn't face the crowd. I just couldn't do it."

"What happened?"

"Nothing. Everything. I went home and I attacked a canvas. I told Aiden it was a talisman, a bit of magic to trap the old, scared self and all her rage. I left it there in the painting, and I walked right on out into the sun." She turned slowly in place, looking at all the art at once. "Augustus John had a bit of that magic in reverse."

"Dorian Gray?" Jo asked. For a moment, Chen's eyes were a blank, but then they fired to life.

"Ah—perhaps! Something like that. He told people things about themselves they wanted to stay hidden. You can't hide in an Augustus John portrait. He painted to reveal hidden truths."

Jo felt a shiver run through her, as though she was wearing skin a size too small.

"Evelyn," she whispered, thinking of her far-away expression, the angle of her eyes that was still wrong, mismatched from her body, "off" somehow. Her body was in a posture of longing. Expectation. The way she seemed both retiring but resisting, the effect of holding back passion. "Oh. Oh no. He painted her in *love*."

A head tilt, a nervous movement of hands, a quickening of pulse; each could be an indicator if you read them right, and each might be hidden or ignored. But once rendered as a painting—one to be hung *with* Lord William and Lady Gwen Ardemore—the revelation must surely have been imminent. Gwen, long-suffering, barren, in what was probably a marriage of convenience and consolidation of wealth . . . maybe she could countenance an affair. But could she hang it on the wall in her own home?

"Did Gwen destroy the painting?" Jo asked. "She couldn't bear to see the proof each day of her husband in love with someone else?" She hadn't meant to say it out loud, but Chen's hand gave hers a squeeze.

"Your uncle Aiden thought so. And now, I think it's time

I tell you a story. Not here, of course. But I know the perfect place for tea and cake."

★★★

MacAdams waited until ten past the hour, ensuring Ashok and Annie would already be seated and saving himself the awkwardness of playing host. They sat at a corner table, sipping still water and chatting idly. Surveillance was the guilty pleasure of the detective, and so he indulged: Ashok was a trifle younger than Annie; he had a fresh face beneath thick black hair and expressive eyes of amber brown. He smiled. A lot. Annie smiled, too, her cheeks flushed by the warmth of the day. Also she was now looking right at him. A sixth sense, he long decided. She'd got him on her radar somehow.

"James!" said Ashok, who darted up and shook his hand with police-rookie enthusiasm.

"Hello, Ashok. I appreciate you taking the time."

"We ought to be appreciating yours," Ashok said. "I'm so happy to help."

"And it's the only way we'll get you to a meal," Annie added, popping up to mime a cheek kiss.

MacAdams took a seat.

"How's the baby?" he asked. Green had reminded him to send a congrats card for the arrival of young Edward, named for Annie's father.

"Noisy and not sleeping, your average eleven-month-old," Annie assured him. "Tell Green thank you for the card."

MacAdams wondered why they bothered pretending he did any of the usual niceties himself. He had half a mind to tell her he'd changed the curtains. The server came and went while they finished the small talk. MacAdams ordered fish and chips and out came the notebook and pencil.

"Hammersmith," he said.

Ashok nodded and leaned his forearms on the table. "It's a good firm. I know a few of the architects who work for them. Top-notch people who really enjoy the work. But that's what makes their business in York so odd."

"Stanley Burnhope suggested he'd received complaints about Ronan Foley," MacAdams said. "The manager of a certain build in York that went wrong."

"He should, if Ronan was overseeing that development. That site should have been finished a year ago. The designs were simple enough, just a mixed-use space on the other side of the Ouse River—not far from the 1237 motorway. Not even their usual thing. Low-brow, almost." Ashok talked with his hands, and almost upset his water glass. Annie saved it.

"Have they done jobs in town before?" MacAdams asked, moving his own water out of reach.

"Not usually. They did the new facade of a larger hotel a few years back. Modern aesthetics are a little out of place in York."

MacAdams couldn't disagree; the firm seemed better fit for the city center of London in terms of their look.

"So why take on something like this at all, then?" he asked. The food had arrived; he permitted himself chips between questions but hovered over his notepad all the same.

"Honestly? It's been hard all round for that sort of thing. Brexit, various shutdowns, new trade sanctions." Ashok took a healthy bit of his chicken salad before adding, "If you're mainly office high-rises, it's a tough time to be an architect."

Gridley had, in fact, taken a good look at what Hammersmith produced since about 2016. There were golf clubs and art centers, a few theater rehabs and several (very high end) condos, but they won awards for being the cradle-to-grave company for design and construction of tall glass buildings. But their finances seemed very sound, and despite the empty offices, there hadn't been a single layoff in either the architectural or real estate side of things. Perhaps that was unusual in itself. He made a note to check back.

"Are you suggesting they lost interest in the project, somehow? Not good enough for them?" MacAdams suggested.

"Not sure. But they're going to lose the project entirely if the Lord Mayor has a say," Ashok said, and Annie piped in:

"Part of that building is supposed to house a community center. People are angry it's been stalled, and I don't blame them."

"Especially since the city would have to find another set of real estate developers, at expense," Ashok added. "Which means a change in space use."

"To retail, probably," Annie sighed. "Because we need more of *that*."

MacAdams worried the conversation was about to veer toward the state of public programs. He tapped his pencil against the table.

"Would you say delay is the biggest complaint, then?" he asked. "I got the impression that personalities may have been at odds."

"Oh that," Ashok said. *Yes,* MacAdams thought, *that*. "It was fine until the city put pressure on the job manager. I never met the man, but he had words with the council leader and his deputy. You'd have to be gormless, yeah? You don't take the piss when it comes to city council."

"Ashok!" Annie admonished and Ashok blushed to his dark eyebrows. First time MacAdams felt some fellow feeling for the man.

"Sorry! But it's true."

This was the first plausible, business-oriented motive MacAdams had come across, as far as Burnhope was concerned. "How much money would Hammersmith stand to lose on a job like this?"

"Probably not more than they could stomach," Ashok said with a shrug. "It's more about reputation, though."

"Especially if bigger jobs are thin on the ground," MacAdams added. Could Foley have been jeopardizing Hammersmith's position in a new niche? Or did his mismanagement in York do more than annoy the locals?

"Anyway, this Foley hasn't been around all that much. That's frankly the problem."

"Absence, not presence," MacAdams clarified. Foley couldn't very well spend much time in York if he was twice a month in Abington with his lady friend, could he? He dipped his chips in brown sauce, still ignoring the fish. "Tell me, Ashok, what about the property now? Is it still active?"

"I haven't been by it, so I'm not sure. As far as I know the city hasn't pulled the plug yet, so it's not out of Hammersmith's hands."

MacAdams had a sudden desire to see the property himself. If derelict, would it be locked up? Better to go first to York Central Station. If Foley had made an ass of himself, the city wouldn't mind some poking about. He might get surveillance on the place.

"I need to make a call," he said, pushing his chair back.

Ashok pushed his chair away, too. "I need to answer one," he said, winking at Annie. "Be back."

MacAdams watched him disappear in the direction of the WC.

"Don't be scandalized, James," Annie said. "When you have toddlers, it's all potty humor."

"Right," he said, because what else did one say to that? "This has been very useful—today—meeting here."

"And you're about to do a runner on lunch, aren't you," she said, looking at their half-finished plates.

"I'm sorry, Annie."

"No, you're not," she said with a laugh. "I've not seen you this engaged with a case since . . . possibly ever." She narrowed her eyes over apple cheeks and pretended severe scrutiny. "There's something different about you, James MacAdams."

"I doubt that," he said.

"No, it's true. Your slacks have been ironed."

"I *can* do laundry, Annie." He hunted out a ten-pound note for his portion. Annie batted it away, so he stuck it beneath Ashok's plate.

"He's a good man, isn't he?" he asked.

"Yes, he is," Annie said and smiled. "I'm happy."

"I'm glad," MacAdams said. And he meant it.

CHAPTER 17

Jo had lost her way.

She'd been walking for some time, through rabbit-hole alleyways and back streets, body on autopilot, mind in centrifuge. It had started with an opera cake.

"Marvelous, aren't they?" Chen had said, ushering her into a musical little café near the Minster. "Layers of almond sponge in coffee syrup, coated in ganache. Bracing and beautiful."

"But you aren't having one?" Jo asked.

Chen had ordered tea with milk and sugar for both of them, then a large opera cake . . . for Jo.

"I'll be talking. About your father."

Jo dropped her fork. It fell to the floor and slid beneath a radiator.

"My father? Where is he—Who—"

Chen handed her a second fork. "Shush, shush, eat cake," she said.

"But—" Jo began. Chen pointed at the dessert. Jo swallowed her question and took a bite. Then another.

"There's a girl," Chen said softly. "Sugar down those feelings.

And don't interrupt. I'm going to say some hard things now in a minute."

Jo bit the fork to keep from interfering with the presentation. Chen took a deep breath and poured tea into her cup.

"Love. It's messy. So damn messy," she sighed. "That's why I have to start far back. With your grandfather, I mean."

Jo ate cake and listened to Chen, a breathy, soft, humming voice telling her the worst story she'd ever heard.

★ ★ ★

"Alfred Jones was a hard man. He'd spent a few years in service to queen and country, had been stationed with Americans and learned to hate them. But he didn't care much for his fellow Brits, either. He loved very few things. Money was one. Order, another. An order he was sure existed in the past and not now, something lost in the generations since *his* father. Bought things with cash, like his house and his car, and—in 1973—Julia, daughter of the local barrister. The marriage dissolved. Not in divorce, but in a more literal sense. Unhappy for seven years, Julia drank herself to death, and Alfred locked himself into the routine he'd keep for the rest of his life. It might have been right enough, except by then there were two children to think of, a boy and a girl just a year apart. He trained them up on rigor and abstinence; never give in to drink or love or joy. Was a miserable, awful life, and Aiden and your mum clung to each other like babes in a storm.

"Now me, I knew myself by age six. Aiden took a little longer. Twelve years old he had his first crush on a boy, and he told the only person he thought he could trust—his sister, Caroline. Your mother.

"Caroline kept his secret a long time, because if Aldred knew, he'd disown the lad. This went on for another nine years; Aiden finished grammar school and had gone to Newcastle University. That's where he met Thomas—Thomas Oliver Lofthouse. They were together a while, but Thomas couldn't settle. Too pretty, you know. All the boys, and all the girls, too; who didn't want to put hands through his red-gold curls or kiss the rosebud mouth? Does it sound like the portrait of *Dylan* Thomas? It should. Aiden compared him to it often; it's why he took to Augustus John, as an artist. Aiden brought pretty Thomas home with him on holidays. Maybe he thought his flirting with your mum was cover, something to keep him in good with Aiden's father. But Aiden didn't know Thomas half so well as he thought.

"I don't know when the affair began. It certainly went on for some time, Thomas courting brother and sister. But there's a thing about being a woman, isn't there, pet? Some things can't stay hid. Caroline got pregnant, and she told Thomas, and Thomas told *her* he was engaged to be married to the lovely heiress of a packing plant fortune.

"He left Newcastle. He left Caroline. He left Aiden—but not before confessing what he'd done. They should have come together for comfort and solace. But love is painful and messy; it eats up your heart and much of your brains. Heartbroken, devastated and feeling doubly betrayed, Aiden told their father about her condition. As predicted, Alfred threw her out and Caroline fled to the cold welcome of her widowed aunt—but not before getting revenge in kind. She told Alfred that Aiden was gay.

"Alfred Jones never spoke to either of them again. When he died some ten years later, alone, as deserved, he left every penny of his hard-won money to a trust for 'moral education' so that his children could never touch it. Thomas went before him, in the ground before you were more than seven or eight. Pride, hurt, private shame—those are powerful things, especially when there's none left to make a clean breast with. Your uncle and mum should have made amends . . .

"But they didn't," Chen finished.

"He—he tried." Jo heard herself say the words, as if from a long way off. The feelings pent up upon receiving Aiden's letters had not resurfaced; rather, they were the medium in which she was now drowning.

"I think that's why he wanted me," Chen said. "He couldn't connect forward, so he wanted to connect backward. Try to find family that way. And when he saw the ruined painting, he knew it was an Augustus—and that the other two weren't. Which meant there must've logically been something happened—a breaking point between the siblings."

Evelyn reminded him of Caroline, Jo said in the long hallway of her brain. The words never came out, though, and Chen carried on.

"I took on the work," she explained, "and Aiden sat in a chair and watched me, just so. Said I should make sure the eyes were on him."

This piece of information shook Jo out of herself, and she clambered desperately to the surface.

"He *told* you to set her eyes that way?"

"Aye, pet. You don't think I'd do that on purpose, do you? The wrong angle, not by much, but it's there. He told me all these things while I painted, and I think . . . maybe he just wanted someone to see him."

Jo could envision her uncle, already ill and in treatment, hiding some of this even from Arthur, whom he loved. Aiden, telling Chen what he never told anyone else. Aiden, slipping away as Evelyn's painting came to life.

"He went into care just as I finished the painting," Chen said, and now her own voice grew husky and strained. "The last thing he told me was that, if he beat the cancer, he'd give me my painting back. He was done hiding. He'd marry Arthur and sell the York flat, make a clean breast of things." A tear crested the wrinkles around her dark eyes and found its way to her chin. "Imagine. He didn't need the talisman anymore. No more hiding."

These had been the words that broke Jo.

And it told her, again, of a tragedy that somehow was *Wuthering Heights* and *Great Expectations* and *Mill on the Floss* all at once—cast-off children and divided siblings and hopes forever lost in the flood. But awful as it was, horrid as the tale was, what hurt the most was knowing her mother had made it so. Caroline was the one who didn't reach back. She was the one who locked everything away, who kept all her secrets, and who—in doing so—stole them from her daughter.

Stole them. From me. Jo loved her mother. Loved and missed her and didn't know how to also be angry. The feelings wouldn't stay fast. She'd left the café; she'd wandered. Tears already streaked Jo's cheeks, leaving them hot and wet, and a tremor had begun deep in her sinews. She needed to get back to the hotel. The ugly, squat, unappealing hotel, which—when she finally found it—offered itself like hope's own beacon. She threw herself inside, navigating the stairs and feeling the final wave pressing, pressing. *Fetal position. Please.* And wracking sobs the likes of which she hadn't experienced since she'd told Gwilym about her mother's diary.

Thomas Oliver Lofthouse, her long-awaited father, had broken two hearts and then walked away. Married. Divorced. Dead.

Caroline Jones had been betrayed, responded by betraying. She gave birth to a daughter who always reminded her of it, and made sure that daughter would never, ever meet the source of her pain.

And then there was Aiden, who wanted to make amends, but made them much too late—dreaming of future happiness as the cancer ate him away.

And finally Jo herself, who had not managed to make it *into* her room, but was curled up in her black dress on the horrible hall carpet, sobbing for herself, the world and everything in it.

★★★

MacAdams wasn't overfond of York Central Station—and tried to assure himself it wasn't professional jealousy. Upon his spontaneous visit that day, however, he received a hero's welcome from the staff—probably a consequence of keeping the department clear of wrongdoing in his last case.

"Tea? Or coffee—it's one of those fancy machines," said Superintendent Charles Fernsby. He hovered over a small black Nespresso knockoff, with its tiny tin pods. "I'm trying the espresso today."

"I'll follow your lead," MacAdams said, mostly to be polite. He'd rather go for one of Ben's hard-won creations on his brass-topped, ever-breaking-down device.

"I'm told this isn't a social call," Fernsby said, producing two demitasse cups and putting them on matching saucers. If it weren't for the clearly spilled and forgotten sugar packets on the coffee cart, Fernsby's neatness might approach the late, unlamented Jarvis Fleet.

"Murder case; Ronan Foley. And I've since discovered that he oversaw a development for Hammersmith here in town—a sort of galleria south of town," MacAdams said. "I have some questions."

"Yes, the defunct shopping center. As I said over the phone, I am only too happy to help. What would you like to know?"

"For a start, just how much trouble has the property been for the city? I'm told tensions were high, but how high?"

"As in, were they murderously high? I wouldn't say so. We don't get overinvolved in city disputes, but the Lord Mayor descended from on high to make sure we knew his feelings on the matter. So we did a bit of looking in." Fernsby nudged his computer mouse to bring his screen to life. "All the permits are there, and things were off to a banging start. They finished the first three or four floors—then things started to slow."

He beckoned MacAdams to look at his screen, which boasted photographs of a rectangular building, finished with windows and all the trappings to floor four, but with a network of bare iron scaffolding above.

"That's odd, isn't it? Finishing as you go?"

"I'd think so, but the architects tell me differently. Apparently each finished floor level gets a concrete topping—a structural slab that more or less keeps everything below from being weathered on. Thing is, they use it for fast-track jobs, something they plan to complete well before any damage could occur."

"But this job is behind schedule." MacAdams took a cursory sip of espresso—found it better than expected and finished it off. "I don't suppose you looked further afield? Any other jobs running behind?"

"We didn't, no. But we did do an assessment of who was coming and going. Very minor surveillance, I suppose. Again, everything was aboveboard. Contractors were still turning up, machinery still rolling. Just at half speed for some reason. Another espresso?"

MacAdams didn't trust himself to more caffeine at the moment—his brain was whirring fast enough.

"I need dates," he said. "Job start, job slowdown, any protracted stalls."

"Start was about a year and six months," Fernsby said. "With the slowdown occurring in the last third."

Which, MacAdams noted, would be when Burnhope gave the job over to Foley, perhaps as a last chance to prove himself? Burnhope *claimed* Foley was a bulldog, someone who knew what he wanted, a pushy job boss. Yet when his promotion was on the line, he utterly changed tack. Sold his house, spent time in the country with a (possibly now pregnant) lover, stopped doing the requisite work on the York property . . .

"Everything comes down to what happened six months ago," MacAdams said out loud.

"And what's that?" Fernsby asked.

MacAdams pushed his chair back. "I wish I knew," he said. "It's around when Foley got put on the job."

★ ★ ★

MacAdams called Gridley on his way back to the hotel. No, no next of kin had turned up. No, they still didn't have leads on Foley's early years. One plus: they *had* tracked the other burner numbers Foley had contacted. Every last one had been disconnected, but they all lead back to Newcastle. They were still digging.

"Print the obit, send it to papers in Abington and Newcastle," he told her. *Someone* must know the man more personally, and perhaps the girlfriend might even turn up. He tucked the phone back into his jacket before heading into the Astoria hotel. There still wasn't a desk clerk, and the day had darkened such that the lobby looked somehow more forlorn than before. Jo had picked it, and perhaps he ought not to have let her; it looked exactly like the place people went to be murdered. And that was a professional opinion.

MacAdams climbed the stairs and stepped into the third-floor corridor. He expected the assault of red-and-salmon zigzag carpet. He didn't expect to see Jo Jones sitting on it, just opposite the stairwell door.

He was going to ask if she'd been locked out. That was before she looked up at him. Eyes swollen from crying, pink stains down both cheeks, the look she gave him wasn't misery so much as defeat. He'd never, ever seen her that way. Would have thought defeat alien to her nature, even. He wasn't sure what had happened, or what to do, so he knelt down next to her on the same awful rug.

"Hi," Jo said. "I look like I feel."

"And how is that?"

"Not good."

A fair assessment. He set aside his hat and coat. "Can I ask what happened?"

"I think so," she said, but didn't try to get up.

MacAdams sank down next to her, both of them with legs outstretched and backs to the wall.

"Okay. What happened?" he asked.

Jo took a deep breath, then another, like a swimmer before a dive. Then, instead of speaking, she handed him her phone. MacAdams looked down at an obituary for Thomas Oliver Lofthouse, born 1966, died 1994. From the somewhat sanitized account, he gathered there was a car accident.

"That's my father," Jo said. She sounded like she had a head cold; MacAdams hunted fruitlessly for a handkerchief.

"I'm sorry," he said. He wasn't sure if she heard him; her eyes stared into the far corner of the hallway.

"Car accident, officially. Unofficially, he drove at high speed into a literal brick wall." Jo took her phone back and flipped to another search window. "That's the rest of the story."

This was not an obituary, but a series of police reports. "No surviving kin," they read. Because they didn't know. Thomas, it seemed, was troubled. Violent outbursts that sometimes landed him in prison—sometimes in psychiatric hospital—and sometimes put *other* people in hospital. Like his first wife, who was not, MacAdams now realized, Jo's mother.

"Oh."

"He wasn't okay," Jo said.

"No," MacAdams agreed. "Did—did the artist tell you all of this?"

"Sort of." Jo rubbed at her nose. "Arthur told me some. Arthur gave me letters that were my uncle's. And I realized I *could* have met him. And that hurts like fuck."

MacAdams didn't say anything. And Jo didn't say more. So they sat in the hallway in silence for another ten minutes.

"It's really an awful design," MacAdams said at length.

"The stripes don't even line up," Jo said. "I've been counting them."

"All of them?"

"Just the pink ones. There are 341." She paused. "I do that. Counting. Especially when I have an emotion hangover."

MacAdams nodded, hid head bobbing against the paneled wall. He wasn't very good at comforting people; his job usually benefited from the opposite treatment. You wouldn't call him a shoulder to cry on, certainly. But there were a few things he understood pretty well.

"Is it even remotely close to the way one feels after signing divorce papers?" he asked. Jo turned her head to look at him for the first time.

"Yeah, kind of."

"Then I might know a good place for a cure," he said, returning the glance. "At least, it's where I went after signing *mine.* Italian. Greasy pizza and cheap beer."

"True Italian pizza isn't actually greasy," Jo said, wiping her nose. "It originates in Naples and was just an easy way to eat tomatoes and cheese on flatbread."

"Is that a no, then?" MacAdams asked.

"It's a yes," she said.

★ ★ ★

Jo had changed back into jeans and T-shirt, washed her face and was feeling a bit more like herself by the time they returned to the hotel car park. The restaurant, MacAdams explained, was a little out of the way, on the outskirts where York looked less York-like. This meant the buildings weren't a thousand years old and pitching in every direction like plate tectonics, something

Jo enjoyed for obvious charm, but which also made her just the tiniest bit anxious.

"The proprietor's name is Allen. But he'll insist you call him Giuseppe," MacAdams said.

"He's Italian?"

"He is not."

He wasn't American, either, but upon entry, Jo had the uncanny feeling of placement slip. Exposed-brick walls, multicolored lamp shades, the smell of deep dish and—ironically—black-and-white photographs of New York. Tables sported red-and-white-checked plastic tablecloths, shakers of dry parm and red pepper flakes, and she could almost imagine they were somewhere in south Brooklyn.

"James!" shouted Giuseppe-not-Allen. "Haven't seen you in ages! Light or dark?"

"He means the beer," MacAdams explained.

"Dark?" Jo suggested, and a pitcher followed them to their table.

MacAdams rolled his sleeves and poured them each a glass.

"I never lived in York myself," he said. "Found this by mistake while searching for a pub. Came back weekly for a while, despite the distance. Treating the—the emotion hangover, I suppose. Getting used to being single."

"I never had a chance, really," Jo admitted, sipping through beer foam. After her own divorce, Jo had moved to Chicago middivorce to help her ailing mother. "Or at least, taking care of the dying is not the best way to do it."

MacAdams leaned his elbows on the table and gave her a thoughtful look. "I have seen a lot of death. But never the dying. My mother's still with us; my dad had a killing heart attack while I was in training."

"You couldn't see him before he went?"

"No time. He was there. Then he wasn't. But I think that might be a blessing, frankly. We hadn't any scores to settle, my da and I. Good terms." Jo felt a little shiver run across her synapse. It occurred to her that he was telling her personal things, and she wasn't sure he'd ever done that before.

"I had all sorts of unanswered things to settle," she said. "But eight months of hospice didn't actually solve it. So I'm inclined to agree." Jo was testing herself, like testing thin ice. But she'd managed to speak of her mum and not fall through, so she walked a little bolder. "I know what she was hiding now. I even know why. But that hasn't actually solved my mystery for me."

"You mean about Evelyn," MacAdams guessed. Jo wondered if she should clap like Chen did. Instead, she ordered a bacon-sausage-hot-pepper slice.

"Evelyn, why her painting was done by a different artist, how and why it was destroyed. Her death. And—*and* her missing baby," Jo explained. "Aiden knew. Had to have known. At least, I think so. I might be making big leaps."

"Little stories based on clues, isn't that what you called it?" MacAdams asked. "Try me." He'd ordered a far less flamboyant pepperoni, and both slices were now ready to hand. Jo took one very cheesy, wonderful, awful bite before continuing. To be honest, she preferred it to opera cake.

"You ever read *Wuthering Heights*?" she asked.

"Heathcliffe and Catherine. Actually, I saw one of the movies."

"Well, the book is like a—a mirror. No, better; like those nested Russian dolls. Things keep duplicating, but the repeat is a smaller, less impressive version than the first. Anyway, there are two Catherines a generation apart. One of them comes to a bad end." She waited to see that he was following. Between pizza bites and beer swigs, he seemed to be. "Evelyn is Catherine the first. She gets pregnant; now we know it was an illicit affair with her brother-in-law. We *don't* know what happened to her, or her baby, but being buried under a house is a pretty sticky end."

"I think we can agree on that," MacAdams said.

"Right? So my mum is Catherine the second. At least, to Aiden. Pregnant out of wedlock, forced out of the family home. Lost, in her own way. He told Chen that he would 'take Evelyn home.' Like finding his sister, again, I think."

"But he doesn't end up doing that," MacAdams pointed out.

Jo sighed. "No. He died. Chen wasn't even sure what happened to the painting till I told her. There was a *lot* of damage to the painting. Chen worked on it for six whole months."

MacAdams had a new slice halfway to his mouth and stopped cold.

"Six months," he said. "I'm beginning to hate this unit of time."

"Because of the Foley murder?" Jo asked. It was a shot in the dark, but a good one, as MacAdams was technically here to investigate.

"Six months ago, his life altered. We have been told that he may have been on thin ice at his job, but that seems consequence rather than cause. What would you think if a man sold his house, dyed his hair, began—or continued—seeing a young lady and made a sow's ear of his job?"

"That he was having a midlife crisis," Jo said. Because, without meaning to, he'd just described Tony. "My ex was turning fifty-five. Got a gym membership, started vitamin supplements, managed to sell out the publishing house from under me. And, of course, step out with a twenty-eight-year-old publishing employee on the fast track."

"I see the similarities," MacAdams said, but Jo frowned.

"The thing is, I met him, right? And this doesn't sound like him at all. I mean, it's not . . ." She was trying hard to avoid saying *vibe* or *aura*. Her sense of people was actually a lot more like instinct or some subconscious recognition of pheromones. "He didn't *feel* like a Tony."

In fact, she could almost see him now: disheveled, surprised. On recovery, more like a guy in a hurry. He certainly wasn't smarmy or creepy, didn't act like the big man or try to push her around. And he liked Jammie Dodgers, which somehow seemed the antithesis of Tony-ness.

"I try not to discredit your feelings," MacAdams said. "Any-more." He'd dispensed with the tie earlier, and with his jacket off, looked almost like not a policeman. Jo noticed he also had marinara on his chin.

"Actually, you've been really kind about my feelings today," she said, feeling an embarrassed blush starting at her neckline. This was an improvement. She'd been too exhausted to feel embarrassed earlier. "I really appreciate it."

"You . . . are welcome." He seemed to be weighing some-thing in his mind. After a moment, he brought out his phone. "You understand that I am *not* asking you to get involved. But what do you make of this?"

He'd shown her a police-style photograph, white background with a ruler for scale. A golden earring featured in the center, ornate and curiously wrought.

"It's not like anything I've seen," she admitted.

"That might be because it's a thousand years old. Or at least pretending to be."

"It's from the case?" Jo asked, realizing that this was a mo-ment of surprising trust.

MacAdams nodded and took the phone back. "We found it near the body. I don't suppose Gwilym would know anything about it?"

"Can you send it to me?" Jo asked, because even if Gwilym *didn't* the two of them could certainly find out.

MacAdams compressed his upper lip to a fine seam. "I—could," he said. "You aren't to share it."

"Except with Gwilym."

"A natural exception," MacAdams said, sending the image through. He looked up as her own phone registered the mes-sage, and seemed about to say something else—but his phone began triple buzzing on the table. He glanced at the number, then snapped it up in a hurry. "Now? . . . On site? . . . No—no tell them to circle back. I don't want to spook whoever it is." MacAdams motioned to Giuseppe for the bill. "I'll be there." Hanging up, he turned back to Jo. "I have to go."

"*We.* We have to go. What's going on?"

"I just need to check on a property," he said, half out of his chair already. "Someone's there."

"*The* property?"

"Yes, stay here—or, I'll call you a cab." He handed over his credit card and signed.

"I'm coming with," Jo said, getting to her feet and heading for the door. MacAdams was still admonishing her from the table . . . where he was now also checking pockets for his keys.

"In fact," she said, jingling the prize in one hand, "I'll even drive."

CHAPTER 18

He didn't let her drive.

The Hammersmith property wasn't far; they arrived there just after 10:00 p.m. It made up part of a more commercial section of town over the river, and consisted of a mostly finished exterior that looked, to Jo, like an excessively tall supermarket. Three floors were more or less complete; a fourth one was in process. Heavy equipment haunted the grounds; in the dark they reminded her of articulated museum dinosaurs. MacAdams switched off the beams and coasted quietly under streetlights. The building site butted up against the road and had been cordoned off with fencing. A sign on the side said Hammersmith, and someone had tagged it with spray paint: "u wankers."

"Where's the entrance?" Jo asked—because they weren't driving machinery over the curbs. MacAdams looked at the map on his phone.

"There's a road that runs along the rear of the property; it's also the delivery road for a warehouse." He pulled off to the side and parked the car. "I'm going to take a look through the fence. Supposedly there has been some movement over here. Could be nothing."

"Flashlights," Jo said.

"I have a torch in the glove compartment—"

"No, I mean there *are* flashlights," Jo said, leaning across him and pointing. On the third floor of the building, a rapid flicker bounced across the windows. Almost as if they imagined it . . . but then there was another. It helped that her distance vision was quite good, but whoever it was wasn't being terribly careful.

"Shite." MacAdams rolled down his window for a better view, then took out his phone. He pulled up a number, but didn't call, his index finger hovering over the screen.

"Uh-oh."

"What?"

"You're thinking of sneaking up on them by yourself."

"I'm not." MacAdams wet his lips. "I *am*, but only for a look. I don't want uniform—or a squad car—spooking them."

"Is that a good idea?" Jo asked. Because it didn't sound like one. MacAdams handed her his phone, then reached over her knees to the glove box.

"Copy the number. It will call the squad car directly; they are in the neighborhood. Be here in minutes." He pulled out the torch—actually a penlight—and checked battery power. "If anything goes wrong, or I take too long, you have my permission to call."

She didn't need to ask this time. *This* was a terrible idea.

"How am I supposed to know? And how long is too long?" she asked, but MacAdams was already half out of the car.

"Give me a half hour." He took off his suit jacket and left the coat in the back—then shut the door (quietly). She wasn't entirely sure why until he got to the chain link fence and proceeded to *climb* it. Granted, it wasn't very tall. But MacAdams was a lot nimbler than he looked.

Jo was pretty nimble, too. And lighter than him, if also a lot shorter. She knocked her boot heels together and flexed her fingers. How hard could it be? She waited until he was well over, then another few minutes to give him a start.

★ ★ ★

MacAdams crossed in the shadow of the yard. The building's entrance faced west, and he could see a vehicle parked at the north end. Too dark to see make and model, but just the sort of grand SUV he hated, the kind that took up two spaces and too much room on the road. It's presence, however, made the situation suddenly more ominous. The kind of people who drove hundred-thousand-dollar automobiles shouldn't be breaking into a building site with flashlights. It wasn't teens or vagrants, at the least. He crept more carefully to the front doors.

An apparent Hammersmith standard, they were double glass panes, steel handles. If locked, he wouldn't be getting them open, but they weren't locked. They weren't even *closed*. One door had been propped open with a stray brick. What did that suggest?

MacAdams craned his neck but had lost sight of the torches at this angle. Someone was on the third floor; he could tell this, at least.

Were they stealing something? What could you steal from an empty building? If he waited till morning and a search-and-seizure warrant—he'd never find out.

MacAdams turned on the penlight and let it play over the first floor. Not just complete, *finished*. Shiny, complete with an open lobby and what looked like glassed-in shop spaces beyond. And yet, the top floor was a skeleton of spikes and concrete and cables. It made him think, suddenly, of Nagamaki Plaza, though he wished his mind had *not* chosen that particular American classic as a reference point. For one thing, MacAdams was about a stone too heavy to be climbing in the ventilation.

He found the stairwell on the east wall; no lights and no windows. MacAdams followed the penlight's tiny circle up the first flight; by the time he reached the landing, he could hear noises above: a grating noise, like a trolley, heavily loaded. Then sounds of muffled effort, occasional indistinct voices. MacAdams passed by the second floor, heart hammering, and waited on the landing before the third. Two voices, male, one Cockney.

"Be careful with that—fuck's sake!"

"Wot? You fink I wan' be here all nigh'? C'mon. These boxes are bloody 'eavy."

"Fair. All right. Let's get these down."

MacAdams ducked back down the stairs to the second-floor door, begging it not to be locked. The handle turned, and he darted into the black space; he'd gone somewhere windowless and shut off his light.

"Mate, shoulda figured no lift—we're daft getting these down apples and pears."

"You've a trolley, for Christ's sake, lean it on your hip as you go."

MacAdams watched light flicker through the door crack and heard them wrestle their burdens down the flight. Neither voice was familiar, certainly not the kid who sold him crisps from the butty van—nor was either a Geordie, nor Yorkshire bred.

These voices were from out-of-towners. Property workers? Hired hands? If so, hired by whom?

The light vanished and the thuds grew distant. The silence of the building now felt pregnant; he could hear something. Or imagine that he did. Breathing.

A flutter of second thoughts assaulted MacAdams, but he pushed them away. *Get it together*; he needed to see the third floor before they came back. And they *were* coming back.

The third floor offered a large open space. Faint light came through the window wall onto a long central table. It was presently clear, just a metal surface from which a lot of things had no doubt been swept away.

MacAdams dared turn on the minitorch and played the beam along the walls. There were boxes stacked along a makeshift shelving system, all of them taped shut. He stuck the penlight in his mouth to free his hands, then used his serrated door key as a knife and worked through the heavy layers.

A moment later, McAdams was sweating. Beads ran down his forehead as he pried the box apart. He gripped a heavy plastic bag and lifted, shining the penlight on its contents with his other hand, bracing himself to find stacks of cash or drugs or—

Pottery?

Broken pottery, at that. MacAdams lifted a shard; in the dim light he could see complex designs painted on the glazed side. He tore open the next box. Tile, this time, pictographic. Even in pieces, it was possible to make out the semblance of broadleaf plants.

Footsteps. *They're coming back*. But he hadn't made sense of anything yet; he couldn't back away now. He wrestled with a third box; this one made a whisper of displaced contents as it moved. He set the light down this time, hurrying to pull away the tape. When he shone it back inside again, the beam reflected golden. MacAdams couldn't help but stare: before him was a box of earrings, pendants, bracelets, rings—all of it delicate, intricate and almost exactly like the photo he'd just sent to Jo. *Open work*, Struthers said. *Arabesque designs*.

MacAdams shone the light once more on the tile, only now he understood what he was looking at: a mosaic, probably ancient, absolutely black market. He'd just stumbled into a trade, not of illicit drugs or the usual suspects, but—stolen artifacts.

This realization was followed by a whisper of displaced air. The sounds of atoms scattering out of the way as an object went slicing through empty space. MacAdams didn't have time to guess its heft or its shape. It connected solidly with the back of his head and the stars exploded.

He crashed to both knees as his vision turned to gray mist. Through it, he could just make out a shape—a man above him—swinging something heavy.

"Stop! Police!" A light suddenly shone in the dark. The figure froze, the arm didn't swing.

"Drop your weapon!"

He didn't drop the weapon. He threw it at the source of light—then bolted. There was noise, commotion, except MacAdams wasn't sure if it was coming from inside or outside his brain. He groped his hands toward the ground, hoping to find it solid.

"Omigod, omigod—are you all right?"

MacAdams raised his throbbing head. But there were no police. There was just Jo Jones.

"James, *that* was the guy!"

"The—who?" he begged, dabbing at his head and coming away bloody.

Jo got one arm under him and hobbled him to standing.

"The driver of the butty van!"

★ ★ ★

When Jo was twelve, she took on a bully, Chad. He was in eighth grade and big for his age. He used to pick on a boy down the street from her aunt's house. One day, Chad took the kid's bike and then refused to give it back. Jo didn't remember deciding to act; she just remembered taking Chad at a run and shoving him sideways. He lost his balance and fell off. Jo stood over him feeling like some sort of Athenian warrior, despite probably looking more like an angry Chihuahua. Perhaps it was just the shock of it that disarmed Chad. She didn't even get much credit, anyway. The kid claimed she only stood up to Chad because she was a girl and knew he wouldn't hit her. It wasn't true.

Jo hadn't thought of that. She hadn't thought of anything. It wasn't bravery so much as override, self-preservation momentarily shut off.

"That was a very dangerous thing you did," MacAdams said. He was sitting in the back of a police SUV with a cold compress on his head.

"At least I ducked," Jo said, which was true. The assailant narrowly missed clocking her with the pipe he'd thrown—a pipe presently being dusted for fingerprints. MacAdams winced a bit.

"Yes, and good. But I meant pretending you were the police." His words were coming through gritted teeth, and one eye kept blinking on its own. "What if he hadn't been fooled?"

"I had at least already *called* the police," Jo reminded him.

It took Jo rather longer than anticipated to climb the fence; the toe of her Doc Martens didn't fit right into the links, so there had been a lot of scrambling. By the time she made it over, MacAdams had gone *into* the building, and two other people had come *out*. She'd waited in the dark until the ones unloading began making noises of return—then she ran in ahead of them to warn MacAdams to hide. At least, that had been the plan.

"Ms. Jones?" an officer asked. "Can you please give your statement?"

"Now?" Jo looked back at MacAdams, who nodded she should, then looked sorry he'd moved his head that way.

"I had just got into the stairwell. It was pitch-black, so I was crawling up and there were twelve steps instead of eleven per flight. It should end on an odd number because most people step off with their right foot." Jo pinched her own thigh. *Stop doing that.* "Sorry, um." *Architectural Elements and Design, 2014.* "The door on the second floor opened and I saw someone climb to the third."

"Where Detective MacAdams had gone," the officer clarified.

MacAdams made noises of agreement. Jo took a moment to

look back at the building. They had floodlights on it, and the actual electrics inside were on, too. A crew from Newcastle were sweeping through each floor.

"Right. I followed, and I saw him get hit." Jo winced in spite of herself, not least because Ronan Foley had been murdered that way. "I didn't know what else to do, so I shouted 'Stop! Police!'"

"And you say you recognized the man? How?"

"I turned my phone light on when I yelled," Jo said. The hope was to blind him and keep *him* from seeing *her*. There he was, the same sallow, heavy jowls, eyes squinting over grimace. A big brick of a human. "He owns a butty van I've seen in Newcastle and Abington."

"About that." MacAdams pulled out his phone and stared at it blearily. "Green has the license for the *other* butty van. We need to fast track."

MacAdams was now on the phone, and it seemed he'd not been the first to call Green.

"Yes, I'm fine. Mostly fine . . . Yes—all right, yes, I'll have myself checked over at A&E," he was saying. *Accident and Emergency*, Jo translated. She'd make sure he actually did it. "Listen, Green, we have a building full of what I *think* are artifacts of some kind—and a getaway SUV we're still trying to track down."

He looked up to the officer for an update.

"Nothing yet, sir," she said.

"And so far nothing—but the assailant was the driver Jo saw in Newcastle." MacAdams stopped talking for a moment to close his eyes tight. The on-scene medic declared it "not dangerous," but even a minor head injury could cause concussion, nausea, plus a star-spangled headache. "Green—Hammersmith is high profile, so word is going to get out about this. I don't know how fast, but you need to try and capture the other van. Tomorrow morning, ASAP. I'll be there by tomorrow afternoon . . . Yes—"

Jo had been watching MacAdams talk. She wasn't sure how

long she'd been staring at him like that, but now he was looking back. He blinked a few times before going on.

"I'm in good hands," he said.

★ ★ ★

It turns out he was right. Jo knew how to drive a standard, and despite her supposed trouble getting around York, she managed to find the emergency center with no trouble at all.

"I'm not sure it's really necessary," MacAdams said.

"You can't lie to Green," Jo told him, and she was right of course. His shirt had blood on it from the collar and down his left arm, so he put the jacket on despite the fissure of light that kept opening up in his head when he moved his neck.

"Been through the wars," he sighed. Jo was surprisingly quiet.

Follow the Blue Line said the sign on entry. Nine at night and the waiting room had a considerable number of people already. They settled into chairs at the far corner, Jo at a diagonal and still watching him intently.

"I know you have a headache; do your ears ring? Do you feel dizzy? Blurred vision?" She inched forward to stare right into his pupils, "Your eyes are dilated."

"It's bright in here, Jo."

"It's not *that* bright. What if it's a mild traumatic brain injury? We need our brains. You and me especially," Jo said, putting both hands in her lap. They were in little fists. He'd seen her do that before. Angry? No. Nervous. Anxious.

Worried.

"I'm . . . fine. I'll *be* fine," he said, trying to placate.

Jo's head darted up in a way his might never do again. "You might have been very *not* fine! That guy—*big* guy—" she aped a Herculean figure "—had an honest-to-God-*Clue*-murderer *lead pipe*! And I saw him, and I didn't even stop him hitting you!"

Her fists returned to her lap, squashed between knees. She wasn't looking at MacAdams anymore but at the floor, worry lines creasing her brow between strands of hair dislodged from her ponytail. MacAdams could blame things on the incessant pounding at the base of his skull or on the sudden influx of new case information, which included an apparent rare artifacts trade happening in *Yorkshire*, of all places. Or maybe he was just too unforgivably thick to make the realization that—first—Jo just saved his life. Second, on some level, despite having absolutely no grounds in reality, she was blaming *herself* for not preventing the attack. Often Jo baffled him, but especially in this moment. Five feet and a few spare inches of unaccountable behavior. She once jumped out the window of a (burning) building; tonight, she broke *into* one to keep him getting his head knocked in.

"Jo? Can you look at me?"

"Probably."

"Try."

Jo slumped her shoulders and looked up, and the semipetulant expression would have been funny except it wasn't. MacAdams took a breath against his pounding headache.

"What you did was dangerous and reckless. And brave and selfless. Thank you for doing it. And—" There was a compliment swimming around in MacAdams brain. *And*, they would not have taken an interest in the butty van without her. *And*, they wouldn't have known his assailant was connected to it without her. Fucksake, she made a better detective than half the people on the force. How did you wrangle that into words? Jo was still waiting on him to finish, perched forward on an uncomfortable chair with her knees together and her feet apart, all scuffed Doc Martens and dirty jeans.

"Honestly? I'm just glad you're here," he said finally.

"Really?"

"Yes. If I don't look appreciative it's because someone hit me with a lead pipe."

"It's not an improvement on you," Jo said. And it was funny enough to laugh at, but he was afraid his brain might explode.

"James MacAdams?" the desk clerk announced, and he hobbled off to have his war wounds dressed, knowing Jo would be there to drive him back to the murder hotel. And that was just fine.

CHAPTER 19

Sheila Green pulled a long-sleeved T-shirt over her head and tugged on a pair of cargo pants. It wasn't her usual workplace attire, but today wasn't a usual day.

"You all right, babe?" Rachel asked. She was still in her sleep shirt, sitting cross-legged on their bed.

"Mostly," Green said. She looked into the bureau mirror, past her own reflection to see Rachel's. "Do I look enough like a Pennine Way hiker?"

"You look like a sexy lesbian."

"I am a sexy lesbian."

"No, you're *my* sexy lesbian," Rachel said, getting up to join her. A good six inches shorter, she nuzzled her head against Green's shoulder. Green always preferred her natural hair to extensions; the box braids were short and tight—except for the baby hairs along her neck. Rachel already had her fingers coiling around the stray strands.

"I'll give you a call when it's over," Green said, turning around.

"Too fucking right, you will." Rachel planted a kiss on her lips. "You got this. You're the best there is when things get real."

And they had definitely gotten real. When they got through with a building search, they'd found more than fifty boxes of looted history. It wasn't quite as big as the Interpol raid a few years earlier, perhaps—that one turned up nineteen thousand stolen artifacts in an operation that spanned over a hundred countries. But when it came to precious objects of antiquity, size and number were no indication of *cost*. Millions of pounds' worth had been stored in the York building site. Where there was money, there was trouble—and that was before taking into account *where* the artifacts came from. Even without Interpol, York Central was able to source some of the pottery back to Syria, and Gridley's online search turned up plenty on the looting of cultural sites. War. Warlords. In a weird way, Green almost wished they were dealing with drug trafficking instead—less complicated, at least.

Green tied up her boots. She had been trained and licensed for firearms use but set that aside when she became a DS. Neither she nor MacAdams—nor much of anyone else—carried a gun, and she didn't miss it. Except on days like today.

They were walking up to the van—*one* of the vans—in a largely deserted area, which may or may not be on alert already after the break-in last night in York. Green had spent the afternoon in Newcastle with some of her former mates, and her former chief . . . and she'd called in a favor: would they send a few members of the firearms division, just in case? They would. In her opinion, they *should*. They owed it.

When she called the chief in the middle of the night saying MacAdams had been assaulted in an artifacts raid, she didn't even have to ask. The officers would be waiting for her at the station, and they'd brought extra protective gear for her, Andrews and Gridley. Probably this was more caution than necessary. But Green didn't take chances.

The weather had changed again, was wet and brooding and

cool. The van arrived as predicted by nine; Green had watched them park up through binoculars.

"Same plate as the one from yesterday," she said to Gridley.

The registration had checked out just fine, listed as belonging to a Samuel Fordham. Mr. Fordham lived in Bent Road, Newcastle, and had opened his door to police in his pajamas. Yes, he was who he claimed to be—current driver license, no infractions.

Trouble was, he didn't own a van, or a car, either. His identity had been stolen, lifted and applied to the white butty van presently parked down the hill from where Green and the others took positions.

"Firearm team ready?" Green spoke into Gridley's radio.

"Yes, Detective, we've got you covered," returned the tinny voice.

Green patted the vest well concealed under a windbreaker and nodded to Gridley.

"Careful," Gridley mouthed.

Andrews gave her a thumbs-up; they had the road blocked to either side. She nodded, took a break and made her way down the far side of the hill.

She could hear music playing long before she got to the open window and its metal counter. Punk, she thought; not her style but Rachel liked it—possibly Ghost Car, out of London. Green rapped on the counter hard enough to jostle condiments.

"Oi, be there in a minute," came the reply, followed by a pocked face and a shock of red hair. Not the youth they had encountered before—but also about twenty. "What can I get you?"

"Actually," Green said. "I am not here for bacon butty."

His face appeared to be on hold. "What are you here for, then?" he asked.

Green kept her face neutral, body language casual. "Same as you," she said. He didn't appear to be buying it. "Just running late today. It's muddy out there."

"You—you're a walker?" he asked, one hand squeezing down the volume control on a set of portable speakers.

Green felt her eyebrows twitch. *A walker,* he said, when the common term was *rambler.* Did it signify? She decided to commit.

"I'm the walker today," she said, changing to the definite article.

"Haven't seen you before."

"I'm new."

The kid looked Green up and down, and she immediately regretted not sending Andrews, who was youngest of them and looked younger still. For a tense moment, she thought the game was up. Then he reached behind the counter and lifted up a hiker's backpack.

"Your turn," he said, and Green began to sweat. Her turn for what?

"Show me what's in the bag first," she said, heart beating hard against her ribs. He still had one hand on it, firm.

"Ain't how it works," he said. "Gimme the envelope."

Green reached into her jacket, a pretense. *Could she stall further? If she jumped for it, could she grab hold of the bag strap? Should she blow cover and call for backup?*

"Benny? That you?"

Green started at the voice and spun about. Between the punk rock music and the soft, wet earth, she hadn't heard anyone walking up to them. Not just anyone; a young girl in a blue poncho and wellies. She had something tucked under one arm.

"Ah, shit!" Benny, as the pocked teen must be known, had recognized the girl—and also his mistake. He slammed the window shut. Green wasn't fast enough to stop him from latching it, but at the moment, she had bigger problems. The girl had taken off across the moor.

"Stop! Police!" Green shouted, not because she assumed it would work, but to alert the others that the jig was up. The girl had a good start, but Green was fast and in better footwear. She pelted across the trail in pursuit.

Off the trail, the hills were a matrix of boggy earth and hard rock. The girl in blue slid down a muddy incline on her backside, momentarily vanishing from view. Green took the hill at an angle instead, carving to the left and picking up speed as she raced after her.

Near the bottom was a ravine, presently swollen with runoff water. The girl plunged in, tripped against rocks or current or both, and fell face-first into the water. Green jumped in after her, grasping hold of the girl to lift her out. They both semi-collapsed on the grass, the girl still clutching a plastic sleeve.

'I'm sorry—I'm sorry!" she squealed as Green tugged it away from her. Inside was a brown manila envelope. She opened it to reveal a sheaf of crisp bills.

"I'm placing you under arrest," she huffed. "You don't have to say anything—but it might harm your defense if—" But by this point, the girl was wailing. Green stared at wet blond hair and spoiled makeup on what might have been a fifteen-year-old. "Oh for—Are you hurt or something?"

The girl shook her head but continued to cry and, possibly, hyperventilate. Green knelt next to her.

"Okay, okay now. Let's breathe. In and out, slow. You're all right."

"I'm not. All right. I'm not." Her words came out like gasping hiccups. "They gonna send. Me back. Don't want. To go back!"

"Back where?" Green asked. The girl looked up, nose dripping.

"HM," she said.

* * *

HM, Her Majesty's Young Offenders, incarceration for troubled teens, young drug addicts, petty thieves. Green sipped hot tea;

she'd gone home for a quick change after her dousing—she honestly felt bad that the girl couldn't do the same. Best she could manage was to bring in a pair of Rachel's scrubs and a sweatshirt.

"How old is she?" Gridley asked.

"Seventeen. I know, she doesn't look it," Green said. "She finally gave us the name of her guardian; foster mum. We're waiting on legal representation, as she's a minor."

She called herself Rose, though her name turned out to be Rosalind Ellis. In and out of care homes, high school dropout, did some time for stealing.

"Job training center," Gridley said, flipping through the print-fresh file. "Part of her early release; curfew with the foster, get some skill levels at the center."

"Hold up, which one?" Andrews asked. He had two calls going, one on the landline and one on his cell. "Newcastle City Center by chance?"

"Yeah, actually."

"Hold—hold on," he said to the landline call. "Look here. That's where our young friend Benny's been jobbing out of, too."

Green hovered over his shoulder. He'd scratched out a dozen notes on a pad at his elbow: Benjamin (Benny) Wendall, twenty-one, had denied knowing anything about anything, despite an attempt to flee (stopped at the roadblock). But it seemed he had been in and out of the same job center.

"Has form, too," Andrews added, pointing to the mobile phone call ongoing. "Public drunkenness and assaulting a traffic cop."

"Find out everything about the center, then. I want rosters with names before the boss gets in."

"I'm already in."

"Boss!" Gridley flew across the room to meet MacAdams. For a second, Green thought she might hug the man. "God, we're glad you're all right."

"Mostly," he said. He traced a finger delicately along the back of his head. "Better after a sleep, but headache lingers."

Andrews managed to untangle himself from phone cords.

"Now we know why Chief Clapham always said you were hardheaded," he said, because *someone* had to, and it might as well be Tommy. Green found herself grinning anyway, because she was damn glad to see him, too. And at some more appropriate point, she wanted the details about how exactly Jo Jones came to be the one to ensure it. There was something about her that made Green want to root for her.

"Got a lot of debriefing to do," she said. "And we're waiting on chaperone for a minor; want a coffee?"

★ ★ ★

"I met the firearms unit," MacAdams said as they took plastic chairs in the kitchenette. "You took no chances, I see."

"We don't know who we're dealing with yet, do we?" Green said, a trifle defensive. "Gold earrings are one thing, but they found a quarter-ton limestone plaque on the ground floor."

"I wasn't questioning your decision," he said. "Honest." Green pursed her lips.

"Right, I guess you weren't."

MacAdams sipped his black-no-cream. "You did right, protecting your people."

"Well. Training." Green cleared her throat. "Anyway, we looked in that rucksack of Benny's. It had two items; one was a horse and rider in terra cotta, and the other a pillar figure made of clay. Gridley found ones like them in a museum collection—Syrian, Euphrates region. And I'm guessing it's part of the loot in York."

"We've contacted the British Museum; they're supposed to send us experts to verify provenance. But it's a good guess that it's *all* Syrian. Looting funds terrorists, and targets include religious sites, cultural institutions and archeological sites to traffic the spoils."

"Fucking hell, boss!" Green bucked her sharp chin. "That's not exactly a precinct kind of problem, is it? I mean, the British and American governments haven't been able to stop it; what are *we* supposed to do about it?"

The answer was: not much. They'd already notified UNESCO—The United Nations Educational, Scientific and Cultural organization acted as the UN's watchdog on such things. Multinational art theft lay with the international police. But of course, Abington CID had problems much closer to home.

"What *we* do is find out how this relates to the murder of Ronan Foley—or the butty van or Hammersmith," he said. His head *was* still pounding. Sort of a background thump, as if a car park were going up just outside his frontal cortex. "Burnhope's been out ahead of us," he added. "As soon as Burnhope had news of our raid, he made a public statement. It's in the paper already, I'd guess. Claimed to have *no idea* that the property had been used to nefarious ends; all Foley's doing, and so on. Appalled, horrified, betrayed."

"He told press it was Ronan Foley?" Green grimaced. "Thank God we managed to get the obituary out ahead of this—but who's gonna claim him as next of kin now?"

Another question to ricochet in MacAdams head; he needed to clear it before they interviewed their young perpetrators. He peered through the interview glass at Miss Rose. Her foster mother had not yet made an appearance, but the youth counsel had. They could start there. MacAdams pushed the door open to face the sad-looking creature before them, still wet-headed but presently wearing Rachel's pants and Green's Newcastle United sweatshirt.

"Detective Chief Inspector MacAdams and Detective Sergeant Green to interview Rosalind Ellis," he said for the recording.

"It's Rose," she sniffed into her teacup.

"Okay, Rose. You were carrying an envelope today. Did you know what was in it?"

The counsel nodded to her client. "You can answer," she said.

"No."

"There was money inside. You saw me open it," Green said.

"I didn't know *before*hand," Rose clarified. "Was just a packet, like."

"Okay. Where did you get it, then?" Green asked.

"Dunno."

"Rose," MacAdams said quietly, "if you don't want to get into trouble, just tell us where it came from."

"They said there wouldn't *be* no trouble!" she moaned.

"They who?" MacAdams asked.

"Just boys. I don't know."

"Boys?" MacAdams asked, but Rose had shut up like a book. He tried asking twice more, but Rose said nothing, and the counsel reminded him that he could not force her to answer. It was a quiet minute, then Green cleared her throat.

"Hi, Rose. That's my shirt; I hope it's warm enough." Rose nodded, so Green went on. "The people who told you; they were at the job center, right? Because someone there told Benny, too. You recognized him, I think?"

That got a response, if a small one. She looked up through her eyebrows.

"I don't like the center. It's hard getting jobs. Not good ones that pay you anything."

"You're right," Green agreed. "Newcastle is hard like that, especially for early leavers." MacAdams noted she did not call the girl a dropout, though it amounted to much the same thing. Good tactic; he let her carry on.

"So somebody was going to give you a better job, right? Some regular pay," she said—only this time, Rose shook her head.

"Not regular. We only had to do it every couple of months. But it was five hundred pounds each time!" That had been the amount in the envelope meant for Benny, too.

"That's a lot," Green agreed. "Would be nice to have. So how did you earn it?"

Rose rubbed her nose. "There's a place to get sandwiches outta van."

"Here in Abington?"

"Nar, in Newcastle. Just on the street, like. I got chips. And this plastic thing." Rose chewed her lip. "It's not illegal."

That was technically true. MacAdams leaned forward, hands spread on the table. If the girl was scared of going back to HM, then they could use it to advantage.

"Can you tell us what you did next? Maybe none of that was illegal, either," he said.

"It weren't!" she agreed enthusiastically. "It's just a train ride, getting here. Then I was s'posed to go for a walk. Leave the envelope in the van and take a bag." Her eyes searched the counsel's face. "That's not crimes, is it? They can't send me back for that, can they?"

"Then what?" MacAdams repeated, trying to mask his impatience. "Who were you supposed to meet?"

Rose only shrugged. "Someone was supposed to find *me*," she said.

A knock came at the door, then, and Gridley entered, but she wasn't alone.

"Sir, Rose's foster mum—" was about all she managed to say.

"Rosalind! I thought we'd got past all this!" said a harried-looking women in tracksuit and jacket. "And you can't interview her without a guardian!"

"We have provided for counsel," MacAdams said.

"Well?" the woman demanded, though it was hard to know

from whom she expected an answer. Rose had retreated further into Green's sweatshirt. She hadn't made the drop; she hadn't even been to the hotel yet—she couldn't tell them any more.

"Do you want to go home?" MacAdams asked. Enthusiastic nodding ensued. He nodded to Green. "Thank you for answering our questions. We may have more; please don't leave town."

"She's not leaving the *house*, is what," the foster said, helping Rose out of her seat.

MacAdams gave both of them his card.

"Does that mean—Am I not under arrest now?" Rose asked hopefully.

"You're free to go," MacAdams assured her. It was the first time she smiled.

★ ★ ★

In the end, interviewing Benny put them at the same disadvantage. He really did work the butty van, and only did the "other" job now and then. Deliver a bag, take an envelope. He knew Rose from the job center, but they weren't the only ones working the gig. There had to be other pairs, but Benny and Rose didn't know them. And neither of them seemed to know Foley, either.

"Fucking evil," Green said. They were seated in the Red Lion, opting for an honest lunch and a pint after all that. "Butty vans and coffee wagons pepper the way between petrol stops. No one questions you stopping. And the kids aren't told anything. Disposable. Itinerant. It's genius in a way; no one on either side has enough info to incriminate you."

MacAdams shrugged. The porter was going down very well and the throbbing had finally ceased. "Genius or reckless? What if a kid steals an artifact? Or pawns it?"

"That's only if you know what you have," Green reminded him. "Okay, the gold earrings are fancy. But half the stuff in

York was painted pottery and such. What's a kid gonna do with that? You said yourself you have to know a network. A big, international one."

"Right, there's the problem," MacAdams said. He had been slow-scrolling through an article about looted antiquities. "Big. Multinational. Plenty of the artifacts are laundered through auction houses, even museums. A buyer could almost be aboveboard."

"Okay," Green said slowly. "So if it's not that hard to source the stuff, why buy it out the back of a butty van?"

"Exactly." He clinked her glass. "There were too many artifacts in the York property for this to be a small-time operation. Efficiency, planning, connections. Hiring troubled teens to port things via butty van is anything but."

"So—it's two problems?" Green asked. "Why would a high-flying, clearly well-lubricated operation stoop to selling on back roads? And who buys their artifacts that way?"

MacAdams still didn't have an answer to the first question. He might have an answer to the second. "Frankly, it has to be someone local."

"You're joking. Who around here would have the money for that sort of thing?" Green asked; MacAdams gave her a thin, hard smile.

"The kind of people who stay at Abington Arms, I would guess," he said.

"Or the kind who join gold clubs in Newcastle?" Green offered. She had as much respect for Burnhope as *he* did for old Clapham. Rich men whose money made bad things go away. Burnhope seemed to be using those riches in the right way, but neither of them were quite ready to let him off. Did that make them biased against the fantastically wealthy? Or just wise flatfoots who'd seen a lot of crooked morals among the great and good? *Wisdom*, he decided, knocking back the rest of his pint.

"Time to rattle Burnhope again, then, too," he said, *And Ava*, he added silently. He waved at Tula for the bill, but she didn't bring it. Instead, she slapped the day's edition of Newcastle news on the counter.

"You just saved me a trip," she said, pointing to the front page. Stanley Burnhope peered up front and center, shaking hands with the mayor: "Local business targeted by black market dealers: Stanley Burnhope seeks counsel of mayor after discovery of building break-in."

"Wow," Green said. "That's a hell of an interpretation."

MacAdams had predicted it, but even he was impressed with how Burnhope spun the story to appear as the victim. Tula, however, wasn't concerned with this particular bit of news. She'd underlined a name farther down the article lead: Ronan Foley.

"That's your dead guy," she said.

"It is," MacAdams agreed. "We placed that ad ourselves."

Tula nodded, sending waves of curls bouncing. Then, she shuffled the pile to bring forward news from the day before, folded to the obituaries.

"Aye, o' course you did. Looking for next of kin, ain't you?"

"That was the plan," Green said.

"Right. Well. Here I am." She pulled up a spare bar stool and sat upon it, hands leaning on the flat front edge of her seat. MacAdams felt suddenly like a trap was being set.

"You. You're Ronan Foley's next of kin?"

"O, aye." She pushed a strand of hair behind her ear. "See, I'm his *wife*."

CHAPTER 20

Jo watched the water run in swirling eddies around the retired Mill wheel. It had been a weird two days. Even for Jo, whose days never seemed to be normal. But reflecting on the last eleven hours was an exercise in mild embarrassment. You weren't supposed to sleep too soundly after a head injury, and someone needed to make sure. MacAdams argued about this and lost, then proposed sitting in the lobby. Its horrible foam sofas would keep anyone awake. Which wasn't true; Jo could sleep anyplace, so she ensured wakefulness by making free with the EZ pod coffee maker in the corner . . . and then eating all the peanut M&Ms from the vending machine. That's when she launched into the history of automats. Did MacAdams know that by the 1920s, some three hundred thousand people had office jobs in Manhattan? (He didn't.) They needed cheap places to eat in a hurry and fast-food chains had yet to really catch on. Germany had the answer: they developed coin-operated diners to dispense with waiters and menus. You could see the offerings behind glass, pay your dime and pull out the food. There were hundreds of them in Manhattan, but the last one closed in 1991, so Jo never had the pleasure. (She had, of course, edited a history about them.)

"Vending machines were invented in Germany?" Macadams had asked.

No, they weren't, Jo explained. Vending machines were designed by Percival Everitt in 1883 for London train stations. Vending machines weren't even related to the German automats—they just associated together in Jo's head. And that's pretty much how things went until MacAdams was permitted a lie-down. She still had to wake him again every hour to ask his name and address, that sort of thing. But she herself had been too full of coffee and chocolate for slumber.

She would have liked to doze on the way back to Abington, but of course, MacAdams wasn't yet permitted to drive. Some sort of sting operation had happened that morning regarding the butty van—or so she gathered from the one-sided conversations he'd had with Green. She was concentrating on the driving part, especially as this was *not* her car. "What's happening?" had been met with "I'll let you know when it's over."

So she'd dropped him off, eaten a cold cheese sandwich from Teresa's coffee cart and spent the rest of her time sitting cross-legged in front of the Mill stream. Waiting. But he hadn't contacted her yet, and it was well after lunch. MacAdams was fine, she figured, or someone would have told her.

Jo rolled over on her stomach, leaning on her arms against bent grass. Was she worried? Technically, he'd worried about her *first*. He'd sat on the floor with her and talked about carpet stripes. She couldn't even be sorry he'd seen her like that, because his kindness was a gift and that would be refusing it. Then, two hours later, he'd been attacked. Seeing MacAdams covered in blood had jolted her clean out of herself. (Noted: adrenaline made a better emotion-hangover cure than pizza.)

MacAdams was fine. A&E confirmed he was fine. Again. Obviously, everything was *fine*. But would it kill him to send a text?

She was being irrational. Jo hated being irrational. *Go home*, she told herself. *Get some sleep*, which also helpfully killed time. She was meeting Gwilym at the Indian restaurant for dinner, and he promised to have all sorts of news about Augustus John. Jo stood, stretched and suppressed a yawn. It was a two-mile trek back to her cottage, but at least the walk was a pleasant one.

Jo followed the river until she passed the cemetery, then began the slow climb up the double lane that led to Jekyll Gardens and the estate. The wind had shifted and the air turned warm and close—and promised rain again. It also brought a sudden crushing exhaustion, as if crossing into home territory kicked away whatever support had kept her upright for the last twenty-four hours. Her overnight bag felt heavy. Her Doc Martens, too. She could hear her heart rushing in her ears and a dull headache promising.

Just close your eyes a minute, she told herself.

It was a mistake. The world did a flat spin, as if she'd been drinking. When had she last eaten? Jo touched grass, literally, and blinked away the cloudiness. From her crouched position, she could just look up over the knoll—the tall grasses that bordered the field and fens. And she saw a yellow raincoat.

Jo bolted to standing, which caused a secondary blood rush, followed by red-green splotches in her vision. When her world came to rights again, she dropped her pack in the lane and ran toward the knoll. Up through scratchy furze she went, waist deep in herbaceous borders. But the field waved beyond, empty.

Dammit. No one on the path above, no one below and no one had passed her by. Jo felt the trickle of adrenaline wick away. A trick of the light, maybe. The brain filling in gaps with what it *wanted* to see rather than strict reality.

That, or the mysterious vanishing hiker had been hill-walking their way into town not far from the trail she'd seen her on before.

Sleep. Jo needed sleep. That was all.

★ ★ ★

Tula Byrne had lived in Abington for ages, owned the Red Lion well before MacAdams and Annie got married. Not a native, she'd had won her way into the center of things with good feeling, excellent business sense and damn fine cooking. Dark complected, despite being Irish, with curly black locks streaked in gray, she presided over the pub—and over Ben—like a good witch, benevolent, vaguely mysterious, not to be trifled with. Usually, he found that amusing. Today, it reminded him that he knew next to nothing *about* her.

"I thought you didn't go in for marriage," Green said—an expression of shock, not even a question.

"Well, not after the last one," Tula agreed. "Catastrophe, that." MacAdams got more to the point.

"You said you didn't know Ronan Foley, Tula. You lied," he said, intending to follow up with how this obstructed an ongoing investigation among other things—but she didn't give him the chance.

"I did no such thing. I *didna* know any Foley. Because that ain't the man's name." She pulled something out of her pocket: a wedding photograph, bent in the center to put the subjects on either side. "Only kept it in case I could identify the bastard someday."

MacAdams took it in hand and Green leaned. Unfolded, it presented a stunningly beautiful Tula Byrne—tresses down to her waist—and a man with Foley's jawline and deep-set eyes.

"That there is Rhyan Flannery. I see he kept the *R* and *F*, but *Ronan Foley*? Wholly made-up name, probably got a fixer to do an ID for him." Tula shook her head. "Damn sot. I married him in 1980, three days after my nineteenth birthday. Regretted it ever after."

MacAdams was trying to take notes and simultaneously thumb-dial Gridley to change their search criteria. He'd certainly had his doubts about Foley's credentials when they failed to find a birth certificate, but had put it down to attempts at assimilation.

"Why didn't you tell us before, Tula?" he demanded.

Tula blinked long lashes and looked at him over imaginary glasses.

"Because I weren't ready, James MacAdams. I hadn't laid eyes on him since 1982—been as dead to me as Charlemagne."

"But you are—were—still *married* to the man?" MacAdams clarified.

"Hard to divorce a bloke you cannae find, James," Tula said. "Listen, now. I had a hint of it all when you showed me that photo; couldn't be sure, though. Time ain't been especially kind to him."

"You were sure enough to drop a glass," MacAdams muttered, mostly to himself. He should have known that the woman who carried eleven pints without spilling a drop wouldn't smash a glass for no reason.

"*Then* I see the obit. No family, you say." Tula's voice stayed light, even jovial. But MacAdams watched the cord in her neck contract like a pulley system. "And *then*—thieving. Well, of course. Had to be him."

"Hold up, hold up," Green said, waving her hands. "What are you talking about?"

"The artifacts in York. Of course, it was all petty theft, fencing goods and minor cannabis dealing back then. We'd not been married a full year yet before I discovered the loose floorboard where he'd been hiding his loot. Gave him hell about it."

"But you didn't go to police, I take it. Didn't you think that might be trouble?" MacAdams asked. Tula laughed at him, but it wasn't the usual musical sound. Harsh notes.

"Let's see—me da was in the IRA, me brother locked up for making pipe bombs. What kind of trouble ought I to have been looking out for, James MacAdams?" Tula twined one finger into her locks. "I should have known, though. It wasn't gonna stop with stealing watches and old trinkets. He started house-breaking with a couple of his boys. They got in with a gang, and soon it was every weekend. Right up till he knocked over a petrol station and was caught on film."

"Ah," said Green.

Tula gave her a wink. "Greedy fool," she agreed. "That's when I last caught him taking our emergency money from the tin." Tula slid off the stool and took up the paper from the bar. "Police were looking for him. And more dangerous sorts, too. Not to worry, *he'd be back for me.*"

Tula cast the paper down.

"But he never planned to come back. Didn't even warn me I might be in danger myself, but I figured that out pretty quick. Crime bosses aren't exactly a forgiving sort." She gave MacAdams and Green a wry smile. "Lotta bad things about having a thug for a da, but some good. I got out, clean."

"You're saying he left you there to get killed?" Green asked. She looked at MacAdams. "How's this the charming guy who wins over lady colleagues?"

MacAdams didn't have an answer and didn't need one. Tula had hers ready.

"He was just like that. Had a way of *listening* to you, made you feel he hung on every word. With women, anyway. Was a right bastard with other men." She leaned on the bar and cast her eyes over the pub room, as though seeing something else. "If he hadn't got in trouble, I imagine we'd have run off together somewhere, the three of us. Maybe even made a go of things. At least till the next time he got himself in trouble and needed to bug out."

MacAdams had been writing it all down, which is probably why he caught the slip.

"Three of you," he said. For a moment, Tula said nothing at all, her face as hard and bright as jasper.

"There *might* have been three of us. But I was on my own, all of a sudden, and no father coming back. So." Her face relaxed again. "Plenty of water under that bridge; I choose not to regret it. Anyhow, I've all I wanted and more in life. And Rhyan—or Ronan or whate'er he called himself—is right where he was headed all along."

MacAdams managed to break the tip of his pencil, embedding lead in the page.

"To a ditch?" he asked.

Tula leaned over, full lips parted and eyes half-closed.

"I've a motive now, I expect," she said.

She did, and it gave Ben a motive, too, for that matter. Did he think they were suspects? No. Did he need to know their movements the night of the murder? Hell yes.

"Statement. Both of you. And you know what I'll need—"

"To eliminate us from your enquiries," Tula finished for him. "You'll have 'em. But just remember, James, I needn't have told you. And without me, you'd never know." She gave him a wink after that, a touch triumphant because utterly true.

Green let out a long, low whistle. "Fuck me," she said.

"Quite."

"What are we to do with all that?"

"Find previous on Rhyan Flannery," MacAdams said, reaching for his buzzing phone. "And see if our man Foley was preparing to cut and run again. MacAdams here."

He was in for a shock.

"It's the Abington Arms," said the voice on the line. "Your mystery woman just turned up . . . and then disappeared just as quickly."

"Right, Green, call in Uniform; Foley's woman has turned up—" He'd headed back toward the car but Arianna's voice cut into the phone line.

"That's not *all*," she said. "She came here to pick something up."

★ ★ ★

Arianna was waiting for them, arms crossed over her green blazer. As it turned out, the Abington Arms provided lockers to their esteemed returning guests. The idea, said Arianna, was to provide regulars with "convenience." It was hard for MacAdams not to see the potential implications for less-legal activity. Like storing stolen art.

"Why didn't you say this before?" Green asked, despite promising to mostly stay mum. Arianna chose to answer MacAdams instead.

"I didn't know she'd left anything. I'm not the coat check." She led the way to a large room in the back, possibly a sort of livery service at some point. The tall units were large enough to hang several large coats—even a small wardrobe.

"How many of your guests get this sort of special treatment?" MacAdams asked.

"It's technically available to everyone, if they ask," Arianna told him.

Green stepped ever so slightly between them. "That wasn't the question, though, was it?"

"Five," Arianna barked. "You can see that for yourself." She swept a long arm toward the lockers, five of which had been bolted shut. Then she continued to address MacAdams exclusively. "I was at the desk when she arrived."

"Tell me everything she said from beginning to end," MacAdams said.

"Not difficult; she didn't say anything. Just presented me with a ticket for number twelve." Arianna held up the key. "I asked her name. She wouldn't speak. So I told her to wait and came to call you. When I returned, she'd gone. I sent the bell hop running out after, and the security guard, too."

"But she didn't get what she wanted?" MacAdams said, nodding. "Well done. She might be back."

"Not if all the hotel staff are chasing around town for her, and us here in marked cars," Green suggested. And it was a fair point. He drummed his fingers against the locker.

"All right. Arianna, let's see what's inside."

"It's a private client's locker."

"Yes, and you called the police because you know it's a murder investigation—do you want us to wait for a search warrant?" MacAdams asked.

Beside him, Green smiled toothily. "We'll be sure to search the *whole* hotel," she said. "Your boss Evans should like that."

Arianna narrowed her eyes. "Look. I have to resist or I wouldn't be doing my job—and I like my job. But yes, you can have the bloody key. I don't even know what's in there."

MacAdams took it from her. A twist in the lock and the door sprung open.

Inside was a pale pink gown of silk, a fitted jacket in white and a dappled scarf of pink and red and blue.

"And . . . shoes again," Green said. She pulled a glove from one pocket and used it to pick up a pair of wedge heels. "I'm no expert. Are these as fancy as Foley's?"

"Those are J'Adior pumps from DIOR," Arianna said.

"Expensive?" MacAdams asked.

"Oh yes," she said. "What's that?" Arianna pointed to a white envelope near the bottom. MacAdams borrowed Green's glove and lifted it out. *That,* it turned out, was fifteen hundred pounds in cash . . . and a necklace.

"Well, well, boss. I think I know what the earrings were for," Green said, indicating the chain. The pendant displayed the same open design, like a little golden basket of delicate filigree. MacAdams watched its half-moon shape, studded with rubies, glint in the light. Then he turned back to Arianna.

"In fact, we *will* get a search warrant. I want to see inside each of these. And I want the names of who uses them," he said.

Arianna pointed a painted nail at the bills poking out from the envelope.

"It's not the first client we've had who likes to keep cash," she said. "There's nothing wrong with that."

"Perhaps not. But *this* is a Syrian artifact," MacAdams said of the pendant. "And I want to know who else keeps antiquities in their lockups."

"What are you *talking* about?" Arianna demanded, but MacAdams wasn't finished.

"You saw this woman, on more than one occasion. Today, you have seen her up close. I'm calling in a sketch artist and I want you to give them every detail. Understood?" Perhaps it was his tone, or the urgency with which he ordered the sketch artist over the phone, but Arianna seemed to be having a crisis of faith.

"Is she dangerous? Is *she* the murderer?" She flashed a look at Green. "I thought you left Newcastle to get away from this sort of mess."

Green's face remained impassable. "Is that why *you* left?" she asked.

Arianna dropped her gaze. "I left for a promotion in hospitality—"

"In Abington. How convenient."

"I went where there was *work*," Arianna snapped back.

Green tilted her head, as if to recapture direct eye contact.

"I guess that makes two of us," she said, voice flat, placid, yet also white-hot.

MacAdams cleared his throat. "Lock it back up until forensics gets here. They'll bag it for the station. And you have my number if the woman returns." He put one hand very loosely against Green's clavicle and steered her toward the door. She went without remonstrance, but the tension didn't lift until they were back outside.

"Before you say anything, she and I were never, *ever* an item," she said.

"I wouldn't dare suggest it."

"Good." She seethed a moment, then took a long breath. "What do we do next?"

"Repeat the procedure," MacAdams said. "Foley's image turned up Tula. We'll get a composite image and post it here and in Newcastle. Did you notice anything about what's in the locker?"

"Bit fancy for Abington."

"Fancy like Foley's last outfit. Minus the bespoke shoes." MacAdams headed to the car, already rearranging the incident board in his head.

★ ★ ★

Gridley had already opened all the available windows, but the room remained hot and humid, with rain misting through the open panes.

"I think we've a desk fan someplace," she said, poking through the read cupboard. MacAdams was already performing his zoo-tiger stride at the front of the room, divested of coat, jacket, tie, and in his shirtsleeves. The middle of the board had been cleared, and he just waited for the others to take their places.

"Gridley, Andrews, spill the details."

"Yes sir," Andrews said, waving his coffee mug. "First, phone records. We went after all the numbers we could find, and every one of them's a burner. End to end it doesn't help us much, or wouldn't have, until we picked up Benny. One of the burners was *his*."

"Right," Gridley said, sitting on the edge of his desk. "Official proof he's connected to Her Majesty's Young Offenders. These phones were being activated and deactivated over a few days. Kids got their directions off 'em, marching orders, and sometimes warnings."

"As far as the numbers Foley called that weren't burners: the hotel, the offices at Hammersmith—"

"Presumably coworker Trisha Simmons?" Gridley interrupted.

"And Burnhope. But get this, he wasn't calling Burnhope's mobile. He called his *house*," Andrews finished. "An honest to God landline."

MacAdams turned to face Green.

He knew what they were both thinking. *Clandestine phone calls with Ms. Ava?*

Green sucked her teeth. "It's damn well starting to look like an affair, isn't it? Especially since Burnhope claimed he never let business and home intersect."

"Hang on to the Ava-and-Ronan idea for a minute and let us give you the authentic *Rhyan Flannery*," Gridley said, going back to her own desk and swiveling her chair to face the monitor. "Ronan Foley appears after 1998, no form—but old Rhyan had *plenty*. As a lad, he was caught housebreaking. Brought up on charges for pickpocketing, too. There's a hint that he may have been questioned about a series of robberies later tied to a gang called the Belfast Seven. Then he's clean for a few years, no convictions."

"But not because he wasn't doing dirty work," Andrews said. "North-Irish police had been tracking him, figured he might lead them to bigger fish."

"Which he did. Sort of," Gridley said. "There had been a spate of art thefts, the whole Russborough House art robbery thing."

"Foley was tied to Martin Cahill?" MacAdams demanded. "That was a thirty-million-dollar heist!"

"God no. But he was linked to a group trying to fence stolen goods—that clashed with Cahill's gang."

"In fact, some of his set got mysteriously murdered," Andrews added, now sitting on the edge of Gridley's desk. MacAdams wondered if he should suggest they pick a single speaker next time.

"Too right, they did. Police put out a warrant for Flannery/Foley, but chances are good he was wanted by the rival gang members, too."

"He was in trouble every place with everyone. And that's when he split—"

"Rhyan Flannery dies, Ronan Foley–slash–Nathanial Connolly is born," Gridley confirmed.

"That's a *lot* of identities, isn't it?" Green asked. "It can't be that easy to change your name."

"Ah! But Foley's little art-fencing troupe had a side business in forgery!" Andrews said, waving his hands. "It's the '80s, too. Not exactly the cutting edge of technology for spotting a fake."

MacAdams had been born in the '80s. And tried not to take it personally.

"Okay, makes sense. But then how does he end up in commercial real estate? I'm not sure if I should be surprised or not."

"Not," Andrews said with a grin. "Get this. Flannery's father was an architect."

MacAdams had anticipated most of this, but *that* was news. He'd built a picture of Foley's youth along the same lines of Tula's: struggle, poverty, politics. Andrews pulled up an old newsprint on his machine.

"Flannery Sr. ultimately takes a job *teaching* architecture, and we found some documentation for his son as enrolled in engineering. If he'd kept his nose clear, he might have ended up in the same career."

"Instead, he knows just enough to work in real estate development as a bulldog job boss," MacAdams said, turning back to the board. "Burnhope made the man sound like uncultured muscle. Instead, he's got a whole back history in art theft, meaning he *knows* art well enough to value it. He's got some sort of background in architecture, too, and enough brains to keep several identities popping."

"That doesn't necessarily make him cultured," Green said.

"No, but—*but* . . ." Gridley interjected. "He's a bad boy with brains who knows how to turn on charm when he wants, especially with women." Perhaps the exception being, MacAdams thought, Jo Jones; she hadn't seemed to describe him that way at all. But nonetheless.

"All right, let's say Ava found him intriguing," Green said. "Ava wasn't the woman who just turned up at the Abington Arms." She had a point. But MacAdams had an idea.

"Tula gave us reason to believe he was ready to do a runner again." MacAdams dropped Foley's picture down to the cleared space on the board. "Everything changed *six months ago*. So let's start there: six months ago. Foley sells his house. That's approximately, by Struthers's estimate, when he stopped drinking and smoking. It's also when Foley starts coming *here* to Abington, according to his hotel records."

MacAdams moved a photo of the now-seized butty van next to Foley.

"Why here?" MacAdams next drew down a photo of the posh hotel. "Abington Arms has been known for its . . . privacy, let's say. We need to take a long look at the regular guests, especially those that overlap with his stay."

"You think it's related to the art deal?" Gridley chewed the end of her pen. "I mean, it's a good place to hide a love affair, but it meant he could hide his real identity from *her*, too. By Foley's admission, they're going to have a baby. You think he means to cut and run?"

"A hotel willing to protect your privacy is good for all sorts," MacAdams said, somewhat grimly. "But I don't think Foley planned to abandon this new lover like he did Tula Byrne."

MacAdams had started to sweat, despite the fan's feeble attempts to circulate air. He hadn't had time to print new photos, so he drew a picture of a locker, and one of a shoe in dry erase marker.

"At Foley's flat, everything was disposable."

"Boring, even," Green added.

"Just so. Everything except the clothes he was wearing—or, I suspect, planning to wear. And over at the Abington Arms, the locker held a different suit of clothes, fancy attire for a woman and fifteen hundred in cash." MacAdams rubbed the marker between his hands as though trying to start a fire. "They each had a fine set of clothes waiting for them, almost like a bug-out bag. Where were they going?"

"Vacation?" Andrews asked.

"A cruise?" suggested Gridley—but MacAdams shook his head.

"Honeymoon," he said. "Very possibly as Mr. and Mrs. Connolly."

"But Ava is already married," Green said. "Oh. Shit, he's leaving *Ava* for someone else."

MacAdams tapped his nose. "He knows he's in trouble, right? So he invents not one identity but *two.* Both of them were going to flee. But something didn't go as planned."

"Yeah, he got murdered," Andrews said.

"Yes, but *before* that. The mystery woman never picked up her gown from the locker; he didn't get his shoes or suit from his flat." MacAdams closed his eyes hard enough to restart the distant pounding from his head injury. *The plan had been put in motion.* Foley had packed in a desperate rush, toppling shaving cream, grabbing only his shirt. He had come to Abington, perhaps to pick up his girlfriend, but she didn't arrive. In fact, she only *now* came looking for her locker. Why wait? Unless you were afraid.

"We need to find Foley's girlfriend," MacAdams said. "Because I think whoever was targeting Foley means to target her next."

Green had been following along, but with increasingly stiff posture.

"You haven't said this out loud yet, but you're going to. If Ava is the jilted lover . . . then she might have murdered Foley before he could leave her."

MacAdams thought about Ava; above the fray somehow, protected by wealth and position, seemingly beyond mortal emotions. But he also thought of her fierce protection of her maid, and that ever-cool self-possession.

"It's not our job to guess," he said. "It's our job to suspect, and to follow through. Right now, Foley's lover is our priority. Because I suspect she might be in danger."

He meant the mystery woman; of course he did. But without meaning to, he was also thinking about Jo Jones.

CHAPTER 21

When the knock came, it startled Jo out of heavy slumber. She fumbled about, forgetting she was on the sofa, and craned her neck to catch a glimpse of the clock. Was it Gwilym already, picking her up for dinner? The knock repeated. She should jump up and answer it, but the particular couch crevice in which she found herself seemed too good to endanger.

"It's open," she said.

"*Why* is it open, Jo?" asked . . . James MacAdams.

Jo rolled herself to sitting and blinked sleep out of her eyes. He was standing in her doorway in short sleeves. She'd never seen him in short sleeves and stared like he'd walked in naked.

"Well, I'm home and it's daytime," she started.

"And asleep. With the door unlocked." He crossed the room and crouched to be at eye level. "You said you'd quit that."

Jo wasn't sure she'd promised, in fact. She got to her feet instead of answering and pointed to the kitchen. "Tea?"

"Yes. No—actually. I brought you something." He held up a paper bag. "In thanks. For yesterday."

Jo peered inside. A whiskey bottle. Caol Ila, it said. She

wanted to say thank you. Did you thank you for a thank you? She blinked her eyes a few more times and decided she, at least, needed caffeine.

"How about coffee?" she asked, putting the whiskey on the kitchen counter. "How's your head?"

"Fuzzy and tired," he admitted, taking his usual seat in the wicker rocking chair.

"Mine, too."

"Adrenaline leaving the system," he suggested.

Jo ground beans and put the kettle on before trying to talk again. For some reason she was struggling with her mouth-words—so much so that MacAdams, of all people, took the lead.

"We are still looking for the Geordie van driver and his associates," he said over the gentle creak of the rocker. "But I think we've sorted the vanishing hiker for you."

"Really?" Jo wondered if she should tell him about the semi-hallucinated version, but decided to keep mum for the minute.

"Not hill-walkers at all," he said. "Foley seems to have been selling stolen artifacts out of the vans. Using kids as couriers."

Jo absorbed this while watching the French press timer, a minihourglass she'd bought at a curio shop. "If he had a van, why did he need couriers?"

"Small, local deliveries, we think," MacAdams went on. "We picked up a youth, about sixteen. Blond, around your height."

"That one's not *my* hiker. Mine had dark hair. And a yellow raincoat. And she wasn't carrying a pack or anything."

"Well, we gather they used quite a lot of different people," MacAdams assured her. She brought him a mug. No biscuits. After Foley, those felt like bad luck.

"So what's next?" she asked, settling into the peacock-blue chaise.

"For the investigation? Going back to Newcastle tomorrow to follow some leads." MacAdams tilted his head as though looking at her stairs. "Back to Hammersmith—see if the CEO recognizes a drawing of . . . Jo? Did you tell me that Foley took towels and soap?"

"Hand towels, a bath towel and *all* the soap. Why?"

MacAdams hovered the coffee halfway to his lips but was still looking up at the ceiling. Thinking of her "murder room," she guessed.

"Have you used the sink up there since all this started?" he asked.

"No." Jo already put her cup down, because she could see where this was going. "You want to check something?"

MacAdams was on his feet already. Jo led the way into the vaulted attic with its lovely afternoon light (watery light, given the weather). First, he investigated the little WC sink, then hovered over the roll-top bath, sliding a finger along the porcelain. Jo was suddenly grateful that her method of dealing with stress involved serious housekeeping.

"What are you looking for, exactly?" she asked. MacAdams sat down on the tub edge and leaned his arms upon his knees. After a moment, he gave an inward sort of chuckle.

"Ignore me. I just can't turn it off, sometimes."

"Oh God, I get it."

"I came here to thank you, not chase up loose ends." He ran a hand through his hair. "This case is a million tiny details that don't add up, and I can't tell which are important."

"Such as?" Jo asked, pulling up the nearby chair.

"Soap residue. There isn't any. Foley took soap and towels, but he didn't wash up. What did he want them for? Where did they go?"

"Like the missing raincoat and towels and the question of the car," Jo added. MacAdams gave her a weary smile.

"Exactly. Could add you to the CID. This case is all shoes and ice burn." He'd started to get up, but Jo waved her hands at him.

"Whoa, whoa! You don't just drop in things like that without an explanation. Shoes. And ice?"

"I shouldn't have said."

"You did, though."

"Fair," he sighed. First he explained the expensive shoes they found at Foley's flat. The second bit was definitely stranger. "The body was packed in ice. We don't know why."

Why did you pack anything in ice? Jo thought, her brain doing a quick run through of freezer pops, ice cubes for watering orchids, ice baths for tightening skin, refrigeration against spoilage. The freezer had failed in their New York apartment while they were on holiday once. They didn't need a fumigator; they'd needed an exorcist. Plus bodies—even freshly dead ones—had a funk all their own.

"Maybe to stop it smelling?" Jo offered. MacAdams had got halfway to his feet again, but again returned to sitting. He might never leave the tub at this point.

"That's—Why would you say that?"

"Well, if I had a dead person in my trunk on a muggy, rainy night, I might consider some ice." Jo twitched her nose. Did that sound callous? "Dead people don't immediately decay or anything. But stuff happens when you die. Body fluids—let go. It's not especially pleasant."

"You edited a book on anatomy."

"No, on body farms," Jo corrected.

MacAdams made it to standing this time. And pacing. Walking his brain, as it was.

"All right; it's warm and wet, and the victim has a considerable and bloody wound," he said. "In a trunk, you said."

"It's a guess," Jo admitted. "In a trunk, you could get away with just four or five bags of ice. You can't pack ice in an open van or SUV. Or not as well. Also the body might flop around."

"You've a way of putting things." He said. "Okay, in a trunk. It's messy. *And* there's melting ice. And he still has to be dragged out again."

Jo had been following the dance of wallpaper flowers as he

spoke, but in her mind's eye she was considering the problems of vehicular upholstery.

"I know it sounds extra complicated, but what if the murderer was fastidious? Someone that worried about the *smell* isn't going to just put the body on the mats. If they use a tarpaulin, they could drag him out easier, too. Especially with a bit of rigor mortis," she said. MacAdams was following, but waved the last bit away.

"Doubtful he'd been dead that long, as you saw him around eleven thirty, but all fair points. The murderer doesn't want to spoil his car."

"If it *is* his car," Jo added.

"Why would you say that?" MacAdams asked. He'd stopped his circuit just in front of her. She instinctively put her hands on a pretend steering wheel, thinking of their drive back from Newcastle.

"Because you'd be a lot more careful if it was someone else's. I was in *yours*."

"Makes sense." MacAdams extended her a hand and pulled her to standing. "At least, if it was someone you cared about." He blushed and quickly added, "A boss, for example. There would be other eyes looking at it, someone else who would recognize a smell or a stain." He backed away to let her out of the room and she returned to her coffee.

"Still doesn't explain the raincoat, shoes or soap and towel thievery, though," she said before drinking a good half cup at a go.

"Maybe the murderer came to the cottage for it so he could scrub down the car," Jo added. She meant it as a joke, but MacAdams had just blanched gray enough to make her worry about concussion again.

"I'm kidding—I'm not serious."

"Jo." MacAdams walked across the living room to the front door and pushed it open. "The thing is, he *could* have."

★ ★ ★

"That's . . . wow," Gwilym said over his vindaloo. "He thinks the murderer was *actually* here in the cottage, now?"

"It's a theory, although I'm not sure why they wouldn't also take Foley's suitcase with him. Make it look like he really just ran off," Jo said, pulling off a bite of naan. Gwilym had come bearing research and an invite to the India Palace. "And I got a lecture about locking up."

"You really should do."

"I know." Jo winced. How had she gone from New York with ten dead bolts to North Yorkshire and an unlocked door? "I've just got used to leaving it unlocked during the day."

"No offense, but you *are* supposed to have a photographic memory," Gwilym reminded her.

Jo rolled her eyes. "It doesn't work like that," she protested (again). "You have the hippocampus, right? And you also have the frontal cortex. That's your executive command center—"

"For people who have those," Gwilym added.

"—and it's how you sort the important memories from the not-important ones. *And* you have a neural matrix map for retrieving and rebuilding them, but not *everything* is episodic."

"You've lost me."

Jo waggled her fingers, then stuck another piece of bread in her mouth before answering. More slowly.

"You take a prescription, right?"

"Adderall."

"You take it every day, in the same spot, at the same time. Your brain will compress all those memories of taking it into a single, long-running episode. Which is why it's easy to forget whether you did it or not."

"Which is why I have a Monday-through-Friday pillbox," Gwilym said, nodding. "What does that have to do with your front door?"

"Memory isn't stored; it's re-created," Jo said. That was partly what made it a fascinating study (and a very well received book in her once-upon-a-time back catalog). "You have bits and pieces, and you have to pull them together again to make a coherent picture. Usually with some embellishment from context."

"Wait a sec, does that mean you make up stuff to fill in the gaps?" He frowned. "Don't make me doubt you, Jo; it will upend my whole religion."

Jo laughed and assaulted the samosas with knife and fork.

"I don't have the same static and emotional clutter that most people do. I tend to remember details for themselves. But I still use association. Ronan Foley, for instance, is a surprised pigeon in a raincoat." She had to pause long enough for Gwilym to stop laughing before adding, "He didn't look like a pigeon. But he had wide eyes which looked that much wider for being heavy-lidded, and stared at me like he'd just hit a window."

"I'm suddenly frightened to inquire what I remind you of," Gwilym said, rubbing his eyes.

"Well, don't get murdered and I won't need to make a statement. Anyway, they found out who he was without my help."

"I want to see his picture, now. Can I?" Gwilym asked.

Jo shrugged. "I've not seen it. Apparently, they printed his obit. You can probably look it up. But *not now*!" she added, watching him reach for his phone. "Actually, though, I have a photo to show you. It's an earring."

Jo pulled out her phone and called up the image. "Care to comment?"

Gwilym starred at it a moment, turning the phone around and around.

"It's not an earring," he said. "It's a nose ring. Like the ones they found in the Upper Euphrates. You know, Kish? Tell Ingharra?"

"What."

"Tell Ingharra! It's a famous archeological site, third millennium BC."

Jo choked, reached for water and sputtered through a half swallow.

"As in three thousand years *before* year one? What the hell?"

"So, the site kind of *spans* the period, so it might not be exactly as old as that. I mean, that sort of filigree design is all over ancient Egypt, too. And nose rings were pretty popular." He leaned forward suddenly. "Did I just tell you something you didn't know?"

"Yes, a lot."

"Sexy, isn't it?" he asked.

Jo tossed a napkin at him. "How about you tell me things I don't know regarding Augustus John. Like why Augustus did Evelyn's painting and not the others."

"Right, right." Gwilym reached down to retrieve a file from his satchel. "We're gonna have some name confusion, so I'll deal with that first. Evelyn's sister was Gwen Ardemore, right? Well, Augustus had an older sister, too, *also* named Gwen."

"That part I knew, actually. Chen told me—I saw some of her paintings in York."

Gwilym deflated slightly. "So you know he was a famous painter from the Slade School of Art in London, too?"

"I do. But carry on!" she encouraged.

Gwilym slurped up a bit more vindaloo, then pulled out a reproduction daguerreotype showing a beautiful young woman in soft silver light.

"Augustus lived in Paris with Gwen and some other artists, and he meets this lovely lady: Ida Nettleship. They got married and had a kid, so Augustus suddenly needed a real job. He gets one working as an art teacher in Liverpool."

More photos escaped Gwilym's bag. Most were copies of Augustus's early art; red chalk drawings, Moses and the brazen serpent. Jo had seen several of the originals in York.

"His career doesn't *really* take off, though, until he meets the Signorina Estella Dolores Cerutti in 1900 and starts painting her. Estella was an Italian pianist who lived downstairs from Augustus's flat—and here she is!" Gwilym took out a color print-off, and Jo caught her breath. Three-quarter length and in full left-side profile was a dark eyed beauty. She was dressed in cream satin with delicate folds, her hands clasped together at the waist. She did not look *like* Evelyn, but the portraits lived in the same orbit.

"Gorgeous isn't it?" Gwilym asked. "The way the light falls just so, the softness of her hair. Apparently, Ida was jealous and made herself a whole new set of clothes to compete."

Jo could kind of see her point. Estella was majestic.

"Anyway, the portrait helped make his name. At least in artistic circles. William Ardemore would surely have heard of him," Gwilym said, taking a break to finish his platter.

Jo pushed away the remains of her curry and drew little circles on the tablecloth.

"William and Gwen marry in 1906. They have their portraits done that year—or the next. But Augustus John isn't the artist for those." The records kept by her solicitor, Rupert Selkirk, listed a relatively well known and accomplished regional artist, a man in high fashion at the time. "Evelyn comes to them sometime in 1906 or 1907, and William has her sit for someone just making his mark? Is it just because he enjoyed the one of signorina?"

"Maybe. You can see how similar to Evelyn's it is."

"Okay, but then why would Augustus not take credit for it or sign the painting? He's trying to make it in the world, and this is the guy who argued a painter has more rights than the sitter or the owner."

"Ah! I saved the best bit," Gwilym said. He pushed his dish away, cracked his knuckles and prepared to talk with his hands. "In 1903, Mr. John meets an artist model named Dorelia McNeill. Unsurprisingly, she becomes his lover. But it gets better; she was originally his sister Gwen's model—and also *her* lover. She even introduced them."

"The sister and brother shared the same lover?" Jo asked. Somewhat loudly, having temporarily forgotten they were in a public restaurant.

"So Augustus and Ida and Dorelia all set up house together, and he fathers kids by both of them."

Jo put her hands out as if to stop the train wreck that surely must have been.

"So he is living with both women, the same way William is living with Gwen and Evelyn?"

"Kinda yeah?" Gwilym said. "And it wasn't a secret or anything. So William Ardemore probably knew about the arrangement."

"Meaning?" Jo asked.

"Common ground? I dunno. Maybe Ardemore wanted the same thing. You know, not leaving Gwen—"

"And her money," Jo added.

"—and instead figured they could have their own little family unit. With Evelyn being the, um, bearer of heirs." Gwilym cleared his throat over this last bit, but it didn't keep Jo from hearing *chattel.*

"I really hope he wasn't keeping her around as his baby-maker," she said, grimacing in distaste. "And I'm still not sure how this explains why Augustus John didn't make it plain that was *his* masterwork."

"True. Though the guy was *also* broke at the time of painting. He lived in a traveling caravan with an expanding tribe of children, and two women. Maybe more women. Did you happen to look up his bio online? Under children, it just says *various.*" Gwilym scooped up the various photos and started tucking them back into his envelop. "Just saying, William and Gwen were rich, and a little money goes along way for Bohemian painters who keep fathering everybody's kids."

Jo puffed air, sending a loose strand of hair dancing.

"By 1908, Evelyn is dead, the painting presumably ruined, so maybe he just never got the chance to promote it. Plus,

Gwen and William disappeared from society shortly after Evelyn's death, so maybe an Ardemore portrait was no longer high profile to help his career. Who knows." Jo hunted the menu for *ras malai*, little white discs swimming in cardamom milk. They looked like spider egg sacs. She liked them anyway. "Chen said my uncle blamed Gwen Ardemore."

"For damaging the painting?"

"Someone threw acid on the eyes," Jo said.

"The windows to the soul," Gwilym added.

"Exactly. It's a psychological portrait of a woman in love."

"And Gwen couldn't live with it? I guess she didn't go in for polyamory." Gwilym hovered over the dessert menu. "Actually, I'm not sure Ida was all that into it, either. Some accounts say she felt like a drudge, looking after all the kids while Dorelia continued to model."

Jo ordered, then sat back thoughtfully. Two women, one adored, the other rejected. Like the Bible story about Jacob's wives, Leah and Rachel. Was it motive for murder? Was Gwen's jealousy and heartbreak bitter enough to lead to bloodshed? *She wouldn't*, Jo thought. Would she?

"I wonder what would have happened if they *had* lived all together," she said. "Happily, I mean. Or at least openly, like the artists."

"Artists can get away with that a lot better than lords, I think," Gwilym suggested. "Marriages of convenience and secret trysts for king and country."

Secrets. There shouldn't have to be secrets—Jo hated them. Look what they did to her mother . . . to her relationship with her mother, too. Look what had happened to Aiden, and then to Arthur, since he couldn't bring himself to come out of the closet. Look at how the world crushed and squeezed anyone who was different for the sake of "society says."

"You've gone quiet," Gwilym said. Jo blinked at him. Dessert had come and she'd been staring into space.

"Sorry. It's just—you know, my uncle was going to propose to Arthur. I don't think Arthur knows. Chen said he was tired of hiding. Told her he'd even give up the *Hiding* painting—"

Jo's brain ground gears. *He was going to give the painting back.* More importantly, he was going to take Evelyn *home.* Jo jumped out of her seat, remembered they were in a restaurant and forced herself to sit back down.

"Okay. So we all notice that Evelyn appears to be looking the wrong way. It's subtle. Takes you a minute to see it."

"Yeah, because it was repaired, so they looked at a photograph instead of the real thing. And because you said Uncle Aiden wanted Evelyn's eyes to be looking at him."

"I know, that's what we decided. But what if—*what if*— it's more intentional than that? What if it's a *clue*?" Jo almost squeaked the last word out.

"How do you mean?" Gwilym asked, half standing himself now.

"I have an idea. We need to take Evelyn to Arthur's flat," she said, digging out her phone. "I want Chen to be there, too. Are you busy?"

"Selling antiques out of my by-appointment-only in Swansea?" Gwilym asked, twirling his mustache. "Not likely."

Jo hadn't really thought so. She raised her hand as if in primary school to catch the waiter's attention, thumb typing texts to Chen and Arthur with the other.

"We're going to Newcastle first thing tomorrow."

CHAPTER 22

Debriefing occurred at six, Thursday morning. The sun had not yet come up, but at least the office was pleasantly cool. Green looked as mysteriously well-rested as ever; Gridley looked daggers at the clock. Andrews—very intelligently—brought a mother lode of pastry, and MacAdams had taken the initiative to bring everyone's preferred beverage: double-espresso, flat white and Andrews's "dirty" chai. They all looked tired, but perhaps none more so than Struthers, who was just walking in. He didn't take coffee, so MacAdams sent Andrews to make a strong cup of tea.

"Thanks for coming, Eric," he said.

The pathologist smiled weakly. "Would be all right if I'd had a full night of sleep," he said.

MacAdams clapped him on the shoulder in a way he hoped was bracing. After returning from Jo's cottage the night before, he'd called Struthers back to his lab. Knowing the murderer *may* have been back on-site, they needed—first, a much closer time of death, and second, a thorough reexamination of Foley's belongings. MacAdams hadn't been idle, either. He lifted documents from the printer and handed them around.

"Sea change," MacAdams said, taking his position in front. "I know it's tempting to follow the artifact trade, but I don't think that's what got Foley murdered.

"We've been struggling with this case for two reasons. First, we didn't know Foley, the man. Now we do, thanks to Tula Byrne. Second, we had no sense of the murderer apart from seemingly random weapon of choice. Now, we've got a bit more."

"All because Jo didn't lock her front door?" Gridley asked through a puff of powdered sugar. And when you put it that way, it did sound thin. But MacAdams rallied:

"Small details break cases," he said, returning to the board. "Let's make a list. The murderer ice-packs the body, then later returns to the cottage for soap, so he's careful—fastidious," he said, borrowing Jo's word. "What else does this tell us?"

"They're bold? It's a hell of a risk, going back," Green said. "What if someone saw him?"

"Yeah. Plus, how'd he know he could get in, even?" Andrews asked. "*We* know the door was unlocked, but did he?"

"Or she," MacAdams said. Green acquiesced this time.

"It's a good point. You found Foley's key on the nightstand; he didn't even have it on him when he got killed."

MacAdams smiled grimly. "We found it on the nightstand. We *assumed* Foley didn't take it with him." He nodded to Struthers, still blowing on his tea.

"Because we didn't find any trace of blood in the cottage, we knew the victim was murdered somewhere else. As a result, not *everything* had been tested for prints."

"The door?" Gridley asked. Struthers made a half-offended *of course* noise.

"Obviously, but no usable prints from the latch handle. And since both doors were open, with the key to hand—"

"No one dusted the *key*," MacAdams said. "I picked it up from Jo's last night, sent it to Eric."

"A nice fat print, thumb, I think," Struthers said. "Only it doesn't match our victim's."

"It didn't match anyone in the database, either," MacAdams explained. "But it *did* match the extra prints we found in Foley's flat."

"Holy shite, boss. You're saying the murderer *actually* walked into Netherleigh Cottage while Jo was asleep?" Green's eyes hovered in their whites. "What if she'd heard him—what if she woke up and caught him? Also, why the hell did he bring the key back?"

That had kept him up most of the night.

"I don't have an answer to any of that," he said. "Jo *didn't* wake up, thank God. As to the murderer, he may have been looking for something. Struthers has been attempting to find possible prints or DNA on items in Foley's bag."

"We've no clear evidence—yet—that anything had been rummaged," Struthers said, but MacAdams already noted at least two inconsistencies. First, why throw the muddy trousers on top of everything else? Second, the damaged pair didn't look like anything in Foley's closets. Pale trousers, the sort of thing you might wear to deck chairs—and a size smaller than the pair Foley wore when he died. He'd worn them, they matched the description Jo gave, but it was one more inconsistency.

"I don't think the various contents are going to yield us much more—especially as our killer doesn't have prior," Struthers cautioned. "So I spent most of the night reading tea leaves. Viscera, actually. Trying to narrow down the time of death."

"We've got that at between elevven, when Jo last saw him, and 3:00 a.m.," Green confirmed.

Struthers nodded. "Right," he sighed. "I thought I could confirm it with stomach contents. No luck."

"Okay, I'll ask," Andrews said, raising his hand. "How would the stomach help, even?"

Struthers stifled a yawn before continuing. "Well, if you ate something right before being murdered, it wouldn't be digested. It takes four to six hours to clear the gut. I thought we might be able to work backward if I knew his last meal—maybe even work out what type of food, and whether he consumed it here in town."

Andrews put down the chocolate éclair and wiped his hands on his trousers. "Sorry I asked."

"I'm rather sorry I bothered," Struthers said. "Stomach told me nothing. I *still* think he must have been murdered *very* soon after eleven. Liver mortis set in even before we packed him back to my lab."

This time, no one asked—but it was an important point.

"Blood pooling," MacAdams said.

Struthers nodded. "Deterioration of blood cells, more accurately." Still standing next to Andrews, he borrowed his arm and pressed down hard with his thumb. "See how it turns white? In a second or two, the pink returns. When a body's been dead twelve hours or so, the color doesn't change anymore."

"So killer goes back inside with the key," Andrews said, rubbing the depression vigorously. "*And* the murder took place closer to eleven? Doesn't that suggest the murderer went *to* the cottage to get Foley—and back inside shortly after?"

It seemed likely, but not definitive. They had searched all around the grounds and found no evidence of foul play; Foley had been spirited off *somewhere* to be murdered.

MacAdams addressed the room. "In review, this murderer steals soap to tidy up the car and even returns the key. It sounds coolheaded, well planned. Except they doesn't wear gloves, and they kill Foley with an object not well-suited to be a weapon."

Struthers lifted a bin bag onto an empty chair, then took out several glass curios and the ashtray. Several had evidently shattered.

"I was able to replicate the damage with various objects, but only the ashtray worked in a single blow—and most left shards.

I'm convinced now that this was a heavy object, resilient to shattering. If glass, tempered."

"Then it's time to go looking in Newcastle," MacAdams said. "At the Burnhopes'. They are, after all, into the *arts*. What about our other leads?"

"Gimme a sec!" Gridley said, snatching something from the printer. "I got the guest list from the charity ball at Lime Tree Greens. I also spoke for two hours with various art dealers in York and Newcastle to see which of them were big collectors. *And* I cross-referenced with the booking list at Abington Arms."

She had highlighted a name: Gerald Standish. "He's a Newcastle man, made his money in oil and gas. Big giver at the charity."

"Good work," he said. "We'll look him up, too."

From the back, Andrews gave a wave.

"Oi! Sketch artist has a rough copy of the mystery woman ready. You can pick it up at the front desk."

MacAdams fished his keys out of a pocket and beckoned to Green. It was time to pay the Burnhopes a visit.

* * *

They didn't stop at Costa this time; MacAdams and Green chose assorted foods from Tesco and made it to Hammersmith by nine, hoping to catch Stanley, first, then Ava at home. Unfortunately, Burnhope wasn't in. MacAdams half wondered if it was an attempt to avoid them. It wouldn't work. Fifteen minutes brought them to the Burnhope residence, its top floor skylights glinting in morning sun. Green rang the bell; as before, Nanny Maryam was the one to answer. She recognized them this time, but she still didn't smile.

"Please wait here," she directed.

A moment later, Ava Burnhope took her place to usher them inside.

"Trisha Simmons told us you were coming," she said, sweeping along in a floor-length duster of sea-foamgreen, MacAdams would have said, except so desaturated to the point where color words seemed irrelevant. He wasn't just looking at her, however. He was casing the entire house.

"He is working from home, I take it?" he asked, eyes straying to the mantelpiece as she led them through. Two bronze rabbits. A sizable freestanding clock.

"He is. And does," Ava said. "There's a conference room upstairs and he's in a meeting." Ava slow-blinked at them. "You're welcome to wait, though I don't know how long he'll be."

They were in the rear music room again, exactly as MacAdams hoped. He wondered suddenly if it was soundproof. What might happen in such a space with the shades drawn? The glass "muses" stood as before, far too large to be used as weapons. But they weren't the only sculptures on display.

"You two patronize the arts, I understand?" MacAdams asked, choosing a seat. Ava did not like her household disturbed, clearly. But she wasn't rude, either; she took one of the chairs for herself, all poise and social graces.

"Of course. As you have clearly seen."

"What about that one?" MacAdams asked. He indicated a figure in molten silver and orange, the size and shape of a cockatiel.

"Local artist," Ava said. "Part of a series of ten."

"May I?" MacAdams asked, intending to pick it up. Ava stood to intercept him.

"It's fragile. Blown glass, Detective. You can see how delicate." She picked it up herself and brought it gently to his notice—but didn't allow him to touch. Regardless, it was no murder weapon.

"Do you ever purchase anything older? Or foreign?" Green asked. Ava's look remained aloof, if slightly vacant.

"I don't follow," she said, replacing the glass bird.

"Antiquities. From Syria," MacAdams clarified—and watched her eyes narrow precipitously.

"As in a building site full of stolen goods, Detective? No." She stood up. "I am not a fool. We've already answered to York police, and I understand you have questions. But don't pretend pleasantries and don't make assumptions."

Whatever else Ava might be—philanthropist, pianist, patron of the arts, suspected murderer—she was at least impressive about it. And he had to respect plain dealing.

"All right. I do plan to ask about the artifacts."

"I don't know anything about them."

"Perhaps your friends do? Gerald Standish?" MacAdams asked.

"I don't know him, either," she said resolutely. He didn't believe her in the slightest. But it wasn't his last card trick.

"He was one of the collectors on the guest list for the gala. But no matter. Maybe you can help me with this instead."

The sketch artist had produced a rough but serviceable rendition based on Arianna's description back at the hotel. A young subject looked up from the folded paper, peaked chin, round cheeks still in puppy fat. The eyes were dark and large, almond shaped. Hair: black. He presented the image to Ava.

"Do you recognize this woman?" he asked.

"Not immediately. Should I?"

"She's missing, and possibly in trouble. Look carefully," he said. Ava reengaged her attention.

"What kind of trouble?" she asked, peering down with greater interest.

"The kind that got Ronan Foley killed," MacAdams said.

"I told you, I didn't know Ronan Foley."

"That's strange. He called your house several times."

"Well, I never spoke to him."

"You're sure?" MacAdams asked. Ava's gaze could freeze quicksilver.

"I am," she assured him.

Thankfully, Green picked up the broken thread. We're asking because he's been keeping company with this girl," she said, crossing the room. Now she and Ava looked at the sketch together. "Young. Very young, we gather. Vulnerable."

"Is she an immigrant?" Ava asked.

It surprised MacAdams—Green, too.

"Why would you ask that, Ms. Burnhope?"

Ava handed back the drawing and fixed her with those pale eyes.

"I spend most of my time in charity work for refugees. Most of them are young—very young—and vulnerable."

"We think she's in trouble," Green said.

"Trouble is what *makes* a refugee," Ava assured her. "Ukraine, Gaza."

"And Syria," MacAdams said suddenly.

"I'm sorry?"

"That's where Maryam comes from, isn't it?" MacAdams asked. "You said she'd been with you for a year, from Syria." Ava's face remained placid as ever, but the hard edge had returned again.

"I don't see why that is relevant."

"Don't you?" Green asked. "You could scarcely find more trouble than the Syrian crisis. Thirteen years of people displacement—"

"Funding war crimes through traffic in artifacts," MacAdams added. "Like the ones we found in York."

"I *know* of the horrors," Ava said tersely. "Better than you. And I don't condone the looting of vulnerable cultures. But frankly, I don't see what that has to do with Maryam or why you insist on asking me about her."

"All right. Let's talk about Fresh Start instead," MacAdams said. "How many Syrian refugees have you sponsored?"

"Many. Obviously." Ava stood up and walked to the tall windows. "You say you know how terrible it is there. Have you seen it? Have you looked into the eyes of children who have?"

She wrapped her arms around her willowy frame, despite the sun and its warmth. "I suppose for you I'm a wealthy socialite, making good on my charitable giving. Don't think I haven't heard that before."

Her voice changed with emotion; the velvety quality grew somehow stronger, more intense and varied. A symphony.

"We cannot take them all," she said, still looking away over the manicured gardens. "We bring a few, and they weep at night for their sisters and brothers, cousins and grandparents. Why can't we save them?"

When Ava turned about, her glass-like eyes held unfallen tears.

"Do you know what it's like to say we *can't*? Half of Maryam's family remains behind. We don't even know if they are still alive. All this—all *this*—" she swept her arm about the room with its bespoke furnishings "—and we cannot save them all because of paperwork and politics and because no one *cares*."

MacAdams allowed her to finish, and for the silence to stretch. Then he held up the sketch again.

"I care," he said. "Ronan Foley wasn't who he pretended to be. His real name is Rhyan Flannery, and he was mixed up in antiquities trafficking, art theft, forgery and maybe worse. He was also involved with this woman—or girl. *You* say you didn't know him. If it's true, then you have every reason to help me—because this woman is missing, and I think she's in trouble."

Ava's cool exterior had softened when she spoke about the refugees. Now it shattered. She looked no different to the unpracticed eye, but there was a human under there.

"A forger. An art thief," she repeated. "And you say he was Stanley's partner?"

"*And* that he called your house. Repeatedly," Green added.

MacAdams watched the import of that sink in before adding, "There's a connection here somewhere between money and artifacts and murder and *that* girl. If you really want to help, then it's about time your husband finished his meeting."

Ava nodded. It was slight, but resolute. Then she turned around and walked out of the room.

"Follow me, please."

CHAPTER 23

Thursday, 10:00

Jo's hands felt clammy and her heart kept hopping into her throat. She rested one hand on the cloth-draped and carefully wrapped portrait of Evelyn Davies, and used the other to steady herself against the elevator walls.

"Ready?" Gwilym asked when they arrived on the right floor.

Fortuitous, Fortinbras, for fuck's sake.

"Nope, but here goes," she said and they lifted the painting and carried it to Arthur's door. Gwilym rang the bell, but scarcely needed to—the door swung open to reveal an impeccably suited Arthur, Chen in vermillio, and two excitable dogs.

"Welcome, welcome! Come in." Arthur helped them deposit the painting against the far wall. Jo noted that *Hiding* had already been taken down and was sitting next to the breakfast table. There were also four glasses of champagne set out and sparkling in the sunlight. Introductions were made and hands shaken, then Gwilym gave Jo a nudge.

"Ready when you are, Hercule," he said with a wink.

Jo nodded, and the two of them removed the cover and lifted

Evelyn into place. She heard Arthur gasp behind her; he'd never seen Evelyn before. The look on Chen's face was more subtle, like welcoming an old friend. Jo wasn't planning to give Evelyn up, though; this was official business.

"Thank you, everyone, for coming," she said, feeling weirdly like she was about to give the garden opening address again. "We're here today to solve a missing persons mystery."

Solve /sälv/ verb: to find an answer to, explanation for, or means of effectively dealing with a problem. Jo took a breath, and carried on.

"Evelyn Davies fell in love with her brother-in-law in 1906 or early 1907. They started as confidants. They wrote letters. In 1908, Evelyn is pregnant, dies and is buried in the Ardemore House basement, her painting is partly ruined in an acid attack and her lover and her sister leave the house forever. We don't know what happened to the baby."

Missing /ˈmɪsɪŋ/ adjective, verb, noun: unable to be found, to feel the lack of, someone who is absent—lost.

Jo clasped her hands.

"My mother kept secrets. Aiden kept secrets, too. But I think Aiden meant his to be solved." She nodded at Chen. "What did he tell you about the eyes?"

"He asked me to paint them looking a different direction—just slightly—from where they should've been looking," Chen said. "It gives her an uncanny appearance."

"Is that what it is?" Arthur asked. "Something is so strange and haunting about her."

"You're not wrong," Gwilym said. He had managed to befriend Hans, who was resting in his arms. Jo bounced slightly on her heels. It was coming down to it, and the anticipation was sending little sparks of electricity all through her.

"Aiden meant to give *Hiding* back to Chen. He planned to take Evelyn here, and I believe he meant her to be hung on this wall, just as she is right now. He requested Chen paint the eyes like this for a specific reason. *So* . . ." Jo walked to where the small party stood, then turned to face the portrait with them. "What is Evelyn supposed to be looking at?"

"The mantelpiece," Gwilym said.

"No," Chen corrected gently. "What's *on* the mantelpiece."

All eyes turned to look at the Russian doll.

"You told me that was a gift from Aiden," Jo said.

Arthur nodded, approaching it. "For Christmas—our last Christmas. He'd only just been diagnosed, but I've opened it before." He picked up the doll with careful hands. Layer by layer, he dismantled the dolls until all were standing in a line upon the mantel. Gwilym put Hans on the sofa and picked up the last doll.

"This one isn't original," he said, pulling a jewelry magnifier out of his vest pocket. "Antiques are my line of work—eh—*when* I'm working. It's got the wrong color of red. Also . . ." He gave it a slight shake. "The last nesting doll in a series is supposed to be solid."

Jo took the doll from Gwilym.

"If it's hollow, then it opens," she said, turning it in the light. When angled just so against the windows, a faint line appeared. "There's a seam! Look."

Now it was Arthur's turn, but Jo noticed his hands were trembling.

"Sorry, I—You think there's something inside? He didn't say. Why wouldn't he say?" Arthur tried twisting the doll to no avail.

"He wasn't ready to say," Chen said quietly. "Give it here, pet. Welshman, you say it's a reproduction?"

"Yes ma'am."

"Good." Chen dropped the doll on the floor and crushed it with her heel. Arthur gave a little cry—Jo may have squeaked—and both dogs lost their tiny little minds. But Chen merely leaned down, long fingers scooping up something among the fragments.

"For you," she said to Arthur with a flourish. A tiny piece

of paper, no bigger than a cookie fortune. It said "Arthur and Ægle".

"That's Aiden's handwriting," Arthur said, his face suddenly ashy. "The Laing—it's an art gallery. It's the first place we went together after meeting at Chen's art exhibit."

"Who is Ægle?" Gwilym asked.

Jo's brain spit up a volley of factoids; Ægle as one of the Greek nymphs of evening, Ægle and her sisters as daughters of Zeus, or of Hesperus, or—

"An Etruscan queen—in a long-form poem by Sir Edward Bulwer-Lytton, about King Arthur," Arthur explained. "I took Aiden to see the painting *King Arthur and Queen Aegle in the Happy Valley*."

Jo's eyes strayed back to Evelyn's portrait. Aiden had used a painting—to point to another painting—and to remind Arthur of their first date. This wasn't an end. It was the beginning.

"Can we go see it now?" Jo asked.

Arthur looked uncertain, but Chen picked up her umbrella cane and pointed to the door.

"Oh yes, child. *Right* now," she said.

★ ★ ★

The Laing looked like a warehouse married to a church. Their little party stood in a room with arched ceilings and deep blue walls, lost in the faraway snow of distant Alps. "John Martin, oil on canvas, 1849." It had been painted only five years before the artist's death, an alien landscape of crag and tower and cliff under a thumbnail moon and endless expanse of night. In the foreground stood two tiny figures, King Arthur and Queen Ægle. The museum label included a part of the poem, and Arthur read it aloud:

"Still, hand in hand, they range the lulled isle,
Air knows no breeze, scarce sighing to their sighs."

"It's my favorite painting," Arthur explained, a gentle blush forming at his cheeks. "And *not* just because it's also my name. This is the Happy Valley, a mythic place in the Alps where everyone is safe from the changes of the ancient world. But Arthur doesn't stay there; he chooses change—and everything that comes with it."

"Including death," Chen added.

"Yes. But life first." Arthur clasped his hands behind his back, his clear eyes wandering over the painting. "Traditions don't make us safe, and staying the same doesn't keep us from dying." Beside him, Chen lay her jeweled hand against her heart.

"Speaking truth," she whispered—and Jo felt an internal contraction, as though her heart were turning inside out. Arthur and Chen were the brave ones; Aiden knew that, was trying to tell them so. He wanted to change, but didn't know how, and started the journey too late.

"Arthur?" Jo asked. "That day. Standing here. Do you remember what happened next?"

"It was a very long time ago," he said. Because everyone said that—but memory existed outside of time. Memory *superseded* time, squashed it, lengthened it, chunked it, pulled it like taffy. Jo grasped both of Arthur's hands and squeezed hard.

"Close your eyes. Quick, just do it. In your brain is a map; you just need to follow it. Aiden bought Chen's painting. You invited him to see your favorite painting, the one that mattered most to you. Now—" she turned him toward the painting again "—look at Arthur and Ægle and tell us about the day."

Arthur let out a long breath. He was close now, almost close enough to set off alarms—his vision enveloped in layers of oil and varnish.

"It was August," he murmured.

"Good," said Chen—in a far more soothing manner than Jo could muster at the moment. "August 23, and it was raining the night of the gallery opening," she added.

Arthur kept his eyes on the painting, but a half smile worked across his features.

"It was—I didn't have an umbrella. Adien offered to share so we walked together. I didn't want to go back to my car; I didn't want the evening to end. The Laing wasn't far; I asked him if he'd like to see a painting."

Jo could picture them: two men in summer suits, not holding hands but permitted the closeness of a shared umbrella in the rain.

"He didn't know the poem. I think I might have gone on about it for some time." Arthur's voice had grown quieter, husky. "*He* talked about Greek epic and compared the painted sky to a wine-dark sea. And I . . . asked him if he'd like to join me for a glass. God; I'd forgotten that! We went to the Velmont Hotel for dinner."

"Gorgeous," Chen said, patting his arm gently. "Absolute luxury, the Velmont."

Arthur nodded, but seemed slightly unsteady on his feet.

"They had a 1999 red burgundy; the best year, I think," he said with the ghost of a smile. "It was perfect."

Jo hadn't meant to lead a scavenger hunt through Arthur's memories. She wouldn't want anyone doing the same to *hers*. But Arthur had changed, somehow. Gone was the winsome businessman with his sleek hair and impeccable manner. His eyes shone as though misted—and he hadn't released Jo's hand, almost as though he feared to walk on his own.

"Are you all right?" she asked.

"I'm *not* all right," Arthur said. "It feels like dreaming. There are things I'd not thought about. Afraid to think about. I'm not sure. I've not even been back to the Velmont since Aiden passed."

"Then it's time you go again," Chen said, giving him a sideways squeeze.

Gwilym gave himself a once-over.

"Luxury, you said. I'm not exactly dressed for this." He

plucked at his blue jeans. Chen merely offered up her arm, as though for him to escort her.

"Tut, the restaurant does lunch—and my art hangs on all the walls. They won't toss you on your ear, pet."

Gwilym and Chen headed toward the far door, as though the matter was settled.

Jo bit her lip. "We don't have to do this," she said to Arthur.

He just pointed to the Happy Valley and its tiny, fragile inhabitants.

"We *do*, though. I do. And I don't think I can on my own."

CHAPTER 24

Thursday, 10:30

The fourth floor of the Burnhope residence turned out to be a massive solarium with a ceiling of glass. MacAdams really should have predicted as much. The space, almost entirely open-plan, boasted an enormous meeting room, a casing with books and almost as many business trophies as the main office, as well as an extended conference room table. The rest of the house had preserved a kind of warmth, made possible by plants and music stands and the accoutrements of living. The fourth floor had none of this; sleek, modern, it might as well have been a suite of Hammersmith and Company. Burnhope sat at his desk, back to the door.

"Finished with your meeting, I take it," MacAdams said.

Burnhope turned around in a hurry. It was the first time MacAdams had seen surprise there; it gave him a curious open-eyed look.

"I wasn't aware you were here," he said.

"Oh, I think you were," MacAdams replied. He had to walk a line here; they had nothing—yet—to bring him in over. But for once he had an advantage, and he was going to make the most of it. "You surely know we would be coming to ask about York."

"Yes. I already spoke to the Newcastle police about this, and I've made a statement for York Central, too," Burnhope replied easily. "I told them, and I'm happy to tell you: I knew *nothing* about this."

"One of your close colleagues imported millions in stolen goods under your nose, and you . . . just had no idea at all?" MacAdams asked. "You seem too smart for that kind of con."

"There would be records of deliveries, shipments, documents to sign, distribution . . ." Green ticked them off on her long fingers. "Here you are, the boss of it all."

Burnhope's expression was cool, though still amiable.

"Have a seat, Detectives," he said. "First of all, you don't run a multinational company by being the one who checks every invoice and shipping receipt. I already told you that I'd given the York property to Foley to run."

"And he ran it into the ground—and you didn't check up."

"I didn't know I had to. Look at this from my perspective, why don't you? A company and its employees depend on trust and reputation. I trusted Foley." Burnhope folded his hands on the desk and sighed. "He betrayed that trust. He might well ruin our reputation, which means he betrayed all of Hammersmith."

"I entirely agree," MacAdams said, taking the seat he'd been offered. "A company with all these awards—" he gestured to the wall of glittering teardrops "—depends a lot on its reputation. The market isn't easy . . . and everyone knows it's slowed in the last decade. And now you've been betrayed by someone you trusted. One might almost say it was a motive."

Burnhope placed both hands upon his desk. "I did *not* kill Ronan Foley."

"Good, because he doesn't exist," Green said. She opened the file folder she'd been carrying and handed out several photographs.

"What am I looking at?" Burnhope sighed, though MacAdams could see it well enough: a young man and woman on their wedding day.

"Rhyan Flannery," Green said. "Irish. From Belfast."

"I don't know him."

"Look closer," MacAdams encouraged. "You told me you were only in Ireland as a child. You must have gone back now and then, surely. Perhaps you met a man looking for a new start. A *Fresh Start*, let's say."

Burnhope put the photographs down and attempted to push them away.

"I don't know what you're talking about, and I take offence that you'd bring my charity work for rehoming refugees into this."

"Stanley, *this* is Ronan Foley," MacAdams said. And for the second time, he saw the look of shock. It didn't appear to be faked. Burnhope snatched up of the photographs of Foley and Tula again.

"This? Is Foley? And that's . . . his wife?"

"They are still married, in fact," Green said. "Perhaps you knew that. She lives in Abington."

"Look, I knew Foley had *been* married, once. He mentioned it in passing. I didn't know where she lived, and I sure didn't think they were still together."

"Was it because he had another woman?" MacAdams asked. He'd been trying to catch Burnhope out, get him to admit to some knowledge previously repressed. But the man merely gave him a smile, salesman like.

"There had been women, off and on, through the years. Christmas party dates and the like, nothing serious."

"You told me you weren't friends. That he stayed out of your personal life. But he came to Christmas parties."

"Company Christmas parties, Detective."

"Yet he called your house. Your landline," MacAdams pressed.

The hooded eyes remained slack. "Our landline is publicly

available, not that anyone uses a phone book these days. If you say he called, he did. That doesn't make us close companions." The slight brogue had resurfaced, but it was proving difficult to get a real reaction out of Burnhope. Emotion, after all, led to more mistakes.

"Maybe he wasn't calling *you*," MacAdams said.

"I beg your pardon?"

"Mr. Burnhope," Green said, still standing at his elbow with the folder. "I have here a list of times he called your house using a burner phone. Can you verify that this is your home number?"

"It is . . . but that doesn't signify—"

"A burner phone, Stanley," MacAdams repeated. "A person only uses one of those if they don't want to be traced. A person who has changed their name, who is a devious criminal and who—for instance—doesn't want his boss to know he's calling his wife."

The expression on Burnhope's face wasn't one of surprise, not this time. It was stone-cold anger.

"I should kick you out of my house for even suggesting something like that."

"We are not making accusations," Green said, throwing MacAdams a rather pointed glance. "We're just trying to understand why he phoned you eight times when you *claim* you weren't on personal terms."

"I've had just about enough of this," Stanley said. "What is it that you have against me? I run a successful business, I help organize a charity, Ava and I were both *at* a charity event when all this happened."

"By *all this* you mean Ronan Foley's murder," MacAdams clarified.

Burnhope nodded grudgingly. "Yes. Look, the man worked for me for years. Over a decade, you understand. I investigated his references, and they checked out. I didn't know he'd been lying about himself then—and I didn't know he was lying to me *now*. I don't even know when it all started." He drew himself up a little, a man getting his composure back. "Did he call the house? Maybe. People do. Should I have been suspicious? Maybe. But unlike some people, I *trust* my *wife*."

"You don't believe she was having an affair with Foley," MacAdams asked, delivering a poke he hoped might reignite his passions. It didn't work.

"I do not. The two of them wouldn't even have anything to talk about."

Green had never bought MacAdams's theory about Ava. Which was why her next comment surprised MacAdams.

"Actually, they might have plenty to talk about," she said. "Like two million or more in black market antiquities stolen from Syria and on their way to collectors. Rich men, like yourself."

Burnhope got out of his chair so fast that it nearly triggered MacAdams's reflexes. But he was *laughing*.

"Please do look around yourself," he said. "I collect art, yes—modern art. I have no interest in antiquities. And have a look at Ava's music room, if you like. Modern. Regional and local. Now you are grasping at straws."

"Maybe you don't collect," MacAdams said, not willing to let the line of inquiry die out. "But someone does. Someone with ties to you, to the charity, to Abington. Come on, Burnhope. You play golf with these people, you go to balls with them. Black-tie people."

"People like Gerald Standish," Green added.

An indistinguishable sound escaped him Burnhope and he scrubbed fingers through his hair.

"*Dr.* Standish has sponsored more refugees than anyone—hundreds of thousands of pounds spent, lives made better, people changed. He's opened his own home as a halfway station. He serves on two committees for the refugee council. *Why* are you targeting the very people trying to make a difference in the world? Foley was the bad apple. Can't you see that? Let the blame fall on him."

"The consequences certainly did," Green said.

Burnhope's hands had found pockets, probably to keep them still, but his anger was growing palpable.

"Sit down, Mr. Burnhope," MacAdams said. "You told it from your perspective; now I'll give you mine. This isn't some one-off operation. Foley couldn't get the pieces here on his own; he must have connections—a network—in Syria. *You* have connections to Syria. Your charity does, too. And Hammersmith is an international company with its own network, buying power and access to tax havens. At the same time, both you and your wife collect art and know the art world. And then you have friends like Standish, who collect art and antiquities—from Syria. I'm sure you'll agree, that's expecting a lot from coincidence."

"Syria is not a coincidence," Burnhope said. He'd resumed his seat, and simultaneously seemed to deflate. He reached for a framed photo near his laptop.

"Do you want to know why I care about Syria? Why Ava does? Why we both work so damn hard?" he asked. "My children, *our* children, are from Syria. We adopted them five years ago. Look at them."

They stared up at MacAdams with laughing expressions. Dark hair, olive skin. One of them had pale blue eyes. He guessed one to be eight, the other six.

Burnhope was still speaking. "Their village was destroyed. Their families were probably murdered."

"I didn't know that," MacAdams admitted, though it explained Ava's earlier emotional response. It was also chewing a few holes in a few theories.

"You wouldn't. We don't tart them up and trot them about; we work hard to keep them out of the press. They're *children*, Detective." Burnhope presently had the high ground and MacAdams knew it. "I don't care about your 'coincidence' theory. And I don't care for your tone. Do your best to find Foley's murderer, but leave my family out of it. We've done nothing wrong. And if you want to speak to me again, it will be with my lawyer."

"I'm sorry, but we're not quite finished," MacAdams said, without moving to stand. He took the folded police sketch from his pocket. "This is a rough drawing of Foley's girlfriend—possibly fiancée. Ava didn't recognize her, but suggested she might be a refugee. Did she come through Fresh Start?"

Burnhope hesitated. "Ava said?" he asked.

"Yes. She doesn't know much about your business. But you both work in the charity; is that right?" MacAdams asked. He handed him the drawing, and Burnhope took it.

"Yes, we . . . share. Ava cares deeply about refugees." He looked over the image with interest.

"You recognize her, don't you," MacAdams said flatly. But Burnhope didn't bend.

"No. I've never seen her before."

"You sure? We have a witness at a hotel in Abington. She and Foley had been seeing one another for at least six months," Green said.

Burnhope's eyes roved the image, and in the silence, MacAdams pushed their advantage.

"She may be carrying his child," he added. "And she—and the child—might be in danger."

Burnhope's eyes flitted up and back down. "I don't know her. She wasn't sponsored through Fresh Start."

"You're sure? Would Ms. Wagner say differently?"

Burnhope pushed the drawing back at him. "I'm sure. And for the record, Sophie Wagner is above reproach. A model citizen."

"Is that why you are such a big donor for her charity?" Green asked with affected disinterest. Over the past few years, his contributions had amounted to more than seventy thousand.

Burnhope's face closed like a book, personal emotional register snuffed out. He gave them a benign smile.

"You just can't bear the idea that we're the good guys, can you?" he asked. Then he stood and pointed toward the door. "Leave. Now."

"We will. Until we have more questions," MacAdams said. He opened the door for Green and ushered them both down the grand stairs. They hadn't quite got to the bottom when they spotted Maryam coming from the kitchen.

"So sorry. Excuse me," she said, bowing her head over a tray of sandwiches. "For the children."

"We'll be out of your way," MacAdams said. "But maybe you can help me with something?" He began to unfold the image once again, but Green poked him solidly in the ribs.

"Incoming," she whispered.

Maryam curtsied, then hurried past and up the stairs behind them.

Ava suddenly reappeared, her eyes narrowed, and pointed a switchblade index finger. "You have bothered us enough! I told you before, Maryam has been through a great deal. She doesn't like police or government officials. You wouldn't, either, in her shoes. I want you to leave."

Hospitality had its limits, MacAdams supposed.

"Thank you for your time, Ms. Burnhope," he said, tipping a hat he wasn't wearing but force of habit. "We'll be in touch."

She followed them to the door and was sure to close—and lock—it after them.

"What now?" Green asked once they were a good distance away.

"Now, we pressure Ms. Wagner."

"About Burnhope? The charity?"

"All that," he agreed. But he was thinking about the list of donors from the gala, including Gerald Standish; the big "giver" was also an art collector. He wasn't willing to let that go just yet.

★ ★ ★

MacAdams parked the car under the lime trees. Green wagged a finger at him.

"You'll have a sticky mess." He'd forgotten about that; Common Lime—for some reason always planted on estates and along streets, despite the fact that they attracted aphids—dropped syrupy sap, and did not actually produce any citrus fruits. They were linden trees, really, "noble stands" of them in older novels he'd read as a kid. He reparked the car, thinking about what a terrible choice it was for an actual golf course; of course, the trees, like the original stone structure, predated its current incarnation. An awful lot—about an awful lot—was a nod to aristocratic tradition and bygone days and nothing more.

"Detective Chief Inspector James MacAdams, Detective Sergeant Green," he introduced them to the greeter, presenting credentials. "We're here to see Sophie Wagner." They hadn't yet been pointed to a seat when the charming barkeep spotted them.

"Back again!" Simon said. Today, however, he was wearing golf gear.

"Not pouring drinks, I take it?" Green asked.

"Golf lessons. I give them on Thursdays." He winked above a broad smile. "Usually to elder ladies, I fear."

Well-monied ones, MacAdams thought privately. Sophie employed refugees and made ample use of her jack-of-all-trades son. Shrewd business dealing? Or a sign of trouble in the pocketbook? Simon waved a gloved hand and trotted off before MacAdams could ask him to identify the missing woman.

"We'll catch him later," he said to Green. "I'd rather show it round the current Fresh Start staff." In fact, he intended to while waiting on Sophie to find them.

"So, still think Ava and Foley are a thing?" Green asked him.

He had to admit, it was looking less and less likely.

"Gold star to you," he said. "Not a jilted lover."

"Not one who gets revenge on refugee women," Green said. "Particularly not pregnant ones."

"Agreed."

"You fancy Sophie might be?" she asked as they wandered down another corridor. It was a question worth answering. But best answered, perhaps, in her absence. If, that is, they could get any of her many supposedly thankful employees to talk about her.

Finding their way around the club provided some exercise. A sprawling set of interconnected buildings and extensive grounds—kitchens, banquet hall, private rooms. The land Lime Tree occupied made up part of an estate long ago, but was converted to a golf club in the 1890s. Harold Wagner purchased it in 1999, and his wife, Sophie, succeeded him at his passing, raising up young Simon and turning the club—somehow—into the platform for Fresh Start in 2002. The charity grew faster than the club memberships. Then again, this seemed to be an overall trend nationally.

"It's generational," Green said as they peered into a busy kitchen prep room. "Young people don't do clubs and golf."

"Rebellion against their parents?" MacAdams asked.

"Maybe. Or, you know. The world is on fire and hitting a ball with sticks feels a bit silly."

MacAdams shrugged. "It's about rubbing shoulders, though, isn't it?" he asked, hunting the kitchen's flushed faces for recent sponsored refugees. "Business types doing deals on the green."

"People don't have to rub shoulders anymore, boss. It's what Zoom is for. Over there—is that one of them?" MacAdams had just glimpsed Anje, the woman they met on their last visit to the country club. She was headed out through the rear door, toward the patio.

"You take the left; I'll take the right," MacAdams said.

Would she actively avoid them? Probably not. But he wasn't

taking chances, and meeting outside would be less threatening. He'd found the side door, but by the time he crossed the grass, Green had already intercepted Anje.

"And this is Detective MacAdams," Green said, giving him a nod. "We were wondering if you could look at a picture for us, tell us if you recognize the person in it?"

MacAdams held it up, but Anje looked away. "I can't. I have to collect the herbs for tonight."

"Just look, please?" Green asked; she barely gave it a glance.

"I—I don't know. I don't think so. I have to go."

It was deeply suspicious . . . or was it? MacAdams noted that none of the sponsored refugees wanted to look police in the face. And perhaps that made sense. This did not bode well.

"You could really help us if you took a closer look," he said, but his phone had begun to buzz. The number wasn't familiar; he handed the sketch over to Green.

"MacAdams here," he said.

"Oh! Detective? I—I didn't really expect you to answer." The voice was excited, breathy, and not wholly unfamiliar.

"This is?"

"Sorry, sorry! I'm Emma. Rosalind's foster mother. You said if there was anything else, I should call—" she began, and MacAdams nearly dropped the damn phone trying to fish out his notepad. He wedged the mobile between ear and shoulder.

"Yes! Go on," he said, nodding that Green should continue. Anje was already shaking her head negative; she didn't know the girl in the drawing. If Green was asking her about Sophie, he didn't hear over Emma's rapid-fire speech.

"Well, I took her phone away. Rosalind's. That's how they all communicate these days, and I never know what's what."

"Ma'am," MacAdams said, hoping to hurry things up. Several of the staff had just come out to the patio, too. Maybe for a smoke. Maybe looking for Anje.

"I want what's best for her. You understand. And she shouldn't be hanging out with that boyfriend of hers. They get into trouble together."

MacAdams suppressed a sigh and rehomed the notepad. This was going to be an angry parent's witch hunt, no doubt.

"But he has been texting her. I don't know the passcode, but you can *see* who it is. Keeps wanted to know 'what happened.' I thought you should know, because that's how she got mixed up. If it weren't for Domino, or whatever he calls himself, she'd be fine—"

"I'm sorry, what was the name?"

"I don't know how to pronounce it; the texts say *D-m-y-t-r-o*."

"Thank you for your time," MacAdams said, the phone sliding down the stubble of his chin. Dmytro and Artem, those were the names of the other refugee employees he had met on their last visit.

And at the moment, they were both standing right in front of him. He locked eyes upon Dmytro; blond hair, blue eyes, the handsome adolescent most likely to be attractive to young people of either sex.

"Hello there; you're one of Sophie's recent hires—from Ukraine, am I right?" he asked.

Dmytro nodded.

"I'd like to ask you a question about your girlfriend, Rose," MacAdams said.

Dmytro nodded again—he seemed willing to cooperate, to his surprise. *Maybe this won't be so hard after all*, MacAdams thought. And then, before any of them could react, he *bolted*.

★★★

There wasn't time to explain the phone call to Green; there wasn't time for much of anything. MacAdams shed his jacket in a single swift motion and dashed after Dmytro in full pursuit.

He didn't know the grounds, and he wasn't at all dressed for a hotfooted chase, but a year off cigarettes made a hell of a difference. MacAdams had height to beat him stride for stride; what he didn't have was Dmytro's youth and stamina. He needed to catch him *now*, or at least hope Green could intercept before his knees gave out.

Dmytro headed for the golf course greens. MacAdams watched him leap a drystone wall and dash eastward. In a moment, he'd lose him to the topography. *Dammit*; he wasn't hurdling a three-foot wall without breaking something. He slowed on the penultimate and used both hands to vault over, ignoring the grating of palms against stone. Below, he just glimpsed a flash of white disappear among two outbuildings near the water hazard. Did he think to hide there? MacAdams slid down the decline toward the pond and banked right, breathing hard. *Good. Stay there*, he thought. They could flush him out later. Then he heard the interrupted rumble of a motorcycle kick start.

It came from the largest of the buildings; metal sides, a small garage for equipment. The attempted kick start sounded again; the engine hadn't yet turned over. MacAdams held his breath and hoped it *wouldn't*—then he shoved open the unlocked door.

"Dmytro, stop!" he shouted, holding up his badge. "Get off the motorbike!"

Dmytro gave him a wild, panicked stare and gave a heavy kick. The engine sprang to life and a 74 R90/6 BMW lurched forward—directly at MacAdams. There wasn't much time to dodge aside; he spun left and Dmytro stuttered past, almost losing balance but ultimately skidding across the concrete floor and out the door. Right into a broom handle.

MacAdams blinked dust. Dmytro had just been clotheslined off the motorbike, which sputtered forward, died and fell onto its side for lack of momentum.

"Don't even think about it!" Green shouted, getting a knee onto a coughing and nose-bloodied Dmytro.

"Is he all right?" MacAdams asked, getting up from where he'd fallen against old tarpaulins.

"Are *you*?" Green asked, getting the handcuffs out. "Am I, for that matter? Wrenched my shoulder clean out."

It was a blessing he wasn't going any faster. Dmytro didn't struggle; he seemed suddenly spent—though being hit in the chest with a broom handle may have had something to do with it. Green got him to his feet and read him the rights, and MacAdams called for backup. They were going to need an interview room at Newcastle station.

CHAPTER 25

Thursday, 11:45

The Velmont Hotel stood like a palace over the Tyne, great yellow blocks of stone stacked in a rising pyramid of arched windows. Jo felt a wave of nausea as they walked through the opulent lobby; the environment was *perfect*, but she had never been less correctly dressed for a venue in her life. Thank God for Chen, who sashayed in all silver and cinnabar—a lure for those who would otherwise be staring at the neurodivergent misfit in jeans and T-shirt. At least Gwilym had a waistcoat on.

"The restaurant occupies the top floor," Chen explained, still leading the charge. "You can see the whole city."

"Part of it is open—part under a solarium," Arthur said as they climbed into the lift. "We watched the rain fall from a table there. Number 24. We requested it whenever we came back."

Jo pursed her lips. Memory was a curious puzzle box; whole years might be shoved together under a generic cover. Just a four-cornered brick of a thing, uninteresting until the trigger was located, the mechanism sprung. Arthur had been pulling out little treasures, surprising himself that he remembered, shocked that he had ever forgotten. Jo understood. Everything in her own head worked that way; the difference, she supposed, was that she knew it—and could find her way back to almost anything. People laughed about Sherlock's mind-palace, but it was a real strategy, first described in a case about Russian reporter Solomon Shereshevsky in 1968. Events, memories, words had color and taste and form; he built those into structures inside his own head. Jo's memory worked that way, too; for years she thought everyone else's did. She was right, and wrong. The capability was there, but so was interference, the constant turbulent tide of emotion, and something Jo never counted on: the *desire* to *unknow*. Her mother forgot so much. She'd forgotten the times she hurt Jo, forgotten things that were unpleasant to remember. Jo kept them all, but she wondered now if that were a blessing . . . or not.

"Here we are, my lovelies," Chen said as the doors opened to a rich purple interior. As promised, great colorful squares graced the walls—Chen's modernist work.

"I've been meaning to ask," Gwilym said, still escorting Chen, "how did you come to choose Augustus John for study when your styles are so different?"

"Are they different?" Chen asked. "Brush stroke and subject, yes. But I like to think mine are as psychological as his own."

"John grew more expressionist as he ages, too," Jo added.

Chen released herself from Gwilym with a laugh. "Artists change! A concept more than one admirer confuses.

"Jill! We haven't lunched!" Jill turned out to be a robust woman of fifty and the daytime manager for Velmont's signature restaurant. She cheek-kissed Chen and took her by the delicate fingers.

"How *have* you been? Would you like your usual table?"

"Not today, dear; I've brought friends. This is Jo Jones and Gwilym . . ." Failing his surname, she added, "Welshman. And

I think you know Arthur?" Arthur had been lingering behind in the room's foyer. When he joined them, Jill gave a little gasp of delight.

"My God, Arthur! It's been *years*!"

"I know," he said quietly. Chen took his arm.

"Table 24, I think," she said.

★ ★ ★

People spoke about the view of Paris, sometimes of London, and often of New York—cityscapes that had been painted, photographed, framed and studied. Jo had never seen the Newcastle skyline among them, but looking out from the clear glass dome into a horizon of great stone and steel bridges, buildings and an honest-to-God *castle* couldn't fail to impress. Then there was brunch, which included, among other things, caviar and crab cakes.

Arthur ordered a croque madame in honor of Aiden and ate it, misty-eyed. Mostly, Chen did the talking, her voice a gentle hum surrounding them with news of art and of the city. She made occasional clicks as she spoke, not a tic so much as moments of verbal affirmation. Jo began to rely on them, counting like a clock. She could happily listen to Chen all day, a background for a wondering mind. It was Arthur, finally, who broke the reverie.

"This has been a very unusual Thursday," he said, smiling over his finished plate.

"A good one, I hope?" Gwilym asked. "Considering a bunch of strangers descended on you before breakfast."

"Chen and I aren't strangers," Arthur said. "Or at least, we weren't. *Before*." He cleared his throat over the unsaid bit. "And I hope you and Jo aren't strangers any longer."

"Cheers to that." Gwilym lifted champagne, and they toasted to grief and recovery.

"It all seems such an elaborate setup for a brunch, however," Arthur said.

Jo had been thinking that, too. Maybe the table number had been a clue? Maybe one of Chen's paintings? But no one else was looking for them and maybe—probably—there weren't any more clues to find. She wriggled in her chair; sometimes, things simply ended. Sometimes.

But not this time.

Jill had returned with the bill, which Chen took upon herself. But Jill had also brought something with her.

"I had nearly forgotten about this," she said. "Honestly, I might still if you hadn't sat *here*." She placed a paper take-away bag on the white linen—just in front of Arthur. "I had firm instructions, and I promised I would hold onto this until you came back to the restaurant," she said. "Aiden said that you coming back here was the sign you'd be ready to open it, and no sooner. I didn't think it would be five years. You're lucky no one tried to resell it!"

MacAdams reached into the bag and produced a bottle of wine.

"A—a 1999 burgundy," he said, his breath catching.

Jill placed a hand on his shoulder. "Aiden bought the last bottle we had. I was—we were all—so sorry to hear of his passing. There's also an envelope." She pointed to the bag and then retreated from an increasingly emotional Arthur. He'd pulled out a square envelope with trembling fingers.

"I—I can't open it," he said. "Jo?"

Jo took it in hand, another letter from Aiden, posthumous, awaiting fruition. She unsealed it with her butter knife and lifted out a folded piece of paper . . . and a tiny, flat key. It lay in her hand; nothing special, no marks. Too small to be a door key.

"What's it say?" Gwilym begged.

Jo pursed her lips. "It says, 'Go get an ice cream, and this time *you* pay.'"

Finding an ice cream in Newcastle in May wasn't difficult. Little carts dotted the parks and side streets, proffering the usual fare plus not a few rum-raisin possibilities that Jo still hadn't got used to.

"Was there someplace specific you used to go?" Gwilym asked. They were walking Quayside under a warm sun.

"Not really," Arthur said. "To be honest, Aiden preferred pastry to ice cream. He had two favorite pastry shops in town."

"Do *you* like it, though?" Jo asked. The note had been singular imperative; not "let's get ice cream," but "you" get it.

Arthur considered. "I fancy strawberry. Though not for my figure." He paused, smiling. "Hans and Pepper love it, of course. Vanilla."

"Pup cones," Chen observed sagely. "I remember."

They were coming up, at last, to a little blue cart. The sides had been decorated with cartoon children and oversize treats. Gwilym was already ordering an iced lolly. They did have strawberry and Jo purchased one for Arthur and one for herself. Chen declined: "No dairy, pet."

"There must be something," Jo said as they sought a bench to recline on. "Ice cream doesn't explain the key." When Arthur recovered from the initial shock of it, each had turned over the key in careful fingers. Gwilym suggested a bicycle key, Chen a jewelry box. Aiden didn't ride, however, and had only a single ring, worn from his schooldays.

"The wine is special," Jo said. "It's about your first meeting, your first date, your first drink together."

"I'm not sure I remember our first ice cream," Arthur said, helping Chen to a seat and then lowering himself beside her. Jo looked again at the key in her palm.

"It's about more than ice cream," she said. Chen tapped the ground gently with her umbrella.

"Aye. More than paintings or wines or dinner tables. It's about Aiden. And about you, Arthur." She closed her eyes and gave herself a little shake, earrings shimmering. "Arthur and his Ægle. The brave one and the stuck one."

Jo bit her lip; she'd not been the only one to see that, then.

"Only Aiden was done being stuck," Chen went on, eyes open and trained upon Arthur's leading-man features. "Done, I say. Told Jo, and now I'm telling you. He was going to beat cancer and come home a changed man."

"Except he didn't," Arthur said.

Jo had left her ice cream to melt by mistake; she dropped it into the bin and tried to unstick her fingers with a napkin.

"We know that now," she said. "But all this—the doll, the painting, the wine. It's from *before*. Before it was too late."

"I'm not sure it makes a difference," Arthur said, but Jo had caught the thread and was winding it.

"It *does*. I'm an idiot—of *course* it does." She turned in place. *Before it was too late.* It was too late for Aiden to mend things with his sister, Jo's mother. It was too late for him to have a relationship with Jo. Too late for Jo to know her father. It had been too late for Evelyn and William, too. Everything about their family was *too late*. And Aiden wasn't going to let it happen again if he could help it. He had cancer, but meant to beat it. "Don't you see? You weren't supposed to be making this journey with *us*. You were supposed to be doing it with a recovered Aiden. He would have been here."

"Does that mean there's no clue for the key?" Gwilym asked. "Is it a metaphor, like the key to my heart?"

Arthur winced. "Aiden didn't go in for cliché," he said.

"Of course not. This man arranged a painting clue and secret messages!" Jo was flapping her hands at the wrist, looking for an outlet to the restless energy. Her brain was circling something, all bells ringing. They were on a treasure hunt—it had a beginning on a rainy night in August . . . *Inception. Itinerate. Iconography.* It would also have an *end*.

"Arthur, I don't need to know that first time you ate ice cream with Aiden," Jo said suddenly. "I need to know the *last* time."

For a moment, Arthur's face was a blank. Then his mouth drew down, eyes casting away to the distance over the Tyne.

"Oh." He'd balled up his dessert napkin between his fists. "November. One of those strange warm days. He'd been staying with me, seeing the oncologist here. We took a walk, ended up near a stand like this one. I'd brought the dogs and—they had their share. He paid because—"

They waited in silence as Arthur mastered his emotions.

"He said he was selling the flat in York," he said at last. "'I'll soon be flush,' he said. 'So I'll get this one.'"

"Next time, you pay," Gwilym added.

"We talked about joined households. He teased me about my choice in financial establishments—I work there, after all."

Jo felt her breath catch. *The bank*. Arthur's *own* bank. She held up the key, a key not unlike the one for her mother's safe-deposit box.

"Let's go there," she said. "I think something is waiting for you."

CHAPTER 26

Thursday, 12:45

MacAdams dabbed at his palms with antiseptic. If this kept up, he'd need to start carrying first aid around in his car. It was supposed to be a straightforward day: shake Burnhope, pressure Sophie Wagner, track down this Gerald Standish—oil and gas *doctor.* Now they had a suspect in an interview room, and they had also called in Anje and Artem for questioning. They came without the same sort of fuss.

"All set, boss," Green said, leaning through the storage room door.

"Thank you, Sheila." She'd been his best asset; Newcastle police didn't forget one of their own and so far, all their needs had been fairly accommodated without a rumble.

"You really are okay?" she asked, eyeing the scrapes.

"Honest," he said, patting them dry and leading the way to their suspect. He looked worse for wear through the one-way glass.

"I'm glad you didn't render our suspect unconscious for his trouble."

"He'd deserve it. By the way—you're faster than you look."

"Thanks, I think," MacAdams said, opening the door.

Dmytro didn't look up; he kept his eyes on the table in front of him. Green did the usual and started the tapes rolling.

"Do you want to tell us why you ran?" MacAdams asked.

No eye contact, but Dmytro rubbed at his nose.

"You were chasing me," he said.

"Then maybe you want to tell us why you tried to kill a police officer with a motorcycle?" Green asked. A bit heavy-handed, maybe, but it certainly got a startle response.

"I didn't!"

"You might have."

"I didn't *mean* to—he was just standing there."

"Yes, Dmytro," MacAdams interrupted. "A detective showed you his badge and told you to stop. And you were going to run me over for 'just standing there.' You're already in about as much trouble as you *can* be in. So, I'll ask again, why did you run when I asked about Rose?"

"I don't know anyone named Rose."

"We have your mobile; you've been sending texts to Rose for two days," Green said. Technically, they hadn't managed to hack it, but they had Rose's foster mom as witness.

"I just—She's just a girl I met."

"So you do know Rose," MacAdams added. "Do you know she was arrested along with a boy named Benny?"

Dmytro looked at the ceiling, a despairing sound in his throat. "You arrested her? She didn't even know why she was doing it!"

"No. But you do." MacAdams picked up the report from York. "A fortune in stolen artifacts. And that's just what we seized. Your pals got away with more."

"I don't even know them."

"You're working for them," Green said. "We've already taken your photo to the job training center. We know you've been grooming couriers. *Walkers*, you were calling them. Poor kids with no prospects. Kids like Rose."

"It's not like that! They weren't supposed to get involved . . ." Dmytro's words had begun to run over each other, his accent thick with emotion.

"They weren't supposed to get *caught*," MacAdams corrected. "But they did. And that's not all; you understand that Ronan Foley is dead, don't you? You realize that all of you—and all those you brought into this mess—are in danger?"

Dmytro dropped his eyes again and went silent. MacAdams had brought images of Foley, graphic ones. He hesitated to show them; the boy seemed fragile.

"Listen to me, Dmytro. I need to find out who killed Foley so I can protect the others. Rose. Anje. The girl in the sketch Sergeant Green showed you. It's not over until we know who is responsible."

"I don't know. I honestly don't." When Dmytro raised his head again, it was clear he was crying hot tears. "I just wanted to get my family out."

MacAdams exchanged a glance with Green. *His family?*

"Do you mean . . . from the Ukraine?" he asked.

Dmytro nodded. "Me and Artem. We're the youngest boys, both of us. His brother and my father? They're still fighting. Anje doesn't even know where her father is, or if he's alive. And I have sisters." He wiped his dripping nose and MacAdams nudged Green to fetch him something for it. "Mr. Foley said there were ways to get them out."

MacAdams hadn't got his notepad; he didn't want anything to disturb the moment. He leaned forward in his chair, speaking as gently as he dared.

"Dmytro? You're saying Foley told you he could bring people to this country—but not using the charity, as Sophie wanted to do? How?"

"He said there were ways to make it go faster. And he could do the same thing for my family. I just had to do a little work for him. A year, he said. To pay their way. I could save them."

MacAdams felt his stomach drop. There were names for this sort of contract: human trafficking, indentured servitude. "What did you do for Ronan Foley?" he asked.

Dmytro looked up, his eyes wide and glassy. "It wasn't drugs or anything. It was just *stuff.* Statues and things. Mr. Foley called it 'refugee art.'"

"Come again?" Green asked. "He told you it had been made by asylum seekers?"

Dmytro shook his head. "No, the art—the pots and things. They're refugees. Like us. We were rescuing it." He sniffed and rubbed his nose. "But then Ms. Wagner said I was stealing."

"Your boss at the golf club?" MacAdams asked.

Dmytro nodded. "That's what she said. When she caught me at it."

"Caught you—when?"

"On Friday."

★ ★ ★

MacAdams burst out of the interview room and into the hall, nearly colliding with Green.

"I can't find tissues—"

"Forget that. I want Sophie Wagner."

"What about Anje and Artem?" Green asked.

MacAdams kept walking, adrenaline making him forget he'd just sprinted a half mile.

"Wagner knew what Dmytro was up to the night of the murder. I want her. Now."

"Boss—" Green started, but MacAdams shook his head.

"I want her in a room if it takes an arrest, and I want Burnhope down here, too, lawyer and all."

"*Boss*, I know. I'm trying to tell you, Sophie Wagner just called. She wants you to meet her at the club."

★ ★ ★

MacAdams didn't like the turnabout. He wanted Wagner on his turf, in a wired interview room walking distance from overnight cells. Instead he walked into a busy club, buzzing with golfer bar-flies . . . then walked into her business office, a plant-draped oasis against Hammersmith white walls. She stood up when he entered.

"You are aware that we have arrested Dmytro."

"I am." Sophie lowered herself to the chair and placed her hands in front of her, every movement seemingly thought out. "He shouldn't have run. I could have helped you understand."

MacAdams sat down. "You cannot explain this away, Ms. Wagner," he said.

Sophie shook her head violently, her mane of hair showering both shoulders. "It's not—it's not his *fault*. He's vulnerable."

"No doubt that's what made him so attractive to you and Foley," MacAdams said flatly.

Wagner drew herself up. "I had nothing to do with this! *He* did this. *He's* the start of everything going wrong! I didn't know—none of us knew—until—"

"He started it and what? You became his partner? Did you make promises to Dmytro, too, telling him you would save his family?"

Sophie had been working up to a purple rage, but appeared to have stalled, facial expression frozen. "Wh-what?"

"Foley said he could get Dmytro's family here illegally, in exchange for helping him traffic artifacts." MacAdams was talking louder, but managed to keep his body language to a minimum. "Is that one more way you're helping refugees? By trafficking them, too?"

"Stop!" Sophie Wagner was standing. She'd slammed both hands against her desk, and now seemed embarrassed to have done so. Her face suggested something between fear, confusion and anger. "This charity is my life. These people—these kids. They are *my family.* And I would *never* make promises I could not keep. If Dmytro was promised something—"

"Extralegal passage for his family in exchange for labor," MacAdams said flatly. "Selling them to slavery, keeping them here illegally, profiting from misery."

Sophie shuddered and collapsed back into her chair. "*That's* what Foley was doing?" She put her head in her hands, voice coming out muffled. "I swear to *God* I didn't know he was—"

"Selling stolen cultural relics?" MacAdams interrupted.

"*Lying* to *Dmytro*!" Sophie half shouted. "It's evil. It's just *evil*—that boy has already seen so many terrible things, then to toy with his emotions like that!"

"You're angry."

"Of *course* I am!"

"Angry enough to kill him for it?" MacAdams asked. He was putting Sophie through her paces. She had turned an ashen shade beneath the faux tan.

"No!"

"Then you had better work on proving it. Tell me *everything*, in order, in detail. Now." He half expected her to begin shouting for a lawyer, like Burnhope had.

Instead, she nodded. "I'll do better. I'll show you," she said stiffly.

* * *

The club already reminded MacAdams of an airport; now he'd followed Wagner into a concourse. Sophie walked him down a corridor with windows to one side and framed photographs to the other. Smiling children in bright clothes, all of them very apparently immigrants or refugees. It looked like a UNICEF commercial.

"Pathos," he muttered under his breath.

Sophie turned sharp. "Yes," she agreed. "Charity isn't easily motivated by logos."

It was only now that MacAdams noted the nameplates beneath. Each one had a donor name attached, the way you might name a building in honor of the funders. Donations on display—just another way of showing off wealth, getting a tax break and looking pious at the same time. He was suddenly glad Green didn't have to see this.

"I know you don't appreciate the work I do," Sophie continued. "Or don't trust it. My own father would be as skeptical. I married into money."

"You're going to tell me a rags-to-riches story?" MacAdams asked.

Sophie had turned the corner into a lounge space; it wasn't as fancy as the others.

"No. Comfortably middle-class. But I'm trying to explain—I have seen both sides of wealth. And when I had it to do with as I pleased, I decided to help people like Dmytro. He came to us early this year, just seventeen. His father and brother were both enlisted in the Ukrainian army and he has three younger sisters, one of whom is disabled." She had crossed the room and now stood before a bank of lockers. "They sent Dmytro here, seeking asylum. To protect him, you see, as the last male in the family, meaning no one expects his father and brother to make it. He hoped to find work, save money and bring his mother and sisters—but it isn't that easy."

"Because?" MacAdams asked. His mood had softened slightly, and he wanted to guard against it. She could be lying. Or, she could be telling the truth—and the truth was motive for murder.

"Visas are hard to get if you don't have family already here and background checks take ages. We sponsored Dmytro, who applied for asylum instead. But you can't apply for asylum *from* the Ukraine; you need to be here already."

"That doesn't make sense."

"The system doesn't make sense," Sophie explained. "But there is a logic to it. You apply for a visa from your home country; you seek asylum because you already fled, in fear for your life."

"So either Dmytro's mother and sisters wait in line, or they have to make it here on their own?"

"Or with sponsors," Sophie said. "But we can't take everyone. And it's even harder because his sister has *special needs*."

MacAdams was aware that this wasn't the proper terminology for disability anymore—but then, Sophie saw everything in terms of needs, didn't she? He was starting to lose his patience.

"You haven't explained what you know about Ronan Foley. You said he wasn't involved in the charity, but here we are."

Sophie stopped and took a breath. "He wasn't. *Anymore.* He came round, early on, offered to help out. But he took too much interest in my young women." She grimaced. "I didn't know he *also* threatened my young men."

She opened the nearest locker. Inside were shoes, a hoodie, what looked like an iPad and a bundle of dirty shirts.

"This is Dmytro's locker. I provide these for the staff." She reached in and folded over the edge of a T-shirt. Something vaguely metallic shone from beneath. It was some sort of antique figurine. MacAdams followed her lead, pulling back fabric without touching the object itself. It was made of bronze, about the size of his hand and human shaped, a seated woman with a tambourine. As the others, it wasn't especially ostentatious, no gold or jewels. But it had all the hallmarks of being a Syrian artifact, and therefore priceless. He turned to face Sophie Wagner.

"Start talking," he said.

"On Friday, before the charity event, Dmytro missed an all-staff meeting. He *had* been missing them, but this was *important*; I went looking for him myself. And I found him here, trying to hide this in the bottom of the locker."

"And you didn't think to tell the police?"

"I didn't know what it *was*," she explained. "It could be a hood ornament for all I know."

MacAdams took a second look at the figurine. A deity, perhaps. A muse, but rendered in bronze. Behind him, Sophie continued.

"It was his behavior after being caught that made me suspicious. He just broke down entirely, and everything came tumbling out—some of it in Ukrainian." Sophie leaned against the locker. "When I . . . encouraged . . . Foley to stop coming round the clubhouse, he gave his number to Dmytro. Said he had a job for him. Could he carry a package for him across town?"

"Here in Newcastle."

"The first time, yes. Then a few just a train ride away. Regional."

MacAdams dug out the notepad. "Who did he deliver to?"

"Ah. No one. He dropped them at various places. Hotels, pubs. Like a courier service, but always to a place where someone was supposed to pick up later."

Of course, MacAdams thought grimly. They would try to get the locations out of Dmytro, but chances were good no one who held the packages knew what they were. If they could ID someone . . .

"He got paid a bit of money, and for a while that was it. Then he was asked too often, and Dmytro didn't want to miss work."

"Let me guess. Dmytro recruited other people," MacAdams asked.

Sophie pursed her lips. "There is a job placement agency that sometimes helps find work for our asylum seekers. He met people there. But it was Foley who asked him! He didn't mean to get anyone into trouble."

"Let's talk about the day you found it," MacAdams said. "It's Friday. You are having a gala—and you have just uncovered a crime. But you don't call police. Did you call *Foley*?"

"Why would I?"

"Because you just found out he'd coerced a kid into stealing for him. Come on, Ms. Wagner. You know that's no hood ornament." He stood up to face her, and she struggled to meet him eye for eye.

"It's . . . not," she admitted, "It's the Syrian goddess Anat."

"Ms. Wagner, I'm arresting you on suspicion of artifact trafficking—"

"Wait! I didn't know that when I first saw it!" She'd thrown her hands up as though MacAdams meant to tackle her the way Green had tackled Dmytro. "I swear to you, Detective! I—I just took a photograph and did a reverse image search."

"Meaning you knew Foley was smuggling," MacAdams said, still menacing her with arrest. "*So*, did you call him? Did you demand he meet you somewhere?"

"Who? Foley?" Sophie shook her head in evident confusion. "No. I told Dmytro to leave it, and I locked it up with my own key. He's a good boy, Detective. I knew he didn't realize it was wrong. I meant to deal with it—but not Friday. I had an event to run."

"So you catch Dmytro stealing, and Foley trafficking, and you decide to do . . . nothing." MacAdams might not have the fullest range of facial expressions, but there would be no hiding his complete disbelief.

Sophie looked at him, full of pleading. "Getting into this

country is hard; getting kicked out is easy. I didn't want to do anything to jeopardize Dmytro. I thought I could handle it myself, one way or another, without alerting anyone."

"Not even Stanley Burnhope?" MacAdams asked.

Sophie looked horrified. "Especially not! I couldn't do any of this without him—his donations, Ava's connections." She'd said it with feeling. But the picture it painted was *not* an exonerating one.

"Foley's actions have endangered one of your refugees, while also threatening your position with the Burnhopes. Is that right? And you were, what? Planning to return this stolen treasure to him and ask him to go away quietly?" His eyes strayed to the figurine again. Was *that* heavy enough to be a murder weapon? He'd have it bagged and sent to forensics.

"I wasn't sure what I'd do with it, and that's the truth," Sophie said. "I was about to have hundreds of people descend on the biggest fundraiser of the year. Ronan could be dealt with later."

"Ronan *was* dealt with later," MacAdams said darkly.

"Ms. Wagner, where you were last Friday night between 11:30 p.m. and 3:00 a.m. on Friday night?"

"Here. With Burnhope and a room full of people."

"Do you have concrete proof of that?" he asked. "Not just the glad-wishing of your favorite donors?"

Sophie tilted her head—then, unexpectedly, she smiled at him.

"Yes. Yes, I do. We had a camera crew cover the event for marketing. It's been flashed to a drive. Six hours of footage—and you'll see I'm always there."

That was highly convenient. MacAdams would be sure they went through every frame.

"I'll take it with me," he said.

"Back at my office. Shall I bring it to you?"

"I'll follow and wait," MacAdams said, not that he expected her to bolt. Rather, he had a last question. "I want to ask you about one of your patrons. He was at the charity ball, and I take it he's a big donor: Gerald Standish."

It could be his imagination, but Sophie appeared relieved.

"Oh *him*. He's here, I imagine. He keeps bar hours every day between two and four."

CHAPTER 27

Thursday, 14:00

Jo held her breath. A wooden box lay upon the art nouveau table next to the champagne they'd abandoned that morning. The lid was carved in roses and darkened with the patina of age. It had come from Spain, purchased on an art-buying trip and had spent the last five-plus years in a safe-deposit box.

Arthur—who knew more about banks than Jo could ever hope to—explained that only four of them still offered safe-deposit boxes, and one of them was in fact *his* bank. He'd protested that he, at least, did not have a safe-deposit box. But it seems he did, in fact. By what means Aiden had worked this minor miracle was a matter of speculation (and possibly the forging of Arthur's signature), but he returned with the prize now before them. Midafternoon sunshine slipped through the windows and left squares on the carpets; they'd spent the day searching, but finding always felt a little anticlimactic, in the end.

"Do you know, I'm afraid to open it," Arthur said.

"I think it's time, though," Chen suggested. She'd been sitting on the sofa with Pepper, resting "old bones," which had nonetheless almost outwalked the rest of them. Now she stood and took her position next to Arthur. "Let's finish that journey."

"I'm glad you were here for it," Arthur said, placing a gentle kiss on her forehead. "I never meant to drift away."

"Oh, you meant to. But now you're sorry, and that's enough." She guided his hand to the box latch. "Don't keep us in suspense, darling."

Arthur lifted the lid.

"Oh," he said, a tiny sound. He lifted out a small velvet pillow and its precious cargo: a ring, and a note: "Will you marry me?" A shudder passed through Arthur, then he collapsed into a dining chair and *sobbed*. Chen cradled the man, whose hoarse voice escaped in a broken question:

"*Why*—why didn't he ask me? Before the end?"

Why set up an elaborate game only to hide it? It was raw and painful and hard to answer. But Jo thought she knew. *Miss Havisham.*

"Arthur?" she asked quietly. "You remember the letter? Aiden couldn't wait to meet me. Then nothing happened." She'd pictured him then, waiting for a young Jo who never arrived. Now she imagined Aiden buying rings and wine bottles. "He was supposed to get better. When he didn't—" Jo struggled to find the right words "—he thought you would be happier if you never knew the loss of joy."

Arthur lifted his head to look at her, his firm jaw trembling.

"He was *wrong*," he said, swallowing hard. *"He was so wrong."*

"I know," Jo told him, sinking to her knees by his chair. "But he's told you *now*."

Arthur reached tentatively forward to pick up the ring: white gold set with twin stones, yellow and deep red.

"Topaz and jacinth," Arthur said softly. "The stones of Excalibur." He put it upon his left ring finger, a perfect fit.

"It's everything," he whispered.

Chen picked up a champagne glass and set it next to him.

"Congratulations, love." She tipped her glass against his, a tiny chimera of tinkling crystal. Jo wasn't sure she could do champagne on her emotion-knotted stomach, but reached for a glass to toast. That's when she noticed the spine.

"There's a book in there," she said. Beneath the paper and to one side, a corner peeked. Leather, hard-bound, overstuffed and wrapped with string. She lifted it up and out. "A journal, I think?"

"Open it," Arthur encouraged. Jo handed it over and his fingers worked at the knots, but once released from tension the pages surged. A folded sheet fell to the floor.

"I've got it," Gwilym said, bending down.

Arthur let him, and instead opened the inside cover with Jo looking on. "Family history," it said, and beneath, in Aiden's careful print: "William, Gwen, Evelyn . . . and Violet."

Jo lingered over the last word, her own sticking in her throat. *Oh God.*

"Jo?" Gwilym asked, lifting of a sheet of weathered paper. "It's Ardemore's insignia."

Arthur took the letter and tucked it back inside the journal. Then he closed the cover, wrapped it once, and held it out to Jo.

The bound book hovered above the Persian rug, a bright apple on the stalk of Arthur's outstretched arm.

"I think this belongs to you," he said.

★ ★ ★

Gerald Standish held court at a corner table beneath an enormous painting of a fox hunt on the moors; it didn't go with the modern decor, but it *was* vaguely familiar. Standish sat near enough to the bar to be carrying on a conversation with two men seated there, but far enough to shout it. Shirtsleeves and a tweed vest, with exactly the sort of trousers golfers wore circa 1960, he had a flushed face, red nose, gray-white tufts of unruly hair and appeared to be in his late sixties. He didn't look like a respected physician. To MacAdams he was the perfect representation of a harmless old fool.

"May I join you?" MacAdams asked.

"Eh? Certainly! New member?" he asked. MacAdams unfolded his police identification, but this didn't put a damper on his welcome. "A detective. Well, we've had a fair few of those, too, in our years—haven't we, boys? Pint?"

The *boys* were all at least ten years older than MacAdams, who declined the drink.

"I actually want to ask you about art," he said. "I understand you collect."

"I do. This one, see?" He thumbed to the oil painting behind him, which like the posters in the concourse bore a little gold plaque. The artist's name wasn't present, but Gerald's own. "I lent it, you know. Like it? It's of the countryside just north of Abington."

MacAdams took a seat. "You've been there?"

"Good course over that way. Do you golf, Detective?"

"I solve crime."

"Ah, of course. I bet you've come to ask about ancient artifacts." The surprise must have registered on MacAdams's stiff features. Standish made a great show of cleaning his glasses. "I do have a *doctorate* in the subject," he added.

That was unexpected.

"I thought you were an oil and gas magnate."

"Oh-ho? Surprised an industry man managed a degree? I've a PhD from Cambridge, archaeology, I'll have you know."

Laughter like gunshots erupted from the bar.

"Watch out, Officer, he'll have you to his museum!"

"Jealous, every one of you," Standish said with a grin. Then turned a surprisingly keen eye upon MacAdams. "You'll need expertise. You might have called *me*, you know. I've never been part of an investigation. What a treat!" He replaced his well-rubbed lenses. It did give him a vaguely professorial air. "The papers didn't say region or era."

MacAdams presumed there would be no harm in providing detail. Possibly Standish could be of use. If he *was* presently a suspect. He decided to set the bait.

"Syria. Eleventh or twelfth century. Gold. Pottery. Mosaics," he said, watching Standish narrowly. *Tell me something I can use.* Standish merely wiped his mouth on a napkin and told Simon (again the barman) to put it on his tab.

"Tell you what, Officer. Let me take you round my place; it's not far and we can have a proper chat."

⋆ ⋆ ⋆

Standish lived less than a mile from Lime Tree Greens. It wasn't an estate like Burnhope's, but an old, well-pedigreed town house of brick and stone. They entered through enormous double doors into a foyer of chessboard tile and mahogany walls. Flanking the stairs were two ebony statues, doglike with highly pointed ears. Anubis, he supposed. Jo would know.

"Don't be fooled," Standish said, closing the doors. "Those are replicas created in the early 1800s. *Not* from the ancient world. I don't collect Egyptian art; it's a bit overdone."

He led MacAdams through to a large reception room. Some sort of wooden mask hung over the fireplace.

"That comes from the Krahn people, Liberia." Standish hitched his trousers higher. "Nineteenth century again, if you're wondering."

"I thought you collected antiquities."

"Oh I do, son. But I'm not leaving them out in the front room, am I?" He chortled to himself and beckoned him on. "We'll take a turn in the study, shall we? Have a nice port in there."

MacAdams found himself trying to make sense of the man's easy manners.

"You know I am investigating a crime," he said. "Not just the trafficking of stolen artifacts but also the murder of Ronan Foley."

"Ah, sad business, that. Played golf with him once or twice."

"So you knew him," MacAdams clarified, his hand itching to pull out the battered notebook.

"Only knew he was terrible at golf," Standish said, then led the way into his study.

This was a room of private opulence. Two chairs in bomber leather and brass studs flanked the far corner. He'd flicked a switch that illuminated several brass lamps; the room had a single window, but it had been well shaded. It smelled of woodgrain, leather, pipe smoke and alcohol and offered up the antithesis of Burnhope's residence. No glass except the decanter of port, but every surface held a precious object of stone, pottery or precious metal. MacAdams pointed to a small star-shaped amulet with floral designs.

"Arabesque open work," he said.

Standish clapped his hands. "Oh very good!"

MacAdams felt a sudden heat in his gut.

"So it's from ancient Syria, like the stolen ones," he said sharply.

"Tut, now you're guessing. It's *not*. Iran, in fact. Ilkhanid period, 1256–1353. And you'll find I bought it at auction." He swept his hand about the room. "That's where most of this comes from, you know. Auctions, private collectors, museums in trouble—" he winked "—and eBay."

"You just make your bids, I take it."

"Oh yes." Standish poured himself a glass of port. "You won't join me? No, of course. Let's say I want something specific. And I *do*, at that. I can search, or I can hire people who search."

"What people."

"Online people." Standish settled himself into one of the leather chairs. MacAdams was meant for the other. He declined that offer, too. "Some men my age don't like new technology. I find it all *fascinating.* I could pull up three websites dedicated to sourcing rare objects."

"Such as?" MacAdams asked.

"You'd hardly be impressed if I told you. The best things are often seemingly the least significant."

MacAdams was far from impressed by this banter. "I want a list of every place you've purchased from."

Standish let his eyes drift from one antique to the next.

"Heavens, Detective, I don't keep records of every purchase."

"Provenance, then."

"I haven't got it. Not for every piece."

MacAdams said the next bit through gritted teeth. "Can you prove that you obtained these legally?"

Standish smiled. Benign. Grandfatherly.

"I think the question is, can *you* prove otherwise? Don't be angry, old boy. The British Museum itself can't tell where it got half its treasures. The important thing is that they're *safe.*"

"How do you figure that?" MacAdams demanded.

Standish set down his port and leaned forward as if trying to explain a lesson.

"*Because* they won't be bombed or looted or destroyed. Saved for the next generation, and so forth. Collectors do the world a service. It's practically charity."

MacAdams flexed his fingers, anger rising. He'd been here before. It was even what Foley had told Dmytro. Blind men gloating over their triumphs and their sticky morals. *Focus.*

"Charity like Fresh Start?" he asked, keeping his voice even. "Burnhope says you're a model donor. Doing your bit."

"Exactly, that! Lifting up the downtrodden, investing in the future." Standish bobbed his head, pleased with himself.

MacAdams swallowed before continuing. "Bringing in kids from war-torn countries," he said slowly. "Where the sale of artifacts buys bombs and guns. This *isn't* a victimless crime."

"It's just art!" Standish blustered. "What harm can art do?"

"Ronan Foley was *murdered*. And right now, I have a kid named Dmytro in lockup because he was helping him smuggle illegal spoils. Now he might lose his status in the country. How's that for harm?"

MacAdams hadn't expected this to make an impression. He turned to go, trying to get outside before he said something *very* off the books. But Standish had followed him.

"Dmytro?" he asked, the levity gone. "They won't deport him, though? Surely?"

"Not for me to say."

"Well, but . . . we agreed—"

MacAdams turned on his heel. Standish looked as though he wanted to reswallow every word.

"We *who*, agreed *what*?"

"I—It's nothing, really," Standish said, backing away.

MacAdams followed him step for step.

"Nothing would please me more than dragging you to the station for this," he said. "I am running out of patience."

Standish heaved a sigh and patted his sides. "We all like that boy, you know. Good lad. Burnhope thought we could keep it tight—why should he take the fall for a man like Foley?"

"Burnhope," MacAdams repeated. "Not Sophie."

"Oh, Sophie always gets the job done, certainly. But it was all Stanley's idea."

MacAdams had Green on the phone before he got back to his car. "Bring in Burnhope," he demanded. "And I want the receipts on Burnhope's career. Rumors. Anything. Clear? He's up to his neck in this. *Somehow.*"

He hung up, still fuming—and hadn't noticed that Standish followed him out.

"Detective? A word—"

"No more words. You're lucky I'm not taking you in with me."

"I want you to."

MacAdams flexed his fingers in exasperation. *"Why?"*

"To be there for Dmytro, of course." He meant it, apparently.

MacAdams could not stomach him.

"Good afternoon, Mr. Standish," he said, opening his car door. He flopped into his seat and was about to shut the door.

"Nose rings," Standish said. Which made no bloody sense at all.

"What?"

"My holy grail, the thing I'd been searching for. Just a small, perfectly common nose ring. But so very ancient. That's the stuff of human civilization itself." He was turning back toward his front stairs. "Hardly a crime, now, is it?"

CHAPTER 28

Thursday, 17:00

Jo had spent the last few hours in a haze.

Aiden Jones was a man of secrets, meticulous habits and a singular, abiding special interest. Like the receipts and backs of envelopes she'd found in his archive box, the book had been written in, written on, written *around*, with text creeping up the sides when a new fact needed to be added in place. Interleaved between the dense-packed pages were letters, photocopies, newsprint, timelines, obituaries, photographs and enough minutiae and ephemera that would make Roberta Wilkinson blush.

Jo assumed the portrait of Evelyn drove his quest. She was *wrong.* Aiden had been reconstructing the entire family tree, a great flowering of data that put the genealogy sites to shame.

Chen had made green tea. Arthur needed time with his thoughts; Jo needed no walls and an open sky. She and Gwilym walked to the park and sat beneath old trees and green boughs. Even hyperlexic speed reading had been no match for Aiden's curious scribbled spirals. There were places where the text opened up, became ropy and loose—a mind working faster than a pen. There were places where it narrowed, stuttered, shrank from cramped fingers afraid of losing a thought. Explosive excitement as he made connections, winnowed details, solved the miniproblems of lost family lines.

And as she went, a mantra repeated in her head: *he was like me, he was like me, he was like me.* She'd lost Aiden even before her mother, but reading his words, she'd never felt so close to anyone. She'd found the family she knew must be there. And through him, she found one thing more.

Her name was Violet. Just like the flowers decorating Evelyn's portrait or those that sprang up over the buried hope chest: humility, grace and *delicate love.* From scraps and letters, ancestry searches and medical records, Aiden pieced together the skeleton of the story. Evelyn had indeed died in childbirth.

But the baby survived. And as for the answer Jo had been seeking all this time: Gwen had given the child away.

The travel records before her now revealed that William was in London on business when Evelyn went into labor; he returned to her corpse. Did Gwen tell him the baby died? It seemed likely. Why not keep the baby; why not raise it as her own? She thought better of it, eventually. Strangely, Gwen's own letters, preserved in Aiden's notebook, were the first clue:

November 1910, Gwen to someone named Tomlinson: "Please," she wrote, "if you know or can discover her whereabouts, I would be happy to pay for your trouble . . ."

January 1913: "I can pay for travel to abroad, but I cannot go myself. I have my reasons."

Another came in the form of scrap paper, a note scrawled in uneven script, but not by Aiden: "Flooding—must get Hobarth."

Jo looked at the torn paper, it's edges rust brown. Aiden provided a caption: "Written by the midwife. Evelyn needed a doctor."

—whom? Jo found some more notes that clarified Hobarth as Dr. Ida Hobarth, the only modern physician in Abington, the same one who, in another letter, told Gwen she was barren and could never conceive. Jo understood the meaning of the other word, too, and it wasn't about the creeks rising. *Flooding* stood in as the lingering Victorian word for preeclampsia, a hypertensive, multisystem disorder leading to severe convulsions and hemorrhage. By 1906 physicians could manage the condition with magnesium sulfate. Hobarth would have known that; she could even have performed an emergency C-section, risky as it was. But she didn't. She never came. Because no one called her.

Aiden wrote more in the margins of these factual notations, as if trying to imagine the scene himself: Evelyn lying above in the secret nursery, alone, in labor, and everything going wrong. The midwife had written the notes to *someone*, but if it had been the good doctor, then there would be records. What happened?

Jo thought she knew. Ida Hobarth would know the baby was William's, which meant she'd learned of the affair. To call her would be to invite calumny and shame. Did the midwife send that note to Gwen? Upon refusing to do as asked, did she stand in her nightdress at the bottom of those grand stairs and let her sister die? Or did she leave the house so she wouldn't hear the cries?

Aiden filled in the details on his own:

Maybe she told herself Evelyn would survive on her own; perhaps she lied to her conscience. The midwife was local, low-class. Someone poor who could be paid off. She couldn't save Evelyn. Managed to save the infant. Evelyn's last words were the child's name; call her Violet. Gwen forced the midwife to take the child with her. When it was over, the house was silent—so silent—too silent. Or did Gwen still hear the ringing of a babe's weak cry?

Gwen didn't murder her sister with the twist of a knife, but she killed her all the same. The greater crime came next; she rejected the baby—hid it from its father, sent it away. Records of work done by the gardeners reveal a cold cellar dug in the basement. It had only begun, but served as the perfect grave for Evelyn. And when the deed was done? Jo imagined Gwen standing before the painting of Evelyn Davies where it hung in the library.

Letters, in the autumn years: April 1931 to "a friend":

William stays so often in Allerton; we rarely speak. This house is so very empty, Ethel, and I am sick at heart. Won't you come see me? I cannot stand to be company to myself, and you know so much of my history. You'll come, won't you? I think this place is haunted, yet.]

January 1935 to "Dr. Jack":

He won't rise again. I went in to see him, but he turns from me. You tell me to take heart, but I must know. Is this the end? There are things I need to tell him. Please don't preserve me as a lady; the world is already so dark, death is a shadow against night.

February of the same, a letter begun and never finished:

He knows. I know he does. He will not forgive me.

Jo had thought this whole time that Gwen destroyed it out of jealousy, but it wasn't so. She couldn't bear the judgment of those eyes. She couldn't stand the guilt. The garden was still in its glory, then, well fertilized no doubt with phosphates. Perhaps she found the sulfuric acid in a potting shed, property of the gardeners she was about to get rid of. Maybe she even blamed them for the deed. Daughter of a steel magnate, she would, of course, know exactly what such a corrosive would do.

Aiden ended Gwen's tree, a solitary branch. But for William, the lines went on. Violet had become Viola. She'd been given the last name Taylor at a home for orphans—and then shipped, with hundred of other "home children," to rural Canada. She'd been "received" by a farmer in Quebec in 1913 at the age of five. The trail went cold until after the First World War; Aiden located a marriage license: Viola Taylor and Edmon Bouchard to be wed in April 1922. The tree branched in 1923, 1925 and 1928. Three children.

"Three," Jo said out loud. Her eyes had clouded, and she blinked at the sky to try and clear them. "Noah, Olivia and Emile."

"Last name Bouchard, right?" Gwilym had been fighting to access his genealogy sites via mobile phone.

"Yes, but Noah died in World War II. He was a pilot, flew with the Royal Canadian Air Force, and later the British RAF." Jo scanned the last pages. The handwriting grew weaker, the entries further apart. The last entry wasn't about Viola's children at all; it was a record of her death at the age of fifty-one. Survived by her husband, buried at Notre Dame des Neiges Cemetery. Jo checked the date; Aiden himself would have died a month after the last entry. He must have known it was coming, and that his hope for the wedding proposal wasn't to be. Mortal, he concluded with Viola's mortality, then locked it away beneath a ring he'd never give his lover.

"God, this is—this is . . ." Jo sank her face into her hands.

"A lot?" Gwilym asked, patting her gingerly on the back. Succinct. Correct. But not nearly enough to cover all the feelings Jo had swelling up.

"They're out there," she said, looking at Gwilym through her fingers. "At least, maybe their children are, if they had them. I have *family*." Gwilym gave her a curious look. Then he leaned on his knees and looked Tyne-ward.

"You know, Jo. You *have* family. I mean. There's Arthur, he counts. And Tula. Imagine what she'd say if you *didn't* think of her that way." He hazarded a glance in her direction. "MacAdams, even. And me. I hope you count me."

Jo found it suddenly hard to swallow. *Do not*, she warned her cry muscles. There had been one meltdown this week already and that was plenty, so she forced the sob into something more benign.

"You're my friend, Gwilym. I'm not entirely sure I've even had one before," she said. "Not a real one."

"Those are the only kind worth having," he said. Jo felt a temporary impulse to hug him. Instead, she stood up and offered a hand in pulling him to his feet.

"I want to take Evelyn home," she said. *Her* home. Abington—and Netherleigh Cottage.

"Good plan," Gwilym agreed. Jo handed him the book; she needed to put her sweatshirt on. The day had been warm, but a cool wind was blowing and brought with it a chill. It was nearly six in the evening, and though the sun wouldn't set for hours, the sky had grayed. If they crossed the next street, it would be a short walk back to Arthur's flat; she'd taken that route the day she encountered the butty van driver.

"We should see about getting this into Roberta's archive," Gwilym said, tying up the twine.

"If Arthur lets us," Jo added. "Today might not be the day to ask."

They stood at the corner, checking for traffic, but someone had just run ahead of them into the street. Gwilym said something about the risk of it—at least she thought he did; the world had just fuzzed out. It happened in moments of hyperfocus: the hi-fi rush of pinpoint attention as everything else desaturated. A taxi stopped to let the crosswalker go by, everything in slow motion. When it all snapped forward again, Jo didn't think, she just reacted: *follow*. Across the road, amid honks and shouts and Gwilym cursing in Welsh she went—because out in front was the woman in yellow, the one who had vanished on the moor.

★ ★ ★

Stanley Burnhope wore a pale blue sport coat of linen which nearly matched the walls of Newcastle's interview room. His lawyer, a woman in deep black whose lapels, heels and facial expressions were all equally sharp, looked like she might spit venom. MacAdams took a seat, though Burnhope was first to speak.

"I'm here as a free agent and of my own volition," he said. "I want to help Dmytro."

MacAdams made him repeat it for the tape. Then he opened the file, the one with blunt trauma images of Foley.

"Good. You can start by telling the truth," MacAdams said. "This morning you pretended to be shocked about the seizure of artifacts. But you knew Foley was dealing in stolen goods, and you knew Dmytro helped him. For all I know, all of Hammersmith is in on the deal and those were *your* goons clearing away the evidence in York."

"You have just accused my client of a crime. Do you wish to retract?" asked the legal.

MacAdams leaned toward the recording device. "No, I don't wish to retract."

"My client does not have *goons,* as you put it," she said.

MacAdams ignored her and looked instead at Burnhope. "Sophie caught Dmytro Friday morning. But she wasn't alone, was she? You and Gerald were there, too. How convenient. But you promise to keep Dmytro out of trouble. Why would you do that? Worried we might trace all of this back to you?"

Burnhope settled his gaze on MacAdams. It was hard to read what might be going on there; when not surprised, he was very good at hiding emotion. Almost as good as MacAdams.

"Foley's crimes have nothing to do with me, except that I'm Dmytro's only protection. He is vulnerable," he said, smoothing a curl behind his ear. "Artem is older; he's a solid lad. And he's engaged to Anje. Dmytro—he's much more alone. I took him under wing; he needed a father figure."

MacAdams noted that none of this answered his question, but he was willing to be patient. Just not *very* patient.

"Go on," he said flatly.

"He struggled. And his behavior had changed in the last few months." Burnhope's hands had been folded on the table; now they wandered, restless. "Sophie cornered him, and after he told her, they both came to tell me, his sponsor."

"On Friday," MacAdams repeated for the tape.

"That's right. He admitted he'd been doing work on the side for Foley, *a courier service*." Burnhope cleared his throat. "He's not a stupid boy. He knew it was wrong, but Foley promised to get his family out of the war zone."

"How would he do that?"

"How would I know? They were lies."

"You have been telling lies, too," MacAdams countered. "The meeting with Foley last Friday, that wasn't about a promotion. You already knew what Foley was hiding in York."

"No, I *didn't* know about York," Burnhope said, his brow twitching in annoyance. "I didn't have the first clue—how would I?"

"There is a stolen artifact in Dmytro's locker," MacAdams said flatly. "You could have reported it. You could have had Foley arrested and put away. But you didn't." MacAdams tapped the tabletop, then slid forward the more gruesome of the photos. "Almost as though you knew Foley wouldn't be a problem anymore, regardless."

Predictably, Burnhope's lawyer was ready to interrupt.

"You are insinuating a crime," she said.

"No," MacAdams countered. "I'm solving one. Tell me, Mr. Burnhope. Why the lies?"

Burnhope released his grip on the table and forced his hands back to a neutral clasp. Possibly, this was to make him appear more at ease. It had the opposite effect of highlighting contents under pressure.

"Do you *know* how difficult it is to bring refugees into this country?" he demanded. "There's already a stigma. People are against anyone who wasn't born here, and you know it. Dmytro will be lucky if he's not sent back to Ukraine. Fresh Start will be lucky if we don't lose our certifications—"

"So you were willing to ignore felonies to save face?" MacAdams interrupted.

Burnhope did not relish being interrupted. "To save *lives*!" he half shouted. "To bring these people out of war—that's what we *do*."

MacAdams let a few seconds of silence fall between them and this last exclamation. Then he leaned forward on the metal table. "Let's try this again. Friday. What happened at that meeting?"

For a long moment, Burnhope said nothing. MacAdams thought he might not proceed at all, and that the interview would terminate, intractable. He was already thinking through scenarios for keeping him in the interview room—even arrest, if that were possible—when he spoke.

"I didn't know what Dmytro had stolen. I didn't know why, and the last thing I wanted was to bring suspicion on the poor kid. I thought—maybe—there was some other explanation, and I already had a meeting with Foley." He looked from MacAdams to the tape recorder. "I didn't lie about that; we were discussing his promotion."

"The promotion he'd emailed you about. The one you didn't plan to give him."

"We never even got so far," Burnhope explained. "I demanded answers. He didn't have any. Instead, he said Dmytro was a liar and a delinquent. He said they were *all* delinquents."

"And then what? You argued? It got heated?"

"No. I was angry but could barely speak. He said he was leaving the country—with a woman. I told him good riddance."

"Was she a refugee, like Dmytro?" MacAdams asked.

Burnhope shook his head. "I don't know *anything* about her," he insisted. "I got suspicious when you showed me the sketch. I hope to God she isn't. I just wanted Foley gone, out of the business, out of our lives—out of Dmytro's life. Hasn't it occurred to you that *he* is the one most likely to pay for Foley's crimes? An outsider, barely an adult, a refugee?"

Burnhope's voice had elevated slightly. MacAdams watched his pulse tick at the vein in his neck.

"Is that why you killed Foley?" he asked.

"Mr. MacAdams," shouted his legal counsel, but Burnhope held up a placating hand.

"He *knows* I didn't kill Foley. I was at the charity ball on Friday night, with more than a hundred witnesses." Then he fixed his gaze on MacAdams again. "You asked me why I didn't report Foley—why I didn't reveal this to you even after his death. It's because if I did, it would endanger Dmytro. And I was right."

★ ★ ★

Every detective was a cynic. It couldn't be helped. Humans, even when best intentioned, *lied constantly*. They lied to others; they lied to themselves. Three eyewitnesses couldn't tell you the same story standing next to each other. There were biases and vested interests; a witness to a vicious attack suddenly remembered that he *tried* to help; of course he did. A witness to the regular beatings of a wife by her husband would claim there was nothing to suggest he might one day murder her. People made up endings and filled gaps always with a view to present themselves in the best light; truth was relative and up for revision.

MacAdams walked away from the interview room where a charitable businessman with a supposedly impeccable record claimed his worst fault was in service to a vulnerable teenager on the cusp of adulthood. Even if he wanted to believe him, MacAdams couldn't afford to take his word. But Burnhope did have an ace; he *was* at the charity ball. And Green was presently checking the footage.

He found Green surrounded by a cluster of young officers and detectives. Heads down, they were watching Sophie's footage, with Green offering commentary to eager listeners. It was rare he caught her so candid, and not for the first time he thought she ought to be running a department somewhere.

"What news?" he asked.

"It's not favorable," she said, eyes still locked on the time stamp. "Not to us, anyway." She motioned to the picture, which was surprisingly clear and focused. Sophie—and Burnhope—stood on the stage welcoming guests and announcing the silent auction. "I haven't gone over it minute by minute yet. But he gives the farewell, too, just like he said."

"And Sophie Wagner?"

"Yup, she's there the whole time."

"Not our murderers?" MacAdams sat on the edge of the desk, chewing pride and indignation—and his lower lip. It didn't mean they were clear of involvement, but they had just been bumped back to square one. Who dealt the killing blow?

"We've got other problems," Green said. "The Lord Mayor's office called. They want to know why we're holding Stanley Burnhope."

"We're not," MacAdams said, aware that it came out a bit like a growl.

"Well, thank God you've preserved your good humor," Green replied, but she wasn't happy, either, he knew.

They *had* to let Burnhope go. But of course, he wouldn't go far. He was Newcastle's golden boy, after all. There was an empty desk nearby; MacAdams threw himself into the chair with enough force to make the springs squeal. What did they have? A terrified kid who had seen too much but somehow not enough to help them, and who was now in danger of prison time or deportation.

"Gerald Standish. I'm sure he's our receiver," he muttered.

"Can we prove it?" Green asked.

"No. Not yet." *Maybe not ever,* he added silently. "But there's more that bothers me. He seemed utterly shocked that we'd picked up Dmytro."

"As in, surprised the kid got caught?"

"As in, that he was involved. Apparently, he and Burnhope are sort of sponsoring him. And to be honest, I don't think either of them would risk involving the charity."

"Foley working alone somehow?" Green considered it a moment. "There's no way, right?"

A golden rule of policing: big jobs are never lonely jobs. The one thread they could follow was that Foley must have plenty of connections. He must have somehow used Fresh Start to make contacts in Syria; that was at least somewhere to begin. Sophie admitted Foley had been involved in the early days; he'd ask Newcastle to call Home Office and have every record checked. Sophie would be brought in for questioning, too, and Burnhope was right—they may very well lose whatever license permitted them to sponsor incoming refugees.

"He's got people. For one, he has the Geordie—whoever he is." They didn't know the van driver, not even with cooperation from Dmytro, and they *still* didn't know who killed Foley. At present it seemed their excursion to Newcastle had done more harm than good. MacAdams looked at his palms; he'd been reduced to, literally, going home to lick his wounds.

"Boss?"

MacAdams looked up to see Green. She'd removed her suit jacket, too, and was presently stretching her left shoulder.

"You all right?" he asked.

"Hell of a wrench, but I'll live," she said. It occurred to Mac-

Adams that if it wasn't for Green and Jo, he might be in hospital. Things could certainly be worse.

"Let's get back to Abington. I want to go over that video frame by frame," he said—or tried to. A local DS had just started shouting at them.

"Sir! Uniform just found a butty van—matches your description!"

Green jumped up ahead of him. "Where?" she asked. The kid handed her his mobile, coordinates on GPS. "Ah *fuck*," she said, handing it over to MacAdams. To him, it was just a dot on a map.

"What's the trouble, Sheila?" he asked.

She grimaced and spoke through her teeth. "That's a dumping ground," she said.

MacAdams stood on the overlook of a quarry-turned-landfill. He'd thought Green meant fly-tipping, the rather notorious practice of trashdumping on an out-of-the-way property. He hadn't realized it was an actual garbage dump, nor one that provided for a steep dropoff if you were bold enough. The butty van driver got full marks for that.

"Locals reported the smoke," Green explained. "Had mostly burned out by the time anyone got here."

They picked their way down to the vehicle itself, awash in the smell of petrol and smoking rubber. The lettering had crisped and peeled, the delivery window smashed in on impact. MacAdams half expected Struthers to climb out of the wreckage, but instead it was a short woman in her late fifties.

"You want the bad news first?" she asked, peeling away a glove. "I'd say they took a blow torch to surfaces even *before* dousing, lighting and giving the heave-ho. Black as sin in there. I'm Lori Peterson, by the way."

"James MacAdams," he said by way of obligatory greeting. "Is there any good news?"

"No bodies," she said with a shrug. "I did find something

potentially interesting. It's a shoe. I think I found the other, as well, but it's melted to the frame." She motioned to a baggie off to one side.

MacAdams knelt beside the evidence wrapped in blue plastic. Not much to look at; possibly canvas—a sort of walking shoe.

"Can you tell what size that is?"

"Wouldn't fit me," Peterson said. "Little feet, whoever they were. Why?"

"I need to know if we have a match," MacAdams said. Because he was thinking of the fancy heels back at the Abington Arms. They had been a 37 Euro size—about a 4 in UK.

"I'll see what I can do," Peterson agreed.

Green came abreast of MacAdams. "What are you thinking?" she asked.

MacAdams pursed his lips into a tight line. He was *thinking* about Jo Jones . . . or rather, about her way of sensing incongruity. Little details mattered.

"The hiker, the one Jo said vanished. We assumed she was another artifact courier for Foley."

"You don't think so?" Green asked.

MacAdams shook his head. Jo told him—he just hadn't really *heard* her.

"The woman, according to Jo, wasn't carrying a rucksack the way a hill walker would. Jo sees her walk toward the van; the Geordie claims he hasn't seen anyone. Now we find lady's shoes inside? Too much of a coincidence."

"Shite. We're talking about Foley's girlfriend, aren't we?"

MacAdams started back toward the car, his brain leaping forward onto the new trail. *Girlfriend* wasn't quite the word.

"We're talking about a refugee that Foley managed to shuttle around in a food truck," he said. One he'd apparently gotten pregnant and made promises to—one he was *supposed* to meet in Abington the night he died. "She's in danger."

Green's brows furrowed, a sign of the gears turning within. "Okay, let's think. She went to the hotel; she could still be in Abington."

"The van is *here*," MacAdams said, opening the driver's door and leaning on it. "Which means the Geordie is here, and the girl, too. I suspect we're looking for a big black SUV now—like the one in York."

"Right. But without make and model, we can't even send out a search." Green climbed into the passenger seat. "What do they want her for? If she witnessed the murder, surely she'd already be dead."

MacAdams agreed. There was something else afoot. Was she a threat? A bargaining chip? Something else?

"It would help if we knew who she was—even where she was from," he said.

Green buckled in. "I think I know," she said. "I at least know who to ask. Ava Burnhope. I've been chewing over something she said."

"I believe we've been kicked out of her house," MacAdams reminded her.

Green merely gave him a sly smile.

"Just let me do the talking on this one," she said.

★ ★ ★

The day was getting late when Green rang the bell—and this time, Ava answered it herself.

"No. You don't get to come in and you don't get to ask questions. My husband has been down at the station for hours and—"

"He's been released," Green interrupted.

"Well, he's not home. And you aren't welcome." Ava moved to shut the door. Green wedged her foot and shoulder into the crack before she could manage it.

"You *cannot* do that!" Ava exclaimed. "Unlawful entry—"

"Do you want me to get a warrant? Because I can. And I won't be quiet about it, either, Ms. Thompson."

"It's *Burnhope*," Ava corrected. Green didn't retreat.

"It was Thompson first. And you might be glad of that, eventually. I saw you perform—everyone here knows you're brilliant. You're above him."

MacAdams hung back, a spectator. And so far, he'd not anticipated a single one of Green's moves. Apparently, neither had Ava.

"I beg your pardon?" she asked.

Green pushed the police sketch through the door.

"This woman. She was trafficked by Foley into this country. The van they kept her in was torched at the dump. We know because her shoes were in there. She's still missing and in trouble. Now . . . you said you cared, and I'm asking you to prove it."

Ava didn't say anything for a moment, as though each of Green's sentences had to make an emergency landing in her mind.

"Her shoes," she said finally, and opened the door. "God."

Ava was wearing the same shimmering duster from earlier in the day, but her gait was no longer ethereal. She walked, heavy soled, on the earth the same as anyone, stopping when she reached the kitchen.

"Do you want tea?" she asked, and MacAdams had the distinct impression she was speaking only to Green.

"No, thank you."

"You won't mind if I have some," Ava said, pouring from a carafe into a nearby mug. She wrapped her fingers around it, held on without drinking. A talisman, or something for her hands to do. "What do you want, Detective?"

"The truth," Green said. And Ava . . . laughed. It was an empty, sad sound. The only sound. MacAdams realized he could hear no children.

"Doesn't everyone," she said. "They aren't here, if you're wondering. I sent the children to my mother's. And Maryam, too."

Green walked farther into the kitchen and leaned against marble countertops.

"You're angry, aren't you?" she said quietly to Ava. "But not at us. I'm guessing you didn't know about Dmytro and Foley."

"Stanley told me this morning, after you left." The pale lashes closed slowly before opening again. "Because he knew I'd find out eventually."

"Foley wasn't just bringing artifacts into the country. He was bringing people. A person, anyway. And she's carrying his baby."

The mug hit the counter hard enough to spill tea over the lip.

"Everything I've worked for is wrapped up in refugee work," Ava said, turning away. She delivered the rest while staring at the cupboards. "I gave up my career for this—for my children and people like them. For Maryam. For the charity."

"When news of this gets out, it's going to play hell with reputation," Green said. "Stanley lied. Sophie lied."

"To protect Dmytro!" Ava said, snapping back around.

"Yeah?" Green asked. "Why him? Why not think about all the others? He's put everyone in jeopardy, and not just at Fresh Start. What about Maryam? What about your kids?"

Ava made a noise of disgust, almost a bark.

"I asked him that, myself," she said, finally drinking the tea—possibly to hide a look of white-hot anger. It reflected in her eyes, anyway.

"Did he give you an answer? He didn't, did he? He didn't give us much of one, either." Green unfolded the sketch again. "You know what I think? I think this woman is key to a whole lot about a whole lot. I want to know who she is, and I want you to tell me."

MacAdams braced himself, but Ava didn't erupt. She looked honestly confused.

"I told you, I don't recognize her," she said.

Green nodded. "I know. And I believe you meant it. I just don't think it's *true*." She held up the page to the light. A rounded face, strong jaw but pointed chin, broad nose and almond eyes beneath dark brows. "Do you remember what you said? You asked if she was a refugee. Why?"

"It was a guess—she had dark hair, dark eyes—"

Green bucked her chin. "You said it because you *do* recognize her, unconsciously, at least. She reminds you of Maryam."

Ava bristled. "Because she's Syrian? So what, you're saying I think all Syrians look the same?"

"Ava, listen to yourself. I didn't say this woman was Syrian. But you just did."

"It's where the artifacts came from, the papers said. I just—It's coincidence," Ava remonstrated.

"Is it?" MacAdams asked. "Or are these matters all connected? You saw that face and you thought of Maryam. We told you this girl is in trouble; you said all refugees are in trouble. So maybe you should tell us why Maryam remains frightened of the police?"

"It was just a filing error—it's been sorted—she has a passport and everything!" Ava said, which told MacAdams at least half of what he wanted to know.

"Her entry into this country was complicated, is that it?"

"But not illegal!" Ava said, though without the firm conviction she'd used a few days before.

Green nodded in her direction. "Well, *something* illegal is happening here. And meanwhile, we have a missing person on our hands. If I were you, Ms. Burnhope, I'd get a solicitor. For yourself, the kids and Maryam, too."

Ava's glassy eyes held unfallen tears, but the line of her mouth was surprisingly resolute.

"Call me Ms. *Thompson*, please."

CHAPTER 29

Thursday, 18:37

Jo stared down an empty street. They had been following the yellow raincoat for ten minutes. Yellow like Caution, or Slippery When Wet; it should have been easy to track. It wasn't. The woman never stopped, rarely slowed and moved with erratic cadence . . . almost as if she knew someone followed behind and had every intent of losing them.

Now she had.

Jo leaned against a light post and overlooked Grey's Monument.

"Gone," she muttered, lifting her left foot. There had been entirely too much walking all day, and a newborn blister was forming. Gwilym rolled his shirtsleeves. The evening promised to be cool, but they'd both worked up a sweat in the chase.

"Maybe she went into one of the shops?" he asked. Jo looked at her flagging phone battery and frowned.

"According to GPS, we've been heading south and east pretty directly," she said, showing the blue line of their recent movements. Gwilym had tucked Aiden's notebook under his arm and followed along on his own mobile.

"So not as random as it felt," he said. "She must have a destination in mind. I mean, she might even live around here."

"But we first saw her in Abington," Jo protested.

"Honestly, all I saw was a yellow blur. How can we be sure it's even the same person?"

"It's her. I saw her face. Also, the coat doesn't have lapels; you don't see a priest's collar on a rain slicker very often," Jo said. But there was something more, too, something that assured her even if she couldn't quite explain it. It *felt* the same. Both times she'd seen her Jo had the same strange presentiment, the long-shadowed feeling of dread. It wasn't a superpower, but pheromones . . . And according to recent scientific study, it wasn't even rare. Humans evolved to pick up emotion chemicals; they simultaneously evolved to forget that's what they were doing. Chemical signatures shared through sweat glands: *I have a bad feeling about this.* The woman was afraid . . . and on some subconscious level, Jo could smell trouble.

"We need to find her before something bad happens," Jo said finally. And to his credit, Gwilym started hunting the map for possibilities.

"Welp, if she keeps on south, she'll have to cross a bridge." He looked at his watch, then back to the phone. "We might be able to catch up."

They headed south, not quite jogging down Grey Street with Gwilym in the lead.

"Okay, decision time," Gwilym said as they circled a roundabout in a nest of stately sandstone buildings. "High Level Bridge or Swing? Those are more likely for pedestrians."

"Let's do both. I'll take Swing and meet you on the other side."

The High Level Bridge arched above them, meaning Gwilym had to backtrack. Jo stole another look at her own map before heading toward the river.

Swing Bridge took the middle between High and the stately

auto bridge; it was, however, the far more humble construction. The pedestrian way wound *outside* of the supports; no rails or bumper between pavement and a short drop to the water. Safe enough, she guessed, as fat drops began falling. Jo pulled her hood in place as pedestrians ducked under awnings on her side of the river. The far side appeared empty; no shops, no one traveling the bridge, not even a passing car. Certainly not a woman in a rain slicker. Jo headed across anyway.

The drops became a steady—if light—rain by the time she reached the end. The south side of the river had a wholly different feel. On the hill she could see a hotel; street level offered mainly spray-paint-tagged garage doors of closed shops. The wind had begun to blow, sending a chill down her damp spine. Gwilym would be coming from the west, so she chose to go east and south.

Bottle Bank Street ran next to a stone wall and the separation of the river. There had been crowds all day, everywhere she went; the business corridor felt strangely blank and lonely by contrast. She stood at the next intersection, a prickle raising hairs on the back of her neck. *Text MacAdams*, she thought. She'd meant Gwilym. Until she didn't.

Jo pulled out her phone and scrolled to *M*. We've found and lost the vanishing hiker, she typed. Send. Send. *Send, send, send* . . .

The screen blinked and turned off: dead battery. Jo huffed and tucked it back in her pocket, eyes straying down the cross street and its identical apartment lofts for rent—and a single flash of distant yellow.

"Wait!" Jo shouted, but she was far ahead of her. The street headed away at an angle, past the hotel. *Service drive*, Jo thought. Garbage bins and maintenance vehicles, and probably no trespassing, but the girl had just vanished around the corner. Jo followed, ignoring her screaming blister—but the road dead-ended at a parking garage. Jo stared at two square doors and warnings about low ceilings. There wasn't anywhere else to go; she *must* have run inside.

"I should not be doing this." It had never worked before, but she felt obliged to say it anyway. Then she held her breath and crossed into the shadow of the building. Jo half expected to be accosted, or at least to set off some sort of alarm; she saw no one, heard nothing but a distant drip of water somewhere farther within. A row of parked cars ran down the one side, one of them surprisingly *American*—an SUV as big as an Escalade. Jo stared at her own reflection in its tinted windows, and then, the engine turned over. Jo started and spun around, ready to dash for the entrance, but someone stood just behind her. A man. A man who shouldn't be there.

"Can I help you, miss?" he asked, coming closer.

Jo's voice came out in a gasping whisper: *"Ronan Foley?"*

19:00

Newcastle's CID grew considerably quieter in the after-hours. Green and MacAdams had borrowed desk space and were currently going through the charity ball footage frame by agonizing frame. MacAdams had taken a break to refresh their coffees; when he returned Green was hanging up the landline.

"They're keeping the kid overnight in a cell," Green was saying. "Worried he's a flight risk."

"He'd have every reason. He doesn't want to go back to the Ukraine."

"We still have Sophie, too," he said, though they couldn't keep her. He'd repeated the interview and taken her statement, but lying about someone else's offense wasn't the same as committing one.

"Speaking of." Green paused the footage and reversed it. "There's Sophie on the night of."

Dressed in sequins, she'd be hard to miss. She worked her way through the ballroom. A banner had been hung above, and tiny white lights twinkled against exposed stone walls. Smart-clad staff filled champagne flutes, and Sophie gave her wide, breezy smile to black-tie guests. Time-stamp: 21:12, just after 9:00 p.m.

"That's the city CEO she's taking to—Ava's father," Green explained. "And that's the Lord Mayor in the back with the whiskey glass." The guest list had included plenty more from city governance, but also three MPs and a representative from Home Office, along with not a few local celebrities and the city's top-earning businesspersons. "They skimmed the whole top layer for this gig. And *there's* Burnhope."

MacAdams squinted at the freeze-frame. He'd given a speech at the outset, about eight, and hadn't been around much since. Now, four people stood in front of him posing for a photograph and mostly obstructing the view. Stanley said something to Sophie, then he was out of frame again.

"You know, while you were suspecting Ava, I half thought the two of *them* were carrying on," Green said. "Sophie and Burnhope, I mean."

"They did fly to Syria without Ava," MacAdams agreed, settling back in his chair.

"Right? But it's like with Trisha and Foley, maybe. One-sided."

"You think Sophie was keen and Burnhope wasn't?"

"Or didn't want to risk it. A wife like Ava and all those fancy connections would be a lot to jeopardize."

"Yet, he *has* jeopardized them," MacAdams said. "If we can find evidence he was part of this mess, he stands to lose just about everything. Then again, what if this case isn't about the artifacts at all?"

"Didn't we seize a small museum's worth of the stuff?"

"Yes. Technically," MacAdams said. "But it hasn't helped us make sense of Foley's murder. What's the motive?"

"Money, in'it? Makes problems go away. And trafficking anything makes money," Green reminded him. MacAdams drank his coffee. Obviously, following the money was just good policing. Then why did it feel wrongheaded?

"I know the gold is worth something on its own. The pottery, though. The bronze statue in Dmytro's locker. Our going theory is that most of the objects that the kids trafficked didn't 'look' expensive. They would be valuable for a select few."

"It would to the right people, though," Green said, looking at her screen again. "Standish, for instance."

"Him and his nose rings. But even he's not buying a whole warehouse full. That's the sign of a big operation. Trafficking anything requires a network. It's global. Hammersmith is global. And yet, this butty van business, the use of the kids, the Geordie driver—"

"With his lead pipe," Green added, and MacAdams grimaced a smile.

"Ye-es, with that. It's all small. Unprofessional." Beside him, Green pushed her chair back and swiveled toward him.

"*Ah.* That's why you still suspect Burnhope. And what, this other stuff was Foley cutting corners?"

"Maybe. He made a mess of the York property, too. As Burnhope himself told us, no head for business. But if Foley isn't the trafficking mastermind, then we need to open up our motives again." He set his mug down. "Leave the video for a minute. Let's go to the whiteboard. What are our possible scenarios now?"

Green rolled up her sleeves and tapped her chin with one finger.

"Number one: Foley is running it all—dealing with trade and with the front end, in Syria. Gets in over his head. Tries to do a runner but doesn't make it."

"Meaning the murder is UNESCO and Interpol territory. Okay, next?"

"Two: Burnhope and Foley are in it together. Foley was his heavy, the dark horse to his golden boy, and the York property was a place to warehouse artifacts before distribution," Green finished, but MacAdams wagged a finger.

"*Except* Burnhope knew that the York property was behind schedule and had been called by the Lord Mayor of all people. Ashok said they could have lost the property if the right strings were pulled; that's no place to keep secrets."

"Maybe he's just that brash?" Green asked.

MacAdams stared at the photos pinned to the board. Burnhope, with his hooded eyes, smooth manners, important friends. Foley, with his faux black hair, his habit of bullying men and wooing women and his propensity to bug out when things got hot.

"No. Burnhope is bold. He's cool under pressure. But not brash. I don't think he knew the artifacts were in York. If he had, and he was part of the deal, he would have cleaned the place out immediately, not three days after Foley's death. But that's not all." MacAdams drummed the table. "Burnhope said it himself, in a way. Foley did the dirty work, the hands-on business of dealing with contractors. If Burnhope is in on the trade, Foley is the middleman. And Burnhope himself doesn't want that job."

Green drew her brows together, thinking.

"Did you just clear Burnhope of murder?" she asked.

"No. But now you see why I don't think the motive has to do with the artifact trade."

"Okay, then what about Foley corrupting Dmytro?" Green suggested. "That's a motive for Burnhope and Sophie. And what about Gerald Standish? He's a sponsor or whatever, but isn't he still a likely buyer for the butty van art?"

MacAdams set his coffee mug aside. "Okay, now *that* makes sense. Small-time operation, that would be the sort of thing that works local. Granted, he still has plausible deniability. He could say he didn't *know* the back-of-van objects were illegal."

"Yes but only because Foley is dead. He can't plea-bargain and spill it. But he can't be our murderer, either," Green said, returning to the computer terminal. "He's right here on the tapes . . . and he never even leaves the bar."

The alibis were really starting to gall. Green restarted the video and MacAdams peered over her shoulder. Ava had entered the frame. She wore a gown of shimmering silver, her platinum hair wound up in a complicated braid. The piano had been largely obscured by milling humans; now a spotlight shone upon it, and Ava took her place at the keys.

"You know, I may have had a mild crush on her," she mused. "Back in Newcastle. She was a joy to watch, even if not exactly my type."

There it was again: *type.* He found himself thinking of Arianna—and her taunts about leaving town.

"Do you miss it here in Newcastle?" he asked.

Green lifted her head and smiled faintly. "Sometimes," she said. "But I left for Rachel."

On the screen, Sophie had announced the silent auction—and Ava began to play. The long, willowy arms seemed to float above dancing fingers. They had the sound off, but it was captivating anyway.

Green leaned on her hand. "Rachel was seeing someone else when we met. Arianna Templeton. Don't look at me like that—you *knew* I'd tell you eventually."

"I made no assumptions," MacAdams protested.

"Well, the split was messy. And when we got together, Arianna was furious. At me, not Rachel."

"Because you replaced her?"

"Because I'm a *cop.* The queer community isn't exactly police friendly, and I don't blame us for it. But that wasn't it. She said I'd doomed Rachel to a life of worry and pain and looking out windows wondering if I'd come home again." Green's smile faded. "*Then* I lost my partner to a bad call-out. So I left Newcastle because I didn't want to make Rachel a widow."

MacAdams noted the gut punch of irony—to leave dangerous city cases only to end up where you started with trafficking and a murder on the side.

"Rachel's lucky to have you," he said. Then, after a pause: "So am I."

Green didn't reply; he didn't expect her to. But he was glad he'd said it. On the screen, Ava played on, hands weaving a spell rather than playing music. The light glanced off her pale skin, pearlescent, translucent. Her eyes, he noticed, appeared half-closed; a face of concentration, a face of rapture.

"She's beautiful to watch, isn't she?" Green asked. "Wait till you hear her." She increased the volume and notes spilled out of the speakers.

"Complicated piece."

"No shite. That's Piano Concerto No. 3 by Sergei Rachmaninoff," Green told him. "It's her showpiece—one of the most difficult to play. She stopped touring five years ago; this would have been a big draw to this crowd."

MacAdams wasn't familiar with classical music, but agreed her performance was incredible.

It was also *distracting.* All eyes were upon Ava—including their own. MacAdams forced himself to search the crowd.

"Where's Burnhope?" he asked.

"He steps out of frame at nine-twelve, remember?"

"Right before a signature performance his wife hasn't given in years?" MacAdams paused and scrolled back, then forward. Stanley Burnhope left; he didn't come back. "This is the only camera angle?"

"Yes. Unless you count CCTV; we collected it from the parking lot, and from the rear hall. It's loading and storage for the booze. Expensive shipments with bottles that tend to walk away if you aren't watching."

MacAdams was still scrolling forward, partygoers speeding along in jerky treble time. Sophie glinted in and out, Ava too—dancing at one point with her father. No Stanley.

"Queue up CCTV on the second monitor," he said.

Green scrolled to a secondary jump drive. The first view offered a parking lot with nothing but sheets of diagonal rain.

"Switch to the rear door."

"Whew. Lots going on here," Green said.

The camera had given them a gray-and-white view of the hall behind the annex kitchen. Crates stood on the floor, stacked double. Three uniformed staff members were busily unloading—a fourth slipped by precariously with a tray of glasses. She disappeared to the right, and in her place appeared a man in a mackintosh.

"Hold! Stop it there," MacAdams said. Frozen, the image was less distinct, but here was a man with his collar up and an umbrella in his left hand. "It's Burnhope. It must be."

"But we know he's back on stage to give the farewell address."

"That's half past midnight." MacAdams checked the coordinates on his phone. "You can make it from here to Abington in an hour and ten. Faster if you're really pushing it."

"Okay, but saying he left at nine-twelve, he'd not get to town till almost ten thirty. Foley was at Jo's by then, and she's with him till just after eleven."

"Burnhope could *still* make it back to give the speech," he said. "By quarter past midnight at the latest."

"Boss, you're counting *from* 11:00 p.m. Think about it. First he has to lure Foley out, then kill him, wrap him in ice for some reason, drive to the back road and dump him. That takes time. Like, a lot of time."

Dammit. She was right; he'd got caught up in the minutiae. MacAdams slumped back into his chair, pressed both palms (gingerly) to his eyes and heaved a sigh.

"Sheila. I hate this case," he said. "Nothing adds up."

"I know." Green put down her coffee and fished around in the bag at her feet. She emerged with assorted biscuits from

Tesco—what Jo called cookies—and offered him one. "This would be a lot easier if Jo last saw Foley an hour or so earlier."

"You're telling me." He accepted her offering; his stomach had been making noises of protest for an hour.

"Well. Here's a thought, boss. What if Jo is *wrong*?"

MacAdams gave her what he hoped was a look of incredulity.

"Jo Jones, who details the minutiae of absolutely everything and can cite chapter and verse?" he asked.

Green swallowed biscuit and chased it with now-cold coffee.

"Nobody's right all the time," she said. "Even Struthers was gonna put time of death earlier, remember?"

"Only because he can't be more precise. None of the other tests were conclusive—" MacAdams stopped midsentence. *The other tests.* He dug out his phone and speed-dialed the pathologist.

Green watched him, sharp eyed. "What—what have we missed?" she asked.

"Scroll to Burnhope's last speech and zoom in," he said.

"Struthers here," came the voice on the other end of the line.

MacAdams watched the footage. Burnhope stepped onto the stage at twelve thirty-two. Now that he was looking for the right thing, it was hard to miss.

"Eric, we've got a problem."

"What sort of problem?" Struthers asked.

MacAdams lifted the biscuit until it was eye level, a little round shortbread with a sticky, jam middle.

"Jammie Dodgers," he said.

CHAPTER 30

Thursday, 19:50

The man standing in front of Jo wore a tailored suit; hair perfectly set, shoe leather buffed to shine. But his eyes had just widened in their sockets, pulling hooded lids into wells of excess skin folds. Pigeon. Window. Smack.

"Ms. Jones?" he asked, his voice rising on the last syllable, the sharp note of disbelief.

"You're dead," Jo said. Because that was the first thought that came to mind, and at the moment shock wasn't permitting any others.

He opened his mouth, failed to speak and closed it again. Then he gestured to the car door.

"I can explain," he said finally. "I know it seems incredible, but there's—there's an answer. A solution. A very *simple* solution. Can you? Just come with me, please."

The sentences came out half-formed; a theory, a question, an imperative. Jo did not like it.

"I'm going to go now," she said. Except she didn't. Her eyes kept straying to the dark windows; he followed her train of thought exactly.

"You're looking for the girl." He took a step forward—Jo took a step back. "I'm trying to protect her. She's in trouble.

"Then you should call the police," Jo said. She thought: *Thirty steps to the parking ramp.*

"I will. I'm going to." Foley had recovered from the shock of seeing her. His manner smoothed. "But I don't want to get Lina in trouble."

"Why would she be in trouble?" Jo asked.

Foley sighed. "Because the system is broken, that's why. She's an asylum seeker." He waited for Jo to understand. She didn't. "Undocumented, I suppose, you'd say. She fled to the UK and applied for asylum. But she's been denied."

Jo was backing up, slowly.

"What does that mean?"

"It *means* she'll be deported. But Lina is safe with me." Foley looked over his shoulder and gestured to the car. "Do you want to meet her?"

Jo could smell the exhaust; whoever started the engine, it wasn't Foley. And that bothered her. Everything bothered her almost as much as the not-dead Foley. There were questions she ought to be asking, but they'd bottlenecked: *Why was he here, who was the girl . . . who was the* dead *guy*?

What she said was: "Let her out of the car."

Foley stood with his hands in front of him, palms open, facing out—nonthreatening. He took a step backward, his face near the window of the passenger side. It was, Jo noticed, cracked open.

"Lina, do you want to come out?" he asked. Jo's breath came quick in her throat as she watched the rear of the SUV. Her brain felt itchy. Something wasn't right. On the other side of the vehicle, Jo heard a door open and shut. *Run*, she told herself. *Run and don't look back.* Jo spun around and sprinted for the garage doors; she could make it to the street then back to the bridge—

"Gotcha!" Two arms wrapped tight around her middle, and the force almost sent her colliding with the pavement.

"Let *go*!" Jo shouted, writhing and kicking.

"Put her in the back," Foley said. He remained exactly where he was, unhurried, arms folded. Jo threw her head backward, trying to find a nose to break.

"She bloody feral," the man growled. "Open the door!"

Jo saw the back of the SUV in mental flashbulb: black leather seats, black interior, blacked-out windows, and cowering in the far corner was *Lina.* Under the yellow coat she wore an oversize shirt and leggings. She wasn't hurt, but the look on her face was one of hypervigilant attention—and possibly confusion. These men were *not* her rescuers. Jo raised both her knees, shifting the center of gravity. Her captor arched backward to compensate, and Jo kicked down as hard as she could, Doc Martens connecting solidly with both shins.

"Fucking hell!" he squealed and Jo wrenched free.

She didn't get far. Two rough hands closed on her shoulders, lifted and tossed her into the vehicle as if she was a cast-off rag.

"Nebby hinny, yar?"

Jo caught a glimpse of the man's heavy jowls and squared-off shoulders before the door closed. The Geordie. She dived for the handle, only to hear the child-safety locks click into place.

"For your own protection, you understand," said Foley, now from the passenger seat. Jo couldn't reach him; the SUV had been fitted with a caged partition. The other man—the one she'd kicked—climbed into a seat just in front of it. Jo threaded her fingers through the grate and gave it a shake.

"This is kidnapping!" she shouted.

In the front seat, Foley turned to face her. "I promise, we can work all of this out," he said. And then, to the man in front of her: "Close the curtain."

Jo watched as he tugged black fabric. Her window on the world closed by degrees until there was nothing but darkness.

Then the SUV lurched forward, knocking her onto the bench seat. Her phone was dead, and no one—not Gwilym, certainly not MacAdams—knew where she was. Jo felt her chest constrict with the urge to hyperventilate . . . and then, a small hand reached out and clutched her own.

"I am afraid," whispered the girl in yellow.

Jo stared into puffy, red eyes. She couldn't be more than eighteen. *Get a grip*, Jo told herself. *Vagus nerve. Autonomic stimulation. Four belly breaths and hold* . . . She gave the girl's hand a squeeze.

"I'm Jo," she said.

★★★

Sherlock Holmes would count the turns in the streets or identify route by sense of smell. Jo didn't know Newcastle well enough for any of that to matter, but she paid special attention to the *time*. Thirteen minutes from where she'd been; that was the radius. She tried to think of the GPS map and scale; it included a lot of ground on both sides of the river, but they were still in the city's center . . . somewhere. The vehicle came to a halt in a pouring rain; Foley opened the door, holding an umbrella.

"I need you both to come with me," he said.

"No way," Jo said, scrabbling backward—into the broad chest of the Geordie.

"Ye dee as yer telt!" he boomed.

"Tie you up if it was up to me, an' don't tempt me," said the third man, guiding them out of the car.

Two men on both sides of her, one behind, all within touching distance. Jo's skin crawled. *Focus on the ground*, she told herself. New asphalt, wet streaked beneath the black umbrella. A parking lot, but in a moment they were under the awning of a building. She heard Lina whimper: "Where is Habibi?" The word teased Jo's memory; she'd heard it before.

Foley just answered by saying, "Everything will be fine."

The umbrella came down once they were inside; the space was *cavernous.* Polished stone, cut glass and a fountain in the center. Atrium? Office building?

"Why are we here?" she asked.

"I have something to attend to," Foley said. "It won't take long." He led them to an elevator, and when it dinged open, the Geordie herded them in behind Foley—but the other man stayed behind. He turned to go, and in the barest stripe of visual before the doors closed, Jo could see a handgun tucked into his waistband.

Oh shit oh shit oh shit, she breathed as the floors counted up—*six, seven, eight* floors; *nine, ten, eleven.* The elevator didn't open to a hallway, but a whole floor.

"Make yourselves comfortable," Foley said, pointing to a sunken area with shiny sofas and a heavy coffee table. "Would you like a cup of tea?"

"Are you serious?" Jo asked. Lina just stared at him, wide-eyed.

"Where is Habibi?" she asked again.

"Let me get you that tea," Foley said. "And then we can talk about everything." He stepped up to the peculiar platform that circled the room, a sort of display area for various awards. To one side was a small counter and tea maker. Jo looked for the door but found the Geordie instead. He stood in front of it firm and joyless as a salt pillar. And for the first time, Jo noticed the sheath buckled to his belt. It wasn't a gun, thank God. It was a knife, which was almost as bad. Jo swept her eyes back to center.

"You kidnapped us."

"I invited you," Foley corrected. "Do you take milk? I'm sorry I don't have any biscuits to offer." He set two cups down, one for Lina and one for Jo. "You were more hospitable, I know."

Jo was afraid to drink it. Lina wasn't in a state to deny; she gulped it thirstily.

"This doesn't feel like an invitation. Someone's blocking the door. And the man downstairs had a—"

"A temporary arrangement," Foley completed.

"Nar, us has a *deal*," said the Geordie. "Got to get gannin; wot you waiting 'ere for anyways?"

Foley clenched and unclenched his hands against the blue blazer, then turned back to Jo in smiling composure.

"Ignore him. I just have some paperwork to take care of. Then we can talk about—everything."

"Can we talk about who the dead man is?" she asked.

Foley's smile went brittle like plastic. "It's just a misunderstanding," he said, but Jo wasn't having it.

"There is a man in Abington morgue, and he's not misunderstood," she said. "He's dead."

"Dead?" Lina rose to her feet. "Who is dead? *Please* not Habibi!"

Habibi. The meaning escaped Jo before but returned in a flash. She'd seen it on the cover of an Arabic language-learning book she'd edited; it was a term of endearment. It meant *my love*. Jo's brain skipped forward to MacAdams's kitchen; "Foley had a girlfriend." The girlfriend was the missing hiker. The missing hiker was Lina, who begged for news of her lover. The man standing before them *was* the same man who arrived on Jo's doorstep in the rain. But he was *not* Ronan Foley.

21:00

The case had never made sense, because the very first piece of evidence had been wrong. Ronan Foley supposedly shut the attic door between himself and Jo Jones at 11:00 p.m. on Friday. Since then, it had been questions with no answers: why Jo's cottage instead of Abington Arms? How did he get there? Where was his car? Why was the body iced? Why the stolen towels and soap?

Green had said it best; the case would make more sense if Jo got the timing wrong. She didn't. Instead, she'd mistaken the *man*, who had convinced her he was someone he wasn't.

It wasn't possible for Burnhope to get from the charity ball to Abington and back if he had to hunt down and murder Foley. But it *was* possible to *dump* a man he'd murdered and iced earlier that day. Much earlier, in fact. MacAdams had checked with Struthers first: the stomach contents test had failed because the stomach was *empty*. Jo's guest, on the other hand, ate a package of Jammie Dodgers.

Next came the trousers. The muddy ones were a size too small . . . because *they* belonged to Burnhope and not Foley. A side-by-side comparison on film proved it: he returned to the stage in trousers that bagged off his more slender frame. Not counting on the mud, he'd ruined his and needed to take from the dead man. Then there was the raincoat. They hadn't found "Foley's" because it wasn't Foley's at all. It was Burnhope's, because Stanley, not Ronan, "rented" a room in Jo's cottage. Once that domino was set to fall, the others followed:

Why had Burnhope called the Abington Arms? To see if Foley was expected.

Why had he wanted to know if the hotel was busy? A busy hotel might not notice an impersonator, especially if he laid on the Irish accent a bit thick. He was in for a surprise, however; staff had never heard of Ronan Foley; he'd been there under an alias. Then Arianna, mistaking his question as a need for peace and quiet, suggested a cottage rental.

Why the ice? Because Foley died at four thirty in the afternoon and had to keep it from smelling for the rest of the night—which also kept him fresh enough to have died much later. He packed him into his car, then used Foley's phone and credit card to book Netherleigh Cottage. He might have stopped there, but he didn't—not Stanley Burnhope. Too clever for his own good, he determined to collect a duffel of Foley's clothes. A random assortment, a hand-grab of toiletries. First stop: dump the body where Foley's connection in the butty van was sure to find him. Then he drove to Jo's cottage, intent on leaving the duffel as further proof that he was still alive while Stanley was at the charity ball. He'd planned to be back well before the closing remarks—and if things had gone to plan, they'd never be the wiser. But Burnhope hadn't counted on torrential rains and muddy ditches—and he hadn't counted on Jo Jones.

"Warrant granted!" Green shouted from across the room. "Uniform are ready to back us up."

"Good." MacAdams threw on his jacket and checked his watch. "Burnhope should be home by now; we'll approach from the side street." The Burnhope residence was twelve minutes away—and they had a search warrant, too. All the soap and towels in the world wouldn't stand up to a forensic investigation.

"You realize this means he kept a dead body in his car for *hours*," Green said as they sped down the A167. "Damn cool headed."

"That's why he needed to scrub it out," MacAdams said, thinking of Jo's comment days earlier. "He's married. He might even share the car with Ava."

MacAdams had to admit, Burnhope made one hell of a villain. Yet he'd lost his composure when they told him about the York building. Why? Because he thought he didn't know about it. MacAdams didn't have all the pieces yet: he was sure now that Burnhope and Foley were in the trafficking. But Foley must have been double-crossing, doing a side business. It made sense of the two types of operation: professional and international, sloppy and local. No doubt Burnhope thought ending Foley fixed everything—but the York business? One more of Foley's messes he'd have to clean up, and it threatened everything else, too. Burnhope was a man unused to paying for mistakes. How far would he go to cover his tracks?

The radio brayed to life: "We're getting close—do you want to make first approach?"

MacAdams very much did. He switched to fog lights and coasted to a halt on the corner. They would walk up.

Once again, they found themselves on the well-trimmed drive. The lights were on downstairs. MacAdams rang the bell and waited. No answer.

"Think he has the wind up?" Green asked as he rang again—but this time, they heard the slide of a lock. It was Ava.

"Oh. It's you." Her whalebone cheeks had color for the first time; they had been pinked with wine. She waved a half-empty glass at them. "He's not here. Not even a phone call."

She took in the intensity of MacAdams's and Green's expressions, and fear flickered across her features. She could see something was wrong, even through the cloud of Pinot Grigio, and backed away from the door. MacAdams walked right inside behind her.

"Could you give us your husband's license plate number, please," he asked.

"No need. Car's in the garage."

"Both vehicles are here?" Green asked.

Ava's hair had been hastily pulled up, but a strand kept falling against sharp cheekbones. She tucked it clumsily behind her ear before going on.

"We just have the one. His solicitor—or barrister, whatever you call the criminal defense—took him to the station and never brought him back. And—" she took a long drink "—*and* he hasn't called. I think I said."

MacAdams exchanged a glance with Green. Ava was more than a little tipsy, and if they didn't get her to a sofa soon she might well be on the floor.

"Would you like to sit down?" he asked.

She laughed. "How kind. You'd think you lived here. You've

probably been here enough." She made a gesture toward the adjacent sitting room, then a reasonable attempt at leading him there. Green provided a little support, and at last she was resituated on the white leather camelback. A laptop was open on the coffee table. She'd been looking up "family law"—divorce lawyers.

"Ms. Burnhope—" he began.

"No."

"Ava," MacAdams corrected. "We have a warrant to search the house and vehicle for evidence. We also have a warrant for Stanley's arrest. If you have any idea—"

"I've lots of ideas. But I already tried the club. And his mother. And my father. And all of our friends."

"His solicitor?"

"Oh, I *definitely* called her."

"What about a confidant—someone from work?" Green asked.

"If you mean Trisha, you're wrong. And you still have Sophie at the station. And frankly—" Ava's eyes wandered till they found Green's "—if he had a lover, I wouldn't be likely to know, would I?"

MacAdams had messaged the officers; they'd start the search soon, and that would likely put Ava off. He knelt to be nearer her level.

"Do you think he might have?" he asked.

"No. But until this morning I didn't know about Dmytro's theft, or that this Foley person was—doing whatever he does. Or that Maryam's papers only got authenticated a month ago."

"Wait . . ." Now Green was kneeling, too. "Maryam's papers. You mean she wasn't legally here?"

"Oh. She is *now*. Funny, I thought bureaucracy was to blame. That's what Stanley told me; just messy paperwork. But no."

"She wasn't sponsored by Fresh Start?" Green asked.

Ava shook her head. "She applied for azslm—excuse me,

asylum—instead. It's—It takes a long time." She swallowed wine in a gulp. "And s'not guaranteed. But we could have appealed, for fuck's sake."

MacAdams had missed something. He backtracked.

"Are you saying her asylum status was rejected?"

"Yes—no. I don't know." She rifled through the papers on the coffee table. "I just know *this* is new." She handed him a document MacAdams didn't understand, but the date was clear enough. Maryam might be legal now, but Burnhope had done it through the back doors. Had he greased the wheels?

"Why would he lie to you about her status?" he asked instead.

"Apparently, that's what he does," Ava muttered bitterly. Then she seemed to think better of it. "Not to worry her. Not to worry me. Or—he knew I wouldn't let him take a shortcut. *Pisser.*"

"Ava," MacAdams interrupted. "I know this is a lot all at once. But please think back. How often did Stanley travel for Hammersmith?"

Ava picked up the glass, saw that it was empty and put it down again. "He didn't. Practically lived in his office downtown," she said . . . and MacAdams felt another puzzle piece click into place.

"Ava, have you ever *been* to the Hammersmith building?" he asked.

"Not—not since the kids," she said.

"Not for five years. Why might that be?" he asked.

Ava clasped her hands in front of her, forearms leaning on her knees.

"If you'd asked me yesterday, I would have told you I wasn't interested in architecture—or that I was busy with the kids and the charity work. Just separate spheres and all that. I'd have said it, and I'd have believed it, too."

"And what's your answer today?" Green asked.

"I just don't think he wanted me there. And I can only think of terrible reasons why not."

MacAdams could hear the officers as they made their way through the house: footfalls upon the stairs and in and out of rooms above them. But they were in the wrong place.

"Green, back to the car. We need to get to Hammersmith—*now.*" He'd already run for the door, nearly colliding with forensics coming through.

"Why there?" Green asked as they made it outside. "You don't think it's the scene of the crime, do you?"

"Both crimes," MacAdams said. "That's why I asked if he traveled."

"I don't follow," Green said. They'd made it back to the car and MacAdams belted in and started the engine in a single motion.

"Burnhope never gets his hands dirty. Foley is the one who does the deals—he's a liability. But there's a paper trail somewhere, and Burnhope must know we're getting close to a warrant."

"He's going to destroy the evidence," Green said, smacking her thigh. "Shite."

MacAdams couldn't agree more. He'd largely retraced their earlier route, though they needn't go as far as the station. He could already see the round glass sides of Hammersmith's tower above tree-lined street. There were lights on up there, glowing sodium yellow against the haze of rain.

"Gotcha," he said, pulling into the car park. Beside him, Green gripped the dash.

"Boss? We better call for backup," she said. Parked to one side, not far from the entrance, was a large, black SUV.

CHAPTER 31

Thursday, 21:20

MacAdams and Green hugged the wall near the door, just in the shadow of the oversize glass awning.

"Security lights only down here," Green said. "A place like this must have night watchmen or something, right?"

"Not if Burnhope doesn't want anyone to know he was here," he said.

Green had one shoulder around the curve of the entry. Now she crept forward and tried the door.

"Locked," she said.

"I figured." MacAdams liked to be prepared for road hazards and other unexpected obstacles—for which he kept a sizable toolkit in his car. "Stand back."

"If you set alarms off, he'll know we're here."

"It won't," MacAdams said. "He doesn't want witnesses—human or electronic. He'll have turned off the security cameras. That should also mean the alarms aren't wired."

At least, he hoped so. MacAdams lifted the hammer, an old

claw variety. One benefit of Burnhope's love of glass was how easy you could break it. He pulled his arm back.

"Whoa, whoa, boss!" Green held her arm out, almost in peril of being struck. "Someone's coming."

A torch beam stabbed at their eyes, and a tinny voice came through a speaker above them: "Get gone, or I'll call police!"

"We are the police," MacAdams said, holding his identification up to the door. The man came for a closer look, then they heard the buzzer sound.

"Sorry, mate. Been a spot of bother—kids. Security, me. Can I 'elp?"

"What's going on upstairs?" MacAdams asked.

"Nobody up there."

"The lights are on," Green said. "We can see the whole floor lit up."

"They leave 'em on purpose, like. Cheaper than the on-and-off. Anyway, no trouble 'ere." He'd begun to close the door again; MacAdams took a page from Green's book and wedged his foot in the gap.

"You're security? What time did you get here tonight?" he asked.

"Look, mate, I've a job to do—rounds. Le' go."

"Answer the question," Green said.

"Em? Six. And no one's come round. No trouble, I'm sayin. *So* . . ." He shoved the door, hard; MacAdams grimaced at the pinch, then nodded to Green. They both shoved on the door at once, knocking the guard backward. MacAdams stepped inside first.

"Arrived at six and haven't noticed the black SUV outside?" MacAdams gave him a swift looking-over. White shirt, canvas pants. No tie, no nameplate. "Where's your uniform?"

"Got my ID right here." The man flashed a plastic badge and key swipe. "Now look you, I can't 'ave you wanderin' round."

He'd been backing up all the while, putting a bit of distance between them. MacAdams closed it.

"You remind me of someone, you know that?" he said. "About your height. Voice like yours. He was carrying a load of antiques down the *apples and pears*."

"You got it wrong, mate," he said. "I don't know nofink about that—" His right hand slipped backward as he spoke. Backward and hip height.

MacAdams wasn't sure which of them acted first, but they saw the danger as if with a single mind. MacAdams rushed him, hitting him in the chest, but it was Green who flipped him, stripped him of the gun and got a knee—hard—in the middle of his back.

"Ge' off me!" he squealed as she cuffed him.

"Just a hard-working security guard," she said. "You have the right to remain *fucking* silent, you son of a bitch."

MacAdams removed the cartridge. Touching the steel turned him cold. Illegal handgun, semiautomatic.

"You're under arrest," he said.

"Fuck off!"

"Big words from someone on his belly," Green replied.

"Leave him for Uniform," MacAdams said. "He's not going anywhere, and it's Burnhope we want."

"Fuck 'im too," the man spit. "King Dick up there with his girlies. Wouldn't *be* 'ere otherwise!"

"Girls? What girls?" Green demanded, leaning on him again.

"*Ge' off me, for chrissakes!* The foreign one and the nosy American—"

★ ★ ★

MacAdams would never be able to describe the sensation; like ice water, like skin shrink-wrapped to bone. He didn't need to be told; he *knew*. Upstairs, Jo Jones was alone with a murderer.

Again.

Burnhope's office was on the eleventh floor. They needed to get there *before* all of Newcastle police came screaming down the motorway. If Burnhope knew they were coming, it could turn into a hostage situation. Or worse. *Don't think that.* What in hell did Burnhope want with Jo?

But of course, he knew: *Jo knew that Burnhope wasn't Foley.*

What was his plan? To buy her silence? That was a biological impossibility; Jo told the truth. Even when she shouldn't. He wasn't sure she could do otherwise.

A bright spark, an unsinkable, unshakable, infuriating miracle of a human—and Burnhope wanted to shut her up. Man with a clean record, golden boy of Newcastle, how far would he go? He'd murdered someone already—broke the most sacred of laws. And once broken . . .

MacAdams ran for the lift, but the buttons were locked down.

"There must be a work-around," Green said.

"No time! *Stairs!*"

He burst through the rear door and into a copy of the steps he'd climbed in York. He'd take them three at a time.

CHAPTER 32

Jo stared at the man who was not Foley.

"You—who *are* you?" she asked, backing away from him.

"I'm trying to fix things," he said through tight teeth. "To *help*." He had settled Lina back onto the sofa and given her Jo's untouched tea.

"That doesn't answer the question," Jo said.

He took a breath. "I can explain everything, but I can't do it now—"

"Yes, you absolutely can." She had put the sofa between them.

"All right, fine. My name is Stanley Burnhope. This is my building." He paused in front of a long shelf. "Won two city's best and one architectural design for it. And all those—" he said, pointing to pyramidal glass trophies, polished prisms gleaming in the light "—are humanitarian awards. For doing things *right*."

Jo ignored this. "You said your name was Foley."

"No, you *guessed* it was. Foley made trouble. I am trying to clean it up. Why can't you understand?"

Jo gaped at him. The utterance surpassed irony.

"You pretended to be a man who is dead and now you've

trapped me in a high-rise so you can do paperwork. How am I supposed to *understand*?"

Burnhope mastered himself, then crouched next to Lina on the sofa.

"You like Lina, don't you? I help people like her. We sponsor them—there are things we can do. But Foley didn't want to play by anyone's rules."

"Your rules?"

"Yes, *my* rules. He could have left Lina alone. But no." He stood up again. "Now I have to fix that, too."

Jo was clutching her thumbs hard enough to hurt them and an internal tremor was causing her right foot to bounce uncontrollably—but she wasn't the only one feeling restless. The Geordie had stepped back into view.

"Hadawy Burn'ope—gan on with it!" he sneered. "'Av it away before somebody naps us—and gis me the money!"

"For God's sake, all of you be *quiet,*" Burnhope snapped. "And you, just do your job."

"Was his job to kidnap me?" Jo asked, turning to face the hulking figure. "Did he pay you to do this?"

"Nar!"

"That was just a freebie, then? Part of the service?" Jo should *not* be speaking this way; he'd tried to kill MacAdams with a pipe, and he presently had a knife on his belt. But her mouth just kept talking. "You work for him, is that it? Do his dirty work?"

"I divvent wark for 'im!"

"Then who *do* you work for?" she demanded. He adjusted his posture, somehow looking bigger and more square than before.

"Neebody."

"Then let me out!" Jo said it as firmly as she could, though her voice sounded small and strained.

Burnhope grasped Jo by her arm and turned her about.

"Quiet—can't you be *quiet*?" he demanded, but the Geordie seemed up for answering now.

"What divvy ye wanna wi' her, anyhow?" he asked. "Who is she, e'en?"

"Shut up!" Burnhope shouted—really shouted. She could see the vein standing out in his neck. Then he took a breath. "I have loose ends to tie up. That's all. Then Lina can go."

"Just Lina? Why? You're guessing she's not going to go to police?" Jo hadn't actually made the connection until after she'd said it . . . But it was true. "Oh my God."

"Are you physically incapable of silence?" he demanded, coming toward her. Jo backed up, keeping to the raised walkway.

"You know she won't tell anyone. But me—but me?" Jo's words were coming faster, trying to keep up with her heartbeat. "You don't have anything over me."

"We can talk about this," he hissed, still approaching. "Be reasonable."

Jo glanced over his head; Lina stood in the sunken center, watching wide-eyed.

"Or what?" she asked. Because this wasn't about kidnapping. And this wasn't about Lina. Jo was the real liability. She'd backed up onto the raised floor that circled the room. There weren't any windows she could jump out of this time.

"I can fix this," Burnhope insisted. "I can offer you—what you want. Just come here. Can you do that? I need to handle something."

"Did you handle Foley?" she challenged, her back against the trophy wall. He looked ready to lift himself up by his own hair.

"*Foley* is why any of this happened! Don't you see?" He was moving forward again, reaching for her.

"Don't touch me!" Jo picked up the nearest glass award. *For your humanitarian efforts.*

"Don't you throw that," he said. Then turned to the Geordie. "Come get her."

The Geordie stayed put. "Die it yerself."

"For fuck's sake—can't *any* of you see that I'm trying to put it right? It's Foley who did this. He's the only reason you're even *here*."

"*Foley* is *dead*," Jo said, and pitched the bauble at his chest. Too heavy, it didn't go far enough but crashed to the floor instead. Behind her, Lina began to wail.

"You stupid *cunt*," Burnhope hissed, but Jo had picked up the next one.

Shaped like a football, she lobbed it like one. It went wide, splintered the decking and cracked in half, but Burnhope had sense to retreat. He'd made it as far as Lina, who was prostrate and still howling with grief.

"Stop it! I said *stop*!" he demanded, lifting Lina to her feet. She clung to his lapels.

"Why? Why is he dead?" She was wrenching at his clothing with claw-curled fingers, still half sinking to the floor. Burnhope grappled her around the waist and lifted her off the floor.

"I can't deal with this now," he barked at the Geordie. "Take her, for fuck's sake—take one of them or I swear to Christ you'll not see a pound out of this." He'd shoved Lina into the man's arms. The Geordie, to his credit, hung on loosely; Lina herself went suddenly silent and watchful half-clasped to his side.

"Now you," Burnhope said, spinning around. He didn't look cordial anymore. He looked panicked and angry. "You will sit down and *shut up*."

Jo had never sat down and shut up. Not once in her long memory. And recent events had taught her that submission was deadly, and being utterly terror-feral had its benefits. She'd picked up an oddly shaped award, straight on one side, the other like molten glass. It was damn heavy, but she held it aloft.

"So you can leave me in a ditch, too?" Jo shouted. She wasn't tall, but the platform gave her both height and leverage. She stood above and raised the heavy trophy over her head. Four feet and she'd strike him. She could do it. Below her, Burnhope froze.

"Don't," he said, voice a ragged whisper. "You'll—you'll kill someone."

Jo's arms were shaking, the heavy base trembling above her. It *could* kill someone. She'd never seen the body; she'd never even seen the *victim*. MacAdams said his skull had been crushed in by something heavy and irregular.

"My God. This—*this* is how you killed Foley?" she whispered.

"You!" shouted Lina.

"Look out!" shouted the Geordie.

And Jo let go of the murder weapon. It fell corner down, turning to one side and punching a hole in the platform floor. Burnhope had turned around to face Lina, who was now suddenly charging at him, her small frame carried forward by the force of her final exclamation. Jo barely had time to register the knife she carried before Burnhope crumpled to the floor.

★ ★ ★

"Boss!" Green panted as they reached the eleventh floor. "Backup is coming, but we don't know if these people are *armed*!"

True. And yet. MacAdams pulled out the disabled gun; he'd tucked the empty gun into his waistband, where it was chafing a hole in his back. "They don't know that *we* aren't.

"Fine. Then give me the gun," Green said.

"What?"

"I'm cleared for firearms and you're not," she said, taking it from him. "Even unloaded, you aren't supposed to be waving one around."

"You're not on the tactical unit anymore," he whispered back. She gave him a severe look that somehow managed simultaneously to be motherly.

"I'm sure my *chief* will stand by me if I'm cited. Come on." Green pushed open the stairwell door, arms at right angles, gun barrel pointed skyward. The stairs had exited to an adjacent hallway with a single door into Burnhope's office—the only one they'd encountered so far that wasn't made of glass. Green tested the handle. It wasn't locked.

"On three," she whispered. *One. Two . . .*

★ ★ ★

They burst into a room of chaos, broken glass . . . and blood.

Jo Jones knelt in the center over the body of Stanley Burnhope. She'd stripped off her hoodie and was pressing it hard against his abdomen—and standing over her was a dark-haired woman with a short-handled sheath knife.

"Leave it—leave it—" coaxed the largest, squarest man MacAdams had ever seen. He seemed to be trying to disarm the woman, who shrieked and made a wild slash at him.

"Jesus," Green said out loud.

The Geordie turned about, eyes immediately fastened to the gun in her hand.

"Whe?"

"Police!" Green replied. "You, on the ground."

He complied, leaving MacAdams to make sense of everything else.

"Jo? What's—what's happening here?" he asked. She kept her hands pressed down, but let her eyes wander up; they were wide and glassy and adrenaline spiked.

"James," she said quietly. "Meet Lina."

"He killed him. He *killed* him!" Lina's eyes were rimmed, face contorted, mouth an open rectangle of grief. "He dies now."

"Lina, can I come closer?" MacAdams asked. "You are Ronan Foley's girlfriend?"

She shook her head violently, spittle forming at the corners of her mouth.

"No, his *zawjah*!" she shouted. *"Zawjah, habibi!"*

"It means wife," Jo said. "I think. James? I can't—I can't do this a lot longer." He could see that her arms were shaking, but also that she'd managed to stop the bleeding. Burnhope's eyes were open, but unfocused, his breathing stertorous.

"You were married," MacAdams said, coming closer. Lina made a slash at him, though without much force or venom. "And he—Ronan was the father of your baby?"

Lina heaved a sob, her free hand finding her abdomen.

"You were going to run away together, weren't you? Got married in secret, and then you were going away."

"On—on a boat," she hiccupped. "Far."

"To build a new life. He'd done that before—he could do it again. You met when? Six months ago?" MacAdams asked. He should be watching Lina. He was watching Jo instead.

"He loved me," Lina whispered. From the platform, Green agreed.

"I believe he did," she said. "And he wanted better for you."

"Much better," MacAdams said. He was close now. Closer enough to take the knife—not fool enough to try. "He didn't want you to live in hiding. Not you or the baby."

Lina sobbed—and sagged on her feet. MacAdams took a step nearer.

"Give me the knife. You don't want to kill this man. You have your child to think about," he said, and was surprised to hear a gentler sobbing . . . from Jo.

"The *baby*," she said, tears welling up in her eyes. "Do you know how much you'll matter to her? She needs a mother. Her own mother, not—not someone else."

"Come on, now," MacAdams urged.

Lina looked at Jo. *"Scared,"* she whispered.

Jo nodded, bloodied hands still trembling at their work. "I know. But I promise you won't be *alone*."

★ ★ ★

MacAdams felt the words somewhere deep in his gut. This was Jo talking about her family—about Evelyn's baby—and about herself. It hurt him, for her sake.

Lina heaved a sigh, dropped the knife and sank to her knees. MacAdams went for Jo, but Green was already there.

"I got it," she said, taking over providing pressure on the wound. "And I've radioed for an ambulance, too."

Jo leaned backward, tried to get up, and fell in a heap against the leather sofa. She was shaking *everywhere* now, teeth chattering in her head.

"It's okay, it's okay," MacAdams said, scooping her up. He didn't know what else to do except get his arms around her and hold on tight. Jo was a ball of clenched muscle.

"Tighter. P-please," Jo said. "P-pro-pr-ia-ception. D-deep p-pres-ssure c-can—"

"Shhh," he said, resting his chin on her head and squeezing her close. He could do this. Because it's all he'd wanted to do, almost since meeting her. Hold on. Hold on, and not let go.

Outside, he could hear the blessed sound of sirens.

CHAPTER 33

Saturday, midafternoon

The Geordie had a name. And he was very forthcoming, even if it required a translator for all the Geordie dialect.

Billie Bowes met Foley some years ago. At the time, he'd been selling sandwiches out of a cart, trying to make a living after being in lockup for dealing cannabis. Foley came regular, a businessman who didn't mind buying bacon butties from a former criminal. They got to be friendly enough for a pint, and Bowes felt honored that a city-boy type in nice suits would bother. That's before he knew Foley had been in some trouble himself. It's just that Foley hadn't done time; he'd skipped town and changed his name. Then one day, he asked Billie if he'd like to make a little side money. *Yar.* All he needed to do was to take a package and hang on to it. Someone would come for a butty, and he'd give him the package as well.

It wasn't *drugs*, Bowes was keen to tell them. It echoed Dmytro's earnest admission, too, as if the fact made the trade not truly illegal. It reminded MacAdams of the old days of car stereo theft.

Someone turned up with a radio, someone else bought it, no questions asked. It was, as Bowes said for the record, a *canny job.* He'd have been happy with that, or so he told them. But Foley had bigger plans.

"And that's where we begin the last six months," Green said. She and Gridley were sharing a basket of chips outside in warm sunshine. They had traded the beloved Red Lion for the pub near the airfield—principally for its view of the river. Possibly it was all the time spent near the Tyne in Newcastle, but a riverside beer garden just felt right.

"Well, as far as Billie goes, yes," MacAdams agreed. "But Burnhope and Foley go back a lot further than that."

"I can see how Foley and Bowes get on. But I'm still surprised a rich boy like Burnhope got mixed up with Foley. He's not the criminal type."

The golden boy wasn't as spotless as he pretended, though nothing was ever *quite* a crime. The Eton rumor was probably well-founded and there was further suspicion of cheating at Oxford, as well as a bust-up over illegal betting on sports. But that was practically clean-nosed by comparison.

"That, I think, was the point." MacAdams flagged the waiter for the bill. "He as much as told us: he hired Foley to be the heavy at Hammersmith. Someone who could bully and push people around when necessary." He nodded to Andrews, who'd just arrived with brown ale, more chips and a bacon butty. A dish MacAdams was certain he'd never eat again.

"Did I miss anything?" he asked.

"Nah, it's just getting good," Green told him, plucking a plastic cup of extra curry from his tray. MacAdams moved over on the bench.

"We have to make a few guesses on this side of the story," MacAdams said. They couldn't ask Burnhope, who was still in hospital and presently in an induced coma. They expected him to pull through, but in the meantime, MacAdams had pieced it together pretty well. "We have to start with Ava."

Burnhope had everything: A beautiful home, a beautiful wife and, as of five years ago, two kids. MacAdams assumed Ava had given up her musical career for motherhood; he was right—and wrong. Unable to have children of her own, she determined to adopt. And that's when Ava went to Syria, a trip both profound and life altering. She'd found her purpose, and she bent her will and her efforts—and Stanley's, too—on bringing over as many refugees to the UK as possible. It was Ava who sought out Sophie and Fresh Start. But the trip to Syria impacted Stanley, too.

"Burnhope is an art collector. Maybe he brings something back—maybe he doesn't declare it at customs. Guess what? It's easy." In fact, he and Green were learning just *how* easy; the UK had surprisingly lax laws by comparison to the EU. "Business had just hit a downturn, so he decides to use his various connections to bring artifacts in for distribution."

"Entrepreneurial spirit," muttered Green.

"Charity, practically," MacAdams said. "That's what Gerald Standish told me. Thinks of himself as a mini–British Museum. The people who buy it—even Burnhope, who trafficked it in—don't see it as a crime."

"Oh yes, they do," Green said, dusting salt from her fingers. "Otherwise, you don't need the *heavy*."

MacAdams pointed a *bingo* finger in her direction. Foley had told Billie Bowes about his past life; chances were good he'd told Burnhope, too. A semireformed criminal made the perfect partner.

"Exactly that. And I am guessing the two of them ran the business for at least four years. Burnhope made connections with the art world and cleaned the books; Foley handled the shipping. They weren't rivals, as we'd suspected, but true partners." It put

Foley's last email to Stanley Burnhope in a whole new light. It really *was* a partners' meeting. It just wasn't about Hammersmith or architecture.

"So Foley's got the East London connection," Green said, meaning the Cockney presently in lockup. "The shipments came through there."

"Okay. It's coming in through the London ports. But what's the loot doing *here*? The van was in Abington," Andrews pointed out. MacAdams understood the confusion all too well; the case had sent them in circles.

"Golf," MacAdams said. "Foley played golf with Standish, but not in Newcastle, where he was under Burnhope's thumb. They played at the course near Abington Arms."

It's probably where Foley first heard about Gerald's interest in antiquities, where he got the idea about cherry-picking the best artifacts and selling them off on his own for cash and where he discovered there was a very fine hotel with rich clientele who might be buyers.

"Can we nail Standish?" Green asked.

"I wish," MacAdams said, shaking his head. Bowes didn't give them any names, but even so, he'd been the start of Foley's endeavor, not the end of it. "Foley, we now know, had a tendency to get in over his head. Gerald was just one man. To really expand, he needed a way station. A place where he could go through inventory at leisure. He might have been older and wiser than he was back in Belfast, but he hadn't shaken his gambler need for *more wins*. So he takes over a build in York and starts off-loading some of the shipments there."

Green had a mouthful of food but waved her hand. "Time to expand," she said, swallowing. "Get's the Geordie a van. Then two vans."

"Is that when he starts using Dmytro?" Gridley asked.

"No," MacAdams said, leaning on his elbows. "That's when he meets Lina."

It had taken some delicate digging, but Ava had been very happy to help this time. Maryam, the Burnhopes' nanny, had not come as a sponsored refugee but as an asylum seeker. And she hadn't come alone. Maryam had a sister named Lina.

They'd come on their own to Fresh Start because refugees were welcome there. Sophie helped with the paperwork and both applied for asylum. Thus far, all was aboveboard. Except asylum seekers are prohibited from entering the workforce . . . and Burnhope needed a nanny. He told Ava she'd been accepted as a sponsored refugee. Lina, meanwhile, remained at Fresh Start on government support. She was young, attractive and had time on her hands. Foley was single, knew enough Syrian from his travels to be semiconversant, and—unlike Burnhope—had an easy way with women.

"They fell in love," MacAdams said.

"Or something," Green said.

MacAdams ignored the addition. "Then, six months ago, both women had their claims rejected. Burnhope can't face telling Ava he lied, so he deepens the hole he's in. Makes an appeal and greases some palms to make sure things move quickly for Maryam. Foley naturally expects him to do the same for Lina."

"But he doesn't, you're gonna tell us," Gridley said rolling her eyes.

"Right. He's not willing to risk it. And that's when Foley decides he's going to bleed him."

Billie Bowes confirmed that part; suddenly he was driving the vans all over, selling something daily, sometimes for far less than the things were worth. Foley didn't care. He sold up and started banking what he could, ready to fly.

"That's when he tapped Dmytro, and Dmytro tapped the other kids. Right under Fresh Start's nose."

"Rash," said Gridley.

"Desperate, even. Which is how we get to the murder bit,"

Andrews said triumphantly. "Dmytro gets caught stealing, Burnhope finds out about the double cross and wham."

"You're forgetting our man's psychology," MacAdams said. "Stanley doesn't get his hands dirty. He originally hired Foley to be the asshole on job sites. No, he isn't planning to kill him. He needs him."

"So what happens?"

"You have to remember," Green said. "It's Foley who asks for the meeting. A *partners'* meeting, his way of saying *this is about the artifact business.*"

Andrews threw his head back. "The shoes and suit—Foley was ready to split on him, wasn't he?"

"He's already married Lina. Now they are going to run away and leave Burnhope behind," MacAdams explained.

"What a guy," Gridley sighed. "Deciding not to abandon his pregnant lover this time."

MacAdams had made note of that, too. And also his kindness toward Trisha, the single mother. In some way, leaving Tula must have haunted him. So much so that Burnhope knew of her, even knew her name (despite his denial). That's why it pleased him when Jo mentioned her living in Abington. Someone would be able to positively ID the body.

"Burnhope thinks he's getting the drop on Foley, confronting him with his betrayal," Green went on. "Instead, a smug Foley says *you first.*"

MacAdams could well imagine it. Foley was a bully when it came to men; it's what made him useful to Burnhope. Now he bullied Burnhope in turn. "He wouldn't help Lina the way he helped Maryam," MacAdams agreed. "Now he thinks Burnhope owes them a wedding present, which he plans to get by blackmail."

"Okay, I get it," Andrews said. "He demanded hush money not to reveal Burnhope's part in it."

"To the tune of several million, according the Geordie," Green added. "He'd been carting Lina around, a mobile hide-out, and was supposed to get a percent for his time."

This was all true. But still only part of the story. And here was where Foley really showed his colors.

"Let's go back to that York shopping center," he said. "A bad job. Stagnant. Behind schedule."

"Right, because it was just a warehouse for his loot."

"Would you actively court the ire of the Lord Mayor over a building you planned to store stolen goods in?" MacAdams asked.

Andrews had a chip halfway to his mouth. "Um, no, I suppose not. You would want to go under the radar."

"Exactly. Instead, Ronan Foley fights with the city, causes problems, and ultimately the city halts the work and calls Burnhope." MacAdams shook his head; they had all underestimated Foley. "He *wanted* to cause problems. Because they were going to be *Stanley's* problems. Give me two million pounds, cash, or I will ruin you. He just has to make a telephone call to the York police."

"Damn."

"Exactly," Green agreed. "Stanley doesn't have time to think about it. Foley's standing there with his burner phone, saying wire me cash *right now* or everything you love goes up in smoke. The York building might as well have been filled with dynamite. I'm kind of surprised he didn't pay up, to be honest."

Gridley slapped the table with her napkin. "He couldn't! We looked at all his finances, remember? It's tied up in house and business and the charity. No liquidity."

"Unless you count Ava's money," Green added. "So the choices are—let Foley ruin you or take money from your wife, which will still ruin you. Or you pick up the nearest heavy object and smash him over the head."

"That, my friends, was the point. This was about money. But only partly. Foley has a soft spot for women, certainly for Lina, and a conscience well-haunted by Tula of all people. Burnhope got his nanny into the country by pulling strings but left Foley's lover out to dry. Getting Burnhope over his head and in trouble with Ava was the *point.*" He could imagine him flaunting it, even. Laughing when Burnhope said he wouldn't pay, couldn't pay. In the end, Burnhope had more to lose than Foley.

That was, in fact, the only thing Foley hadn't counted on: he'd pushed a rich man too close to losing it all, and Burnhope wasn't going quietly.

MacAdams knew what his defense lawyers would say; heat of the moment, unintentional manslaughter. But there was no doubt Burnhope could be cold and calculating. Once the deed was done, he planned his next moves like an expert villain: He would make it seem a living Ronan Foley was in Abington well after their meeting, at a time when Burnhope would have an alibi. They didn't look alike, but they shared an accent, were of similar height, and both had dark hair. In most cases, a witness wouldn't recall much else on first meeting.

But most witnesses were not Jo Jones.

That was the loose end he hadn't counted on. In other respects, luck continued to smile on Burnhope. Bowes's last duty was to take Lina to the Abington Arms. There, she and Foley would assume the identities they had been building up, change into new clothes and then leave with faked IDs for the continent. Bowes parked with Lina on the hiking trail, waiting for a call that never came. He turned up again the next day, and the next. That's where Jo and Gwilym saw him—and Lina, too, at least for a moment. Spooked, Bowes returned to Newcastle, only to hear that Foley was dead. Panic set in, and Bowes sought help from Burnhope, who conscripted him to clean out the York property with the East London Cockneys.

Stanley Burnhope must have slept better, thinking this last mistake was tidied over—only to be surprised by police inquiries the next day. He'd killed Foley already; now he murdered him in public opinion, claiming no knowledge of his crimes . . . and the papers, at least, believed him.

But of course, there was Lina. And, as MacAdams and Green told him, Lina was pregnant. Bowes had gone to ground after the York bust, leaving Lina on her own in Abington. Burnhope coaxed him back with a promise of cash—if he could bring the girl back. It wasn't hard. Far from helpless, she had managed to return to Newcastle on her own. Bowes texted her the coordinates to the parking ramp.

"What was his plan with Lina, anyway?" Andrews asked. "He wasn't gonna cosh her over the head, too, was he?"

"I don't think so. I suspect he planned to bribe her with the promise of papers. She had the baby to think of—and like Maryam, Lina doesn't trust police. Not much of a loose end."

But MacAdams could imagine the shock—the utter dismay—seeing Jo again in Newcastle must have caused. Stanley could have denied being Ronan Foley right then, told her she was mistaken. But Jo caught him out. Lina may have had nowhere else to go, but an American with connections whose face he'd seen in the local papers? Burnhope couldn't buy his way out of *that*.

The waiter had returned. MacAdams paid for their current fare (and another round, just in case). Then he stood to go.

"Hang on, you didn't even finish a single pint!" Andrews said.

Green slapped his shoulder. "Got better places to be?" she asked, pointing to MacAdams . . . who was wearing the Jekyll Gardens tie. He didn't reply. He did tip his hat, fold his jacket over one arm and head to his car.

★ ★ ★

Sunlight streamed through the larch trees, leaving dappled shade across the garden path. Jo had traded Doc Martens for light walking shoes, even if that made her even shorter. She had never quite mastered the art of sundress; too many fussy attributes, so had settled for a light gray T-shirt dress. The afternoon had agreed to play nice, and in almost every respect, was a perfect twin of the previous Saturday. Minus a murder. So far.

"Welcome to the Jekyll Gardens opening, take two," she said as MacAdams approached the gate.

"Better late than never."

He was in shirtsleeves again. Jo wondered if she was ever going to get used to that. He also carried a basket.

"Lunch," he said, handing it over. Jo peered at cheese and olives, a half loaf of bread—and a bottle of white wine.

"That's not the clowslip kind, right?"

"New Zealand Pinot Grigio," he said, smiling. "I even brought glasses." Which was excellent because plastic cups and drinking . . . anything . . . was a stretch for Jo. Lip plastic was almost as bad as lip Styrofoam. *Shudder.* "Did you want to visit the violets?"

"Actually, no. There's a gazebo in the center now." She led the way along bright cornflower, bluebell and columbine. The May flowers were starting to fade, but the roses would soon be blooming everywhere. "It's the one thing that wasn't original, but what's a garden without a gazebo?"

"Perish the thought," MacAdams said as they entered the shaded structure. He'd already filled her in on most of the case details. Dmytro would be treated with leniency. The charity might yet escape being shut down. Stanley would live, even if that also meant standing trial.

"That part is all down to you," MacAdams had told her. And she'd replied with the date and page count of the book on first aid she'd edited once. Because she couldn't seem to stop doing that.

"What about all the artifacts?" Jo asked. Partly because Gwilym was dying to know.

"Interpol will be handling that; hopefully most will returned to Syria. They may follow up on the drop-off locations Dmytro provided, but I have my doubts about whether it will ever lead to arrests. It so rarely does."

"Right. Because the buyers can claim they didn't know, or that the seller lied to them about provenance. Actually plenty of them really *don't* know what they're looking at. Which reminds me . . ." Jo took out her phone and called up the photo of the Arabesque work. "Your earring isn't an earring. It's a nose ring."

MacAdams gave her an open-eyed stare. "A very *old* nose ring?"

"Oh yeah. From Kush, between three thousand and two thousand years BC—" Jo stopped talking. Because MacAdams was . . . laughing. "Are you all right?"

"Oh Gerald, you just couldn't shut up," he murmured, wiping his eyes. "Jo, you are a miracle."

"It was Gwilym this time, actually."

"Both of you, then. And I change my previous answer. I think, in fact, we might just get a conviction or two," he said, smiling. Actually smiling. Jo smiled back and wondered if she was blushing again.

They hadn't talked about Thursday night, or the fact MacAdams obediently held her close until paramedics arrived. And then, that he'd carried her to the elevator and out to the waiting ambulance to be looked over. He'd had to leave her right after that, and spent the night and next day processing things in Newcastle—so Gwilym had driven her home on Friday in her own car. Now, they had time to spare and plenty to say. And she couldn't think of anything.

"We are going to do all we can for Lina," MacAdams said as he poured wine. "Her actions will be considered as under duress, a bit like self-defense. Ava will be a good advocate. She's already remunerated Maryam, who at least has a visa now."

"And Lina's baby will be born here, in the UK," Jo said, a little wistfully. MacAdams leaned forward to chime his glass against hers.

"Yes. I have been meaning to ask you about that."

"About Lina's baby?"

"About Evelyn's."

Jo drank the wine. She wasn't very knowledgeable about vintages, which suddenly bothered her. *Make a note.* But it was crisp and dry and smelled of pears.

"Violet. Later *Viola*." Jo had built a picture in her mind's eye, though they only had the one image, blurry in newsprint from her wedding day. Tall, willowy, but with eyes like Evelyn's. "She lived most of her life in Canada, believe it or not. Montreal. I was within striking distance when I lived in New York and never knew it."

"You have family there, then?" MacAdams asked, and the question sent a sudden shiver through Jo. He noticed it, too. "I'm sorry, I didn't—"

"It's not an ugly shiver. It's more like turning on a light. A little bit of current. I'm just not used to thinking about *having* family. That kind of family. Instead of all of you, I mean." Jo stopped and frowned. "Um, none of that came out right; can I start over?"

"Please do." MacAdams refilled her glass.

Jo took a breath. "Aiden didn't get as far as living relatives. But two of Violet's children married. One of them actually returned to the UK in the 1960s, but I lost track after that. I don't know if they are still living, or if they had children who might be. It's exciting and scary at the same time, but it feels different now."

It was partly what Gwilym had said (and what Aiden and Arthur and Chen proved): *family* and *blood* weren't the same thing. It was partly knowing that Evelyn's kin had treated her so evilly, sent away by the father, seduced by her brother-in-law and refused medical help by a jealous sister who later gave her baby away. But most of all, it was the realization that Jo herself didn't feel alone anymore.

"I want to find them. I plan to," she said. "But I don't *need* to. Aiden spent so much time hunting for our family that he missed out making his own with Arthur. My mother never learned to let go of anything, and ended up bitter and alone. I don't want to be like that."

MacAdams had been listening attentively. Something he was very good at, she decided. Now he looked over her head to the garden and the open sky where Ardemore House used to be.

"Yes, I think I've had similar revelations," he said. "I stayed married a long time after I wasn't married anymore. So to speak."

"I still haven't met Annie," Jo said.

MacAdams finished his glass. "You will," he said. It wasn't a speech or anything. It wasn't particularly poignant. But Jo was blushing suddenly and her fingers felt tingly.

"Oh. Good." Jo cleared her throat and decided to eat cheese before putting any more wine on her oddly buoyant spirits. She made double portions. "I do have something planned. Sort of."

"A party?" MacAdams asked.

"More like a funeral," Jo said, and MacAdams choked wine.

"Sorry?" he asked after a minor coughing fit.

"Check, I won't call it that," Jo said, nibbling Brie. "It's just that we haven't buried Evelyn yet. And I also want to celebrate Violet, her daughter. And introduce Arthur. Maybe I should call it a baby shower?"

"That might likewise confuse people," MacAdams said. He

stood up and walked about the gazebo. "You're bringing Evelyn home. You could call it a *homecoming*."

He'd completed a circuit and now stood just in front of her chair. His tie had fluttered to one side. Jo stood up and straightened it.

"James?" she asked. "That's perfect."

CHAPTER 34

A Sunday in August

Longside Cemetery had never seen a party like it. Probably it had never seen a party, period, though Jo didn't know why. It offered lovely rolling grounds, mature trees and the bonus of carved headstones going back several hundred years. *Her* party was taking place under the long-stretched arms of an English oak, and almost everyone she knew had turned up.

"Ready when you are," Tula said. She'd come with Ben—and with Lina. Foley's estate, or what remained that hadn't been confiscated by police, had come to Tula as his (until death) lawful wife. It had been enough to sponsor Lina, who now lived with them at the Red Lion, where Tula had transformed the attic into future nursery space. The baby, expected to be a girl, was—so she said—the "only good thing to come of Rhyan Flannery." But she said it with the pride of an expectant grandmother.

Jo walked to the tree's broad trunk. She could see Arthur in the front, wearing the ring and sitting next to Emery, who was pointing it out to Rupert with great enthusiasm. Roberta had chosen her seat next to Gwilym, but had to share him with Chen: tweeds next to waistcoat next to sherbert chiffon. Green was there with her wife, and Kate Gridley and Teresa, Tommy Andrews and a box of doughnuts. There was also a smiling, apple-cheeked woman in the center aisle trying to keep track of two small children with the aid of her equally smiling partner. That, she knew, was Annie and Ashok, because they had introduced themselves like a thunderclap and shaken her hand so much she felt slightly seasick.

"I'm ready," she said to MacAdams. He was standing by, ready to remove a red cloth from a brand-new headstone. Jo took a breath, then let it out through puckered lips. Then she stepped forward.

"We're here today to celebrate Evelyn Davies—and Aiden Jones," she said, and MacAdams drew away the cloth. Underneath, pink granite had been carved into a bouquet of flowers. "Abington is Evelyn's home now. We're her family."

Arthur and Gwilym stood from their chairs and stepped forward to pick up a mahogany box just large enough to hold Evelyn's skeletal remains. They carried it forward in silence, then lowered it into the space beneath the stone.

"She was survived by her daughter," Jo went on. "Violet. And Violet was survived by daughter Olivia, and son Emile."

Arthur lay roses into the grave. Gwilym left violets specially procured by Annie for the day.

"Aiden Jones was my uncle. He's the reason we know what became of Evelyn. He rescued her painting and left her at Ardemore for me to find. So, I think he belongs to Abington, too." Jo wasn't going to do it, but could scarcely help herself. She hazarded a glance in MacAdams's direction. *"Just like me."*

★ ★ ★

It wasn't anything like as draining as the Jekyll Gardens speech, but she might have received wilder applause for it. And, because of Teresa's tea tent, there was almost the same amount of cake.

"Brilliant," Gwilym said around several mouthfuls of it. "Bloody brilliant as ever."

"You'll keep looking for Violet's children, won't you?" Teresa asked as she handed over milky tea.

"I think so. I'm not sure," Jo admitted.

"Everyone needs a hobby," barked Roberta. "You're backing up the line." She thumped her stick against the ground, but no one moved much faster. Jo found her way to MacAdams's table, under a string of party lights.

"You don't need any more hobbies," he said.

"No, Gwilym doesn't need any more hobbies. I just need fewer murderers to get mixed up in mine."

"Fair." He reached out and gave her hand the briefest squeeze. "What's next, then? Now that this is complete?"

"Well. I could take up antiquing."

"Please don't."

"Or I could rent the cottage attic again."

"Antiques seem like an excellent choice," MacAdams agreed. Green had just found them, and gave Jo a wave.

"Hate to be the one," Green said. "But you got a call from the superintendent."

MacAdams rolled his neck. "What *now*?"

"Honestly, he didn't say. Only that you were wanted." She lifted a punch cup. "Benefits of being chief, eh?"

★ ★ ★

MacAdams wasn't chief. Or not exactly. Then again.

The trouble with looking at old cases was that the light

glanced off things differently at distance. Most especially the cases dealing with Admiral Clapham, father of his and Green's old boss. It started with a revisit of Abington Arms guest list and their promise of being "discreet." There had been a few odd cases involving clients there; loose ends, bits that didn't marry up. Two gun safes with historical pieces had been emptied over a weekend. A robbery, but no real investigation. Labeled an isolated incident. Except it wasn't. In another housebreaking, it was jewelry that went missing and a farm hand had been detained; then all charges were dropped, not another word spoken. Insurance fraud? Or ways of dodging taxes? It was hard to say, yet the threads kept running back to the hotel and, MacAdams suspected, to the admiral. He went hunting a little deeper—but bottomed out against closed files and permissions requests from other stations. A detective chief inspector could only do so much. But a chief, now. That might open doors. Especially doors some might like to leave closed.

So, in between sewing up the Burnhope case and a few local bust-ups, he'd been working on his résumé and application for the superintendent. MacAdams stepped away from the merry-making to make the call back. He'd positioned himself between two headstones, facing south for signal. It rang. And rang. And gave him the perfunctory "party is not available, leave a message."

"It's James MacAdams, returning your call—" he started.

"Hello, Detective."

It hadn't come from the other line, but behind him. He turned to see a woman. Not any woman. Cora Clapham, as though thinking of the admiral had somehow conjured his old boss into being. She wore a sleeveless blouse in pale green, but stood with the same straight-backed ferocity as she might in full military dress.

"Surprised?" she asked.

"I . . . am. When did you get in?"

"Last week. Been living in the estate house." She sighed and uncrossed her arms. "It needs work before I put it on the market. I heard from the gardener about the *homecoming.* I take it proper channels were followed for that burial?"

They were. MacAdams didn't feel like he owed that detail, however.

"How long will you be in town?" he asked instead. But Cora knew how to be evasive, too.

"You were ringing Superintendent Bradford," she said. "I'm the reason he phoned for you, I'm guessing. I left Southampton." She smiled at him, broadly. "As I understand you are yet without a chief."

If Jo was there, she'd have read a great deal on MacAdams's face. He wished she was, suddenly, and that she could translate.

"You. Are the new chief?" MacAdams asked. She half turned to face the party just beyond.

"New old chief, yes. I have come home. We can't run from our problems, can we? Even when those problems are our fathers." She smiled. "You have gone from strength to strength, what with this Burnhope case."

MacAdams was still processing the news and not taking it very kindly.

"Thank you. It's still processing. There will be charges brought against a local art collector when we're through, as well." He paused. "It's not often the great and the good are forced to pay for their sins."

Cora turned back to face him. "Not often. But not never. You've ended up on higher radars than the super, too. Antique trades and human trafficking. I'm not surprised you didn't take the chief job yourself."

"But you're not."

"No. You know where you shine, James. Where you're best.

So do I." She walked away, but not toward the tents. She was going, he knew, to her father's burial plot.

"Welcome back," he said, without much feeling, and long after she was out of earshot. Then he returned to the homecoming that mattered.

Jo was waiting.

★★★★★

ACKNOWLEDGMENTS

Many thanks to Mark Schillace, with whom I brainstormed the twisty bits (on a mountain in France, no less). Additional props to Lance Parkin, Deanna Raybourn, my editor and the artists who continue to make the best covers ever.